PHOENIX RISING

BAEN BOOKS by RYK E. SPOOR

Digital Knight

Grand Central Arena

BAEN BOOKS by RYK E. SPOOR & ERIC FLINT

Boundary

Threshold

Portal (forthcoming)

PHOENIX RISING

Ryk E. Spoor

PHOENIX RISING

This is a work of fiction. All the characters and events portrayed in this book are fictional, and any resemblance to real people or incidents is purely coincidental.

A Baen Books Original

Baen Publishing Enterprises
P.O. Box 1403
Riverdale, NY 10471
www.baen.com

ISBN: 978-1-4516-3841-7

Cover art by Todd Lockwood
Maps by Randy Asplund

First printing, November 2012

Distributed by Simon & Schuster
1230 Avenue of the Americas
New York, NY 10020

Library of Congress Cataloging-in-Publication Data

10   9   8   7   6   5   4   3   2   1

Pages by Joy Freeman (www.pagesbyjoy.com)
Printed in the United States of America

ACKNOWLEDGEMENTS & THANKS

First to my wife Kathleen, for giving me the time

To Toni Weisskopf, for giving me the chance

To Tony Daniel, for giving excellent editorial advice

And to my Beta-Readers, for giving me encouragement and feedback—especially my Loyal Lieutenant, Shana.

This novel is dedicated to three people
without whom it would never have been written:

First to Jeffrey Getzin, author of the self-published novel *Prince of Bryanae*, in whose campaign Kyri Vantage (then Kyrie Ross) was first born. Thank you, Jeff, for one of the most intense campaigns I have been in...and thank you for visiting my own world, and taking Bryanae itself with you, to live a greater and brighter life of its own.

Second to Dana Renee LaJeunesse, for demanding and guiding the original creation of...a certain species (spoilers!). Thank you, Dana, for that and so much more. "Fear Me!"

And third to Robert Rudolph, who helped create Skysand, and who first created a character named Tobimar Silverun. That character's adventures were different...yet the spirit of the character is, I think, very much the same. Thank you for entering Zarathan and leaving it richer than before, Rob—and may I never have to deal with another player so incredibly lucky!

CONTENTS

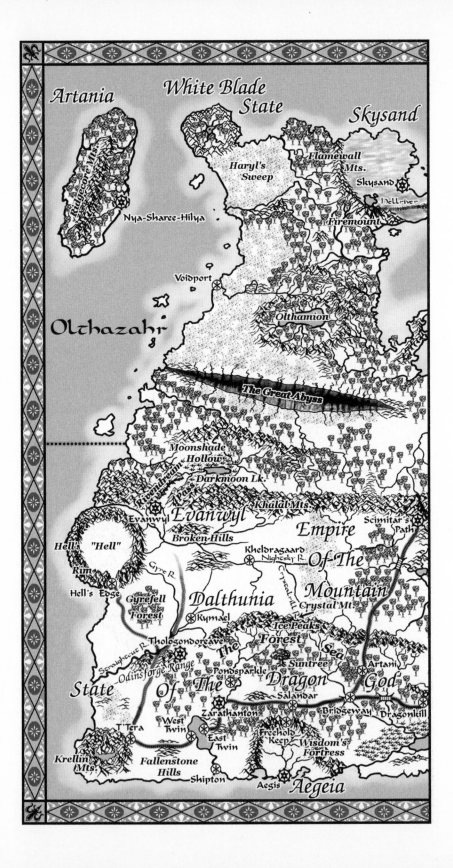

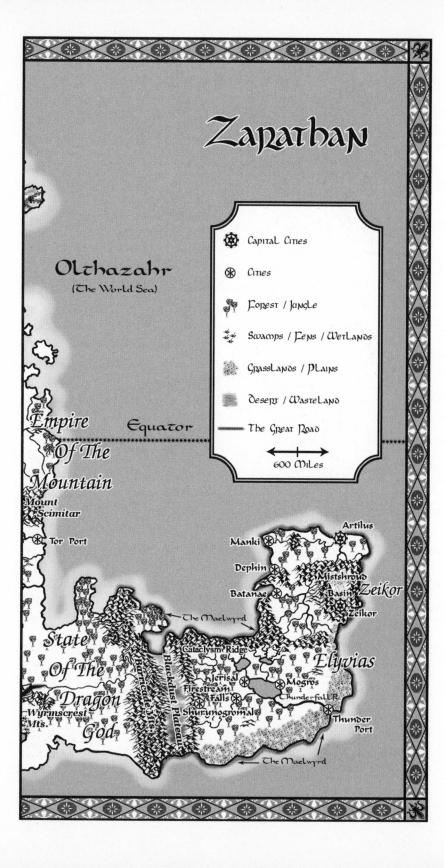

PHOENIX RISING

PROLOGUE

Warm light spilled from the windows of the estate, windows that were set in solid stone, warded with spell and steel; comfort with protection. He gripped the hilt of his sword and swallowed; his mouth was dry, as though filled with sand. "I—I don't want to do this," he whispered.

His companion's grip on his arm was unsettling—a combination of a reassuring squeeze and a warning, angry twist. "Ye're too late fer that, boy," the rough voice answered, barely audible from beneath the other's helmet, covered now with black cloth to prevent any glint of light from reflecting back to possible watching eyes. "Done other things as we been ordered, you have, not so bad, but enough 'tis so you either knew what might be needed, or you been foolin' yerself. Whichever 'tis, you'd best get over it."

"They're not bad people, *sirza*." The word meant friend, brother, father, though not related by blood; it was a word he used only to this man, the man he'd most admired and trusted and followed. "Why—"

"Dragons and curses, kid, you know that doesn't matter!" His mentor's voice nearly rose above a whisper. "We don't know the *why*, ain't got need to know, and askin' could get you what *they're* about to get."

He'd never more wanted to just shed the armor he wore than he did now, but his *sirza* was right; it was too late unless he wanted to go back to the temple and tell the thing waiting there that...

Shuddering, he shook his head and turned his face back to the castle. *No, far, far too late.* "We'll never get in anyway. Doors are shut, the locking wards will—"

"Been assured that's no problem. Just be needin' to break the doors in ourselves. Guards are mostly gone." His companion made three quick hand signals; the others fanned out. "The ones we've come for will be the real problem, boy. Neither soft, both adventurers in their time. But alone, quiet in their upper chamber, guessin' they're takin' advantage with the kids all elsewhere this night." A gentler squeeze to the arm. "Better this way, eh, *sirza*? Better than what *he* would do to them, if we were daft enough to refuse."

That much was true. Their targets thought they were protected, blessed, but he knew how much of that was a lie. *Yes, much better to die at my sword, no matter how horrifying they find it, than . . . than that.*

He took a deep, shaking breath, nodded, and then drew himself up.

"Good lad," he heard faintly. The two of them strode to the doorway now, coordinating their steps, concentrating the power they were given, speeding up, strides becoming a jog, a sprint, shoulders lowering . . .

BOOM!

The twin doors, each ten feet high and five wide, shuddered at the impact; he felt the cloth covering tear, but the time for stealth was over and it was no longer a concern. *He was right, the door-wards are down; all that force would've meant nothing otherwise, and likely alarm chimes and lights would now be everywhere—or something worse.*

They drew back, focused, the power flickering about them in tarnished bronze light before they struck again.

This time the doors flew open, the eight-inch thick beam that had secured them snapped in two, deep gouges in the rimewood panels where their shoulderguards had bitten halfway through the wood.

Two house guards ran forward, but surprise at what greeted them hampered their response—and outnumbered more than three to one they had no chance, anyway. He and the others moved forward now, swiftly. *Thank all the gods that the children are gone.* He spared one more glance towards his companion. *He planned the assault; I'm sure he waited for just that to happen.*

The others fanned out through the house. Sounds of screams, breaking furniture, and curses began to echo throughout the mansion as the two of them bounded up the stairs and smashed into the master bedroom doorway.

A blaze of blue-white thunderbolts limned them and he screamed, thrown back in a momentarily uncontrollable convulsion. *Those wards are still up!*

"Blast them! Threw up a new ward soon's they heard the noise! Go, boy, got to get the door down before—"

"I know!" He gathered himself up and they swung hard, sword and axe slamming into spell-reinforced wood and metal. The hastily spelled ward could not overcome that assault, and though the hilt of his sword tingled, he felt the spell break.

Then the doors were yanked open from the inside, two figures facing them; the grim fury on their faces gave way to disbelief and shock of recognition.

As one, the two invaders lunged forward.

1

The huge double doors of Victoria Vantage's ballroom thundered with the three ceremonial strikes: *Strength, Faith, Wisdom,* they seemed to say, and were flung open from outside. Kyri was already on her feet, along with Urelle, as six armored figures trooped in, three on each side and halted. "Assembled of Evanwyl!" Thornfalcon's voice rang out. "Human and *Artan,* Children of Odin, T'Teranahm and all of the assembled races, the Justiciars of Myrionar greet you!"

Mist Owl's precise *Artan* tones continued from the other side of the doorway. "In the name of Justice and Vengeance, in the name of Truth and Wisdom, in the name of the Creator of All and in the name of all spirits that live, we bring you greetings and glad news!"

Condor and Shrike stepped forward, one from each line, and turned, facing the open doorway. "The Sword is now balanced. On the one hand is Justice. On the other is Vengeance. But between them is Choice and Judgment. A choice and a judgment have been made this day, and where one has gone to the Sword, another has stepped forward to become the Sword of Judgment itself." They extended their arms as one as a figure became visible, striding in from the darkness outside. "Evanwyl and all its people behold! This day we are whole once more, for we and Myrionar give to you—the Silver Eagle, reborn to us again as he has ever been!"

Into the light he came, the Eagle-helm shining like a beacon, the silver and black pattern like wings on the armor and cape that streamed behind, towering dramatically over all the others except Condor, longsword at his hip, walking with a measured solemn step; she could see the mouth beneath unable to restrain a joyous grin. She led the cheer of "Silver Eagle!", but then Urelle burst from her seat, tears streaming down her face, shouting "Rion!", and the entire room dissolved in laughter and cheers. Rion pulled off the Eagle helm and swept his little sister up into his arms. "Now, now, I'm *Silver Eagle* now, Uri!"

"Lad, it might be too much t' expect that your family will be forgettin' your name soon," Shrike said with a chuckle. "Most o' us haven't family, but we all had names, and still have them. Sometimes, we even use them."

"Rion...let me have a look at you." Victoria put her hands gently on the shoulderguards and stood there silently for a moment, then embraced him hard. "Oh, dear, if only your parents *could* be here to see you, Rion. I know how proud they would be, as proud as I am this day."

Rion—*Silver Eagle, Justiciar of Myrionar!*—blushed and looked over at Kyri. "What about you, Kyri?"

She tried to say something, but settled for hugging him so hard the armor creaked, feeling something in her finally completely opening like spreading wings, and crying happily. "I knew you'd do it."

"That's more than *I* knew." He hugged her back, then looked back at Aunt Victoria. "Two parties in a week? You'll go broke, Auntie!"

"Nonsense. Your great-grandmother used to say that one should always have a party just before a great trial, because if things go wrong you at least *had* a party, and if things go right, you have *two*. And so now you have your second. And Kyri actually agreed to dance this time instead of stand around in the corners talking with former adventurers, warriors, and priests!"

Kyri tried not to look embarrassed. But Watchland Velion, the Arms, the other Eyes, and the Justiciars had so many fascinating stories to *tell*...

"Now that we are in the home of a brother Justiciar," Thornfalcon said with a smile, "we are allowed to be...more ourselves." He swept off his own helmet, revealing a long poet's face that seemed naturally mournful until he smiled, a face framed by long straight brown hair. *And that smile...well, I guess I know why he has that reputation with the ladies!*

"Indeed." Mist Owl followed suit, showing the features of the

Artan, that some called Elves, with surprising black-blue hair around a delicate heart-shaped face with eyes almost as large as his namesake's. Kyri was startled by his beauty; Lythos, the Vantage household's *Sho-ka-taida* or Master of Arms, had much of the delicacy of his people in his figure, but a hardness of feature that denied the possibility of beauty being a consideration.

"You won't be dancing in your armor, I assure you," Victoria said, interrupting. "Unless you intend to flatten your partners' feet." She pointed to the side, where one of her servants held a door open. "Change in there."

When some of the Justiciars blinked in surprise, she straightened, giving them the same glare she used to give Kyri and Urelle when they failed to wipe their feet properly. "And *immediately*, if you please!"

Mist Owl looked scandalized, but Thornfalcon backed up a pace. It was the short, squat Shrike who took action. "Come, lads!" he said with a chuckle, leading the way at a double-march pace. "Choose your battles wisely, or the battle may choose you."

Rion stared at her as he was half-dragged away by his new comrades, and Kyri tried to repress a giggle—not altogether successfully.

The crowd did not repress giggles or outright laughter, and spontaneous claps rang out around the room. Kyri, looking around, realized there were even more people here than had been for Rion's "Good Luck" banquet—the great hall of Vantage Fortress was *crowded. There has to be at least one person from every family in Evanwyl for twenty miles! Maybe five hundred, six hundred, more? You will go broke if we do this again, Auntie!*

But now the ruler of Evanwyl was addressing her aunt. "That . . . was quite impressive, Lady Victoria," said Jeridan Velion, the Watchland. His long blond hair was bound back in a careless-seeming tail; having fairly long hair herself, Kyri was aware of just how very much effort, and probably a little magic, went into making that simple style work without becoming a mass of tangles or an impediment.

"Not so much," Victoria said, acknowledging the compliment. "They're civilized, after all, and would be far too polite than to gainsay a woman in her own house. They just needed a bit of firmness to recognize that they should be acting like guests rather than Myrionar's moving statues this evening."

"I am more impressed by the fact that you must have appropriate clothing waiting for them—as I am sure they did not come prepared." The Watchland's smile was warm this evening. *It's odd,* Kyri thought to herself. *Some days I've felt very comfortable around the Watchland, other days... he seems very cold.* There wasn't anything she could put a finger on, but he did seem to go through different phases; she reminded herself to ask Urelle if she'd ever noticed anything like that.

Victoria laughed softly. "I should have known you would be thinking a step farther ahead, Watchland. When you've been an Adventurer for, oh, thirty years before settling down, you learn to be very prepared indeed. I would expect you would be similarly ready, eh, Jeridan?"

An incline of the Watchland's head acknowledged the compliment. "Perhaps, perhaps. But you have a far more... formidable reputation than I."

Victoria looked pleased. "Thank you."

"As would be expected," Byll Kontrul said affectionately, then his tanned farmer's face shifted to a mischievous grin, "from the V—"

Aunt Victoria's narrowed gaze cut him off before he could quite complete the phrase—as she had managed to successfully avert it every other time someone had tried to say it in Kyri's presence. She had *guesses* as to what the rest was, but no one would ever confirm or deny, and Aunt Victoria staunchly refused to elaborate. It had *something* to do with her Adventuring days, of course.

Politely ignoring the byplay, Watchland looked over at Kyri. "And will you be following in your aunt's—and your parents'—footsteps? Or will Arbiter Kelsley's hopes be fulfilled?"

"The Arbiter?"

Her obviously confused response caused Jeridan to smile apologetically. "I seems Kelsley told me things more private than I had thought." He glanced over, where the Arbiter—highest priest of Myrionar—was speaking to Melni Andris. *Oh, Balance, they lost Elodi in one of the patrols.* The memory *hurt*; she and Elodi were the same age, had played together a lot when they were young; her death was the one dark blot in this wonderful week. *And Melni still came? I can't imagine coming to someone's party if my daughter was killed!*

But the Watchland was continuing and she forced herself to

listen. "He has been very pleased with your attentiveness in the Temple, with your memorization of the Way of Justice, and other work in Evanwyl, and it's clear to me that he is hoping you will become a Seeker soon."

He is? The thought made her feel warm inside, despite the lingering empathic ache for what poor Melni must be feeling. "I... I am honored that he would want me as a Seeker. But I haven't decided my path yet." *I really need to speak to her.* "Would you excuse me, Watchland?"

He followed her gaze, nodded emphatically. "Of course, Kyri. Please, go."

She reached Melni and the Arbiter just as the holy man of Myrionar was bowing his farewell. "Melni—"

Melni's tired, red-rimmed eyes met hers, and the sting of tears overwhelmed her. "Oh, Myrionar and Terian, I'm so *sorry*, Melni..."

The older woman embraced her, and Kyri heard a small sob before Melni caught herself and pulled gently away, brushing back her gray-streaked brown hair. "Thank you, Kyri. And don't you tell me I shouldn't have come," she said, as Kyri was about to say exactly that. "El...El would have been *furious* if I didn't come to Rion's celebration. And Balance knows I need some light and cheer in my life now, really."

Kyri smiled and blinked the tears away. "I...thank you. Melni."

"Besides," Melni continued, with a deliberately light tone, "I have so many customers showing off here. Business, you know."

If she wants things to be normal, I certainly won't stop her. I suppose she's already done a lot of the crying. "Of course I do," Kyri said, and gave a little showoff spin of the long-sleeved green and aqua dress. "Look, your dresses makes even a mountain like me look good."

The laugh was weak, but it wasn't forced. "Oh, fishing for compliments, are we? Balance, child, you're impossible to make look *bad*. I could put you in a pile of *leaves* and you'd make most of the others look as though they were wearing *sacks*."

Kyri felt her cheeks go warm. *I'm not nearly that pretty, and the way I tower over everyone...* Fortunately, she saw movement at the far side of the room. "Oh! Here they come."

The Justiciars emerged to renewed applause, which she joined enthusiastically. Thinking on it, she realized that she'd never seen any of the Justiciars without that mystical, ancient, ceremonial armor that was both their badge of office and, it was said, the source of much of their power and protection against many forms of harm. What was most surprising was Condor; *he can't be much older than Rion... well, four or five years older, I guess,* she thought, *which makes him no more than eight or ten years older than me.* He and Rion were almost of identical height, six foot six inches, although Condor was considerably broader across the shoulders, past which fell brilliant red hair. Shrike, Condor's constant companion, was a grizzled bear of a man, nearly a foot shorter than his friend but if anything slightly heavier, with none of it fat. She saw Condor glance at her and mutter something to Shrike, who grinned and said something back; she thought she caught the ancient word *sirza*.

Skyharrier was also startling; he was one of the *Saelar,* the Winged Folk, but the armor usually restrained the great white, bronze, and gold wings that now stretched wide as he bowed to the applause, hair of the same bronze-white-gold shades tumbling around his face as he did. Bolthawk, as compact and strong as his namesake, was one of the *Odinsyrnen,* Children of Odin, the shortest of the Justiciars by far but no less formidable, with a sharp, pointed little black beard, short-cut dark hair, and twinkling black eyes like polished onyx.

Everyone was seated mostly according to plan (there were always a few people who decided to switch seats), the huge ballroom filled with multiple tables to hold all the guests. The largest table, of course, was reserved for the Justiciars, the Watchland, and a few others, including of course the family of the newly chosen Silver Eagle. Kyri also kept an eye on the two large tables on either side; those were the traditional Server's Tables—set aside for those who spent time serving the other people attending. Serving was hard work, but those doing the work were supposed to take shifts and had some of the best food set aside for them. Vanstell, the Master of House, saw her looking and gestured for her to pay attention to her own table. She smiled and nodded at the small, perfectly dressed pale-skinned man. *Van will make sure everyone gets their share.*

Rion was at the head of the table, of course, with the Watchland to one side and Aunt Victoria on the other. This put her next to the Watchland and across from Urelle, who sat beside their aunt, bracketed by Thornfalcon on the other side. Sasha Rithair, one of the Watchland's Arms and also Evanwyl's only summoner and trained mage, sat on Kyri's left. The others ranged down the table, ending with Skyharrier at the foot of the table so that his wings would not crowd anyone else.

Thornfalcon smiled at her with green-brown twinkling eyes. "I am indeed blessed," he said, with a comical exaggeration that made her laugh. "Here I am with a lady on one hand and two across from me; what other man at this table is so fortunate? Save, of course, you, my lord," he added to the Watchland, "as is only proper."

"Hmph," Victoria sniffed, but she, too, had a spark of amusement in her eye. "Compliments are always welcome, but you'll keep your wandering gaze from my younger niece, Thornfalcon. Your reputation precedes you."

"Alas," he replied, even as more chuckles rippled around the table and the first course—shaved raw pricklepine fish with mixed fruit jelly dip—was laid down, "my reputation also *exceeds* me, I am afraid; as with so many heroes, the deeds attributed to me overshadow the reality. But then I take your statement to mean I can extend my wandering gaze to your *elder* niece." He leaned on his elbows and let his eyes go misty and worshipful, such a caricature of a lovestruck youth—even though he had to be at least thirty-five—that she almost choked with laughter.

"Oh, go ahead," Rion said. "If she doesn't like it, she can always break you in half."

"With the legendary Vantage strength, yes, I suppose she *could* break a man." A pause. "If he was lucky."

Her brother was the one coughing out his last mouthful after that, accompanied as it had been with a leer so extremely exaggerated that she was at once blushing and giggling. *And if he wasn't so old, I might wonder if he's* serious.

The dinner continued, and she began to get a sense for the Justiciars as people; Shrike and Condor were, of course, like father and son. Oddly, Bolthawk—the squat, blunt-talking Child of Odin—and the quiet, almost ethereal Skyharrier seemed close. Thornfalcon sometimes fell quiet, and his serious gaze at those times made her suspect that the gangly-looking Justiciar played the clown and troubador because otherwise he would be too shy to speak.

Mist Owl was the oldest, and as an *Artan* he spoke most with

Lythos, the Vantage *Sho-ka-taida* or Master of Arms, and the only other *Artan* she knew of in Evanwyl. Mist Owl was...not *cold*, exactly, but his eyes took in everything and his expression gave back nothing. She had the feeling that he could see through everyone and everything. *Come to think of it, that may just be normal for* Artan; *Lythos always seems to see everything and he almost never smiles.*

As though he was reading her mind, the *Sho-ka-taida* looked up and directly at her...and then, with no one else to see, gave her a tiny smile and the quick hands-grasping gesture that said *together it is accomplished.* Her own smile was not small, for what the taciturn and perfectionist *Artan* teacher had just told her was that he believed her assistance—being one of Rion's main sparring partners—had helped Rion to this wonderful achievement.

Thornfalcon did show his more serious side as he discussed the dinner. "That first-taste was truly exquisite, Lady Victoria. I think I have only tasted such fine *An-su-ni* in Nya-Sharee-Hilya itself. And this with *freshwater* fish?"

"Why, thank you, Thornfalcon," Victoria said. "But the compliments should go to Feszinal, our head chef. He devised this entire feast and that dish, in particular, I know he prepared himself."

"I will certainly remember to convey my appreciation. I am also impressed with the roundcut of hill quillstrike—not the least because they're not the easiest thing to catch!"

She listened as the discussions flowed around her like the food. Privately, Kyri preferred what Victoria called "Southland" cooking—complex delicate flavors that were supposedly popular in Zarathanton and other parts far south—but she knew that Aunt Vicky's "stone and sea" approach was better received here, and she had a top-flight set of chefs. *And I can't complain unless I'm going to learn to do the cooking in between my religious disciplines and combat work, not to mention a little magical study, history...*

She realized she'd drifted when the chiming bell-notes of a Winged Harp sounded. *Oh no, the dances* already? *But who—*

As Rion took her hand and led her out, she realized *that* question had already been answered. "All right, brother, I'll dance with you. But no side balcony walks for you."

He grinned, leading her in a leafwhirl dance appropriate for the music. "What, I'm not pretty enough for you?"

She laughed. "I don't want the other girls getting jealous. We've had you to ourselves up until now, right?" It was pretty much true; Rion hadn't spent any time dancing, flirting, walking, or really even talking much with anyone outside of his training.

"Well, true, but now I'm a Justiciar. Have to be serious and devote myself to Justice and Vengeance."

The words were not nearly as serious as they sounded, and she couldn't keep an almost teary-eyed smile off her face. "Oh, Rion...you don't know how good it is to see you like this."

He didn't pretend to misunderstand. "Yeah. I...wasn't very easy to get along with after Mother and Father..."

She still couldn't quite keep the sadness from her face. "I wasn't, either."

He snorted wryly. "*You* weren't the one that was about to go charging out into the forest, waving a sword around without knowing your target."

Kyri remembered that. She also remembered how Aunt Victoria had responded to his determination to kill the people who had slain their parents and left their home a burning ruin: "An admirable plan, Rion Kervan Vantage. Such detail and attention to execution: 'Bastards! I'll kill them all!,' indeed. I trust you have some idea as to who 'they' are and, by the way you are running with such decision, knowledge of where 'they' may be found?"

Apparently the same memory had just replayed in *his* memory, because their eyes met and they both burst into laughter, even while shifting to the one-two-three of a Railwind Cross dance. "I was really *stupid* then, wasn't I, Kyri?"

"No," she said. "We all felt the same. Urelle too," she saw her little sister, now twelve, dancing and laughing, and remembered the eight-year-old Urelle staring, fury and emptiness and shock mingled in such a venomous brew that sometimes she wouldn't speak to anyone for days at a time, wouldn't eat...or would cry and cling to Kyri in the middle of the night, not letting her go. "Why do you think we've *all* been training every day with you, with Lythos?"

"I know." He smiled at her, and gave her a quick hug in the middle of a spin. "But we're better, now, I think. A lot better."

"Risen from the ashes," she agreed.

"Just like your favorite bird." He looked around. "Justice's *Name*, I think Victoria's actually starting to *line them up* for me."

Kyri giggled—a sound she tried not to allow to escape in public, but Rion could almost always get her to do it. "You know, there's nothing wrong with enjoying yourself at your own party."

He blushed. "Er...well, no, but it's a party about becoming a *Justiciar*, the living weapons of Myrionar, embodiments of Justice and Vengeance—a high and noble calling and all that, you know."

The two of them nearly stumbled—the fact that neither danced much was, unfortunately, too obvious—but she still managed a snort of laughter. "I hear that this doesn't stop Thornfalcon."

"True. I think he should've been a wandering entertainer if he wasn't such a monster with that rapier of his."

She glanced at the tall, melancholy-faced Justiciar with his slender wading-bird build. "He's that good?"

"*Hellish*. I think he could manage a cut or three on Lythos with that speed. Oh, Lythos would then carve him into a wall ornament, but he'd have been touched. Shrike, he's an Elemental. Not literally, but like living rock. You get a good swing at him and it just bounces off—Bolthawk's like that too," he performed a clumsy hand-around spin that almost tripped them both, then continued, "except that since he's purely a hand-to-hand man he tries to get up and pound the justice right out of you. Condor—"

"Condor is asking for the privilege of your sister's company to dance away the next song," Condor said over her shoulder. "If you'd be interested, Kyri?"

She smiled, a little awkwardly. "Well..."

Rion grinned mischeviously at her and glanced around. "I'll notice no one had to work at lining them up for *you*." He bowed out and let Condor take over, even as she was staring at what did appear to be a...rather large group of young men that kept looking in her direction. *That...many?* She recognized Zant from Myss Timbers, and three sons of the various Arms—*including Torokar Heimdalyn? Balance! We'd both look ridiculous, me over six feet and a Child of Odin barely over four!*—and that was Rairlsey Yindar, from all the way over in Gharis...*I think I'll just concentrate on the Justiciar in front of me.*

For a few moments she just tried to follow; the next song's rhythm was different, and Condor was clearly not much more experienced than she was, but was trying hard. They settled on a dance her aunt would have called a jink, but she preferred to call a quad-step. "Um...Condor..."

"Aran," he said quickly. "That's my name. Aran."

A nice name. "Aran. I like it. I wasn't sure the Justiciars kept their names."

"Well...yes and no. We're our Justiciar names most of the time. You understand the idea; by keeping the same names and the armor we imply the immortality of our justice."

"Well, yes, of course." It was actually more fun dancing with Condor than most boys she'd had to dance with. For one thing, he was actually taller than her by three inches, which was something that almost no one except her brother matched. And Watchland Velion, of course, but *he'd* never ask her to dance.

"But when we do get the chance to be out of armor—as we do at our own Temple, and at the houses of our own people—we have names like everyone else. We just don't say them much." A four-step turn, a sidestep, another. "Would you mind if I asked you something?"

"You just *did* ask me something." She grinned. "But no, go ahead."

"I see I had best watch my words around you just like your terrifying aunt. I was wondering...well, actually, *all* of us were wondering why in the name of the Dragons themselves you chose to use a *greatsword.*"

She laughed, slightly embarrassed but pleased that the conversation wasn't going in directions she didn't have experience with. "I'm...not completely sure myself, I suppose. I mean," the song ended, another began, but they continued without interruption, "...well...hmm...my brother went for the shorter blade because he felt the bigger blades would slow him up too much. I've always been a little faster than him, and I thought...well, I guess I wanted to prove I could handle a weapon that was too much for him."

"Ha! That was what I thought." He grinned to take the potential sting out of the words. "You aren't letting him be first if he won't fight for it. Ever."

She felt her answering smile which felt more relaxed somehow. "That's it. That's exactly it, Co— Aran."

He gestured to the other room. "And you remember *my* sword, so it's not like I don't have the same issue. Shrike uses that night-damned axe that looks big enough to cut down trees with a stroke, so I had to go get a weapon that looked even bigger."

She laughed. "So we're both competing with our older brothers?"

"Seems like." Up close, his eyes were a startling green, contrasting with red hair that he kept trimmed to an almost reasonable length in front. *He's ... really handsome, actually,* and was startled to recognize that thought. It wasn't that she hadn't noticed anyone before, but the Justiciars were symbols, not *people* most of the time.

And at that moment, another voice spoke. "Condor, you cannot monopolize the time of the loveliest lady in the room."

To her utter astonishment, it was the Watchland. Even more to her surprise, Condor seemed almost afraid as he yielded his place. "Certainly, sir. My apologies."

From the Watchland's expression, *he* wasn't quite sure why Condor was so apologetic either. But he turned to her with measured grace and bowed. "I hope you do not object. If you do, of course, I will be off."

"Object? Um, sir, oh, no, not at all ..." *This is why I hate these kind of things! I'm sounding like a stuttering ninny and I'm going to end up stepping on his feet.* Unlike her prior partners, the Watchland was a master of the dance floor. Which, she realized as he led her gently in a round-round, meant that he was going to make her look as though she knew what she was doing.

"I have to say I am terribly pleased to see your brother—and you—recovered as you are," Velion said quietly.

She blinked. "Recovered?" Then she remembered her prior conversation with Rion. "Oh. Thank you, sir."

"Perhaps it was not evident to you; indeed, it surely was not. Yet the Vantage family are Eyes of the Watch, second only to the Watchland, and harm to them is harm to our country; but more, your mother and your father were much beloved and your family is—has always been—one of the hearts of Evanwyl. The grievous blow you suffered seemed, for a time, to have taken your own hearts away and left only grief and anger. Becoming a Justiciar is not Rion's true achievement."

I had no idea the Watchland ... well, watched *us so closely.* "You're right, sir."

He laughed softly. "Sir? Dear me, I suppose I must be that old to you."

"Old? I ..." She didn't want to say anything insulting, and really, he didn't *look* old at all. "You ... well, you've been around since I was a little girl."

"Yes. Yes, I have. That must make me a bit old in your eyes, I cannot deny it. Still, could you call me Jeridan?"

It finally dawned on her that this was not simply a social dance. The Watchland did not dance casually, although he danced often. *Me?*

It had never occurred to her that she would even be noticed by the Watchland. Now that it seemed to have happened, she wasn't sure what to think.

But he was waiting for a reply, so she pushed the considerations of future issues aside. "Of course, um, Jeridan."

"Thank you." He seemed aware of her discomfiture. "Is this too embarrassing for you?"

"That...would not be the right word. Confusing in a way."

Another gentle laugh. "As straightforward as your father and mother. Good. I understand the confusion. You are not quite seventeen, and I barely on your side of thirty. In many ways it would seem we have little in common. Yet appearances may be deceiving."

"Meaning no offense, sir, but you don't know much about me, or I you."

His smile had a slightly sharper edge. "The latter may well be true, but the former may not." He guided her in an in-and-out twirl, which she only managed by remembering her training with Lythos. *Martial skills can be applied to the ballroom. I have to remember that. Coordination and focus.*

But the Watchland was continuing. "I observe everyone in the realm that I can; those on whom I rely—and who rely upon me most directly—I try to learn a great deal about." He saw her nod, and continued. "And when such a tragedy befell one of my own Arms? I have made sure to watch your family—and watch *over* them—as much as I could. So I am afraid that I do, in fact, know much about you—how you pushed aside your own grief to help your sister and support your brother, how you tried to take up your father's patrols when you were barely thirteen, your training alongside your brother with your Master of Weapons to the point that you became one of his best sparring partners—and he now Justiciar!—and your..." he saw her staring and almost stumbling, smiled again. "As I say, I know far more than you thought, obviously. Enough," he said, looking more serious, "to make it, perhaps, very wise that I give you the opportunity to learn more about *me*. I have mentioned this to your aunt and while she has some doubts, I am sure, she only said that any further interaction would be entirely up to you."

There it was, a sledgehammer blow delivered with the delicacy of a butterfly landing. Before she could form a reasonable reply, Thornfalcon begged the privilege of a dance in so comical a fashion she could hardly refuse.

And at the end of the night, she was bewildered to find that the sight that stayed most in her mind was not her triumphant brother holding aloft the Eagle helm, or the Seven Justiciars all arrayed before them, but instead two pairs of eyes; green eyes behind a helm, smiling into hers...and the blue eyes of the Watchland, intense and somehow lonely against the darkness of the night, looking back at her as the door closed.

2

"The least of her sons presents his compliments to the ageless and wise Lord of Waters, and asks if she would hear him at this time." The black-haired youth knelt before the woman whose white hair had a very few strands of similar midnight still visible.

There was a gentle laugh. "May the Spring of the Court flow ever for you, my son. The Lord of Waters is pleased that her son would seek out such an aged and infirm woman whose final years are doubtless close upon her, and would hear what wisdom of youth he may have to bring before her." Another laugh. "Close that door and have done with that prattle of tradition, Tobimar. By the Water and the Sand, what brings on such formality?"

Tobimar swallowed but managed a smile as he closed the door. This would be difficult, but his mother seemed in a good humor. "It's ... something I need to talk about, Mother."

Talima Silverun had not been the ruler of all Skysand for forty years without being able to hear what was unsaid. "And this something is not merely of mother and son, but of Lord and one of her heirs." She shook her head, an uncertain but affectionate smile playing about the corners of her mouth. "You are scarce fifteen, Tobimar. What is there of such grave import that you could have involved yourself in? Have you thrown salt into the Court Fountain?"

Tobimar winced; as well ask if he'd dropped his pants and relieved himself on Terian's altar. "Of *course* not, Mother!"

"Then have you killed one of the Warders in practice? No? Sold

19

the Seven Sacred Scrolls? No? Well, now, we're swiftly running out of possibilities, my son. What could—"

She broke off, staring, as he held up the card that had been hidden within the long sleeves of the silver-trimmed black robe. Slowly, unwillingly, she reached out and took the thick, ancient plaque, unable to take her gaze from the image. Then she closed her eyes and bowed her head.

Tobimar knew what she saw: Terian, the Mortal God, Lord of Stars as the Dragons called him, Infinity as some of his followers preferred; a human figure with a face shadowed in glory, in black with a flowing cape clasped with a golden sidewise-eight shaped sigil. The deity their family had followed since before Skysand had existed, and—some claimed—whose power ran within their veins, Terian was said to be one of the greatest of all the gods, and according to legend was a man who had discovered the very key to the power of Creation itself.

But in the reading of the Mirror, Terian's card did not mean a blessing. Not for those of the Silverun family.

"There is no mistake?" she said finally. It was the voice—not of the lord of Skysand, but of his mother, whose other six children were grown, all now helping to keep Skysand a place of safety and beauty amid the all-encompassing sand.

"*Nomdas* Ferril did the reading himself." There could be no mistake when the *Nomdas* of Terian performed the reading.

His mother closed her eyes again. When she opened them again, they were hard and clear, a deep blue that mirrored his own and that only they shared, of all their family. "The Lord of Waters then must speak plainly to her youngest son."

It's as bad as I feared. Yet...I feel so much more alive. Will Mother understand?

"The least of sons awaits the words of his most honored and wise parent, the Lord of Waters, as he would a drink in the very heart of the desert."

A tiny flicker of humor answered his extravagance, and then the Lord of Waters spoke. "The Lord of Waters earnestly inquires of her youngest and most beloved child as to whether he understands in fullness the meaning and import of this seemingly unimportant card, plucked from a deck at seeming random by the fingers of a priest?"

"Oh, Lord of Waters, your youngest son believes that he does, as much as any child can understand such things, for is it not written in our legends that when the face of Glory is revealed to one who stands between the innocence of childhood and the duties of a Lord, then the command of Terian is laid upon that one that he seek for that which was lost until it is found? And," he continued before his mother could begin the next question, for he didn't think he could bear to keep drawing this out, "is it not also written that ever since we fled from the Darkness that pursued us in the years of betrayal and loss, none of the Silverun may seek that which was lost except that they must leave Skysand and not return until their seeking is over, for in the act of seeking shall they draw the eye and will of the Darkness upon them, and upon all Skysand if they remain?"

"The Lord of Waters hears her youngest child and . . . and sees . . ." she broke off, took a breath, and composed herself. "And sees that he does well understand that the command of Terian lies upon him, and that he must leave his home, his city, and his people, not to return until twenty-four years have passed, or until—beyond all hope—that which was lost lies within his grasp and the Darkness is confronted by the Light.

"By our ancient laws, our child must know he has but a single day from the moment the card was drawn. More, he must know that he may taken nothing but what he may carry upon him, and that without the aid of any magics or powers not his own."

He nodded. *I know.*

It was a truth drilled into the Silverun from the time they could walk, the truth that lay beyond, beneath, behind the existence of Skysand itself. Once they had been a great people, a proud people with a land that was truly their own; but in the last Chaoswar something had *happened*—enemies monstrous and fell, demonic or worse, had fallen upon them, driven them from their lands.

And because of the effect of the Chaoswars themselves, the details of their heritage were forgotten. The clear records only spoke of the early years here, in the great and burning desert on the northwest of the huge continent, and the struggle to survive. None could say where the true homeland was, or even the true nature of the enemy.

But they still wait, and when we begin seeking . . .

Thousands of years ago, the first of the Mirror readings on the Skysand had chosen Vancilar Silverun, and it had been a moment of joy; for Terian was their patron god, their protector, and for any other family the face of the Mortal God meant good fortune, victory, protection. The *Nomdas* had told Vancilar he must begin the search for that which was lost, and—as he was the Lord of Waters, ruler of all Skysand—he bent to that task with a will, preparing the entire country to search for its lost land of origin.

Catastrophe struck the very day he was preparing to launch the first ship; an earthquake sudden and violent, followed by a wave that the wizards and priests could only blunt, not stop. Vancilar paused in his quest to repair his country, but did not forget his holy mission; a year later he stepped foot on his flagship, and in that instant the dormant volcano at the head of the bay exploded into violent eruption.

Concerned but still aware of his holy mission, Vancilar stayed to deal with this new emergency, and at the same time prepared to send out other agents to begin the quest. The moment the first group passed from the gates, a cloud appeared on the horizon, grew, and enveloped the city in raging dust filled with howling, water-stealing demons.

Battered by repeated perils, Vancilar could see the pattern; he demanded answers from the priests who had told him of this mission, set his wizards—those who had survived—to tell him why he seemed unable to so much as *begin* the work that, he was told, was the command of the gods. He got his answer . . . and knew his fate.

"I know, Mother," he said aloud. "Our enemies laid upon us a curse, one that used the very power of the Chaoswar to drive us from our old lands. It is a curse upon our people that they can never know their past, and a command and destiny laid upon some small number of our family to seek that past. If we ask our people to assist, the curse will punish them—punish Skysand. Any who are truly part of Skysand will share in their anger and the danger. Only by leaving our people behind, by leaving our *family* behind, only by that can we escape the curse and yet fulfill the command of the Lord Terian."

The Lord of Waters nodded slowly, seeing that he understood both with head and heart the reason and necessity for his quest. She glanced to the door, assuring herself it was still closed, and then came as close as he had ever seen to crying; she buried her face in her hands and sat still for long moments before she dropped her hands and looked up. "Where will you go, Tobimar? My son, what will you *do*?"

Suddenly he laughed and grabbed her hands, knelt in front of her. "Mother, Mother, please don't cry. Don't worry. I know you're afraid—*I'm* afraid, some—but...I never wanted to be a Lesser Lord of a city, or even the Lord of Waters myself."

The eyes looking back at him were suspiciously bright, as though tears hovered there waiting to be shed. But her lips slowly turned upward. "The youngest son becoming his grandfather's image... not to be, then?"

"More of my father and—perhaps—my mother in me."

She laughed, still with a hint of tears. "Perhaps indeed. Was it so obvious that this robe chafes at times?"

"To your children, I think so, Mother."

"Then what will you do, Tobimar?" She studied him. "You are a marvelous quick study with a sword."

"And I've learned from Master Khoros."

She looked grim for a moment. "Yes. He said you had much power of the spirit, to use the spirit to see that which might be invisible, to touch that which lay beyond your hands. And he gave me something when he left..."

"What? What is it, Mother?" The question was not just for what the mage might have left behind, but what bothered her so much.

"I wonder now...if he knew, somehow, even though not all the priests could have seen what was to come. For he said that it was for you 'when the time came.' And what other time could he have meant?" She rose and crossed to the miniature vault set in her chambers, touched the door, which opened. Inside were many things that he strained to see, but when she turned back all she held was a sealed piece of parchment...no, it was a leaf, as Master Khoros had often written upon, a leaf from the Mynoli plants that grew near oases, tough, flexible even when dry.

"Take it...but do not open it until you have left. He said also that 'wisdom comes only to those who seek it, never to those who demand it. Listen to what is said by your heart.'"

That was Khoros, all right. He took the leaf-parchment and tucked it away inside his own robes. "So...I'll do what I can, Mother. I'm a swordsman and a Silverun; I'll help people as I can. And I'll find what was lost. One day I will be able to tell you who we were, and show us where to go."

She suddenly embraced him. "I will pray to Terian that you do, Tobimar. I will pray every day, so that my son will one day stand before me...as my sister never did again."

3

Tobimar stood at the rail of the *Lucramalalla* and stared at Skysand, the great capital city sharing the name of the entirety of the gem-scattered mountains and golden sands of the country itself. The rising sun struck the seven Lesser Towers and made them seem forged of gold, while the central Great Tower, which was in fact gilded, blazed as though poured from a furnace of auric fire. Sparks of other color shimmered in that light, the light of his departure; glittering hints of ruby, argent, sapphire, emerald, other colors more exotic and rare from the mystical gems that were set as both decoration and defense in the towers and walls of Skysand.

Wind-whipped strands of long black hair across his face, hair that had somehow escaped the band he'd used to tie it back with, and the combination gave him an excuse for the tears that trickled from his eyes. It wasn't that he *needed* an excuse, exactly; it was just that a part of him was *glad* he was leaving, as he'd said to his mother, and crying didn't quite make sense to that part of him.

But the other part was afraid he would never see his mother Talima, his brothers... Vanilar, Terimur, Donalan... his sisters Karili, Mindala, Sundrilin... or Skysand itself ever again. He had never imagined that he'd *miss* the endless gray-gold sands, broken by outcrops of black stone, occasional oases... but he would. Skysand was his home.

And yet... it isn't.

That internal voice had spoken to him before. It wasn't so much a different voice as a different part of himself, something deeper, something that had no clear reason or history behind its existence. *Or a history that led me to this.*

Now the sun had risen higher, and the black polished obsidian of the Seven Lesser drank in the light and returned only small, brilliant highlights around the Lord of Waters' Great Tower. He looked at the highest point of the Tower, pretending for a moment that his eyes were sharp as a Dragon's and he could see his mother standing there, watching from the Spire of Legacy, the solemn, empty room at the very top of the Great Tower.

Finally he sighed and turned away, wiping away the traces of the tears. He made his way towards the cabins across the wide silver-gold zhenwood decks; above, the Captain's deep voice sent T'oltha's commands echoing to *Lucramalalla's* crew. *I think T'oltha probably* means *"Captain" in Ancient Sauran, because I think that was the name of the other Sauran captain I met when I was a kid, and it can't have been the same one.* The huge draconic creatures' names tended to be long and descriptive, difficult to remember and sometimes even harder to pronounce. *Or...maybe it* is *the same one.*

The wide stairway down to the cabin level was darker than outside, but still lit by lightstones; Tobimar shook his head in bemusement. Skysand made good use of many forms of magic, but this vessel—five hundred feet long, two hundred or more wide, and with only enough mast and sail for emergencies—was a wonder in itself. "Built only two centuries after the last Chaoswar," T'oltha had claimed. Tobimar wasn't sure he believed that—it would make the *Lucramalalla* something like twelve thousand years old—but then again, it was known that the Saurans themselves lived for thousands of years. It was possible that T'oltha was simply speaking of something she'd *witnessed.*

He reached his cabin and entered. It was reasonably large, but spare in its furnishings; a bunk, a writing desk made fast to the floor, a simple locker which, despite being not overly large, still had ample room for the few possessions he carried.

Tobimar sat down and took a deep breath. *Now.*

From the inside pocket of his robe he took the Mynoli leaf, inscribed with the peculiar rune-like symbol that Khoros used as a signature, and unfolded it.

Clear white light poured from the leaf, dazzling Tobimar and causing him to nearly upset his chair. He blinked as a figure rose out of the light. "M-Master Khoros?"

"Tobimar." The immensely tall form of the wandering enchanter nearly touched the eight-foot ceiling of the cabin; the strange wide, five-sided, peaked hat that Khoros wore obscured, as always, the details of his face; and his staff with the complex gold-crystalline head chimed softly. "Do not make the mistake of believing I am here. As with many things, what you see is less important than what you believe.

"As you are receiving this message, there are two possibilities. The first, and least likely, is that you have ascended to the Lordship of Skysand; you are, then, the Lord of Waters. If that is the case, I shall be before you soon, as you shall be in grave need of my advice.

"Far more probable, however, is that you have now left Skysand on the quest that only a Silverun may complete, at the sight of the card of your patron." The half-hidden mouth gave a smile that Tobimar found extremely disquieting. "It was evident to me that if any in your generation was to be chosen, it would be you." As always, Khoros offered no explanation; he spoke in pronouncements, riddles, and questions. "You have the best chance of any of your people to succeed where all the others have failed, Tobimar Silverun. And it is terribly important that you do, not merely for the sake of your exiled and lost people, but for the entirety of the world." Tobimar felt a slow, creeping dread as the white-haired mage paused and pointed the chiming staff at him. "Remember my lessons of history, Tobimar."

What the . . . he's not even here *and he's expecting me to answer him?* Tobimar searched desperately through the hundreds of hours of instruction Konstantin Khoros had given him, in history, meditation, the power of the mind, the theory of magic, the interaction of the powers . . . "You taught a lot of lessons, Master Khoros."

For a moment he was convinced that—despite the earlier warning—Khoros was, indeed, present, because at his response the old wizard shook his head as dolefully as ever he had in life. "You need to be quicker, Tobimar. A lesson does no good if it is filed away somewhere in your head only to be drawn out by being told to you again." He sighed. "Never mind. I am as much at fault; I tell only that which I dare, and it is never enough.

"I mentioned that over the past several centuries, the number of gods seen intervening in direct and spectacular fashion had decreased. I have spent many of those years trying to determine if this was a pattern that indicated a change in need—if, in fact, the gods simply were not being called upon to act as much as in years past—or a change in behavior, or merely what might be termed an artifact of chance." Despite himself, Tobimar nodded. He remembered this very clearly, now that Khoros had reminded him of it. *Which echoes what he said; it does no good if I have to wait for someone else to remind me.*

"It has, however, become clear to me that this was in fact no coincidence, nor was it a matter of decreased need," Khoros continued. "Indeed, in some cases, the lack of intervention where it would have before been expected has led to terrible disasters." Khoros' deep, sonorous voice was grim. "And now I understand why.

"Twelve thousand years ago, the last of the Chaoswars was fought—a world-enveloping series of conflicts which seemed to erupt almost at once, triggering mystical cataclysms of tremendous force and lingering effect. It is of course known that there have been many such wars in the history of Zarathan; what is not known, however, is how they come to happen, and how often." The sorcerer's image leaned closer. "But *I* know. Every twelve thousand years, more or less."

"Terian's Light...but that means..."

"Exactly so. The next Chaoswar is nearly upon us, and I believe it is much, much closer than merely sometime in the next few centuries. I believe it is within the next few years."

"But what have the—"

"And now you ask what the gods' behavior has to do with this."

If this is truly a message recorded months ago, his ability to be annoyingly correct is even more impressive than I thought.

"I have sources close to the gods, when I dare use them, and in this case I felt it necessary. They confirmed what I feared. There is a pact, now, between virtually all of the gods, an agreement that they shall not intervene directly in events on Zarathan, save only for those gods who have an undeniable and inescapable physical presence on this world. How exactly this pact was arranged...I have yet to determine, for even I dare not tread too far into their realm unless I am willing to confront them. Something which," he smiled wryly, "I would prefer not to do at this time. But its existence convinces me that I am right about my timing. Even though the power unleashed in a Chaoswar can, and does, affect even the gods, without them to assist, the results could be even worse. Even the gods of evil, in general, are not in favor of the complete and total disruption of a Chaoswar, and the few that are would normally be kept under control by the others."

Khoros rotated his hat absently in the ritual manner Tobimar had seen so many times, with the five points of Earth, Air, Fire, Water, and Spirit following in turn. "You must find that which was lost, Tobimar. It is not that it is your destiny, although you may choose to make it so, for destiny is choice, not choicelessness. It is that the powers of destruction gain strength in such times, and those things which failed to utterly destroy your people in their flight will once more walk the world. Your people have kept traditions, yet forgotten the truths. You were deprived of your homes, your power, your freedom, and your allies—and they, of you, so that all are now but feeble shadows of what they once were, and where you once ruled is now darkness. That must not be allowed to happen again—for it shall."

"You *know* where—"

"You must find these things on your own." Once more it seemed as though Khoros knew already what would be said, long months after he had left. "I can only tell you this: that you must learn what you once were before you can decide what you will become; that you must pursue lies to discover truth; and that the only route to your triumph is to serve both justice and vengeance, for both are your people's due. All else is but your choice—to trust or not, to lead or follow, to have faith or lose all. But when all else fails, you may find strength in childhood prayer, for there were, indeed, the true words of Terian himself, as given to your forefathers in the first days of their strength."

That old prayer? Tobimar felt vaguely embarrassed, and yet he remembered the words as though he had never stopped saying them, and they still carried the echoes of his childhood faith as he found himself repeating them with Khoros:

> "Seven Stars and a Single Sun
> Hold the Starlight that I do Own;
> These Eight combine and form the One
> Form the Sign by which I'm known.

The Good in heart can Light wield;
The Length of Space shall be thy shield."

"Two Chaoswars past, your people rose to the heights. In the last, they were felled; in this, Tobimar, they shall either reattain all that was lost and more...or they shall cease to be." The ancient mage bowed deeply. "My hopes and blessings go with you. May the Five and the Seven and the One be ever with you."

And he was gone, the leaf dispersing like the last of the crystalline light that had surrounded him, the echoing chime of his staff fading into the sounds of the surrounding ocean.

4

This was absolutely not in my plans today, he thought as he gazed down into the cavern, yellow-gray stone tinted orange and red by unnatural fire burning in the center of the cave. Figures moved around the fire in an orderly, menacing progression, muttering in a language he didn't understand.

But he didn't need to understand much; he'd only dabbled a little in magic so far, but what he saw now...a huge five-pointed star, carven into the bedrock of the cavern, inlaid with metal and dark gemstones and—at each point of the star—a pathetically twisted body impaled straight through the chest as though by a spear that penetrated the living rock below...*that pretty much tells me all I need to know about what kind of magic this is.* He grimaced and closed his eyes, setting his jaw and feeling his hands grip the hilt of his new sword tightly, but he couldn't shut away the sight of those five murdered people. *Rushsong, Shapeclay, Foamcloak, Divedeep, Tipstone...I knew them all.* Five disappeared. Five dead.

It had all seemed so simple this morning; he'd gone to the temple to pray, as were most of the others with five of their own gone. Everyone had been offering help, planning to assist in the searches; as usual, almost no one had noticed him. That happened a lot when you were that small, a runt who had to literally climb onto the prayer stones instead of squat down like most of the others.

So he'd had to wait until everyone else left to catch old Barkboat's attention. "Hey! Hey! Priest!"

The old priest made a great show of looking around in puzzlement. "What? Are the prayer stones talking now? Oh, it's *you*, little one."

"Five of us gone. One of them my first teacher. No one hunts us. We do not hunt our own. This is...very strange, very bad. This isn't a time for being silly, Barkboat."

"Tsk, tsk. We are taught that even the darkest times may call for the light of laughter. What brings *you* here?"

"I want to help."

Somewhat to his surprise, the priest had not laughed, but gravely considered the offer. "Were the times normal, young one, I would have told you to simply stay close and stay out of trouble—hard though the latter would be for you. Yet...your elders and your larger peers have searched far and wide. They have probed the Burning Waters and the Evermists, searched beyond the Rainbow Mountain. Perhaps...perhaps you could see what they cannot." He rocked back and forth, a sign of uncertainty. "It's true that you have much more of the adventurous spirit than most of us; you have even spoken of leaving the village." The priest still seemed uncertain.

"Please, let me try!"

In the end, the priest had agreed, and had even dug around in the castoff and donated odds and ends until they found a suitable weapon—barely a dagger to anyone else, but a mighty blade for someone his size. He had trained with small sticks before; he hoped he wouldn't embarrass his teachers.

Looking down at the scene before him now, he realized that embarrassment was the very last of his worries. *I could turn around. I found this tunnel myself, and I don't think anyone else has used it. But...*he looked again. *Mazakh, snake-demon men. And...other things I don't know, look like bug-spider monsters. Smoke and fog, can't see whatever's leading this clearly.*

But, his thoughts repeated again, *what would I do? The others aren't really fighters any more than I am. No adventurers in town. If I go back, the others who come here...will get killed off.*

It really began to sink in then, as he watched the creatures continuing a ritual which surely meant something far worse. *If I leave, no one's going to do anything. At best we'll have to send someone to the Suntree, or Zarathanton, and that'll take...way too long, that's for sure. Then Foamcloak, Divedeep, all of them, they'll have been abandoned. It's really up to me, Duckweed. A one-name runt with a tiny sword.*

He studied the cavern more carefully now. *Two doors in the walls. They've been here a while. Maybe a LONG while.* Now that he thought about it in those terms, he seemed to remember there being a few other disappearances in this general area of the woods not far from the Evermist.

That might explain why he didn't see any guards near the doors. Everyone in the room was in this ritual-thing. They'd been here a long time and never been found. *So maybe I can at least get in and do something.*

Climbing down from this point probably wouldn't work. The wall was pretty sheer, and while he was good at climbing, it was a *long* way down for someone his size. *Might not really hurt me . . . or might, but the fall might draw attention. Don't want to draw attention. Those guys stand like eight times taller than I do even if I stretch up on my tippytoes. So let's go check out that branch tunnel.*

The "branch tunnel" was a side passage which he'd ignored because he could see a faint light down the main passage he was following—a light that had led him here. But the side passage, if he was lucky, might lead him to some other part of these caverns.

It was pitch black in the tunnels, and he really wished he could have some light, but even if he'd carried a torch or something with him, he would've needed a way to carry the sword at the same time . . . and using a light in here might call attention to anyone at the other end. *No, just squirm along and let my skin and my sword guide me.*

After several minutes of scuttling and wriggling through the dark side passage, he began to see a dim light. A few moments more and he was at a small opening in the side of a much larger tunnel. Sniffing, he could catch the smell of heated rock, snake musk, the undefinable spicy aroma he associated with large insectoids. *Same caverns!* He peeked cautiously up and down the cave; nothing in sight except greenish lightglobes stuck to the walls at intervals. He moved out and chose to move to the left; that was the direction he thought the main ritual chamber was in.

He moved very cautiously, sword out, even though he wasn't sure what he'd do if he were caught. *A swing with any of their weapons will cut me in half. I need to do this sneakily.* He remembered that wandering mage giving him some general pointers on magic, and one fact stuck in his mind: the crucial importance of the array or symbol used for a ritual or summoning. *That gives me a real* strategy. Sort of. Well, it's really more of an idea for what I want to get done. Is that strategy? No, I have to get those monsters out of the room, or at least confused and moving around to get away with it. And I have to do it without them seeing. Now...how am I...

Suddenly he became aware of multiple footfalls behind him. Duckweed glanced around in panic. *Can't get back to the hole!* The cavern was rough but there were no rocks to hide behind, no open doorways (two closed ones, but the latches were far above him and the fit of the doors far too tight to squeeze under).

Only one chance. He pushed up against the wall and squatted down, seeing vague shadows just starting to come around the gentle bend. *Oh, drought and dust, my* sword...

There was no time to do any thing fancy; he stuck the sword underneath him and sat on it. *Please don't look down, don't look down...or if you do, just see nothing unusual...*

Three figures moved down the rough corridor. One was a *mazakh*, said to be a cross between snake and demon, a venomous reptilian creature on two legs that moved like a striking snake, a long, flexible tail trailing behind it. The other two were ant-headed, with savage cutting mandibles, and armored black-and-red chitinous bodies that also stood on two legs, but had no tails, but did have hard-polished wingcases.

The three were talking quietly and moving purposefully towards the far end of the corridor—where, he suspected, the ritual was taking place—when one of the insectoids' glittering compound eyes swept the area lower down. With a sudden chittering hiss it shrank away from Duckweed, causing its companions to instantly draw weapons and look around for the cause of the panic.

Duckweed resisted the almost overwhelming urge to pull out the sword. *Not a chance. If they just don't* notice *the hilt...*

The *mazakh* hissed something and then smacked the insectoid that had seen Duckweed with the flat of his blade. "Idiot. That's the third one I've seen here this week. Not like the ones we've been capturing. Of course, if you want to waste your time..."

The insectoid chirp-rattled something which somehow sounded sheepishly apologetic, and the three went on, having decided that he was just another harmless native of the cavern.

Which, Duckweed thought as he was slowly allowing himself to breathe again, *isn't all that unusual.*

After all...I'm just a Toad.

5

Once his heart slowed to normal, Duckweed looked up at the doors. *Have to get through the one... or the other, maybe. Wonder what's through there?* He'd seen that the door at the end of the corridor was, as he'd suspected, one of the two into the big cavern. He moved off his sword and hooked it in the little loop of leather tied around his body; if he was going to make a habit of this, he needed to figure out a better way of doing that.

The *mazakh* were going to be the real problem. The big bug thingies apparently had the instinctive fear of his people that many insects—giant and otherwise—did. He could startle them, make them do stupid things if he worked at it. The *mazakh*, however, would just as soon eat him as look at him. *And at my size, I'm barely a mouthful.*

The side door looked like the better bet right now. He still wasn't sure exactly how he was going to accomplish his first goal, which was to either get the monsters doing the ritual in the big room to come out, or at least throw them into a lot of confusion and panic so he could get in unnoticed. And in not too long a time, either; no telling what they were trying to do with that ritual, but he'd bet his tongue it was something really bad.

Focus. You're a Toad, you can handle this. We survive. We always have, even before the Great Dragons, before the Demons, we were here. I can deal with these newcomer scalies and their bug-eyed friends.

Of course, he had to admit as he scuttled over to the side door, *we survive as a group and by usually not getting involved. Adventuring has a way of getting people killed.* Why *was it I wanted to do this again?*

The handle was about three and a half feet from the floor. The one at the end of the corridor had opened without noise, so hopefully it was kept well-oiled. He judged the distance and leaped.

It wasn't the highest leap he'd ever done, or the longest, but it was a hard jump to judge, and he was a little low. He managed to *just* catch the handle with his slightly webbed hands and pull himself on top of it. As he did, his tiny sword-blade rapped against the metal of the handle with a clear, if low, chiming noise.

He froze.

Movement inside! I can hear it! What do I do—

The handle began to turn, tilting downward on his side. He scrabbled desperately, then gave up and dropped down. *As soon as the door opens...*

The heavy metal-bound door was yanked open and a *mazakh* glared out, hissing, a jagged-edged sword in its clawed hand. But it was looking out into the corridor, not just by its own feet, and the little Toad took the chance to gingerly ease by the creature's front foot. He froze again as he noticed the contents of the room.

Three other figures were near a moderate sized table in the center of the room. One, another *mazakh*, had risen and half-drawn his weapon; the other two—one an insectoid like the others Duckweed had seen, the other apparently human—were still seated, looking at the snake-man near the door with bemused expressions.

Duckweed was partially hidden from the group by the *mazakh's* three-toed rear foot. If he moved out from that, he'd be visible. Maybe they wouldn't notice...but at that range, *mazakh* were usually very, very good at sensing motion, even if the others weren't. He held still, watching, controlling panic. *If I lose control for even a moment, they'll catch me in seconds...and then I'll be* lucky *to just get eaten.*

"Well, Lassish? Anything?" the human asked in a bored tone.

"There *seems* to be nothing." The *mazakh* named Lassish still stood immobile, looking up and down the corridor, sniffing suspiciously. "But I *know* I heard something. Metal, sounded like, striking the door, like someone was trying to slide the latch."

"I heard it too," the other *mazakh* agreed. "One of those passing to the Great Summoning, perhaps, brushing by?"

"There was no one in the passage when I opened the door, and the door to the Summoning was closed." Lassish hissed in annoyance, and abruptly let the door swing shut and turned.

The little Toad found himself following as closely as he dared on Lassish's heels; it was the only thing he could think of, to let the body and tail of the seven-foot creature hide him as he scuttled across the room. The tail and feet were hideously close and threatened to crush him with every stride, but Duckweed was committed now.

The *mazakh* reached the table and pulled out his cutout-backed chair, appropriate for a tailed creature; the Toad moved completely under the chair as Lassish sat down. "Finally the Summoning, and *we're* stuck here," the human grumbled, opening his warcard box and checking the positions; the four had apparently been in a match when Duckweed's impromptu knock had interrupted.

"Gladness I feel; wisdom for you, likewise should you feel." The insectoid's voice was a buzz and chatter. *He also smells very tasty. Tough, though, probably.*

"Why's that?"

"Because, smooth-skin, a Great Summoning is perilous even for the trained. Sometimes, despite all the sacrifices and preparation, the *mazolishta* demands more than was expected ... and then the Summoners must restrain it, or become sacrifices themselves."

Mazolishta? Duckweed had heard the word before, but never thought he'd have heard it in a real, living context. *Great Black-wart, they're summoning one of their Ruling Demons!*

The human's voice was tense. "What? Are you telling me that what we're calling up might just decide to eat *our* souls instead of help us?"

Hissing laughs. Duckweed eased himself from under the chair and moved along under the table. *These guys have gotta be guards. And that means ... yep, there's an opening back there, an archway.*

"Did you think dealing with one of the *mazolishta* was *safe?*"

"I figured the boss knew what he was doing."

"Possibility granted; present in this location, is not the 'boss.'"

As they were focused on their conversation, Duckweed cautiously made his way out from under the table. Now that he knew what was going on, there was even more urgency. He glanced behind him and shifted his line a bit, trying to keep the wider form of the human between himself and the others as he moved towards the archway. He could see several alcoves on each side of the passage.

Duckweed gave a silent sigh of relief, letting himself sag down so he looked like a brown puddle with warts for a moment, as he reached the first alcove and ducked around the corner, now completely out of sight of the four guards. Inside the alcove were several strongboxes with crude locks holding them shut. *But not tightly shut. They've got enough slack, I think, so I could get the top open a little.*

He was able to insert his little sword between the top and bottom and lever upward, the lock and hasp allowing slightly less than an inch of opening. Peering in, he saw rows of cushioned spheres of glass with reddish liquid inside. The liquid appeared to glow very faintly.

The little Toad shivered. He knew what that had to be. *Fire essence. Cases of it. They're armed for a war. Against us? One case of that would be enough—most of us wouldn't fight, just run. But north of here...*

It was insane, of course. The *Artan*—elves, as the humans called them—of the Forest Sea might be the youngest of the Great Races, but they had proven how tenacious and indomitable they were as soon as they had appeared. Still...

He lowered the top of the case quietly and withdrew his sword. *Can't open that without making noise. Let's check the other alcoves.*

He systematically searched the other three, taking care to not be seen as he quickly moved from one to the other. More weapons, lots of them, varied in style and type. He paused to admire one rack of *Zachass*, wristblade launchers, with their intricate clockwork mechanisms that allowed the *mazakh* to fire several of the balanced, circular blades in quick succession. Duckweed loved clockworks and other complicated devices. Gears, levers, springs, pulleys, little assemblies that moved in precision... he'd built a few clumsy devices along those lines himself, but the parts that made up these were works of art. Deadly art though... He shrugged and moved on. Crossbows... slings... *What are these little cases?*

The cases in question, about his own nose-to-rump length of five inches square, were packed along with slings and slugthrowers, which used little round bullets of lead or other heavy, hard material. *These are locked too... but I'm another alcove down from the guards, and they're busy with their game...*

He examined the box carefully, and finally—almost holding his breath—slid the sharp point of his blade in where he thought the latching mechanism was, and twisted.

Toads can be quite strong for their size, and Duckweed was experienced in using what he had to the utmost. The latch resisted, but he managed to slide the blade in a little farther, braced his feet on the sides of the big chest the box was sitting in, and *heaved* as he twisted with both hands on the hilt.

The latch gave with an audible *pop* that surprised him; he paused and listened, but there was no sign that any of the guards, even the sharp-eared Lassish, had heard.

Inside the case were blackberry-sized spheres that mirrored in miniature the much larger ones in the first chest he'd examined, packed in soft cloth. *More fire essence in bullet-sizes now. This is bad.*

And he was running out of time. Yes, a summoning ritual like that took time, but no telling how long it had already been going on. He had to *do* something. He gazed around in growing desperation.

And then his golden gaze alighted on the *Zachass* again.

He paused. And then he smiled, a slight upturn of the almost-immobile lips. *If I can have just ten more minutes...* He gave the same hop-and-bob that everyone gave when they entered the Temple, and imagined the immense obsidian statue that loomed behind the altar. *Blackwart, give me just ten more minutes, please, ten more minutes to work in.*

Because if they didn't finish their ritual in ten minutes, the little Toad was pretty sure he could make sure they never would.

6

Duckweed lowered himself slowly down the cord. *Ritual's still going on... Maybe, just maybe...*

It wasn't easy. Two bags were now tied onto him with some of the same string he'd gotten from the fourth alcove, bulky bags that were fairly light but almost as big as his own body. His sword was in a hastily wrapped semi-scabbard on his back. Rigging everything in the alcoves had taken him ten minutes, but it had taken another five minutes to figure out how he was getting out of there past the guards. Fortunately, the rooms had been cut out of natural cavern and he'd finally noticed in the upper corner of one a small crack which he and the bags had *just* been able to squeeze through; apparently no one thought it was worth the trouble to block up. He'd set things going and then gotten out of there.

Getting very tight on the timing I think... Gotta get to the ground before everything starts happening. Normally he'd just drop—it was a long way down, but he'd also long since found out that someone as small as he was could fall a lot farther than the big people without getting hurt.

But that was, of course, *not* a good idea right now.

The ritual was clearly reaching a crescendo. Three ranks of monstrous figures were circling the great pentagonal array, the inner moving to the right, the middle to the left, the outer to the right again, all repeating invocations in lockstep rhythm in a language that made Duckweed's skin prickle. And the rhythm was speeding up. It wouldn't be long now at all.

Only good thing is that means most of them are completely focused on their nasty ritual. He was still worried about the few guards inside the room who *weren't* part of the ritual. He was descending from the same little passageway he'd been in before, and it was in a shadowed part of the room...but *mazakh* had good eyes in the dark, some said they could see heat. Not much heat in a little Toad, but all they needed to do was notice movement...

Only ten feet to go. But time was passing. Had it been five minutes? Seven? He'd been able to rig the clockwork, but no time to be sure of the exact timing. He *thought* he'd given himself ten minutes, but he couldn't be sure...and there were no clocks in here, so he wasn't sure how long it had been. *I feel like a Newleg, stuck between the Swimmer and the Leaper.*

Five feet. Finally he could relax a little. A giant stalagmite now obscured him from the guards. He slid the rest of the way and landed gingerly on the cool stone. *Now I just have to get over near the doors...not too near, though.*

He scuttled from rock to rock, trying to keep from jarring the bags too much. *Still, they* should *be okay with a little banging around.*

One of the *mazakh* suddenly loomed up, pacing slowly around the perimeter of the room. Duckweed froze, pressing himself against the rock, trying to look like a lump of brownish stone.

Either it worked, or—more likely—the demon-snake never looked down. The little Toad waited, fidgeting. *He has to get far enough away so he won't hear me. I think I'm close enough to the doors, but if I try this and I get caught, it's not going to work! And I'm almost out of time!*

The green and gray-scaled creature paused, sniffing suddenly, and Duckweed swallowed nervously.

It shook its head slightly and turned, moving away. *Almost... almost...now!*

He unslung one of the bags, opened the top, and carefully judged the direction and angle of the floor. Then he emptied the bag with a single crescent-shaped movement that sent its contents rolling across the floor towards the two doorways. The second he spread between the doorways and the pentacle, the chanting approached a new crescendo. *Oh, snakes and fisher-birds, I hope I didn't set everything for too long, it would suck bottom-mud if I—*

The entire cavern shuddered, and there was a thunderous echoing blast that sounded like the rage of an awakened Dragon. A blaze of orange fire spurted from the little tunnel he'd just exited. *Oh, ow, that would have hurt!*

Hisses and chittering screeches of consternation echoed through the room, the ritual movement and chanting now ragged. A loud voice—*human, I think! They're everywhere, those creatures*—shouted, "Keep going! *Dhokar morred zshenta vell...*"

A second concussion rocked the cavern, sending fragments of stone sifting down from the ceiling. A huge stalactite suddenly plummeted down like a divine spear, crushing one of the insectoid creatures.

That was enough for the rest. Abandoning such a ritual was dangerous, but it was clear that something worse might happen if they didn't. The three circles broke and ran for the doors.

As they did, some of them stepped on the tiny, blackberry-sized glassy spheres the little Toad had scattered in their path.

A series of fierce detonations erupted, shattering bodies, incinerating limbs, scattering corpses left and right as the compressed fire essence was liberated by the impacts and unleashed the quintessence of devouring heat upon all around it, just as had happened in the alcove rooms moments before when the *Zachass* Duckweed had rigged had fired one of its razor-edged missiles directly into one of the cases of fire-essence warspheres.

A third case must have detonated just then, because the first door suddenly bulged inward as another blast echoed through the cavern's very bedrock, sending a cascade of larger stone fragments raining down. Shrieks and roars of consternation filled the air, and Duckweed hopped desperately forward, dodging falling rocks and moving between running legs. No one was looking *down* now at all. *I haven't seen anything but* mazakh *and those insect-things, which means...*

And then, just behind him, half the cavern roof caved in with a rumble and a juddering roar that dwarfed even the explosion that triggered it. The blast of air and dust and pebbles from the impact blew him off his feet, and smoke and flame belched from the mass of rock as the remaining fire-essence sought release from within the rockfall. He tumbled uncontrollably, fetching up with a jolt against the base of another stalagmite.

Slowly the rockfall slackened from a fall to a stream to a trickle of sifting dust. Duckweed righted himself gingerly and listened. Everything was deathly silent except for the slow grumble of settling stone and the faint hissing of dampness boiling away from the heat of the fire essence. Dust clouded everything and for long moments he couldn't see anything; only the eerie rock-fire in the center provided light at all, and it was half-buried and slowly, slowly starting to fade.

But as the dust gradually cleared, the faint breeze showing that some small outlet, at least, remained to the surface, Duckweed became aware that there was another source of light. A glowing sphere floated about fifty feet away, near a shadowy upright silhouette.

"So near. So very near. By the Gods Below, how could this have *happened?*" It was the same human voice, filled with disbelief and rage. Muttered arcane words, and a wind ripped through the remaining cavern, clearing away the dust as though it had never been. Only some small clouds remained, seeming to glow in the unnatural light.

Duckweed could see now, in the flickering light from both rockfire and magical glow. Human, all right, long brown hair in carefully arranged braids, a set of three long, fine white scars in parallel on his bare upper right arm. He wore some sort of leather protective garment that left his arms clear. His lower half was dressed in black cloth pants with tough-looking leather boots.

Much more worrisome for Duckweed were the eyes, which were now focused on him.

"Could it be...?" The man studied him intensely; abruptly, a strange carven crystal implement was in his hand, pointing in Duckweed's direction. "Speak now if you can, Toad, or I will incinerate you where you sit."

The little Toad debated the question for a moment, but as the tanned hand began to tighten on the crystal, hopped forward a pace. "All right. I'm speaking."

A hiss, almost like that of a *mazakh*, escaped the man. "Surprising. Surprising. Would I be correct in surmising you are responsible for all this?"

Duckweed shrugged. "Well, some of it. I didn't really mean to bring the whole cave down. You had *waaaaay* too much of that fire-essence stuff."

The man gave a very small humorless grin. "So it would appear."

Duckweed blinked. It looked as though one of the clouds of dust was getting bigger. And the color looked...wrong.

"Your people are usually such lazy cowards. What fortune brought me *you*? One willing to risk such dangers as you cannot even *imagine*... and with such magnificent timing! You have ruined years of work, and with but seconds to spare." The wizard—for he was clearly some kind of magician—shook his head slowly. "Truly, I would like to take weeks to devise a suitable punishment for—"

"*Sssummonnerr...*"

The voice was faint, distant, yet cut through all other sound as a blade through grass, a hiss and a scrape as of metal claws climbing a cliff of granite. "*Summoner...*"

The man whirled. Scarcely ten feet from him, the thing Duckweed had taken for a strange dust cloud had grown larger, a perfectly circular pearlescent gateway, and within it something of polished black armor, bladed, edged, eyes that glittered with facets, mandibles and cutting, grasping mouth, something huge and terrible and very, very near to entering indeed. "*My Lord...*"

"*Complete... the Summoning...*"

The wizard glanced around. "I...I cannot. My pentacle is—"

"*Ssspeak my Name, human. Sspeak it and I shall be free.*"

Duckweed was appalled. All he'd done, and the summoning could *still* be completed? With a broken pentacle? *No, no, that's not just bad, that's very, very bad, like a drought that makes the whole lake dry up bad.* He had his sword out, but he didn't have any delusion that he could fight... *that.*

The wizard did not speak immediately, and the shape within the cloud stirred impatiently, revealing the shimmer of reptilian scales on the body. "*Did you not wish to summon me? Speak my name!*"

"Do you want fools as servants, or think me a fool for a sacrifice alone?" The man's voice was tense. "An uncompleted ritual like this? What guarantees do *you* offer to make it worth my while to risk my life and soul that way? *You* and your allies—whoever they were—wanted this as much as we. You have some reason for this, something much greater." He straightened. "Swear that, though the wards are broken and no spells laid upon you, that you will aid me as though the wards whole, the spells complete, and at the end of the service will seek no harm against me or mine. Swear it in the name of Kerlamion himself, his TRUE name."

The *mazolishta*—for Duckweed knew it could be nothing

else—hissed again, but somewhat to his surprise—and apparently the wizard's—the hiss sounded almost pleased. "*Wiser than many. Good. We have need of you, then. H'ved schkalavis mokhteth dergschokh, Kerlamionahlmbana!*"

Oh no. Duckweed tensed himself. *One last chance, I think.*

The wizard cast a terrible triumphant grin at the little Toad and turned back to the shadowy demonic presence. "Then come forth, Voo—*ARGH!*"

The wizard staggered and fell, clawing at his neck; Duckweed leapt from his shoulder, withdrawing the long, narrow blade he'd plunged deep into the man's back, evading the grasping hands, somersaulting above as the wizard hit the floor, turning, coming down, twisting his body, the human's eyes widening, hand reaching, brushing the little Toad's body, and then—

A terrible impact smashed Duckweed aside into the wall and everything seemed to go dark for a moment. He rolled painfully, groggily, to his feet. *Ouch. Rib broken. Maybe more. Moving hurts.* He blinked. *It is a little darker...*

The glowing sphere of light the wizard had summoned was gone. In the dim light of the demon-portal and the still-flickering rockfire, the reason was clear. The wizard's corpse lay, still twitching, on the cold stone, with the hilt of the tiny sword protruding from his throat.

Slowly the little Toad dragged himself over and yanked the sword out. Then he looked up.

The demon's portal was still there. Beginning to flicker slightly, but still present. "*Speak my name.*"

"What? I didn't summon you."

It laughed, a screeching sound that sounded like tearing steel. "*You stopped them, for I would have performed their bidding and your people—and others—would have died. Now you may gain that power for yourself. I will swear the same oath to you I did to this one. Give me my freedom and you shall have that power.*"

"Sorry." The little Toad wiped the sword clean on the dead wizard's pant leg. "Besides, I don't know your name, so I can't do it."

"*Easily remedied. I am Voorith.*" The name echoed through the cavern like a threat of fear. "*Though your god and I have ever been at war, I care not for that, if only you free me.*"

The Toad looked up and suddenly stuck his tongue out. "Go

back where you came from, until Blackwart comes and eats you. You look like a bug so I'll bet he'll find you tasty!"

The demon screeched in frustration, and with that final denial began to truly fade, its summoners gone and its last chance of escape having rejected it. *"Then tell me your name, Toad, as I have told you mine. Our fates have been intertwined, and one day we shall speak our names to each other again."*

Name?

He suddenly realized that *this* was the moment. He was small, but no longer was he young. But what to choose? For in that choice he would be defined, and there was no changing once chosen. He thought back over the entire adventure, for this surely would give him the answer...

And saw the answer, the moment that defined the point when he became who he was. He looked up at the fading demon and smiled with the corners of his mouth. "Poplock," he said proudly. "Poplock Duckweed. Remember it."

"Oh, I shall." The voice was a whisper, a promise of impotent doom. *"And so shall others. For this was not my plan, nor theirs, and you have inserted your tongue into something far more perilous than you can even begin to imagine... Toad."* And the gateway was gone.

He blinked and glanced around in the fast-fading light. *Got to get out of here. But...*

Some minutes later, he eased his way from a narrow crack into the lowering light of the setting sun, near the Evermist of the Burning Waters. With him he dragged a small pouch from the wizard's waist, stuffed with the few objects the little Toad could find before the light went out. Without light, the fresh breeze had been his real guide.

"Not a bad first try... for a small adventurer."

Cheerfully, Poplock Duckweed headed back to the village. He had quite a story to tell... and then a much bigger world to go find.

7

Tobimar squinted across the water. There was nothing to see, just more water, as the *Lucramalalla* continued through the five-foot seas. Of course, that was part of what bothered him; until now, the huge Sauran-built ship had sailed always just in sight of land, able to see ports and cities as they passed, ready in case they were hailed or if there was some need to stop. But sometime during the night, it seemed, they had swung far out to sea.

Still, even that didn't seem enough to cause his unease. He *felt* something was wrong, almost could *see* it, like heat-ripples from the sand, but he couldn't put a name to it. He looked around the ship.

To his mild surprise, he saw T'Oltha standing alone on the second deck, high above the first, immobile as a statue, looking out to sea as he had been. *Well, there's my best source of information.*

It only took a few moments to make his way up; the eight-foot creature was still standing where he had seen her. "A good dawning, T'Oltha."

The draconic head turned slightly. "A good dawning to you as well, questing prince."

Of course the ship's captain knew exactly who he was and something of the errand he was on. He just hoped it wouldn't be general crew knowledge; better to avoid too many questions that he didn't invite. "If it is no secret, why do we sail so far from land this day?"

The Sauran gestured with her taloned hand. "For this day, and for many more days, indeed, we must sail by guidance of stars and the gods, for there lies Elyvias."

That made sense. He hadn't realized they'd come so far already; yes, they had left Tor Port, a major city of the Empire of the Mountain, quite some days ago, but the great inacessible peninsula of Elyvias jutted from the southernmost reaches of the continent. "So we cannot even sail in *sight* of the land?"

The headshake was like the weaving of a snake. "The Maelwyrd extends full forty miles from the land, with but three miles nearest the land safe to sail for those who live there."

Tobimar glanced up. He had heard something of the latter, but never spoken of with the matter-of-fact certainty that T'Oltha used. "How do you know there is such a safe zone?"

T'Oltha gave a rumbling laugh like distant thunder. "Twice, under the guidance of the Lady of Aegeia, I sailed the shifting maze of the Maelwyrd and found my way safe to Elyvias. I have sailed those waters, young prince, seen what was left when the Archmage and Dragon King duelled at the end and sank part of the continent beneath them."

"If you have sailed them before—"

"Only under the Lady of Wisdom's guidance," she said, emphatically. "And only following the partly known paths through. Here we are on the northern frontier of Elyvias, a narrow shore backed by the Northern Cataclysm Ridge, and where the *mazakh* have a stronghold. We still must follow the currents and land in a general sense, and so shall turn northward again to round the portion of the peninsula that projects in that direction. But only in the southernmost waters has the Maelwyrd been mapped at all, and only with the Lady Athena's guidance, or that of S'mbanullah or Elbon Nomicon himself, would I attempt even that route, let alone seek to penetrate the uncharted Maelwyrd here." The weaving shake of the head again. "No, we shall make no port again until *Olthamian' a' ameris.*"

"Shipton."

A snort. "As you and the other *derntera* call it, yes, as you remove the poetry and meaning of *Fanalam' T' ameris' a' u' Zahr-a-Thana T'ikon* and say 'Zarathanton.'"

Tobimar grinned, but had to admit that the Sauran had something of a point. Changing "City of the Sea of Stars" to what amounted to "place with ships" did seem rather a step down. On the other hand, as the name of the capital city illustrated, the Sauran names could get to be long enough to need a couple of breaths to finish. "We are blessed neither with your longevity nor your lung capacity, o T'Teranahm," he said.

That gained him another deep laugh. "Truly said, little human. Truly said. As long as you *remember* the poetry that lies beneath, then the surface is of no matter, or so S'her once said."

He looked up at the ancient reptilian captain again. The Saurans had inhabited Zarathan for longer than almost any other race of beings (save of course for the Dragons, their forebears and possibly one or two others), and—though they had, of course, had their own epics of betrayal and tragedy—had always been a force of stability and wisdom for the younger races; Khoros had often mentioned how much he had learned from the dragon-descended creatures.

That decided him. "T'oltha, you know something of our quest. Where do *you* think I should start my quest? Which port?"

To his surprise, the Sauran captain bowed to him. "You ask my advice? It is well. For know, that while my ship has carried many of your questers, since first I took this ship six millennia agone, none have ever asked. Your mother's sister chose the northern route, landed at the White Blade. Before her, a man, Karilar, and his choice was Tor Port itself, to seek an audience with the Archmage. Others, many others, yet none asking of me what my thoughts were." She looked up to the sky. "All sought in places of peril, of distant lands; one even took passage through the Maelwyrd to seek on Elyvias.

"I say instead that you begin in the city where all once began, and where one of my people still sits atop the Throne that is older than all the *derntera* combined. Go to the First City, take ship with me all the way to Zarathanton, and there I think you will find, if not answers, the path to your answers."

The capital city? Greatest of all cities? The idea made sense. He had thought before of Shipton itself, the great port, or of Aegeia, isolated and proud deiocratic state whose ruler was, it was said, the living incarnation of one of the gods of Wisdom. But T'oltha's advice resonated, fit with the part of him that could find a safe path across a room in total darkness.

"I thank you, Captain. Then I am with you to the end of this journey."

"The end of this *voyage*, young one." The Sauran smiled, showing a fearsome array of teeth. "My journey is far from ending, and yours has not even begun."

8

The room was large and open, of polished marble and obsidian worked with patterns of gold and sapphire and silver, but few decorations outside of these. A bed was set back against one wall, with a locked chest at its foot, a small dresser nearby, all looking rather small against the expanse of the room with its twenty-foot ceiling. A short distance away sat a table, draped in cloth so black that it seemed to drink in the light, leaving the area nearby in inexplicable shadow; a single chair was placed at the table. Two spheres of blue light glowed, suspended in nothing, above the farther corners of the table.

In the center of the table was a scroll, partially unrolled and locked in a mounting that held it still, a scroll two feet high and opened four feet wide. A scroll that seemed made of purest gold, a scroll that shone like a metallic mirror—or, to be more accurate, like three mirrors, for the unrolled piece of enchanted metal was engraved such that it was divided into three equal portions. The engraving scrollwork, on close inspection, consisted of powerful symbols, runes, and mystical metals inlaid into the reflective surface, which within those three portions was inlaid with platinum or silver, shining white against the gold.

The man seated at the table glanced back at the bed and dresser and smiled faintly. *Well, one appreciates austerity on occasion, and a passage at austerity makes one appreciate luxury the more, as well.*

The door was closed, but not locked. The others knew not to

disturb him in this chamber. Though they were, perhaps, his equals in many things, they knew that he directed their actions, that *he* was able to direct the favor of their patron as well. If any of them dared disturb him while that door was closed . . . *well, it had best be deadly important. Or else it will* become *deadly important, indeed.*

He looked at the gemclock; its shimmering symbols showed that the time had arrived.

And now the polished auric and argent metal did not reflect his face, did not show the mostly empty room. Instead, three other beings looked out from the reflection of other rooms than this.

Beings—but not *human* beings.

The central of these—a presence of pure blackness, a humanoid shape in a chamber so dark that the figure should have been invisible, save that the thing also had eyes of a terrible blue flame and its darkness made that which surrounded it appear merely the gloom of dusk—slowly surveyed the others. The man knew that while he only saw three other participants, each of those three had others—their second in commands, their assistants, advisors, or strategists—watching, perhaps even waiting to speak. *It is a most deadly fence to walk,* he thought. *To say nothing risks little; to speak could gain you favor . . . or cost you your life.*

The same was true of the other two visible in the meeting-mirror, of course, but they had power of their own, and long history in speaking to that dark presence which commanded the central mirror.

"Some of you," the dark thing said, and its voice was the deep rumble of a vortex descending to unnameable depths, overlaid with the scream of tortured air. "*Some* of you have already heard the rumors. We have commanded this meeting to examine the situation, and determine a course of action."

The blacker-than-black figure glanced to the left, at a creature that combined the worst features of lizard and mantis, or perhaps warrior ants. "Voorith has reported considerable losses of his forces, at a moment when we had been preparing other forces to move." The burning blue-white gaze was unblinking, frightening even to the man seated at the desk, and he wasn't the focus of that deadly regard. "We are most disappointed, Voorith."

The *mazolishta* bowed, chattering in its own tongue. The apology was long and detailed, and there was no mistaking the fear in the insectoid demon's voice.

"Enough of the apologies. They do not matter to us. How much has been lost?"

The King of All Hells is no more fooled than I; all that apology was an attempt to evade giving these details. It must be worse than we had heard—and I had heard things were very bad. The being in the third portion of the mirror—humanoid in seeming—met the watcher's gaze knowingly; the man returned the gaze with a nod, for this was his patron. It smiled as Voorith replied, "...there have been...significant losses, O Consuming Star."

The eyes if the black thing in the central mirror flared slightly. "Evasions gain you nothing either. How much?"

"I..." Voorith shuddered, recognizing it had no recourse but the truth. "All was lost, Majesty."

"*All?*" the human-seeming figure in the third panel repeated, its voice startled and amused. The man at the table kept himself under control, but it was a shocking revelation. *I'd realized Voorith must have suffered quite a humiliation, the summoning falling through and its consequences, but to have lost all of the gathered resources and thus not even prepared...*

"Yes, *all*." Voorith gave vent to a curse. "It was intervention, I feel sure."

As Voorith recounted exactly how everything had fallen apart, the being in the third mirror did not bother to restrain a laugh. The man did not quite dare join in, but inwardly he was laughing indeed. *Oh, my, yes, this is most amusing.*

The black-on-black thing with the blazing eyes did not apparently see the humor. "Restrain your amusement or leave this council. I concur with Voorith's assessment. The Golden-Eyed God arranged this."

Stifling another chuckle, the man's humanoid patron nodded. "It would seem likely. Though it could simply be poor luck. Still, if the old Toad-God wasn't involved before, we can rest assured he's noticed this undersized menace by now, and he'll be in the game." It narrowed its eyes, with an expression *just* short of reproach. "And if I understand correctly, the Toad-God is *not* subject to the little arrangement you managed to convince most of the other Powers to agree to on pain of cataclysm."

The black thing seemed to tower up in fury; the figure raised a single finger in admonishment. "This plan is of my devising, O Kerlamion. It is of course in service to *you*, as are all things here. But I will not be treated as though I were no more than one of your millions of guards. I shall speak when I wish, and how I wish. And we would be wise to keep to the subject. Better these scrying scrolls are than meeting in person, yet still those with enough power, perception, or fortune might recognize that a hidden council is being held."

And the fact that it can speak thus to Kerlamion, King of All Hells, is what convinces me I have chosen my patron very wisely. The seated man decided now was an opportune time to join in. "Then by all means, let us speak of the subject. How long of a delay does this incident create?"

Kerlamion's blazing-fire eyes had not yielded to the calm azure gaze of the third mirror-figure, but he spoke. "Voorith? You have knowledge of what was arranged, what will be needed, and so on. Your *honest* estimate of time?" Kerlamion's glare finally shifted, and the seated man once more had to restrain a smile. The emphasis of the word "honest" meant that Voorith would be held responsible for keeping the timeline offered. Of course, if he offered too long a timeline, there was always the possibility that the King of all Demons might simply choose another to do his job... and Voorith would have more immediate concerns of survival.

After a hesitation, Voorith sank to the floor of its own chamber in a submissive bow. "It...will take at least four years, O Consuming Star of the Uttermost Destruction."

"Four years..." To their surprise, Kerlamion gave vent to a laugh of his own, an eerie and frightening sound indeed, as of the air itself being rent and destroyed. "Satisfactory, yes. Four years it shall be. Voorith, if you succeed in this, by four years from this day, then shall I reward rather than punish you."

Voorith's voice was shaken and puzzled, but there was relieved gratitude in every tone. "Of course, Lord."

Kerlamion leaned back, its throne barely visible. "The lands have their unwitting reprieve. All other plans shall be adjusted. You will attend to that personally." He glanced at the figure in the third mirror.

"Indeed I shall, great King."

"Do any others have anything to add? For know that now is the time to speak, if any of you believe anything threatens the plan, especially with this change in timing." Kerlamion's tone was moderated from its initial leashed anger, and he was clearly demanding honest responses now.

The man in the chair considered briefly. *Well . . . a few things to discuss with my patron, but nothing to bring up with . . .* him.

Several others did speak, asking questions, clarifying requirements. Even though he understood the overall goals, the man watching still felt a chill of . . . awe? fear? simple excitement? . . . as he heard the mention of carefully devised strategies against every possible stronghold of the enemy, and realized that all of these plans were to culminate on the same day, four years from this moment.

Soon the discussions were finished, and the black-glowing figure surveyed them all one last time, and nodded.

"Then this council is at an end." Kerlamion vanished, as did Voorith. As he had expected, the third figure remained, and smiled.

"What fortuitous timing," it said. The human-seeming fingers brushed back light-colored hair which, the seated man knew, was no more real than the reflection itself.

He had to admit that this last remark escaped him, however. "I confess that I don't quite understand."

It smiled, a glitter of teeth perfect, white . . . and not quite human. "Let us say that while Voorith does not know why four years is a fortunate period of delay, I do. A *most* fortunate coincidence, especially for Voorith himself. The Lord of All Hells is far less tolerant and forgiving than I am."

Controlled as he was, the man in the chair could not—quite—prevent himself from glancing down at what was both evidence of that tolerance, and reminder of just how terrible it could be, if that tolerance were worn thin.

It didn't miss that glance, either, and the smile widened momentarily. "*Far* less tolerant. You very nearly caused me, and my plans, inconvenience some time ago . . . but you have learned well. Kerlamion tends to deal with failure . . . poorly." Its gaze became intense. "You do also understand *our* position?"

He nodded tensely. "I . . . believe so." It was astonishingly hard to say the next words, though he had realized the truth some years before. "You . . . have a deeper plan than that of the Lord of All Hells. That is, your plan given to him has some other levels of its own. One that has something to do with—"

It cut him off with a sharp glare. "Do not say names. *Any*

names. I *believe* this mirror scroll is proof against spying... but not, perhaps, completely so." It looked at him steadily. "Are you willing to continue, knowing that you risk playing so deep and very dangerous a game?"

He nodded, managing a smile of his own. "I am. I believe you know precisely what you are doing... even in this case."

The humanoid's tone became cordial. "Excellent. Then I trust you are... enjoying your first rewards?"

The man smiled more naturally. The being he spoke to might not share all the same interests that he did, but it certainly did not mind *supporting* them as long as he never forgot who he served, and did not fail it. *And one day I may be* like *it.* "I am *tremendously* appreciative, my most generous and supremely devious patron," he said, "and I hope—as time goes on—that I will continue to show you that I am worthy of the full reward you have offered."

"If all goes well..." it chuckled, and the lights at the edge of the table *flickered* as though in fear, "if all goes well... it is quite possible. Sooner than you might think, in fact.

"Now, it will be a challenge to delay things, my friend, especially where you are. Remembering that except when I personally present myself to you, you cannot—*none* of you can—approach or speak to me in any way that indicates a special familiarity. I will thus be relying on you to keep everything... going smoothly for the next four years."

The man grimaced. "Speaking honestly—as you have always demanded—that will be a difficult challenge. There is an immediately complicating factor that you know—"

"—and one I wish treated with *extreme* caution for now. There must not be the faintest breath of suspicion of your actions." It held up a placating hand. "I understand your concerns, my friend. I will make it easier; I do not expect to need you and your allies' services for most of that time, and so I promise not to call upon you for at least three years, possibly the entire four, so long as *you* tend to any... pernicious growths, shall we say?"

That will *make it* much *easier.* Still, there were a huge number of unknowns... and the game they were playing here might attract the wrong sort of attention at any moment, no matter how careful he might be.

At the same time, there was no point in pretending to be

reluctant. His course had long since been decided. *Take what you must.* "I will do so." While normally he would finish such a declaration with a name, a title, or at least "Sir," the other's instructions had been made very clear; no reference to it directly, not even a title of respect other than words such as "patron"—nothing that gave any clue as to the nature, rank, or even sex of the being.

The being smiled at his simple agreement. "I am pleased with your acceptance—and I know the challenges that four such years, without my assistance, may bring. Know them better than you, in fact, for there are things I have had to address which you have not even been aware of." It nodded in decision. "I shall be, in essence, giving you full authority here—to direct our operations, to control those under our command, and to make the decisions I shall not be present to make. For that, of course you must have the *power* to enforce those decisions, take those actions. So let us advance your fortunes."

He felt a surge of disbelieving joy. "You . . . you mean it?" A natural caution took over. "And . . . there will be no . . . untoward prices?"

His patron laughed. "Wisely cautious, my friend—but no, not in this case. I find it most useful to keep my word to those who are, themselves, useful to me, and betraying you with the poison-pill of legendary wishes is hardly in *my* interests.

"There *is* of course *a* price, but you have already begun paying it, and you seem not displeased with the results."

"My soul is being . . . transformed, yes?"

"Slowly, carefully, and in no way that will affect *who* you are, only *what* you are, yes. If you wish to become one of my people, to gain our powers and strengths . . . you will of necessity be giving up your essence as a human."

He almost laughed aloud. "You have said I will retain my true self, my interests, my knowledge, my skills—and from what I have seen, from what you have hinted, I will but become all the greater."

"There are those who would see the change . . . in not so positive a light. But speaking with entire honesty, I do see it as you say, and I believe you shall, as well." It straightened. "In that case, I have no more time to waste. Unlock the scroll and place it on the wall, hanging sideways."

It took only moments to do as he was instructed.

"Stand back," his patron said; as soon as he had done so, his patron spoke a single word in an unknown language, and the scroll blazed with golden light, expanding to the size of a doorway—and through that doorway stepped his patron. "Remove your armor, my friend."

He was already doing so; he remembered the last time, and *this* part he was not, entirely, looking forward to. "Now," his patron said with that disquieting smile, "brace yourself. I strongly suggest you look away from yourself, to the wall, to the scroll or anywhere but down." The smile widened. "This will hurt."

It did.

For a moment it felt as though five lances of fire-essence had impaled him through the guts. He tried to scream, but the pain was so great he could not even manage that. He could feel something dark-ice cold dwelling in the heart of that fire, an ice that spread through his body and soul, the agony of freezing fire saturating every nerve, and he wondered for a moment if he had trusted this monster in vain.

But then the ice warmed, and the fire cooled, and something else began to flow. A trickle, then a flow, then a flood of strength beyond anything he had ever felt, even when using the powers he and his brethren were granted by right of their brotherhood. The dimly lit room brightened, his vision sharpened. He could see the smallest detail on the walls, the ripples where a chisel had shaped the stone. More, he felt he could see *more*—there were colors for which he had, as yet, no names, and a sense of other powers nearby—the souls of the other Justiciars currently at the retreat.

And he could sense that there was something wonderful he could *do* with such souls.

His patron stepped back, studying him narrowly for a moment. Then it gave a quick smile and nod. "You have survived. Most gratifying. Many would not have lived through that infusion... but with the changes we had already begun, you were *just* able to do so."

He tested his balance, leapt half across the room with a single motion. "By the... Will this stay *with* me?"

"It should, for the most part. Oh, there is a certain...flush of the initial change which will wear off soon enough. But there are ways to regain that strength, ones you already suspect. I do not begrudge you such advancement, when you are in truth dealing with problems which would otherwise be mine, and which I now leave to you." It turned, striding back towards the scroll. "Be cautious. Do not betray your nature—even if you are in combat, you must not reveal the fullness of what you have become. Now," it continued, "I must prepare my own works in service of our King... and," that deadly smile flashed again, "in our own, of course. Do not attempt contact with me again. I will contact you when I am ready."

The light flared and dissipated, and the scroll was blank.

He picked up the scroll and carefully returned it to its normal place. He put his armor back on, slowly, carefully, as though it were a ritual. All those moments, he savored the *changes*—the exquisite sensitivity of all senses, the ability to detect traces of power in the very air, the physical and mystical strength that filled him nearly to bursting, and he finally laughed aloud.

Then he thought more carefully on his situation. The smile did not disappear, but became less manic, more calm and focused. *I must not allow these senses to be active most of the time. It would be far too easy to betray myself through knowing, sensing something I shouldn't. In battle or on a hunt, yes, that's one thing, but I must remain mostly the "self" that others know.*

His patron's warning to not betray his nature was a warning he had no intention of testing. A being which could grant him such power—and who could supply the power that gave their entire group their unique abilities... such a being was one to heed well and completely when they gave such quiet and definite warnings.

Still... with my patron gone, and his resources no longer available... I may have to expand my own resources. For a moment he backed away from that thought, for he knew it could be his doom if his patron thought he was plotting against it.

But, he reminded himself, *my patron is quite different from the others.* The King of Hell undoubtedly would be suspicious of an underling amassing a power base. Voorith, likewise. Most of the beings of this dangerously unstable alliance would feel similarly. But his patron... no. As he thought on it, he realized that his patron would *expect* him to build his own power base, the better to be effective—and to be able to act outside of the brotherhood he still belonged to.

Then it is time to gather my own forces, my own allies, he thought. *Getting them here ... concealing them ... these will be challenging, as will this most difficult masquerade I must play.* He sat down and leaned back in the seat, his smile broadening. *But ahh, the rewards when the last curtain comes down!*

9

Kyri set her brush to a slow dry, brushing the long black waves into place as the simple enchantment gradually reduced the heavy dampness from her bath to the lighter flow of cascading black. *Victoria says she managed to do this while on adventure, I suppose I should at least do it while I'm at home.*

She pulled on a houserobe and continued to brush the hair dry as she walked down the wide stone steps of Vantage Fortress. Kyri paused on the first landing and looked out of the wide, high north window, a habit any of the Eyes would have.

The first thing she could see was Evanwyl, the city, itself. *Not,* she admitted to herself, *really a* city *from the point of view of the other countries.* The Vantage estate was almost due south of Evanwyl, with the Watchland's castle-fortress directly opposite to the north-northwest on a corresponding ridge of the Evaryll's valley. The Evaryll, moderately wide but swift-flowing, was the focus of the town, three bridges crossing it at different points.

The buildings below contrasted starkly with the fortresses; they were open, airy, with light, strong doors almost the width of the walls that could be closed against wind and rain but were usually open. She could see the Monn, Jessir, and Tukal farms in the distance, the layered leaf roofs distinctive green-touched gold in the middle of the wide fields—*Oh, I think Tukal's got a crop of gravelseed almost ready to bring in; that gray-blue color's so distinctive.* The town buildings were roofed with split zuna wood but were still mostly open. When the night temperature never got below "cool," you didn't need to exclude the air.

Of course, they were still made of the strongest, lightest woods, and there were heavy bars for every door and window, and the reason lay beyond.

The immense spires of the Khalal range loomed in the distance, a wall of mountains that cut across the entire continent, ranging from the comparatively low peaks she could see—Harlock's Spire at twenty-seven thousand feet, Urudani at twenty-three thousand feet, a few others—to the incomprehensibly high Mount Scimitar, sixty thousand feet in height, throne of Idinus of Scimitar, God-Emperor of the Empire of the Mountain, a wall of stone and peril unbroken for over three thousand miles.

Unbroken save for one narrow passage, directly in the center of the view from the north window, the reason even the smallest house could lock its doors, the reason every man, woman, or child knew how to swing some sort of weapon from the time they could stand, the reason she, as one of the Watchland's Eyes, always took a moment to look to the threatening north. Even from here, the dark green of that gap looked different, the color shadowed and at the same time somehow more virulent, a green that only faded to normalcy a short distance from the Watchland's Fortress. The Riven Forest was not a safe place, no, and it was merely a hint of the horrors on the other side of Rivendream Pass.

She shivered slightly, then turned away. *Almost impossible to believe that was once called Heavenbridge Way, before the Chaoswar.*

She shook off the concern. *There hasn't been much of anything out of there in years*, she reminded herself. The Eyes of the Watch—the Vantages, the Hightowers, the Thalindes, and others—had not relaxed their vigilance on the Pass, and with the help of the Watchland, his Arms and their Armsmen, and of course the Justiciars anything that tried to escape was driven back or killed.

At the bottom of the stairs she turned and started for the breakfast room, when she noticed the door to the underfortress open. *That's odd.* With only her aunt, herself, and Urelle living here full time—Rion now spent most of his time with the Justiciars—there wasn't any need to make use of the underfortress. Even Victoria's servants rarely had to go there.

The lightglobes glowed with soft, clear light, showing that someone had gone down deliberately. "Hello?"

"It's me, sis."

"Urelle?" She went down the steps quickly, putting the brush in the robe pocket. Cooler air greeted her like slowly wading into a sunlit pool. "What are *you* doing down here?"

At the bottom of the stairs the underfortress continued back beneath the rest of Vantage Fortress; she knew there was at least one level below this one, but she'd never actually seen it and she seemed to remember Victoria saying they'd locked it off years back. "I'm in here," came Urelle's voice, and Kyri could see light from the open door at the far end of the hallway, a hundred and fifty feet down.

Even Kyri's bare footsteps caused faint echoes to chase themselves down the corridor and back; the polished marble was chill enough to send a hint of gooseflesh up the backs of Kyri's legs. She paid scant attention to that, because of the sheer surprise at where her little sister *was*.

"I don't think you've *ever* been in this room before," Kiri said as she reached the doorway.

It was a huge room, extending another seventy feet from the doorway, and thirty feet on either side of the doorway Kyri stood in. Lightglobes shone brightly at each corner and one, larger globe illuminated the center of the chamber, which was carved of the native gold-speckled granite and floored with the same light pink marble as the corridors.

"No...no, I never was." Urelle looked nervous, a little afraid. "But...it's been long enough. I'm still a *Vantage*, aren't I?"

At the proud yet uncertain question, Kyri felt a sting of tears, bent and hugged her little sister. "You are most *definitely* a Vantage," she said.

The room was cluttered around most of its perimeter with an assortment of what looked like the most worthless junk imaginable; pieces of half-burned timbers, twisted, blackened metal, crates with objects so melted or burned you could barely discern their original shape as cups or knives or shelves. There were stones covered with soot and broken by heat; a piece of what looked like clay with half a bootprint in it; a scorched length of wood with savage cuts through it, clearly one half of a similar piece that lay next to it, the middle splintered and broken.

In the center of the room, two doors of metal and wood, untouched by fire, a broken bar across their center. And on one wall were two shelves, and beneath the shelves, a small altar to

Myrionar: the Balanced Sword, a sword held upright as the point of balance between a pair of scales. On the lower shelf, seven ornate jars; above them, two simple marble containers carven with the Vantage symbol of a tree and a hill.

Even after all these years, even being moved down here, it all still smells like smoke and iron.

"You are a Vantage," she repeated. "And this...is our heritage. What's left of it."

Urelle shivered, looking at the one wall. "That's...Mother and Father. And Garrick...and Toll. I remember Camberi..."

"They've all gone to the Balance, yes."

Urelle bit her lip, then gazed at the mass of wreckage. "And... well, I can understand why we're keeping *that*," she pointed to a crate with half-melted but still glittering gold cups, "but...why all the rest?"

"Because," Kyri said, and her voice was suddenly hard, "we still don't know *who*, or *why*, and we are *not* destroying the evidence we have. Maybe we've missed something. We couldn't preserve the whole house, but we all searched for anything that might tell us something about what happened."

"I..." Urelle looked down. She didn't speak for a moment, then looked back up. "Kyri, can I tell you something?"

"Of *course* you can."

"I guess..." she hesitated, then like a swimmer nerving herself to dive into icy water, took a breath and plunged ahead, "...I guess I didn't want to think about it. And I was awfully young. Anyway, I can't remember really *anything* from the weeks afterward. I..." her voice trembled, "I remember we were so happy, me, you, and Rion, walking home, and then seeing the fire and you screaming. And... nothing really after that, until, oh, I don't know, it must have been a long time, because I was in Auntie's coach and I looked out the window and saw that the house was all gone and the black, dead spot in the grass and I started crying." Urelle's face crumpled and she sounded like she was going to cry again.

Kyri knelt down and hugged her little sister. *Myrionar's Justice, I'd never realized she'd forgotten everything.*

"Is it true," Urelle said, voice wavering but obviously trying to move on, "that we had an *Adjudicator* here?"

"What? Sword and *Balance*, Urelle, you *can't* have forgotten meeting *him*!"

But her sister's gaze showed that, somehow, she had.

Kyri shook her head. "I...yes, we did. An old adventuring companion of Auntie's, she called him 'Bridgebreaker.' You really don't remember?"

"No, really, I don't. 'Bridgebreaker'?" Urelle giggled. "Why would she call *anyone* that?"

"Because a small bridge literally *did* break under him, when they were running for their lives. Get her to tell you the story, it's both very funny and very scary at the same time. His real name is...let me see if I can get it right...T'Oroning'Oltharamnon ʰGHEK," the last sound sort of an inhaled choke or cough, "R'arshe Ness."

Urelle's expression of disbelief set her laughing. "I know, a ludicrous name, isn't it? He let us use the very shortened form of 'Toron,' though."

But Urelle's next words showed she *had* kept up on her studies, because she recognized the *meaning* of a name like that. "Oh my *gods*, Kyri, he was a *Sauran*?"

"More than that, an *Ancient* Sauran, Master of the Marshaled Hosts and cousin to the Sauran King."

Urelle looked mortified. "And he was a companion to *Auntie* when she was young? And I met him and *forgot*?"

"I'm sorry, Urelle. But you were...very unwell. And very upset." She laughed again. "Not so unwell you refused to shout at him about his failure, though. He took it well, even apologized."

Embarrassment and thoughtfulness chased each other across Urelle's face. "You know...I think I vaguely remember that, now. Being very mad and shouting at something that looked as tall as the Fortress."

"That was exactly it."

"And the Justiciars and the Adjudicator Sauran, they couldn't find *anything*?"

"Oh, they found *some* things. Enough to scare everyone concerned. But not anything that told us what we really *needed* to know." She walked over, picked up a twisted black metal shape that broke even as she lifted it. "Oops. Well, this was part of the dining-room door. Had fire enchantments on it, you know, but it *burned* anyway. That told us whoever did this used fire essence, not just ordinary torches and oil or even a simple magic spell." She dropped the piece back into the box. "And for the frightening...there's the front door." She pointed to the twin doors in the center of the room. "The wards and seals were *removed*. Not broken, not dispelled, but *removed* as though they had never been. Toron said the doors felt as though they had never been enchanted."

"But...I thought that wasn't possible, sis," Urelle said after a moment. "Every spell, every mystical conflict, every act of the gods leaves its mark, or so my teachers always say. According to them, someone like an Adjudicator can read the truth of history in almost any shard or fragment that has been present at the events you seek."

"Toron," she said, remembering, "pointed out that almost nothing was actually *impossible*, just very, very hard. But he didn't know exactly *how* this was done, but it was something very powerful and dangerous; the Chaoswars do that to everyone, even the gods, but to target something like this...well, that was what worried us. And that's what we learned from Toron and the Justiciars and anyone else. Things like that. We learned how most of it was done, but nothing that really told us anything that we could *use*. But maybe...maybe one day something here *will* tell us something."

She turned away, took Urelle's hand. "Come on. It's way past breakfast time, I'm not dressed for down here, and if you don't even remember everything, I think Auntie Victoria should be talking to you, not me."

The strain of having just admitted to a secret she must have been keeping for a long time, and of the discussion itself, was enough to make Urelle less argumentative than she might have been; it didn't take more than another few minutes to get her upstairs.

But Kyri found she couldn't forget that storeroom—or the heart-wrenching discovery that her little sister had blotted out the events of half a year from her mind. The images and questions crowded her mind, nagging her as she ate her breakfast, continuing as she did her quick patrol of the nearby neighborhood, and refusing to go away even as she faced Lythos in the training field. She saw Lythos' narrow gaze, the *Artan* weaponsmaster's disapproval clear in the deep violet eyes, as she made a novice's mistakes.

Balance and Blade! Enough of this!

She focused, drawing on that inner turmoil, *channeling* it instead of letting it churn queasily in her gut. *We are beings of passions,* she reminded herself, quoting Lythos' own words. *But we must* rule *those passions, must never be ruled by them. When anger threatens to overwhelm you, turn it aside into strength,* guide *it, just as you guide the strike of your enemy and make his power work against him, turn his might into your own ally. When fear seeks to paralyze you, take its tightening grip and harden your body against danger, strengthen your own grip on your weapons and skill. When worry circles your mind like carrion birds, circle with it, turn its aimless curves into the smooth arcs of combat.* She traded blows with Lythos, felt the impact of a cut, but brushed the feeling of inadequacy and failure away, sent it spinning into the center of her mind with the other concerns. *Take them all, dark and light, storm and calm, hope and fear, hate and love, fury and peace, bring them to your hands, armor your self with their power, realize that they are* you *and that only you control them, find that peace and certainty within you, and there you find the key of paradox.*

And then—in that single instant—she *felt* it, felt the paradox of the Calm Storm, the Ninth Wind, just for the most infinitesimal moment, as Lythos had told her she could, and time seemed to halt. She could *see* the *Artan*'s silvery blade in its perfect and inimitable path, gliding past her feeble defense, straight for her heart. She saw his silver hair streaming sideways, wind and his own motion making it spray out like a splash of argent foam from a stone; a leaf, falling from the quilli tree above the training field, seemed frozen in midair, locked in place as though the very atmosphere were crystal.

And in that endless instant, she had all the time of the universe to understand, to see, to decide, even as the strength of that perfect moment welled up within her, rising inexorably to furious motion.

She saw, and acted. She turned her head, swung her body *just so*, and the blade passed harmlessly over her shoulder, so near the whisper of its passage through the air was like silken thunder. But she was still moving, her path of action laid out before her as though she had planned it ages before and practiced it a thousand times. Her own blade was deflected, yes, but along with her body she dragged her arm, pushing around, the pommel now leading her hand in a strike.

Lythos' eyes widened—the first time she had ever seen an expression of surprise from the centuries-old master—and he

tried to duck, but he seemed astonishingly slow; the pommel
of her greatsword actually *struck* the slender *Artan* and Lythos
stumbled, chose to fall and roll.

She followed up, letting the fear and anger and pain flow, but
flow as *she* channeled, as *she* directed. Lythos came up, a shield
now raised, and she focused the power of her spirit into her hands
as he had taught her, dropping her sword, seeing his eyebrow rise
like a wing of a startled bird, and *smashing* her hands against the
shield with an impact that sent the weaponsmaster staggering back.

Now the expression shifted, and there was the tiniest of smiles
on the ancient, yet unaged, *Artan* face, as he came to meet her.
For a moment she stood toe-to-toe with a being who had been
fighting since before the days her grandparents were born, and
she did not give in.

But she began to think, try to look beyond the moment—and
she saw Urelle's face, and suddenly an iron-hard hand *whacked*
into her head.

She went to her knees, trying to defend. To her surprise, the
expected attacks did not materialize. She looked up to see Lythos
standing with arms folded, studying her.

"You are one of the most *maddening* students I have ever had,
Kyri Vantage," he said, finally. "For a moment—just a moment—
you achieved the *Ninth* Wind. I saw it. I could see it in your
eyes, watch its flow in your movements, that for just a moment
you touched the eternity within the soul." He shook his head.
"Something, I will tell you, that not your brother, nor your father,
nor your mother *ever* achieved, and indeed precious few in all my
years have I ever seen achieve it, even for such a brief moment."

She was amazed and felt a flood of warmth rushing through her,
an elation she had never expected, at a compliment so extravagant
from the man whose usual comments of praise were drawn from
words such as "adequate" and "not terribly bad."

"And *then* you suddenly lose that focus and forget the other
Eight in the bargain!" Lythos tossed his hair back and traced the
curve of his ears in the same habitual gesture she remembered
from her youngest years. "You *could* be one of the finest warriors
I have ever trained, but you need something to *focus* you. You
have to learn control, and constancy, and not rely on this excellent but most unreliable instinct to carry you through a combat."

"I know, *Sho-ka-taida*," she said contritely. *That rather adequately snuffed out any overconfidence I might have gotten from his com-pliments.* "But..."

The *Artan* master of weapons sighed. "Yes, I noticed. Some-thing weighs upon your mind. Perhaps it is just as well that you tend to whatever distracts you; practice without focus can do as much harm as it could possibly do good, even if on occasion it produces admittedly spectacular results. I will not often be this lenient. You will have double practice tomorrow, and I will require meditation in at least four of the Eight Winds."

"Yes, *Sho-ka-taida.*" She bowed and left, feeling his curious stare boring into her back until the door closed.

After paying respects at the shrine, she wandered slowly around the room, touching smoke-damaged wood and overheated metal remnants, pausing as something struck a chord of memory or to puzzle out the identity of some object that had been burned almost beyond recognition. A small object caught her eye and she found her hand reaching out, picking it up. She smiled fondly down at the little scorched box of toy figures—a golden phoenix, a dignified looking bronze griffin, a lightning-blue thunderbird, a sparkling dragon. *They were my favorite toys when I was little, playing with Rion... We'd pretend they were adventurers, I always took the phoenix and Rion the dragon and we'd share the others.*

She put the box down gently and looked around the room again. *What am I looking for?* she wondered. It wasn't as though these items hadn't been examined. The Justiciars had all combed through the wreckage. Rion had helped others sort through the pieces. Toron, an Adjudicator of the State of the Dragon King, had searched every piece, and none of them had found anything. The gods had been terrifyingly silent, even Myrionar, with its usual power to see through falsehoods and name truth, even Elbon of the Diamonds and the other dragon gods of the Sixteen had not spoken the answers to its child and servant Toron. *What am I expecting to find down here?*

She found herself standing, as she always did when she came here, before the two doors in the center. She remembered how she'd done the same thing when it happened, stood staring for some unmeasured time at these two doors, the only things left untouched in the midst of devastation, portals that should have barred the entry of any hostile force, but that had somehow allowed them to break through, without the faintest alarm being given.

But having stared at them for so long, she also was annoyed by what she saw. *The* inside *of the doors haven't a clue to offer.*

She understood why they lay that way—the bar which had held them together would make them rock unevenly if they were laid over it—but she preferred to look at the part where the house had actually tried to keep out the killers.

She bent over and lifted. *Balance, they're* heavy.

With a grunt, she hefted the first door—eight inches thick of wood bound with enchanted steel—and tipped it over. The other one followed a few moments later, crashing onto its back with an echo like doom. She stood still for a moment, catching her breath. *They talk about the Vantage strength, but that's* still *hard to do.*

The two doors shone in the lightglobes, smeared in places with soot and ash and dirt, but mostly still clean and smooth, marred only by the deep crescent-shaped gouges where whoever—or whatever—had killed her parents had battered down the door. She moved slightly to the left, and the light reflected back from the gouges, one set nearly a foot lower than the others. They looked faintly silvery, just as she remembered.

"Who's down there?" came Rion's familiar voice. "And what in the name of the *Hells* are you doing?"

"It's me," she answered.

"Kyri?" Footsteps, and her brother entered, the glittering armor of Silver Eagle still on him, beaked helm under his arm. "What brought you in *here*?"

She chuckled slightly. *We repeat each other.* "Urelle came down here earlier today, then I couldn't get this place out of my head."

He nodded, blond hair slightly matted from the helm but still shining in the light. For some reason Rion had gotten all their father's traits—the light hair, the lighter skin, the blue eyes—while she and Urelle were both very dark, black of hair and with eyes of stormcloud gray which came from their mother's side of the family. "Yeah, I sometimes get that too." He sighed. "Not that I ever find anything," he said, shrugging the shoulders of his armor, "but it doesn't hurt."

"I suppose," she said, still looking at the doors. Something was still nagging at her. She reached down and traced the grooves. "Did you realize that Urelle didn't *remember* any of what happened for... well, I'm not sure, maybe *weeks* afterward?"

"*Nothing?*" Rion stared at her. "No, I hadn't." He stared off, pensively. "But it does make some sense of a few exchanges I had with her off and on."

Something about this feeling... reminds me of the party for some reason...

Suddenly she was staring at her brother, and he stepped forward, concern writ large. "What? What *is* it, Kyri? You look like you're about to collapse!"

Terian, Chromaias, and Myrionar, it can't *be.*

But even as she thought the denial, she realized that if it was true, it made sense—it explained why nothing could be said, why Myrionar could not reveal the truth, why no suspects could be found. "Rion," she said, and she shuddered herself as she heard the terrible, dead tone in her voice, "Help me lift this door, would you?"

One more glance at her face convinced him to ask no questions, just helped her to raise the righthand door up on its end. "All right, Kyri. Now what—"

She held the door balanced, grabbed hold of his shoulder-guard, pulled. Slightly off-balance, Rion stumbled against the door.

And the shoulder-guard slid perfectly into one of the upper crescent-shaped marks. The marks that shone with a gentle silvery color just the shade of the guards themselves, of the shine-polish used on silver armor. She pushed him down, as though crouching for a second heavy blow, and there, too, his armor fit into the marks... as though it had made them.

She saw Rion look and go parchment-white. "Balance and Demons..."

Silver Eagle.

"It... could be." The words sounded *torn* from her brother's heart, and even in the middle of the cold fury inside her she felt her heart aching for him. "It... it makes sense. If he did this... then to preserve the name, preserve the *trust*, in the Justiciars, if he did this then they wouldn't *dare* mention it, they'd have to deal with it themselves, behind doors at Justice's Retreat, and wait, wait long enough so he thought he'd gotten away with it, wait so that people wouldn't *connect* it with their deaths..."

And they'd have killed all his allies, too, Kyri thought numbly. *Ripped the truth of who helped him, why, and where they were from him with the very power of Myrionar, and then hunted them all down for vengeance and justice.*

He was so hurt—*she* was so hurt—by the thought, the idea that the Justiciars, the living warriors and symbols of Myrionar, the god her family had followed for generations untold, the Justiciars could possibly have had one so corrupt in their number, that she almost wanted to forget this hideous discovery.

But that would not be justice.

"Is...is there any way to find out?"

Rion was silent for a moment, several moments. Then he looked up, and to her astonishment he *smiled*. It was a hard, cold, *dangerous* smile, but it was a smile, and it lifted her up, wiped away despair and horror with hope of vengeance. "*I* am Silver Eagle now," he said. "I am a Justiciar. This is the kind of secret they won't easily tell a newcomer...but the kind they will *have* to tell me sooner or later, just in case. It's been more than three years. They *have* to be getting to trust me now. I will have to be very careful...but yes. Of course there's a way. Even if only a few of them knew, I'll be able to get them to react. Ask the right questions."

"But won't they—"

He shook his head. "Kyri, they're still the Justiciars. I've *seen* them use the powers—healing, speed, strength, truthsaying, others for each of us. The power comes from Myrionar. Perhaps they felt greater justice comes of keeping belief in the Justiciars strong. But for *our* family, at least, we must have the truth. If he did it, we must know. And we must know *why*. I think...if I'm careful, if I make sure they understand how much I believe in Myrionar even with this horrid possibility...I think they'll understand and tell us the truth."

She felt a tiny bit better, a sense of hope emerging from shock. *If we could know the truth...know they had* found *the truth, dealt with the traitor, and simply protected us from that knowledge for the sake of Myrionar and the Justiciars...I think I could accept that. Yes, I could.*

She took her brother's hand. "Then if it's true, *you* have redeemed the armor. Symmetry and balance."

He looked startled, then smiled. "Of *course*. Don't you see?"

And she did. *How else could they apologize, how could they give justice with such a secret? By allowing the dishonored family to purify that which was defiled.* "Rion...it's horrible, yet...yet I feel that we might finally be able to put things to rest."

He smiled broadly. "So do I."

10

Poplock scuttled nimbly down the narrow shaft—*well, narrow for the big lumbering types, actually quite roomy for me*—and headed for the grille.

Something—his long-honed sense of self-preservation combined with a little prickling of his skin—warned him, and he pulled up short. He narrowed his golden eyes, squinting at the area of the ventilation duct just in front of the grille.

Oh, now that could have been painful. Barely visible even to his dark-adapted eyes, tiny symbols were scribed all around the perimeter of the duct. In fact, Poplock realized they were only perceptible because dust had gathered just slightly differently in the minuscule depressions left when they were first scribed; whoever had done it had carefully wiped away all of the original marks as soon as the enchantment had taken hold.

Even more cautious than I thought. Not many people bother securing things this small. Generally, the major worry was either people entering through the existing doors or windows by brute force (through walls, floors, and so on), or entering by magic such as a ghosting spell, teleportation, that sort of thing. A few shells of shielding that negated untuned and unbound magic and you were safe from the vast majority of attempts. Truth be told, most people didn't even go that far. It wasn't worth the effort for ordinary things.

And to go to these lengths—after everything I've already gotten through—well, they've got something pretty extraordinary to hide.

It had been a long and varied road leading him here. After he'd escaped the collapsed underground lair of Voorith's servants, he'd gone home for a little while, but it was, well, *boring*, and he had a bad feeling about the whole thing. Those nasties had been there a long time and he still didn't know what they were after, or why they had gotten so much weaponry together. No one in the village seemed willing to *do* anything, either. For the first time, he really understood the Latecomers' attitude towards his people; they just wanted to soak there in the mud, waiting for some *other* adventurers—Child of Odin, *Artan*, Human, whatever—to come by and take care of it.

"But I just don't think we can wait," he'd said to Barkboat. "That demon, he's already working again, I'll bet a goldbeetle on it."

"It may be, it may not." The priest had bobbed back and forth. "But Blackwart tells us that those who feel the land beneath our feet are the ones to hop forward. The land chafes your feet, Poplock, not ours."

So he'd set out on his search. The problem was, he didn't know what he was searching *for*. The *mazolishta* was behind all of it... well, no, someone else was, Voorith had basically *said* it was someone else's plan. The first group had spent...years? Ten years? More? Poplock had no idea, but it had been a *long* time they'd been building that complex, slowly bringing in their resources, finally setting up the summoning to bring Voorith through himself. After Poplock had gotten in the way, they wouldn't give up—but they'd been about ten times more careful. He wouldn't be just wandering into their next fortress.

He needed to have more resources than small size and a little sword. He needed knowledge. He needed to find allies, eventually, and get the word to the right people. He figured Zarathanton would be the place he could do all of that. The stuff he'd dragged out of the ruins might be worth something if he could get it there.

He'd heard the big city was off to the south, so that was the way he'd headed—down through the Evermist and then through what was supposed to be a small section of the Forest Sea.

Of course, "small" was relative, and "south" was sort of a fuzzy concept. He didn't know *how* long it might have taken him to find his way there if it hadn't been for that magician with the funny hat who'd helped him along the way.

The problem *then* turned out to be getting people to listen to him. He'd been used to it from his people, but somehow he'd thought it would be different in the city.

Yet...as time went on, he realized this might be his best weapon. Voorith knew his name, but couldn't find the little Toad himself. Others didn't even *notice* him, and if they did, they thought he was harmless. A lot of them thought he was a *dumb* Toad. Most of his people were more than twenty pounds, some over a hundred and fifty and four feet from nose to rump. He was not.

So use that.

And he had. He listened where people gathered. Eating and living wasn't a problem in the Great First City—bugs of all sizes, shapes, and tastes were to be found everywhere—so he could stay for days in or near the same place, unnoticed, unremarked.

And he'd learned.

Which brings me to here. He slowly sidled up to the very edge of the spelled area. *Symbolist did these. Not simple runes.*

He reached into the little pack and pulled out a notebook. "Hmm...nope, not fire...fire would be a bad idea, wooden building...lightning...no...Water? That would be silly. Air would be...but no, the sequence is just wrong. Earth...nope. Okay, no elemental...wait." There was of course the final element, but almost no one used that, except...

And there it was, the Sauran symbol of life—which also was the symbol of the first of Dragons. But it was reversed, the lightning-bolt center merely an empty outline, the surrounding sunburst instead a notched circle.

Life-draining. Soul-suckers, necromancers. Eew. This isn't a defense nice people use at all. Definitely on the track of something that's bad.

He *could* try to go around. Or leave and do some more research; after all, finding this much told him that whoever or whatever was here was the kind of person he was looking for. He'd been questing for a long time. He wasn't sure how long, but it was pretty long, a couple of years? More? Old Voory wasn't going to be just sitting on his pincers much longer. And going around didn't make much sense, now that he thought about it; if they were making security this nasty, he'd have better odds arguing an Armorfang out of lunch than of finding an unsecured route in.

Nope. This was the best lead he had; at least half of the *mazakh* in the city had come by this building in the last half year, and most of the rest were *khallit*—self-imposed outcasts, choosing to live with other races in an equal relationship as opposed to the dominant stance the others took. *They might follow another of the* mazolishta, *but I'll bet they know something about what the others are up to, even so.*

Poplock took a deep breath. *This could be...painful. Blackwart, keep an eye out for me, okay? I'm doing this for Pondsparkle.* He had a momentary flash of homesickness, seeing the lumpy houses squatting by the shore, the glitter of the Rainbow Mountain above and the blue of water below, then shook it off.

He turned to another section of his notes and reread them several times. *Tricky. Necromantic magic is theoretically opposed to True Elemental, but I have to call all five elements in balance to neutralize it—or else just pure Spirit, but that could kill me; I'm no spirit mage. Not really much of a mage at all, more a sort of tinkerer. And the demon or necromancer who put these here is probably pretty good.*

But the important point wasn't to destroy the seal—just to keep it from reacting. *The symbols...I think that one means "earth" and it's combined with the boundary symbol...which could mean that it's bound to the rim of the duct.*

Which would mean that all he had to do was *not* touch the rim. Not easy unless he could float, and he had to do that without magic—magic touching on that boundary would *definitely* set it off, unless it was just the right sort of neutralizing spell.

"Float without magic." He gave a wide-mouthed smile. "That works."

The little neverfull pack was the most useful—not to mention fun!—of the purchases he'd been able to make with the proceeds of his loot. Now he stuck half his body into the pack, which would have looked funny to anyone outside, as it was clear he couldn't possibly fit, let alone have anything else in there. He had to dig around by feel—*ouch! Safety cork came off!*—to find everything he was looking for.

A cross-shaped object with a core of screws and gears. A crossbow with clockwork. Bolts about the size of human sewing needles. And wire, a lot of wire. He carefully set the cross in the center of the duct and inserted a crank, turning it slowly and carefully, making sure the arms set firmly. He stopped turning the four-way jack once he could see the pronged metal ends had bitten deeply into the duct's sides. He kicked at it a couple of times; solid. *Good. Now let's hook up the cable . . . good, it's on tight.*

The real trick here was going to be getting the other end anchored. He would really have only one shot at this, because if he missed, *something* would be sure to hit the enchanted area.

He studied the grille again. *Held on by screw-clips.* He squinted across the room through the grille. *Another one across from me . . . about fifteen feet. Should be solid enough.*

He got out what was—for him—a very long pole with a mirror on one end of polished silver and used it to check the hallway. *No one there. Good. This will make a little noise.*

The bolt he selected was unusual—twice as thick as the others. He pulled on the side, causing the grapple sections to unfold, and checked the mechanism. *Impact-trigger working. If I hit it right . . .*

He hooked the cable and cranked the crossbow to maximum tension. One more check with the mirror, and then he brought the bow as close to the edge as he dared, sighted through the grille . . . aim . . . aim . . . relax . . . relax . . . *now!*

A brisk *snap-twang!* echoed through the shaft, followed by a faint whispering whizzing sound as the grapple-bolt streaked outward, trailing metal wire. Poplock winced as he heard and saw the impact of the bolt on the far grille, but luck was with him; the bolt was triggered but, still moving forward, flowered open just as it passed *through* the other grille. Immediately Poplock pulled on the line, keeping it taut, preventing even the slender strand of wire from dropping down to touch the deadly line of symbols.

Ohhhh that was close. Thank you, Blackwart and all the other gods who might be watching.

Still holding tight to the cable with both hands, he reached back with one foot and pulled it through the retaining catch until he could feel the tension on that side matching up with the tension he was keeping on the cable. Then he let go, turned around, and really pulled *hard*, then locked the cable down.

A slender strand of steel now stretched from his cross-shaped anchor to the grille on the far side. He made sure all his gear was secured on his body, especially his sword, Steelthorn. *Don't want anything dangling down.* The practice he'd had at climbing since he was a Newleg made the next maneuver easy, swinging himself onto the wire, thick pads of feet and hands (and his light weight) preventing cuts as he walked himself, upside down, along the wire, right past the mystical barrier. He did find himself holding his breath again as he passed over it... but nothing touched him.

It only took one hand with a careful touch to slide the screw-clips sideways and pop the grille loose; it bounced slightly, held by the wire. Poplock squeezed past it, up, around, and back to the wire, then used his feet to put it back in place; if he bounced too much on his cable he might jar it loose again, but the real key was just to have it *look* okay.

He turned to look down, and suddenly a shrieking alarm cut through the night.

What? How did they catch me?

Just as suddenly he realized it wasn't *him* the alarm was for; the door at one end of the long hallway burst open, and a lone figure burst out, at least five *mazakh* in hot pursuit.

Poplock blinked. *Well, now,* this *will be fun!*

11

Tobimar had no idea where he was going, and he knew that was a very, very bad thing. The *mazakh* had captured him with a stunning spell before he'd realized they'd gotten behind him; he'd been so focused on trying to sense what was going on *inside* that he'd completely failed to watch his back, and the fact he wasn't dead yet was mostly luck.

He'd actually started coming out of his daze while they were still dragging him down a corridor, but he could tell he'd missed a fair amount of time. He'd stayed limp, trying to clear his head and gather his strength as they carried him, but they'd set him down and the order had been given (by something that *wasn't* a *mazakh*, to his surprise and confusion) to strip and bind him.

Gathering the inner light Master Khoros had taught him, he'd suddenly leapt to his feet, twin swords unsheathed, and cut the lights, projecting his essence through the swords, severing the enchantment that kept the glowglobes alight, plunging the room into total darkness. The heat-sense of the *mazakh*, he knew, took time to awaken—like the sensitive vision of a man at night. For the next few moments, they were as blind as anyone.

Anyone except those who could see the light of life itself.

In those seconds he had cut three of his captors down, and seen *something* else in the back, where the voice had come from, a something that vanished impossibly, no flicker of magic, no movement, a cold and eerie entity that was there one moment and gone the next.

But he had no time to think about that; he was running out the door, the three he'd killed leaving a gap wide enough to pass through.

Terian, please! Light unto darkness!

He burst out of another door, hearing the scratching rattle of taloned feet and whisper of trailing tails giving chase. Now he was into a lighted corridor, equalizing sight again. *There's a lot of them after me. Where* am *I? Don't know if they brought me up or down, how large this building is...*

If it was the same building he'd been spying on, it was very large. *If I get out of this, I'm going to renegotiate my fee, justice or no!*

A turn, an angle, through another door, *no! More of them— take the door ahead, no time to turn! Sand and storm, I need Wanderer's luck now!*

A long, long corridor now, lit by glowglobes at intervals and with no side doors, his echoing footsteps drowned out by the hissing, rattling pursuit. *No help for it. I have to make a stand. At the next doorway, if there isn't a mob waiting behind it.*

Tobimar bashed down on the door handle with the hilt of one sword as he reached it, hit the door hard with one shoulder, a jolt of dull pain echoing from the impact as the door flew open.

"*Shiderich!*" The Skysand curse meaning "die without water" was torn from him as he saw the long, triangular room before him, a room with two rows of ever-narrowing perches on either side of the central aisle—an aisle that ended at a double-fanged altar before a looming figure of a monstrous thing, part *mazakh*, part hideous insectoid. And rising from the perch-benches, a dozen of the snake-demons, furious at the interruption of a sacred moment.

Suddenly Tobimar could do nothing but laugh. It was a shaky laugh, filled with more fear and less clear bravado than he would have liked, but it was a laugh, not a scream, not a sob. *Snakes on all sides of me. Then all that remains is to see how many I can take with me.*

Too bad, Master Khoros; I guess your vision wasn't so clear this time. I'm never going to find out where pursuing justice and vengeance would have brought me...because this is as far as I go.

The worshippers were somewhat delayed; their weapons were placed in precise array at each side of the triangular temple, and the creatures scrambled to reach them. This gave Tobimar a minor inspiration; he spun around and brought both swords up and then down and across in a sweeping arc from front to back, sending a cold-iron will pulse through the blades that brought the seven *mazakh* chasing him up short—though, because he could not focus through their own wills, doing them no real harm—and scattered the weapons like straws in a dust-devil, breaking hilts, bending blades, and twisting gears and levers to uselessness.

As the *mazakh* recovered, he drew himself up straight and held the swords level and parallel as Khoros had taught him, and for a moment, looking into the eyes of the snake-things, he saw uncertainty. He forced a smile, the smile he had once seen on his mother's face when the Lord of Waters had offered to duel a troll bandit who had challenged her courage and honor, the smile which had only sharpened when the duel was accepted and when the rock-strong creature had started to realize how terribly wrong its estimation of the Lord of Waters had been.

"The Seventh Prince of Skysand greets you, and offers his blades to still your fear; or keep your fear, and your lives, if you flee." Into the words and level ice-blue gaze, he placed his living will, pressing back on their chill-hard minds with the blazing fire of his soul.

For a fleeting moment, he almost thought it would work. The three in the front wavered, hissing, and the other four stood still. But the twelve behind surged forward, and he had to focus some senses on them, and another figure—a larger *mazakh*, one of the *mazakhar*—appeared behind the first group, screeching orders in their own tongue.

And all dissolved into the chaos of combat. Tobimar spun aside as the seven charged—the advantage of the doorway now a terrible vulnerability, the open space of the temple his only chance—and parried two strikes with one sword, leapt up on a prayer-perch, cut down, impact on scales going through to bone, wrenching the blade free as he jumped again over a spear-thrust. *Parry!* screamed the inner sense, something streaking at him from the side, his sword already coming up, the *spangg!* sound of a *Zachass* disc ricocheting from his own blade almost instantly followed by the meaty *thunk* and a scream from the disc, ending its suddenly deflected course in the chest of one of the attackers. They were trying to herd him, he had to get out of the corner, leap up, on this one's head, flip—

A line of fire scorched its way along his side, and Tobimar realized it wasn't just a matter of sensation—that wasn't a blade. One of the *mazakh* was a spellcaster—maybe a priest, even, and that would be *very* bad. He charged forward, channeling his will into his body, his legs, leapt over the warriors that tried to intercept him with a bound that almost cracked his head open on the wooden beams above, barely kept hold of his weapons and will as dark-blue lightning sparked around him and the scaly priest stumbled backwards, throwing up his arms; it was futile as the razor-sharp swords first took one arm and then half-severed his head. *Three so far, maybe four.*

Impact from the side, sensed too late to block, only roll with it a bit, come up, cut at the legs, back them up, block again, arms hurting, can't stop, turn, disarming spin, jab, he's down, another two on me, stab backwards, missed but they've moved away, jump *up*, by the Sand there's the statue, hope it's not Manifesting right now, land on the outstretched arm, that will make it harder on them . . . Oh *dust and drought* they've all got missiles, spears, *Zachass*, think some of the ones I scattered weren't broken, got to get *down!*

Even moving as fast as he could, Tobimar tried to block two bladed discs, only managed to get one, the other scoring a long cut down his right arm. It wasn't all that serious, but instantly the arm began to simultaneously go numb—and to burn like icy fire. *Poison!*

The Inner Will could disperse a poison, even heal wounds—but if he used that much focus, they'd have him in an instant. All he could do was try to slow it a bit. And keep fighting. Swinging. Cutting.

Finally he realized there was a pause, a gap. He stared around, seeing that he must have killed eight, nine of them already . . . but there were at least eighteen remaining. *Reinforcements.*

The *mazakhar* stepped slightly forward, hissing. "A good fight, boy, and brave speech. But you slow, you tire, and we are many. Nearly all in this house have come. What, then, should we fear?"

And in that moment, when he searched for some words that would mean something, another voice spoke. A voice strange and hollow, echoing around the room, seeming to come from no clear source above or below.

"Fear *me.*"

And the huge *mazakhar* bellowed in agony, clutching futilely at its back as though something had impaled it there. The other *mazakh* whirled, seeking the source of that voice and that pain.

Tobimar didn't know what was going on, but he knew a chance when he saw one. He lunged forward, both swords drawn back, and with all his strength made a double cut; a second, gurgling scream and the leader went down, hands scrabbling grotesquely at his own innards in a useless attempt to keep them where they belonged.

Now there *was* consternation on the reptilian faces, for as Tobimar forced all of his strength into a final whirlwind of cuts, it seemed as though some invisible force protected him, hindering every attempt to hem in the exiled Prince. A spear was levelled at his back, and the wielder suddenly pitched to the ground, clutching at an ankle that was fountaining blood. A blurred, tiny motion, impossible to follow in the shadows and deadly dance of combat, streaked away, and a moment later as Tobimar exchanged blows with a veteran warrior, scales thick and glossy with age, whose skill threatened to disarm the young man at any moment, something tiny dropped from above (or, perhaps, leaped from the floor?) and a silvery flicker of motion jabbed from one side to the other; the veteran's sword clattered unheeded to the floor as the clawed hands were clapped to the throat, impotent to stem the tide of red and the half-seen something bounded away. A murmur of uncertainty began now, and the twin swords spun and danced in lethal rhythm, weariness held at bay with sheer will and rising hope, punctuated now by a pair of chiming *twang*s, and two *mazakh* fell with steam-whistle shrieks as something entered their eyes and began to *burn* with white-fire agony.

That was enough; the remaining creatures fled, unwilling to face the unyielding Tobimar and whatever unknown and terrible force had allied itself with him, even here within their own temple.

In the sudden silence, Tobimar could hear his own ragged breathing, and he glanced around, feeling the poison still trying to work its way through him, dizziness warring with fear and confusion. "Wh-what are you? *Where* are you? *Show yourself!*"

"No need to shout." The voice from down near his feet was the same, but somehow less frightening, almost comical.

Nonetheless, he jumped back, startled, and looked down.

A small brown Toad—with, admittedly, a fair overlayer of red gore—looked up at him and waved. "Hello!"

And Tobimar Silverun, Seventh of Seven, Seeker of Skysand, found himself utterly without words.

12

Tobimar set down the crystal-carved draftglass and signaled for a refill, shaking his head in amazement. "That's quite a story."

The little Toad waved a hand dismissively. "A little luck goes a long way. I'm just a lucky Toad." He lifted his own cup and poured a trickle of a black drink—nearly as thick as honey and with a taste Tobimar unfortunately could still recall—onto his tongue, making the Prince wince with the memory. Poplock had told him, just as he tasted it, that it was brewed from locusts and flame-ants. "Your story was much more interesting. But you didn't really finish yours; you didn't explain what you're still *doing* here. I mean to say, you're on a quest; shouldn't you be doing the questing?"

Tobimar laughed, then thanked the server as he refilled Tobimar's glass. "Well . . . you know, I thought about that a lot. I came here looking for clues to our lost heritage, and I found some. But not really enough to give me an idea of how this connected to what my teacher Khoros said in his parting message." The Toad gave a nodding bob of his body, showing he was listening. "I realized that with dozens of my family, maybe hundreds, having gone on this journey before, they must have come here at some point."

"And your family doesn't really have many clues to the past." Poplock nodded again. "You don't even know how you came to Skysand, really."

"Exactly. We fled there from somewhere, but even the direction isn't clear, just that wherever it was there were many mountains."

"Oh, that's helpful." The ironic tone of the little Toad's voice brought a wry smile to Tobimar's lips.

Mountains were not something in short supply. The entire continent was bisected by the Khalals—something like three to four thousand miles long and a few hundred miles wide, with the Archmage Idinus ruling his empire from the sixty-thousand-foot peak of Mount Scimitar. Then to the south of the Khalals, forming the main border and barricade between the Empire of the Mountain and the State of the Dragon King, were the Ice Peaks, themselves another two thousand miles of mountains, sometimes reaching six miles in height. To the far west and just south of the end of the Khalals, the ramparts of Hell's Rim stood grim and impassible save through the pass at Hell's Edge, while much farther south the Krellin Mountains formed a circle said to house the Father and King of Dragons himself. In the Southeast, the Wyrmscrest was a smaller but still notable range on the way to Elyvias, which was surrounded itself by the Cataclysm Ridge. North of the Khalals, Tobimar's own Skysand was bracketed by the Flamewalls, the White Blade Mountains surrounded the similarly named country . . . there were, simply put, a lot of possibilities.

"Very helpful indeed," he agreed. "But I've found a few reasonable possibilities. Still, what bothered me was that I might be retracing my forefathers' steps; Master Khoros once said 'whenever it seems clear to you what needs to be done to solve some ancient riddle, remember that many others may have thought it clear as well.'"

"Hmmmm. I see. I think. Your old teacher's saying that if it really was that simple, why then, does it still need to be done?"

"Exactly. So I spent, oh, I don't know, *weeks* trying to be clever and think of some new approach." He took a drink of the deep-blue, slightly bubbly Artanian wine and tried one of the baked tineroot chips. "Plus I was trying to figure out what direction I needed to take to follow his awfully cryptic advice."

Poplock's tongue snapped out, snaring a fly that had started an ill-fated investigation of Tobimar's plates. "Mmm. Crunchy. Yes, that did sound vague. Wizards are always like that, though. Follow lies and find truth, go south to reach the north, stand on your head to see things right-side up. I think working magic messes with their heads."

"It'd be easier if I *believed* that, O Sage of Toads. Master Khoros was far too clear-headed, alas." The tineroots were spicy, with an earthy undertone, and dusted with salt. "There's a lot of gods that promise justice or vengeance and no few that promise both; hard to sort them out. Chromaias is one of the obvious ones, the Three Beards, Myrionar, Odin, the Triad...But we're followers of Terian, always have been, so I went to the Hall of Light here."

"Main temple of Terian? That's a big building. Pretty, too. Liked that big statue, but that fuzzy light around the head makes your god hard to see."

Tobimar laughed. "You're not *supposed* to be able to see his face, silly Toad. Anyway, I prayed and then asked the Lurali there for guidance. She meditated and then said that my path could not be guided, for I must make the path my own."

"Oh, ouch, that was useless."

"Not actually." He grinned as he saw Poplock squint one eye shut and warp his face in an expression of incomprehension. "It took a little bit, but I looked at it again from Khoros' point of view. I had to make the path my own. That meant *not* following the same path the others took."

"But," the little Toad said, still puzzled, "they took all *kinds* of paths, from what you said."

"Right. So that meant I had to figure out what they all had in common. What were they *all* doing at the same time?

"So I went out for a walk, to clear my head, after a while—and as soon as I got ten steps out the door, it struck me like the very light of dawn: *that was the answer.*"

Poplock gazed at him with a dour expression for a moment. "*What* was the answer?"

"They were all *looking.* They were all *searching.* Trying to find something on this huge world by chasing around after it."

The Toad blinked, then bounced suddenly. "Oh! Oh! So you had to *start* your search by *stopping* the search!"

"Exactly! Just like when you're trying to think of the answer to something, and it's *almost* there but you just can't quite get it, so you *stop* thinking about it...and then suddenly it comes."

Poplock grabbed a fried beetle-grub from his own miniature plate and chewed on it thoughtfully. "Still, you couldn't just sit down and wait for the answers; the truth of your people's origins never came to your country, and Skysand hasn't been moving much."

"Right." Tobimar leaned back. "So the question was...how

could I work the angles of Khoros' advice? How could I not seek, yet also make sure I was still seeking?" He looked at Poplock to see what he might come up with.

The Toad sat still for a few moments, still chewing. Then he bobbed slowly. "By doing some kind of job that would keep you on the edges of everything strange and dangerous, yet make you respected enough to get access to records that aren't easy for ordinary people to reach."

"And that job would be...?"

Now the Toad grinned. "You followed those hints of justice and vengeance. Bounty hunter with a code, of course. Adjudicator in training, or adventurer looking for steady work in a city. And I guess that brought you to that *mazakh* stronghold."

"You've seen it clearly, Poplock. There aren't all that many Lords Adjudicator, and with the law in the State being mostly composed of 'Don't cause trouble' in different ways, people usually try to settle problems more directly. Oh, anyone can go in and see the King himself, but the cost could be high, depending on what the King decides must be done. There's always a market for a trustworthy independent investigator who's good with blades and able to deal with magic too."

"Oh, no doubt, no doubt," the Toad agreed, with a comically raised eye-ridge, "but how exactly do you convince people you're trustworthy to begin with? That's how any good faceturner makes his living, you know—looking trustworthy. But anyone with the money and resources to hire a good Adventurer or investigator usually isn't going to be that easy to run the turn on." He spoke with the air of someone who—having spent the last couple of years unseen and underfoot throughout the City—had come by this knowledge with experience.

Tobimar grinned, pushing an errant strand of his black hair back into place. "True, but most of them won't put a Starheart on deposit with the *Nomdas* of Terian, or offer to pay for a truthsaying with anyone the client names. I will."

Poplock blinked in surprise. "No...no, I don't suppose many others would. Especially not that last bit about the *client* getting to name the truthsayer. So what about the *mazakh*?"

Tobimar shook his head. "That one was supposed to be pretty simple. One of the *khallit*—Maridras is her name—came to me and asked me to find her eggs; two had been stolen and she and her mate had a clutch of only three. I really only had to *find* them and, if they were still viable, they'd take care of the rest. If the eggs were...unrecoverable, well, they might have had some more work for me, or maybe they'd just have gone straight to the real Adjudicators then.

"Well, even in the First City there's friction between all types; out-and-out prejudice and so on is forbidden, but behind-the-scenes infighting, that kind of thing, goes on all the time. And there's at least two of the races I know of that have a real taste for *mazakh* eggs."

"Ooo! Ooo! I know those too. The Iriistik and the...oh, what do they call them...the *Rohila*, the Artan-that-aren't-Artan?"

"The White Elves?" Tobimar blinked at that. "I hadn't heard *that* one. No, I was talking about *bilarel.*"

"Ogres or trolls...yeah, heard that. But the White Elves do too."

"I'll have to remember that. Anyway, I thought I had a strong lead; there's a small Iriistik nest here that's a colony for the Gold Mother up north, and I picked up some rumors they'd been asking around for eggs. Some *mazakh* will sell their eggs if they're not fertilized, or even if they are and more hatchlings would be a problem, though you almost never see that with the *khallit*—there's too few of them to afford to shrink the population much. I narrowed it down to a Gray Warrior who was seen in the area, and I cornered him last week and after I proved I could probably beat him, he recognized his nest-value lay in survival, not in maintaining secrets.

"So you can imagine how puzzled I was when he said he'd arranged to steal the eggs, but not for him. For some other *mazakh.*"

Poplock shook his head slightly. "Right, that makes no sense. *Khallit* stick together, and the True People—the regular *mazakh*—wouldn't keep eggs of *khallit* at all, they'd destroy them on the spot. Figure they're cursed or something."

"That's what I thought. But the Gray was very certain of what he said, so I started some really careful investigations of the local *mazakh*, and sure enough I found a couple people who remembered hearing something about *mazakh* seeking *khallit* eggs."

Poplock finished his drink and used his rear foot to scratch behind his head. "Hmmmm. Well, you know, there were some pretty nasty necromancers securing that place, and unborn souls..."

"Exactly what I began to guess after a while, especially after I talked to people in the area and managed to find a common thread in the whole affair. The queries and contacts all started with one particular *mazakh* and I was able to pinpoint which one when this old Dwarf—"

"Better not let Odin's Children hear you use that word!"

"I've heard what they call us. They can handle the word 'Dwarf.' Anyway, this old graybeard fighter had seen 'that sneaky hissing lizard,' as he put it, and remembered a mark on his upper arm, three very thin lines like scars. With that hint, I managed to track that *mazakh* down, found out that he was acting as a sort of fixer or arranger for his group, tracked *them* down, and... well, that's how I got into that mess."

Poplock looked thoughtful, almost as though he was trying to think of something. "Something about that... well, it'll come back. Anyway, now what are you going to do, Prince Tobimar?"

Tobimar gave a slight smile. "First I'm going to have to go to my clients and tell them what I've found out. I don't have too much hope their eggs are still viable; if they're using them for what I'd guess, they probably would use them right away. Then..." He looked at Poplock. "We need to do something about your problem, actually. That's more important than my quest. After all, mine's been waiting twelve thousand years."

"With that logic, you'll never finish it," Poplock pointed out with a mocking bounce. "But you're probably right. I'm really feeling uneasy about that old demon; he's had a lot of time. But what can we do? No one listens to me."

Tobimar Silverun sat up a little straighter. "Maybe not, Poplock. But I've made quite a few important connections since I've been here. If we take them the results of this investigation, combined with the importance of what you've got to tell them... I think it just might get us in to see Adjudicator T'Oroning himself, and I've been wanting to talk to him ever since I got here!"

"Well, in *that* case," the little Toad said, "Let's finish up with this meal and get moving!"

13

Once more the gold-silver scroll was set on the desk in the shadowed room, and reflected in the central panel was something far away and terrible to behold. The man seated at the desk, however, found that more exhilarating than frightening, for the fact he was present at these councils—even mostly to observe—meant he was close to the heart of mighty doings indeed.

The glowing-dark figure of the King of the Black City gazed once more out of the central mirror-like surface of the three viewing mirrors before him; the one to his left showed his enigmatic patron, while the right, this time, was but pure, unmarred silver. The King spoke. "All is nearly ready?"

"A few final...adjustments, Majesty," the man's patron answered, casually toying with a deck of cards barely visible in one corner of the mirror. "Credit where it is due; Voorith has worked wonders in the last few years. If anything, he has greater resources now for his part than he would have had without the interference of the Golden-Eyed."

"Have you traced that agent?"

It shook its head. "Not an agent. As is so often the case, a would-be adventurer who proved to have the talent. Which as you know makes him rather difficult to trace; he has the favor of Blackwart upon him, yet none of the power of the gods."

"You are *certain*?"

Ah, the common mistrust and concern of all at such a time. The patron's smile was open and cheerful, yet the room seemed somehow to dim, as though the brightness of the smile drew in all light. "Certainty is for fools, Majesty...as I believe you know well. But I even risked the Cards for a hint."

The glowing eyes widened and then the ebony-glowing head bowed in acknowledgement. "Well enough done, then."

The man was surprised; his patron had shown him those Cards (which it was now idly fiddling with) once, and once only. According to his patron, they made no errors, showed the truth, but if used beyond a very, very limited amount, would give increasingly misleading answers which required ever more caution and cleverness to interpret properly.

When he had expressed surprise that a divination tool would be so perverse, the creature had laughed. "Unsurprising, in truth, as they were meant to serve higher and brighter destinies, and resent being turned against their own." It had smiled with a nostalgic look upon its face that, somehow, made even *him* shiver. "Capturing those Cards...that was one of my greatest triumphs, actually."

But the King of All Hells was continuing: "And did the Cards offer any other insight?"

"The little Toad may well prove an impediment in the future, but not immediately. Alas, my friend, our true opponent is the same as always, and he has set more than one set of plans into motion. More than that I dared not attempt to see, not now."

The hiss of tormented air was the only sound for several minutes, air that shimmered with the same terrible blue-white radiance as Kerlamion's eyes, and then vanished within the blackness that surrounded him. "What of the other components of the plan?"

"All appears nearly ready." His patron's blue eyes met the man's for a split second, as if to say, *Let me handle this.* He was more than happy to stay silent as it continued speaking to Kerlamion, "...and yours?"

The smile of Kerlamion *did* take the light from the room, leaving only the glow of his monstrous eyes and the blacker-than-black half-circle of soulless mirth. "Very soon. Months only."

"Then—"

There was a knock on the door of his room, a door almost never approached by any other than himself, one never to *be* approached save in true emergency. He raised an eyebrow. *This is unexpected.* "Majesty...I must go."

No questions were asked; the King of Demons knew he would not leave so abruptly without reason, and his patron understood even more. The mirror went blank, to ironic silver reflecting only the one seated at the desk. He turned, then. "Enter."

The man who entered was tall, in shining armor of silver edged with black and red. He bowed deeply, dropping to one knee. "Forgive me for the intrusion."

"Forgiveness depends upon reason, my friend. No need to kneel. If your mission is urgent enough, then forgiveness is inevitable. Tell me of the urgency."

"We...have a problem with Silver Eagle."

"A problem?" He frowned. This was *not* the time for problems with the Justiciars. *Only a few months!* "Be more specific."

"He has begun...asking questions. Questions about the past. Nothing too obvious—he is a clever man, sir, very clever—but it is clear that he suspects all is not as it appeared on the outside."

"Aran," he said softly, and Condor shrank back at the use of that name, so familiar and thus so very dangerous, "Aran, my friend, this seems to me far too swift. We have procedures, requirements in place for how you all must conduct yourselves, how the adoption of a new Justiciar is to proceed, how to guide them slowly but surely into acceptance of their new position. More, we have not *had* to perform any questionable acts since his induction. We have been given time, and while it has been clear that he is unfortunately upright and honest, possibly too difficult to turn to our cause, we have all been conducting ourselves as true Justiciars." He looked coldly at Condor. "Have we not?"

"Yes! Of course we have!" Condor was obviously offended as well as worried.

He sighed. "Then...Aran...how is it that he is asking *questions*? Someone has said *something*."

With his newly increased and quite inhuman senses, he could sense the tension and fear in the Condor Justiciar. "No, it's not that. I swear it! You've been *with* us a lot of the time! He's asking about Silver Eagle."

That wasn't the answer he'd expected. Four years was a very long time to continue to keep secrets, and some of the Justiciars simply weren't naturally good at that task, even with their lives and souls at risk.

And his own life and soul might be at risk, too. It was *his* patron that allowed the Justiciars to mimic the powers which they would have otherwise been granted by Myrionar. Something about the Justiciars, or Evanwyl, was crucially important to his patron, and if this brought the masquerade down too soon... "What is our new Silver Eagle asking? Do you have any sense of what he's hoping to find out?"

"I'm not sure," Condor said, "but I *think* he may believe that the Silver Eagle who came before was involved in the attack on the Vantage house."

As he most certainly was, along with the rest of the Justiciars, he thought. *But it's interesting he asks only of Silver Eagle.* "You think he *only* suspects Silver Eagle?"

"Right now?" Condor thought for a moment. He waited patiently, not wanting to disturb the young Justiciar's thoughts.

"Yes," Condor said finally, nodding to emphasize the word. "The way he's been poking around, it's like he's trying to get us to admit something we all *want* to admit."

He frowned. "That... is an interesting approach. And if I think of it from his point of view, it could even make sense. Unfortunately, if he keeps going along that line of thought, it will inevitably force us to the truth. And I do not think there is any likelihood of getting him to let the truth pass by."

Condor shook his head. "No, I don't think so either."

"So. Strategy, secrecy, and safety dictate only one course. Justiciars are often at the forefront of dangerous missions; thus even with their powers they can, and sometimes do, die. I think it has been long enough; arrange the appropriate accident, my friend."

When Condor did not move immediately, he realized there must be more, and his eyes narrowed.

"Forgive me again... but it may not be so simple."

"How so, Condor?"

Condor took a breath so shaky that he felt a faint twinge of excitement and perhaps... not fear, but nervousness. *Truly it must be something of...*

"Today... while he was with myself and Shrike... we came upon a small family, travellers, set upon by doomlocks." He nodded; doomlock spiders were extremely dangerous creatures that sometimes travelled into Evanwyl from Rivendream Pass. "We of course drove the things off, but afterward... before either Shrike or myself could begin, Silver Eagle began *healing* the victims!"

Aran stood still for a moment, taking *that* in. *That changes everything.* As an ordinary man against Justiciars—or, being honest, against false Justiciars who wielded powers equal to the originals—even Rion Vantage, the Silver Eagle, would fall, and fall fairly quickly. *But if he has the true powers of a real Justiciar...*

"You do not think we can...stop him, do you?"

Condor obviously wanted to say he could, but knew this was no time for false confidence. "No. Not certain enough. If he managed to get away, he could reveal the truth. We have a fair hold on Evanwyl, but nothing like perfect control."

"I will...consider this problem. I may have to call in...outside help, I suppose." He nodded slowly. "Aran, unless he seems to suspect you *directly*, it may be well to respond to him in a manner that indicates that you might know something, but are afraid to talk about it. Draw it out a bit; if he believes what we suspect he does, he'll have to eventually realize he needs to reassure you that he won't hold it against the *Justiciars* as long as we...took care of the problem. Getting to that point will probably take at least a few days."

Condor bowed and left, clearly relieved.

He turned and considered the now-blank scroll. He *could* initiate a signal; only a few minutes ago his patron had been visible in the one pane of shining silver and gold. But to reactivate it now might bring him back into the middle of a conference, and the King of All Hells did not at all appreciate people coming and going from his view. Not at all.

More to the sharpest edge of the matter, my patron *has yet to give me permission to contact it again...even using this speaking scroll. And I have been given full authority...*

That decided him. *If I cannot deal with the problems that come before me, what use am I to my patron, or myself for that matter? I have been given the power; I have been making my own preparations for years. I need no other help.*

Yes. That was the proper decision. His patron would not appreciate being called upon—assuming it would answer a call at all, which it might well not—to deal with a problem that he could have dealt with on his own.

Silver Eagle. He smiled, even as he contemplated the next moves. Formidable, yes—he had crossed blades in practice with Rion Vantage, and the young man was fast and deadly. With the actual powers of a Justiciar, even ones newly acquired and thus still being learned, he would be extremely dangerous, and it was vital he not have the chance to communicate the truth.

Still, at the moment Rion was still focused on the idea of *one* rogue Justiciar, hadn't yet grasped—or, perhaps, *allowed* himself to suspect—that all of his cheerful companions had been part of the butchery at the Vantage estate. There were a few days yet. *Just enough time to bring down some...special support from the North.*

Support that I found on my own, bargains I made with my own resources, risking my own life to find and negotiate with certain forces that even my patron has not contacted.

And all the time he thought, his smile grew wider. *Alas, poor Silver Eagle. To be buried again, in so short a time!*

14

Kyri stood, indecisive, at the front door. *I really should be at the Temple.* Still she stood there, unmoving. Something was wrong, and she didn't know what it was.

Rion knew, of course, but he simply wouldn't *tell* her. He had been strangely erratic of late. One day he had come home in a grim mood, silent, almost brusque even with Urelle, and retired to his room without a word after dinner. He'd disappeared for three days after that—and she'd heard rumors of the Justiciars' deeds in that time, including a last-second rescue of a family from Doomlocks—and came home seeming ready to burst with happiness and pride, saying only that now he knew he was truly a Justiciar. Then, later, he came home quiet, contemplative, and over the next few days his mood seemed to become darkly resolute.

This puzzled her. With what they had discovered, she had *thought* they would get answers, that things would get *better* soon, but his reactions were...different.

Then today...with Aunt Victoria and Urelle off visiting around the country...he had come home, walked quietly through the entire estate for hours. Every time she saw him, he would glance up, seem about to speak, then turn away. Finally, she'd cornered him. "Rion...what is wrong?"

The blue eyes, so like Aunt Victoria's, met hers, then looked away.

"Don't try to tell me nothing's wrong! You know you can't lie to me."

"I wasn't going to say that." His voice was pained, both by the accusation and whatever he was hiding. "But I can't tell you . . . I don't *dare* tell you . . . not right now. I have to be sure. I'm very, very close now, Kyri. I . . ." He stopped with what appeared to be a physical effort.

"You can trust me, Rion! I know what you're doing. *I* figured it out, remember. Maybe I can help—"

"Absolutely *not!*" The vehemence was so extreme that she stepped back. Rion hadn't used a tone of voice like that since . . . since their parents died. He shook his head, then continued in a slightly more controlled tone, "Kyri . . . I trust you. I trust my family, believe me. But this is dangerous, and it's my job . . . as a Justiciar . . . to take care of this kind of thing. I . . ." he seemed reluctant, but forced himself to continue, "I *will* tell you everything once I've checked out a few more things. But not quite yet. It's . . ." He shook his head again, then straightened. "Look, I have to go, Kyri. I'll be back tonight, and then . . ."

"Then you *will* tell me, Rion. Or I'll start following you, and you know I can do it."

"You wouldn't." He drew a breath, then sighed. "You would. Of course you would. All right. I'd argue, but . . . all right. I'll tell you. But . . . you won't want to hear everything I have to say."

Without another word he'd left, and she'd been wandering around indecisively ever since. The Balance was that evening, and she had been chosen as the Sword. Kyri glanced at the elaborate clock which was one of Victoria's favorite treasures and shook off the mood. *I'm not going to let Myrionar down; that's not a good way to convince your god to bless your family.*

Decision made, she hurried out, taking one of Victoria's riding horses, Talad, to make up the time she'd lost in dithering around the house. *I'll owe Talad a rubdown when we get back, too, making him stand around waiting for the whole ceremony.*

Myrionar's Temple was bright with light as she entered, just a little more hurriedly than she'd wanted, but she saw with relief that they were just finishing the assembly. The stage was empty, and that gave her enough time to make her way around the back.

"I was getting worried, Kyri," Arbiter Kelsley said, his concerned eyes belying the severe precision of his gray-sprinkled brown hair and square-chiseled features. "You've always been so reliable."

"I'm sorry, Arbiter. Got a little distracted." She took the ceremonial robes, deep blue to either side with pure silver in the center, the gauntlets—also blue on the back, silver on the forearms—and struggled into them as she made her way behind the holy stage.

Just in time. Kyri carefully moved onto the stage, the deep blue of the backdrop identical to the robes; with the side-folds pulled inward and the cowl dropped over her face, she would be effectively invisible to anyone in the congregation—necessary for the Service of the Balance. The effects could, of course, be managed far more easily by magic, or by the power of Myrionar Itself, but the effort and discipline to carry out the ritual without such aids was much more in favor.

She became aware, however, that something still seemed... off. The sense of something larger, of something omnipresent and vigilant, that she associated with Myrionar in these rituals, was... well, not *gone*, but fainter, weaker, muted, and that worried her terribly. Was it her lateness, her hurried entry?

Kelsley was now giving the service, and she straightened, listening for both the meaning and her cues. The exact *words* were not important now; the key was to understand the priest's point. This was one of the traditional services, so the basic point would be one of—or, more likely, all three—of the Foundations, but the exact way in which it was expressed might be of importance.

But Arbiter Kelsley seemed to feel it was best to stick to the traditions closely. Justice with Wisdom, Vengeance with Truth, Mercy through Strength, all three of the Foundations and straightforward. Justice and Wisdom unveiled first—the Fandre brothers, two years younger than she was, trying not to giggle as they kept their arms curved to present the appearance of one of the scales; Vengeance and Truth—Gallire and Lehi Monn, girls of the same age, and then it was her turn, Strength of the Sword, lifting up, spreading the robes to let the silver blaze out, using her hands to raise the bar overhead that revealed the silver backing to join the two sides of the Balance to the upraised Sword.

She took a breath, steadying herself. This was one of the more demanding parts of the ritual, since you were supposed to stay still throughout the remaining several minutes—sometimes up to a quarter hour—of the service.

But now there was a commotion, shouting outside, running feet, and Kyri felt a terrible foreboding, even as the doors burst open. "Arbiter! Arbiter Kelsley, come quickly!"

She recognized with a shock that the voice was that of the

Watchland. Even as she did so, she saw the blue gaze of his eyes across the room, somehow recognizing her, and something in that gaze sent a chill through her, even as the Watchland whirled, drawing his sword, calling for more aid from any who could come, and she heard the three-note clanging of the Watchland's Cry, the warning that Evanwyl was under attack.

Even as she recognized that alarm, an alarm she had never heard rung for real in her entire life, she heard other cries. *Those are screams of pain—and I hear fighting!*

She saw others backing away, the children in the ritual taking cover, looking for shelter, but to do that never occurred to her. Instead she looked desperately around. *A weapon! I don't have armor, but I need something to fight with—*

And it was so obvious, really, the great sword which was a part of the Balanced Sword at the altar. She leapt up and wrenched it free, whispering a prayer for forgiveness as she did so. *Well, I wasn't blasted to ash, so I guess Myrionar thinks I'm doing the right thing.* The greatsword was solid and well-balanced, which was a relief; she'd been afraid that it was merely a show-blade, but apparently the main Temple of the Balanced Sword had felt real weapons were in order.

She sprinted out the door, following the sound. The Watchland was vaguely visible ahead, and suddenly he stopped his run, his sword was up and something—several somethings—were slashing at him. Closer now, and the things were twisted creatures, something like caterpillars grown monstrously huge, but with a humanoid torso, massive arms gripping clubs or maces. The heads were worse, with flowing hair and high foreheads and calm blue eyes...and the mouth of a lamprey below. *From Rivendream Pass. They must be.*

She saw the Watchland's blade dancing back and forth even as she approached, and one of the things fell.

She was stumbling to a halt, frozen now, realizing that this was no sparring match, no fantasy of heroism, no practice, no dream. This was *real.* Those monstrous...*things* were attacking her friends, her neighbors, and she was going to have to face them with weapon and speed—and die if she wasn't good enough.

She tried to make herself move forward, but the fear dragged at her. *Did Rion have to face this? Or was he already prepared, able to face it as soon as he knew the fight was real?*

With a tremendous effort she forced discipline upon her trembling limbs, made her gut steady, repeated the calm and focus of the Way of the Eight Winds to herself: *Speed of East, Guidance of Spring, Light of South, Circle of Summer, Wisdom of West, Flow of Fall, Hardness of North, Cleansing of Winter*. Her heart still hammered, she still felt sweat under the ceremonial robe even in the cool of evening...but she could *move*, and the sword of Myrionar's temple was in her hands. *More screams from ahead—I have to hope Jeridan can handle these creatures!*

She ran past the Watchland, who saw her and gave a quick nod, as if to say *yes, I'm all right, keep going!*

She passed near one of the things and felt a crawling on her flesh—both from the wrongness of its presence and the realization that she would have to fight such a thing and kill it. She still wasn't sure...

But then she realized where the screams were coming from. It was the Monn farm, and she felt a surge of horror, remembering little Gallire and Lehi, the twins who had been Vengeance and Truth in the ritual just a few moments before.

Two children, hiding in fear in the Temple.

Two children away from their homes, while their parents screamed.

Fury surged up in her, fury and memory of her own loss. *No! I won't let them be orphaned! I won't let that happen to* anyone!

The anger sped her feet, and she hurdled a three-and-a-half-foot-tall post fence. The night was dim, only a sliver of a moon showing, but she could see the nightmare shapes ahead, one already grasping a man's shadowy form, bending the head down...

A desperate *leap* and she *slammed* into the creature, impaling it completely through with the sword of Myrionar. It shrieked and gurgled, as blue-white light shone from the wound. She felt a surge of momentary nausea and revulsion as the semi-human torso and arms twitched and shuddered, forced it down. Turning, she ripped the sword clear, seeing two more of the monsters rippling towards her on shuffling pseudofeet, even as she saw Phenre Monn staggering into the farmhouse, helped by his wife Ballu. *They'll be safe there for now. If I can—*

And then she heard another cry of pain and horror, but *this* cry she recognized, the sound piercing her to the heart, sending a wave of cold through her body.

Rion!

"Rion, hold on!" she shouted, and with a pirouette spun past the caterpillar-centaur monstrosities, decapitating one and flowing past the other's grasping hands. *They're slower than me . . . but if they try to chase, I'm at least leading them away . . .*

But her main focus was on the beloved voice somewhere in the thin forest ahead past the edge of the farm, now cursing, and a clash of steel that showed her brother was fighting something in earnest.

She wasted no more breath on calling, just ran, ran with the horrors of the years before shouting at her heels, a terrible foreboding making the run seem slow, mired in oil and tar, as in a nightmare.

Ahead there was a flash of silver light . . . and the light seemed to *vanish*, even as she heard a choked, bubbling cry.

For a moment—the slightest of moments—she thought she saw . . . *something* standing there, something darker than the darkest shadows, with sparks of venomous yellow where there should be eyes, and a monstrous, phantom smile like moonlight through ice. But even as the terror of that vision jabbed like ice through her chest, it was gone—if it had ever been—and she heard and sensed, rather than saw, someone or something else running away, running at a pace that made her own sprint seem slow and lazy.

But she didn't care about that, because on the ground ahead was something else, something silver with black smeared across it. *No, no, no, not again, please, not again . . .*

She could not see, and surely there were still things following her, not far behind, and still with prayers in her heart she spoke the words they had all been taught and the flare-light went up, blazed out, turning what had been black to red, bright, horrible blood-red, and she knew her prayers were in vain, for her brother lay there, the Armor of Eagle rent asunder, blood pooled about him, and the last traces of life were fleeing. She dropped to her knees, taking his hand, saw his eyes flicker open for a moment to catch her gaze with wide-eyed horror, trying to speak—but the terrible wounds gasped with his movement and she knew he was getting no air.

"*ARBITER!*" she screamed, and leapt to her feet, hearing scuttling movement coming up fast. "No, no you will *not* take him, no!" she heard herself saying, voice trembling, tears starting from her eyes, blurring her vision; but she didn't really need to see the misshapen thing, just swing, block, swing again, and it gave a screaming hiss and tried to back away—but she gave it no chance. *More coming*, she thought with fresh horror, hearing more movement from three sides.

She refused to give up. Her brother was not going to die undefended and alone, not now, not *ever*. A club whipped out, grazing her unarmored shoulder, and even that slight contact felt like it broke her arm. She gritted her teeth, refused the pain, focused past the terror and the fear and ducked under the next attack; her blade slid in blue-shining perfection through the lamprey-fanged mouth.

But there were more—not two, three, four, half a dozen, more— and she realized that there was no chance for her *or* Rion now. They were more cautious, not stupid, perhaps even intelligent, and they recognized how dangerous she was. They were maneuvering, ringing her in, and then...

One suddenly fell, convulsing as its head flew from its body, even as the one next to it shrieked, a slender blade flickering through its body from one side to the other, and Lythos continued, jumping over the falling body, blocking two strikes in a single motion and impaling the next creature, a flowing dance of death that showed her just how very little she had yet learned, and why Lythos was called *Sho-ka-taida*, Master Of Weapons.

That was a far and distant thought, though, for now she looked down and her brother's gaze was beginning to glaze, horror still in those eyes and desperation and in his wheezing futile attempts to breathe she heard him trying to form words.

"Let me through!"

It was the voice she had most wanted to hear in that moment, and she moved aside, praying that the Arbiter was in time, taking Rion's hand in hers. "He's here, Rion, the Arbiter's here," she said. "It's okay..."

But Rion's gaze did not shift, even as the Arbiter placed hands upon his wounds and one of the Seekers came to assist; she saw Rion's eyes widen, as though to try to tell her something from the sheer intensity of that look...and then roll and fall shut, the hand spasming and then going limp.

"He's fading!" the Arbiter snapped. He gripped the symbol of the Balance tighter and she felt, suddenly, that presence, strong and certain, and blue light radiated from the priest's other hand, forcing wounds to close, knitting them with power channeled from a god directly into the mortal body of Rion Vantage.

But Kelsley's face was pale, and vaguely, at the edge of her shock and denial she realized there were more shouts of consternation now...other victims...She should rise, she should go to them.

Rion's hand twitched, and for a moment she felt a spark of hope. But that was dashed as she heard Kelsley gasp. "I... I cannot hold him." Seeker Reed—one of the students of the Temple—caught his shoulder. "I will help you, Arbiter...By the Balance, what is this?"

They were gazing at things Kyri could not see, and their faces showed utter horror. "Arbiter, what can we do?" Reed gasped.

"I...I do not know. I have never..." Kelsley swallowed, then leaned forward. "Soul injury. It is spoken of in the texts, but so rare..."

"What is *wrong*?" Kyri demanded.

Even as Kelsley answered, he was busy, focusing more power, pale agony clear now on his face. "His soul itself is injured, cuts across his very essence in parallel with his bodily injuries. Those injuries...were mortal. If I cannot bind...his soul back together...it does not matter if his body is completely whole."

Sweat trickled down his cheeks and Kyri was suddenly aware that the pain he showed was much more real and immediate than the pain of failure. "What are you..."

"Arbiter! Stop!" Reed shouted.

"Reed...I cannot let him..." The Arbiter's voice was weak, but iron-hard in determination, and suddenly Kyri understood. *Only pieces of another soul...could bind together a soul so injured. Kelsley is ripping his own spirit into pieces, into bandages of his own essence...to save my brother—*

"Arbiter...others are injured. And he..."

Kyri looked up at Reed, wanting to rage at him, but seeing only tormented sympathy that struck her silent.

Kelsley's hand dropped to his side and he crumpled. Kyri realized with another dull shock that Kelsley was near death himself.

And in that moment she knew.

Rion...Silver Eagle...Her brother...was gone.

15

Watchland Velion was down off his horse almost before it stopped. "You are still here. Thank the Balance. I was afraid . . . I had missed you."

Kyri took a breath, watching the Justiciars hard at work loading the coach. They had refused to allow any others to help with that—it was their way of mourning her brother, who was also theirs, she knew. *I must answer,* she thought, and turned to face the Watchland. *Another farewell. This is harder than I thought it would be. But staying . . . staying would be even harder.*

It seemed as though everyone in Evanwyl had come at some point in the last few days. *And every one of them so hard to say goodbye to.* She knew them all, every one—one of the Eyes of the Watchland was *supposed* to know them all, and she'd tried. The farmers like the Monns, who had come to offer both sympathies and their thanks; Kochiss the butcher and his wife Minuzi the apothecary, he with huge hands and gentle eyes and she with a dissecting gaze and sympathetic voice; Kell from the Balanced Meal, carrying a load of cookies along with his grief; the Eyes like Zan'Tak and Hightower and Thalinde, almost all twenty-five of the families of the Arms . . . *all so much, all so very much sympathy and support, and yet I* know *we have to leave . . . and now this, one of the hardest of all.*

She looked up into the Watchland's eyes, lighter, more piercing blue than Rion's, but at this range filled with the same concern. *He was so . . . remote, seemed so cold right afterwards. So hard to see as he rode from one side of the country to the other on the hunt. Some say he rode into Rivendream Pass itself, seeking whatever it was that killed Rion.*

"I wasn't sure it would matter," she heard herself say before she could catch herself. *What in the name of the Black City is wrong with me? I know courtesy!*

Victoria, barely in earshot, stiffened, and she heard Justiciar Condor give a grunt of consternation.

To her surprise, the Watchland smiled sadly. "Yes...I am unsurprised. Such terrible events... for many of the last few days I have felt almost outside myself, watching what I have been doing, seeking to make it all right, yet... not able to let myself... truly reach those who needed me most." He took her hand and pressed it between both of his. "We had all too few chances to speak in the last few years, Kyri. So many things to do, for us both. I regret that."

She saw, from the corner of her eye, Condor looking narrowly at the Watchland. *It might almost be funny, if things were different.* "Watchland... Jeridan—"

He laughed. "I am not about to become terribly melodramatic with you, Kyri Vantage, for I have not quite so abysmal a sense of timing nor an overinflated belief in my personal influence. Still I would ask if there is no way we could convince you to stay? Evanwyl will be much lessened without your family."

Kyri looked over at the longcoach; inside, the faint dark shadow of Urelle was visible, unmoving, sitting still and quiet, even as Skyharrier directed Bolthawk in placing one of the wrapped portraits to one side of the coach's cargo area. "There are too many painful memories here right now, Jeridan. For myself... for myself it might be I could remain, overcome them, but I have to think of Urelle." She looked back at him more directly. "And in all honesty, I have to be worried that Rion did not die because he was a Justiciar, but because he was a Vantage."

The handsome face hardened. "Yes. Yes, I suppose you must. It would be unwise to not suspect that as a possibility."

"But," Thornfalcon put in, carrying a long crate of what was probably fishing gear, "does that mean you will return, Lady Kyri?"

She saw Condor glance up again as he headed back into the Vantage mansion for another box, "Possibly." She managed a painful smile. "Even, I suppose, probably. I won't want to give it all up forever. But I have to get Urelle somewhere far away..."

"...Somewhere safer than here," Victoria said, joining them. "Somewhere the poor girl can recover. Kyri's holding up remarkably well, I think you'll agree, but Urelle's devastated."

"You will return, of course, Lady Victoria." It was a statement more than a question.

"Sooner rather than later, but the journey to Zarathanton is not a short one, and not entirely safe even along the Great Road."

The Watchland nodded. "But where is your Master of Arms?"

Victoria's lips tightened and her eyes were sad. "Lythos... blamed himself, felt he failed as a *Sho-ka-taida* of the Way of the Eight Winds. Oh, it's foolish, and I tried to tell him so, but he felt that he could have arrived a few moments faster, or perhaps have trained Rion or Kyri so that Rion would have lasted a few moments longer. He begged to be allowed to return to his home—I presume to heal his own heart, which I hope he shall, and join us again perhaps."

Kyri could see the look of concern in Jeridan Velion's eyes. "But without Lythos... Lady Victoria, I know of course your reputation and skill, and Kyri proved herself full well, but still, you have now none of your guards to spare and you shall be travelling dangerous places, especially as you pass through Dalthunia, which is no longer our friend and ally. Will you require an escort?"

"I've hired a pair of Guild Adventurers to guard us," Victoria answered. "Over there." She indicated the front of the horse team hitched to the longcoach. "And neither I nor Kyri are entirely unable to defend ourselves, as you have already mentioned."

Shrike glanced in that direction. "The Iriistik—Gray Warrior, even! Not a bad choice, but that lavender-haired little boy? Looks t' be not old enough t' leave his mommy!"

Victoria smiled thinly. "That, Shrike, is Ingram Camp-Bel. Of Aegeia."

Shrike's eyebrows rose up so high they disappeared beneath the beak of his helm; the Watchland's rose as well. "Dedicated to the task of bodyguarding nobility, from the Incarnate Goddess on down," Watchland Velion murmured. "And trained in the arts of war from the time they can walk."

"Savagely enough that many of the chosen children die in the process," Mist Owl put in, looking at the slender boy, who in truth did look as though he should just be starting an apprenticeship, with a strange long bladed staff slung across one shoulder and armor of peculiar squarish blocks covered with green fabric. "Then you are fortunate in his presence."

"Yes. He was quite insistent on taking the job once I began the queries, insistent enough that I considered him seriously... and he passed my tests extremely well." Victoria nodded in a satisfied manner.

"What... in the name of Myrionar... is *in* this thing?" Condor's voice was strained. "*Sirza*, give me a hand here before I rupture myself!"

Shrike, seeing the younger Justiciar wrestling with a squarish crate, sighed and walked over. "Young'uns like you always lookin' fer an excuse. Now, let a man take over—" he reached down, grasped the case, and gave a heave—nearly tipping himself onto his face. "*Demons an' dragons*, girl, are you tryin' t' *kill* us?"

Kyri felt her first real laugh since that terrible day two weeks ago come rippling up. "Those are my mother's stonesculpt hangings."

Watchland Velion smiled. "Ah, yes, she was famous for her hobby. I have one of her pieces—the radiant sun relief in my dining hall, in fact."

Between them, Shrike and Condor managed to lift the crate and stagger with it to the rear of the longcoach. "Doesn't want to go *in*..." grunted Condor.

"Put yer shoulder into it, lad," Shrike said; the two Justiciars pushed the crate into place with two ramming blows. "There. Now I hope there be just some drapes or something light."

"Here, I'll help." Kyri followed them, leaving the Watchland, Victoria, and Skyharrier discussing the journey to the south.

As she reached the front hall and paused, looking around to decide what to take next, Condor and Shrike were joined by Bolthawk, Mist Owl, and Thornfalcon. She was startled when all five dropped to their knees before her. "What..."

"My lady," Mist Owl said, his straight and slender figure more tense than usual, "we... owe you a great apology."

"And one that must be given now." She saw Thornfalcon's gaze flicker backwards, towards where—she guessed—he could just barely see Skyharrier. "Now, while our most courteous brother keeps the others in conversation."

Oh, no.

"Your brother..." The slender Justiciar's gentle voice suddenly threatened to break, "He...he had guessed at a most shameful secret. I..."

She saw the others looking, trying to speak, and to spare them the trouble, forced herself to say it. "Silver Eagle betrayed you, and killed my parents."

"Great *Balance*, girl!" The exclamation seemed torn from Shrike. "How...did ye...?"

She smiled bitterly. *More bitter than I knew.* "I was the one who thought of it."

"Myrionar's *Sword*." Condor's voice vibrated with sympathy, a sympathy she nearly rejected outright...but there was no point in inflicting her anger on them.

She was the one who deserved that anger.

"Then," Mist Owl said bleakly, "you have guessed that we found out the truth, and kept it a secret purely from selfish, selfish reasons—to protect the reputation of the Justiciars."

"No," she protested instantly. "Not selfish, Mist Owl. None of you think that! Not *ever!* My brother...and I, and my sister—we've always believed in you. There was nothing he wanted more than to join you—and you gave him, at least, the chance to redeem the armor."

The Justiciars exchanged glances. Thornfalcon looked quickly back, then met her gaze. "But we failed him, and you, again. We had thought we had dealt with all those involved. Now—now we know it was something worse."

"Worse, and deeper than the roots of mountains," Bolthawk said. "We should have realized it. By the Hammer-Father and the Hammer, we should have *known* it would take something much worse to turn one of Myrionar's own and hide it."

"But now we *do* know," Shrike said, "and so, lass, we come to ask ye something we don't deserve at all; that we be given some time to make it *right*. Ye could tell the truth, and we couldn't gainsay y'r right..."

"But," Mist Owl took the words up, "but then all we *have* done...may be undone. We still fight for Evanwyl, for justice; you know this better than any save one of our brothers, for I know your own brother has told you what he has seen, what we have done." He looked to Thornfalcon, who had just looked back again; the slender Justiciar nodded, and Mist Owl continued. "We agree that your family may still be in danger, and you are acting wisely. Will you allow us to continue, to seek those who have now struck our hearts twice, at least until you yourself return?"

The five were staring at her now, eyes beneath the helms as close to pleading as she could ever have imagined. *Allow* you? *I'm the one who caused it this time!* But aloud, she said, "Of course I will, Mist Owl. I won't dishonor my brother's name by destroying what had made him happier and more proud than anything else in his life."

The five bowed so low their helms touched the floor. "Then we all thank you, Kyri Victoria Vantage; your forgiveness both shames and honors us, and we shall strive to be worthy of you... and the memory of our fallen brother."

Thornfalcon made a sudden gesture. "Quick. We have been in here too long and no sign of the actual work being done!"

Despite the heaviness of her heart she couldn't deny a tiny smile for Thornfalcon's exaggerated panic. "Then lend a hand, all of you." She pointed to another crate. "That's the other stone-sculpt crate. I'll get that. None of the others will be that heavy, I'll guarantee it."

She reached down, squatting just as she'd always been taught, and with a smooth motion hefted the crate. *Gods, it's heavy!* It occurred to her now that the two crates were probably about the same weight... and together the hangings had been about eight to nine hundred pounds. *But the pain helps focus, at least.*

Condor and Shrike stared at her momentarily. "Lass, Balance an' Swords, take care! Let us—"

"I've... got it." She gritted her teeth and moved down the path. *Not... going to let them... think I can't handle this.*

Probably should have asked for help. She felt the ground sink under the combined weight, but held grimly on. *Rear of the longcoach. Just have to... lift it... a little more...*

With a supreme effort, she pulled the crate up and practically *threw* it into place next to the first. "Whooo... That'll teach me to try to show off."

"Doubtful. That has always been your problem since you were much younger, Kyri."

She turned quickly. "Arbiter?"

Kelsley sat in a wheeled chair, pushed by one of the other Seekers... Yana, that was her name. "I know you have been terribly busy, Kyri... but we have missed you at the Temple."

I knew it. But how can I say it? "Arbiter...I...I am not sure..."

"I know. Twice now you have lost family, twice to cruelty and evil, and no vengeance yet have you seen. I know."

Kyri was suddenly silent, tears threatening to overwhelm her again, and she realized she was nowhere near as strong as she had thought. *My fault...maybe the weakness of my faith, too...*

"Kyri...I know the pain is great. And it seems there is no reason or justice in the world now. But I beg you, do not abandon your—our—god for appearances. There are many vile powers in the world, and one of their greatest goals is to break our faith, take us away from the gods, and the gods away from us. I *know* of the power of Myrionar, I have felt Its power, and I know Its sorrow, too."

For a moment, she felt that same presence, the one that was sometimes with her in the Temple, and she sensed the sorrow Kelsley spoke of.

"Do not let evil triumph. We need the gods. And they need us. Our faith in times of injustice...brings them strength too, leads them through that which seeks to oppose them, that they can in the end lend us the power to return the world to its right and proper course."

I've lost my mother, and my father, and now my brother! And what has Myrionar given me?

But before she could say it, she looked down at Arbiter Kelsley, still unable to rise for more than a few moments, and—she had heard—likely to need a year or more to recover, and no magic known would avail him. *He held Rion in his arms, and tore his own soul apart to try and save my brother, all in the name of the Lord of Justice.*

That kind of faith, that personal seeking of justice for her and her family—something that could have cost Kelsley his life—could she ignore it? Dismiss it? When the power to even attempt it had come from Myrionar Itself?

When it was I who gave Rion the idea that got him killed?

No. It's hard...but no one said justice was easy. Toron himself said how powerful and hidden our enemies were, even to powers of the greatest of the gods. If I am grateful to Father Kelsley for what he has done and tried to do, some of that has to go to Myrionar for giving him, not just the power, but the courage and convictions to risk all for my brother's sake, even when there was no true hope to save him.

She knelt down and took Kelsley's pale hand. "I'm sorry, Arbiter. It is . . . very hard to keep my faith. But I know what you've done for us, and I won't abandon Myrionar. I will just hope that this time . . . this time we will find the monsters responsible."

"I assure you," he said, and now his voice was cold iron, "I assure you, Kyri Vantage, there is no prayer more fervently made at our temple, and no prayer more fully at the fore of my mind every day. And I know—for I hear all the prayers in my Temple that are given to others to hear—that there is not one person in all Evanwyl who has not said a prayer for you and your family." He gestured outward, and smiled again. "And I doubt not that it is in the minds of all of these present, especially his former brothers; they help you in this movement because they know they have no other help to offer now, and at least with this they accomplish something. See this, and know neither I, nor they, shall give up . . . and Myrionar shall not forget."

"Indeed. Nor shall the Watchland of Evanwyl." Velion was beside her again. "One attack, however terrible, could have been just some single, senseless tragedy. This is far more sinister. A small country we may be, but all the resources I may command will be bent towards finding the truth and delivering that truth to you."

She rose and bowed. "I thank you, Watchland."

"It is the least I can do . . . and far too little, even if I succeed. But you are welcome." He pressed her hand once more, bowed, and returned to his horse. "I have new Armsmen in training, and I must see how they fare. Fare you all well, and take care on the long road."

She waved, then turned towards the Vantage mansion. The sun was setting, and the mansion's front darkened, looking already sad and forlorn.

She went to stand by the door, looking in at the still-silent Urelle, and then looked back at the mansion.

I will be back. Mother, Father, Rion . . . and Myrionar . . . I swear that. I will be back.

16

"Oh ... my," Kyri finally managed.

Aunt Victoria smiled, looking in the same direction. "I've seen it many times ... and never quite gotten used to it." She smiled more widely as even Urelle leaned forward, eyes shining. "Behold the oldest city in the world, built before the Fall itself, in the language of its builders *Fanalam' T' ameris' a' u' Zahr-a-Thana T'ikon*, Zarathanton, home and throne of the Ancient Saurans and the Great Dragons themselves."

The walls that surrounded the first among cities were shining, polished wonders of pearl-gray, uncounted thousands of years old yet as unscarred as though they had been new-polished that very day, two miles or more on each side and five hundred feet high, fortifications spaced regularly along their length, impenetrable above and below. The gates of Zarathanton, open at all times save in war, were more than half the height of the walls, some of the largest portals ever forged, sparkling with gold and *krellin* and a dozen other metals, jewels, and the pearl-gray of unbreakable stone. Within, buildings could be seen, even higher, to the Castle of the T'Teranahm thrusting spires two thousand feet and more into the sky. Crystal and silver, stone and magic fused into testaments of power that had endured throughout every Chaoswar since the beginning, raised by the power of Elbon Nomicon and his Sixteen, and the thought sent chills of awe down Kyri's spine. Memories were faded, knowledge lost, but these walls, this city, had stood since before Myrionar had first spoken Its words of Justice, before Terian had learned the secrets of power, before Idinus of Scimitar had taken up his abode atop the tallest mountain in the world, since even before her people had ever set foot on Zarathan itself.

"Are...are we living *there*, Auntie?" Urelle asked finally, and the anticipation in her voice made Kyri's heart fill with hope. In the weeks of their—sometimes hazardous—travel, Urelle had slowly begun to recover. *Once more, from the ashes.*

And, maybe, so have I. She fingered the phoenix figurine that she'd taken with her on impulse, and looked to the sky, almost expecting to see the fiery actuality somewhere above. *Which is silly—they're rarer than dragons.* But the symbolism of that which dies and somehow comes to live again, was so very strong for her. She still blamed herself, sometimes, for Rion's death—probably always would. But at the same time she knew he wouldn't have blamed her, would have been *furious* at her for blaming herself... and the weeks of sometimes dangerous travel had helped ease the wound.

The worst part is keeping the secret. But I promised, and a Vantage keeps her promises.

Victoria was answering Urelle's question. "Not *within* the City, no, but I've obtained an estate a few miles to the north, at the border of the Forest Sea. We'll be near enough, Urelle." Victoria hugged Urelle. "Near enough for you to see the wonders, and come to know them."

Kyri stared at the crowds as they approached. More and more people—more people just on the Great Road than she'd seen in all Evanwyl, and of so many species. Children of Odin walking within almost *touching* distance of the *Artan* on one side and *mazakh* on the other, an Iriistik talking with a human who seemed comfortable speaking the buzz-click speech.

We're not the only gawkers, she noted with some comfort. Scattered through the crowd were others who stood and stared in awe and wonder and consternation—a wing-shouldered *Valkyrnen* there, a great *shellikaki* all feelers and armored jointed legs and waving, startled eyes from within a huge carven shell, and a bit farther away, on the other side of the road, five young people standing together, all stunned and amazed. They caught Kyri's eye because of their beauty; all five of them startling in their good looks, three boys, two girls, seeming only a year or three older than Urelle's fourteen. One in particular stood out to Kyri, for with his raven-black hair and dusky complexion he looked not unlike Urelle herself.

"We turn north at the next intersection," Ingram said, glancing at Victoria, who nodded to verify his statement. The lavender-haired boy moved forward, weaving his way through the nearby crowd effortlessly, levering others aside with subtle motions of his body and staff-blade weapon.

Kyri shook her head. *We were indeed lucky.* She had seen that weapon, the anai-k'ota, in use three times, striking as a staff, breaking apart into a series of bladed linked sections, slashing and striking and cutting in a ballet of death and destruction that seemed utterly at odds with the quiet, slender boy who, in his spare moments, spent his time reading from ancient books and sometimes peering at a strange glowing square which he hid away before anyone could get a look at it. Not even five feet tall, Ingram Camp-Bel had proven to be fully as formidable as the gray-armored, twin-sword wielding Iriistik warrior who called himself Ele-Kim-ze, which he said meant, roughly, Quester.

Quester was behind them, observing and guarding. Both of their escorts had recognized their skills and thus were willing to rely on their charges to defend themselves for the few moments necessary, if something came from an unwarded direction.

Urelle continued to stare at the City as they headed north, until it vanished behind a hill. An hour or so later, the longcoach pulled up in front of a green and gray mansion, set like a quiet jewel against the background of the Forest Sea.

"And here we are!" Victoria said, leaping down from the roof seat.

Kyri laughed. "Aunt Victoria, you know, you've seemed to be getting younger the longer we've been travelling!"

"Have I?" The older woman glanced up at the mansion, smiling faintly. "I suppose I have. I was a Guild Adventurer myself, and this has taken me back. I'd rather not have had to do it," she said more quietly, with a glance at Urelle, who seemed more interested in watching Ingram unhitching the team, "but as I had to, it's helped wake me back up."

"I think it's helped us all."

"I think you're right, child. I think you're right." Victoria glanced sharply at Urelle as she started towards the mansion. "Stay on the grounds behind the ward-fence, Urelle—and you too, Kyri."

Urelle nodded emphatically. "I understand, Auntie." Kyri stared at the towering mass of jungle, wafting strange, unknown scents into the humid warmth of evening, and nodded also. *The Forest Sea.*

Farther than this, only Adventurers, armies, and the mad or suicidal ventured...or those who were native to the wild. Anywhere on Zarathan, hideous dangers awaited those who left the shelter of their homes, the near and clear circles of the fields and the few fortified areas about the cities, or the broad and enchanted swathes of land about the Great Roads. Though maps claimed huge territories as the Empire of the Mountain or the State of Elbon Nomicon or even Dalthunia and vastly smaller Evanwyl, in truth they were all archipelagos of tiny islands of safety, connected by slender roads that were only mostly safe, surrounded always by wilderness, a hundred species of intelligent beings savage and otherwise, mystical creatures and mobile plants, undead remnants of ancient cities, legacies of ages past and conspiracies of the present, wandering remnants of forgotten gods, or servants of gods so new their names were only beginning to be spoken.

Finally she looked back down towards Aunt Victoria. "Do we have any staff?"

"Not yet, Kyri. Need to set up, get some word around."

Kyri looked over at Quester and Ingram. "I know you're just bodyguards, but..."

Ingram managed a small smile, which lit up his face, making him look even younger. "I suppose for another week's pay..." he glanced to Quester, who dipped his antennae, "we could keep guard here for a week or so." He reached over and with surprising strength hefted one of Urelle's boxes. "And help you move in."

Even with Quester and Ingram helping, of course, it took a long time. Finally, Kyri was left dragging the last piece—the first stonesculpt crate, of course—by herself while Aunt Victoria began to get dinner ready and Urelle, Ingram, and Quester started arranging the rooms to be livable.

What in the name of the Sixteen was I thinking, *bringing these things with me? I swear, they've gotten* heavier! She'd gotten about a quarter of the way up the staircase when she had to put it down and take a rest. *Maybe these should be hung up downstairs.*

She snorted at herself. Upstairs was going to be her own room and Urelle's and she was not going to leave Mother's hangings downstairs. Besides, half of them were already up there.

She sighed and turned back to the crate, leaning on it slightly, slanting rays of sun coming from a side window. She could see the deep impressions left in the wood where Condor and Shrike had finally pushed it all the way to the back. A faint silvery sheen seemed to cover the wood.

Her heart seemed to stop.

Crescent-shaped gouges. Silvery sheen in the slanting sun. One set nearly a foot higher than the others.

"No." She heard herself whisper, backing away from the crate that now loomed before her like a sign of doom. "No, oh, no..."

But those were feeble, impotent words against the implacable understanding that was now surfacing, a hideous truth that a part of her must have already guessed.

Not one *man striking the doors twice, high and then low. No.*

Two men, one very tall, one short, striking those *doors* at the same time.

The understanding—and the realization that those *same* two men had made *these* marks, glowing with bitter cold cheer from the wood—made her stomach twist.

We should have known. Perhaps we did *know, and just didn't want to believe. But it's so obvious. How could* one *corrupt Justiciar hide his true nature within the entire brotherhood? How could he cloak his lies from those who could see truth?*

"No. No. No, Myrionar, *NO!*"

But the memories were merciless, especially the last words of Rion, looking at her with grim certainty—*"you won't want to hear everything I have to say"*—and that final look of utter horror.

How much more simple, how much more sensible, to believe that it was the whole brotherhood that was responsible?

The brotherhood I sent Rion to question!

I SENT him there!

She tumbled backwards down the stairs, scrambled to her feet, sent one more horrified glance at the crate squatting on the tenth stair, indentations glowing like soulless grins in the final rays of sunlight, and turned away, stumbling, tears streaming from her eyes, unable to do anything but run, run, any direction, and repeating the single word *no.*

Inside she knew the answer was *yes*, but she could not bear to hear that voice, and so she ran. Brush and vines tore at her, but she ran on, heedless of anything save the terrible need to escape the heart-rending realization of betrayal more monstrous than anything she had ever imagined. She remembered green eyes gazing into hers, a hand warm on her own, and screamed, half in denial, half in rage, her voice echoing through the jungle and dying away like shattered hopes.

I sent Rion to them. I sent *him to ask questions, to let them* know *someone suspected the truth!*

Rion died because of me!

A part of her, a very distant part, tried to turn her back, knowing she was fleeing into the Forest Sea, but it was impotent before the seething fury and self-hatred boiling ever higher inside of Kyri. Something lunged at her, bladed legs and venomed fangs and a screech of hunger, but that was its one and final error, for without even truly being aware of it, Kyri caught the striking forelimbs, broke them, shattered the carapace, left the thing dying, and ran on, crying now, tears that seemed torn from the core of her soul.

Full dark had fallen and she burst through into a clearing. Shadows of movement were in the clearing, but fled, sensing that the newcomer was heedless, reckless, perhaps mad in truth, and thus a thousand times more dangerous than any more cautious foe. Stars glittered overhead, sparkled in the clear sky, and as Kyri paused she saw the twinkling stars of the Sword and Balance.

The sight was a shock of ice-water, bringing her to her knees. Then she surged to her feet, balling her fists, and screaming at the sky.

"Why, Myrionar? *Why?* We *believed* in you, we called your name, we trusted in Justice and Vengeance and your Wisdom and Mercy! My parents *raised* us to believe!" She reached inside her shirt, tore off the golden symbol so hard the chain left bleeding welts on her neck, but she didn't care. She shook the tiny sword-balance at its celestial mirror. "Even after they *died* we followed you, Rion gave his *life* for you, and you did *nothing!* Your own Justiciars! Your own *Justiciars* betrayed us, mouthed lies and deceit in my own *house,* set foot in your *temples* and you give us not a hint?"

The tears streamed down her face so that she could no longer see the stars, and her furious tirade was full of pain and sorrow as well as smoke-black anger. "How *could* you? Where is the Vengeance or Justice that could explain this?" She hurled the symbol away from her and fell to her knees again, crying, no longer able to scream, just to speak in pain-wracked sobs. "The Arbiter tore his soul to save Rion in your name! Kelsley almost *died*, and Rion *did*, and all for *nothing!* How could you? How could you abandon us all?" She raised her face and glared once more at the distant stars. *"ANSWER ME!"*

Her final cry echoed through the trees and died away to nothing. Silence surrounded her, a silence deeper than any forest should hold, and a chill went down her spine. Not a bird, a single animal, even the buzz and hum of insects was absent, and in the profound quiet the only sound she heard was her own ragged breathing and, under that, the pounding of her broken heart.

"I have not abandoned you."

With the words came the presence, the feeling of something vast and wise that had always been a part of the Temple; only this time it was a hundred times stronger, and the voice itself, though quiet, thundered through her bones, echoed in the ground, a voice that seemed both as unfamiliar as a stranger on the street, yet so familiar that she felt she had always known it.

"I have not abandoned you, Kyri Vantage, and I grieve for all you have suffered. Your faith has been true and even the gods cannot condemn one who is given such cause to doubt."

Kyri, open-mouthed, wanted to scream her accusations anew... but just as she could feel the Presence, so, too, could she feel Myrionar's pain, a sorrow that felt as deep as her own and older, ancient, as though the god had lived with such pain for all of Its existence. "Then...then why, Myrionar?" she said finally, a question instead of a demand or accusation. "Why, and how?"

"Many are the gods, Kyri Vantage. Powers there are greater than mine, and others subtle and cautious who spent ages finding solutions to dark puzzles of their own. I cannot say—precisely— how my Justiciars could be subverted within my own gaze. What I know would be too dangerous for you now, and there is still much hidden from me.

"But not for such useless riddles and half-answers have I spoken to you. You call on me in the name of my last true Justiciar, for the sake of my wounded priest, for the love of your family and for the loss of your innocence, and if any Justice remains in the world, I can do nothing but answer you."

The stars blazed brighter, and suddenly a golden Sword of

heavenly flame burned in the sky, a golden Sword holding aloft a silver Balance of cold-fire beauty, casting aside the night and bringing argent-auric daylight to the clearing in which she stood.

"Kyri Victoria Vantage, hear now the words of Myrionar, God of Justice and Vengeance. If you will have faith in me, I shall in you place all of my faith. Your path will be long, and hard, and filled with pain. But this I promise, this I swear, on the very power of the gods, that if you will remain true through all, if you will be for me the living symbol of Myrionar, then to you I shall in the end deliver all the Justice and Vengeance you desire—knowledge of your enemies, and the will to confront them, and the power to drive them to ruin as great as the pain they have caused."

"Have faith in you?" The words were ludicrous. Moments ago she was cursing Myrionar. "How...how can I? How, when I have seen nothing of your Justice, Myrionar?"

The familiar, alien voice was both stern and rueful, recognizing her plight yet yielding nothing. *"Only you can answer that, Kyri. That is, and has always been, the test of true faith. Can you believe, without proof? More, can you believe still, in the moments when all seems to shout at you that what you believe is a lie?"*

She shook her head slowly. *Believe... have faith in Myrionar. How?*

The treachery of the Justiciars pressed in upon her, and she shuddered. They had been one of the greatest symbols of her belief, and now she knew they had been false, every one of them a lie.

No. Not every one.

For a moment, she almost felt she could hear Rion's voice, and her eyes stung again with tears. *Rion* had had faith, and Myrionar *had* given him the power. He had been seeking justice when he died.

Can I let my brother have died in vain?

And she remembered Arbiter Kelsley. An act of faith and devotion so extreme that he nearly died.

"Be for me the living symbol of Myrionar..."

And what was Myrionar? What was the truth? She remembered the many discussions in her classes, time spent arguing with Rion beneath the starwood tree in the back yard, Kelsley's sermons, even—though spoken by false lips—speeches of the Justiciars.

"There is a reason Justice is always spoken first," she remembered Kelsley saying. "Because Justice is always to be foremost. Vengeance comes only after Justice has been done, after wisdom has found the truth and after careful judgment has guided us to the Just and Right solution, and, if warranted, tempered with Mercy. Only then is the cold and implacable power of Vengeance to be unleashed."

If Myrionar spoke truth...then something inconceivably terrible had happened, arranged and guided by some force so mighty and subtle that a gods' own servants had been subverted in a manner so constrained by power and necessity that even the god dared not alert others as to what was happening.

And was it not one of the most basic of the tenets of Justice that it was easy to give justice to the strong and secure, and thus far more important for the weak, the betrayed, the helpless?

And suddenly Kyri understood, and she laughed—a painful laugh, filled with the ghosts of tears shed and other tears to come, but a laugh. God though It was, *Myrionar* was the helpless one. Evanwyl, the stronghold of its faith, was held somehow by the enemy—perhaps the power that lay beyond Rivendream Pass, perhaps something else—and in Its own name it now came to her...

Because she was the one who would truly understand both what It asked, and why.

It was that which released the terrible knot in her heart. The pain was not gone, but the bile-acid corrosive fury against Myrionar, the foundation of her childhood, faded away. The god asked *her* to help make all these things right, asked her *here*, in the shadow of the First City, far from the corrupting power that had destroyed her family, and she realized that whatever game Myrionar was playing, it was a deadly serious one, one whose price could be the life of a god...or more than one.

She rose slowly to her feet, gazing at the burning symbol. "You swear that if I hold true, that in the end I will have justice and vengeance?"

"By all the Powers that are or have ever been or will ever be, I swear this to you."

"Then..." she took a deep breath, "then I will swear to you that I will keep faith in you, Myrionar. My brother died in your name, died because I sent him into that danger, and I believe in Rion...so I believe in you. I *have* to believe in you."

The Balanced Sword flared so brightly that it seemed to light the entirety of the sky. *"Then you, Kyri Vantage, shall be my one, true, and only Justiciar, the founder of the new Justiciars. Your course will be long and painful, sometimes darker even than the moment in which first I spoke to you; but believe, and hold, and be true to Justice, and there is a way out for you. Follow your instincts but temper them with thought; Justice, Wisdom, and Mercy before Vengeance."*

The Balanced Sword descended, its light drowning out all other sights. *"My touch is upon you, and you shall see it reflected in the morning's light. Find your course, and know my blessing is with you... and my thanks."*

The Sword and Balance rose then, ascending to the heavens, fading... and then there were only the stars shining softly down.

But inside, Kyri felt... somehow at peace, at least for this moment. She knew Rion would be happy, he would approve... and so would the Arbiter.

Two people, against all the ocean of pain and guilt and betrayal.

But they were two people who *mattered.*

17

"Auntie Victoria..."

Victoria Vantage spun around at the voice. "*Kyri!* Good gods above and below, child, you've had us worried half to death!" In the darkness of the night, this far from the City, Aunt Victoria was barely visible as an arrow-straight figure of deeper black. Kyri let the older woman hug her. "Myrionar's Justice, girl, you're shaking! What—"

"Not...not just yet, Auntie, please. Tell the others I'm back and...tell them I saw something, chased it into the forest and got lost. I'm...going to my room. When everyone's settled, I..." She shook her head. "I need to talk to you. But only *you*, Aunt Victoria. No one else."

The tone in her voice seemed to reach her aunt. "Very well. Get inside then and I will call in the others."

Kyri stumbled up the stairs, exhaustion dragging at her every stride; she noticed that in her absence someone had dragged the last crate upstairs. It was astonishing how difficult the last ten steps were; the shock of her terrible discovery, the run through the Forest Sea, the wild extremes of the emotional highs and lows of the last hours had drained more energy from her than any day of training ever had.

She closed the door behind her and dropped into a chair, glancing at the fateful crate which the same someone had thoughtfully delivered to her own room. The room itself was dark, no lightglobes on, and she didn't feel like bothering for now. Despite the quiet and the dark and the softness behind her, her mind refused to slow down. Her body wanted to fall asleep, but her thoughts ran fast and far.

She had no idea how long she sat there, still trying to comprehend what had happened, when there was a gentle rap on her door. "Kyri? Can I come in now, child?"

"Yes, Auntie."

The door opened, her aunt was momentarily silhouetted against the exterior light, and the door closed. "Sitting in the dark? May I give us light, or do we meet here like two thieves conspiring?"

Kyri managed a ghost of a chuckle. "No, Auntie. You can give us light."

"It's taken me *hours* to get everyone back and in bed where they—and by rights we—should be. Dawn is already showing." She muttered something about no lightglobes in this room, and then the shadow of her aunt crossed the room and pulled on the wooden slide, turning the slat-blinds fully open and letting the soft gray light of early morning fill the room. "There. I never enjoyed sitting in the—*Great Balance,* girl, what have you *done* to your *hair?*"

"My hair?" Kyri blinked in confusion, then turned to the full-length mirror that leaned against the far wall, awaiting her decision as to where to hang it.

Her jaw dropped in surprise. The night-black of her hair was gone, replaced by a rich, deep sky-blue, with a flash of pure silver-white in the very center of her forehead. At the very tips of every strand glittered a hint of gold. She heard the voice echo in her memory: "*. . . my touch is upon you, and you shall see it reflected in the morning's light . . .*"

Blue, silver, and gold: the colors of Myrionar, of the Balanced Sword.

She couldn't help it; she began to laugh, a laugh that she realized didn't sound either very comforting or perhaps even entirely sane, and it kept on going, getting louder and louder and less controlled, until all of a sudden a sharp *smack* reverberated through the room in time with a flash of quick pain from her cheek. In startlement she paused, finding her aunt's concerned eyes gazing into hers, Victoria's long, strong hand raised for another slap. "Are you all right now?"

"I . . . I think so. Sorry, Auntie."

"I should hope so. Now are you going to explain?"

She swallowed and took a deep breath, glancing over to the fateful case. "I . . . I know who killed Mother and Father. And Rion."

She saw her aunt's eyes narrow, trying to decide if Kyri were still not entirely there. Then Victoria nodded sharply. "I see. You *do* know."

"Yes." Even now, sure as she was, with Myrionar of the Balance Itself having verified all she knew, it was almost impossible to say. But she had to. She didn't know what to do now, but she *did* know that she couldn't possibly do this alone, without even advice and support from her family—from perhaps the only people who would really understand. She found herself on her feet, pacing, and could feel Victoria's gaze on her as she moved. Finally she stopped in front of the window and opened the shutters wide, leaned on the polished stone and wood of the sill, looking out into the deep black greenness of the Forest Sea, remembering the gold and silver fire speaking to her. She gathered her courage and turned, meeting Victoria's concerned gaze. "It was the Justiciars. All of them."

The color drained entirely from Victoria Vantage's face, turning her white as bone, and she collapsed into the chair from which she had started to rise, her pale lips shaping the same "*No...*" that Kyri remembered herself repeating in futile denial those endless hours ago. Kyri waited sympathetically, knowing that words would be useless now.

But it was only moments before the shock and denial drained away, to be replaced by grim understanding and acceptance... and even a dark, wry smile that startled Kyri. "Of *course*," Victoria Vantage muttered, half to herself. "No wonder Rion had to die. No wonder he didn't want to tell any of us anything. They admitted him to see if he could be brought to their side... and to silence him, if he couldn't. They knew that otherwise he'd be out searching on his own, harder to watch, harder to control, and something might get out." The swiftness of her acceptance and understanding reminded Kyri that Victoria Vantage was a Guild Adventurer and had been for fifty years, since she was fourteen. *I'm awfully lucky she's with us.*

Victoria looked up. "But you've gone far beyond guessing this, Kyri. It's a good guess—a terribly convincing guess, one that explains so very much—but for you, it's not a matter of guessing, you *know*, I can tell. And the simple realization doesn't explain why your parents were attacked, and certainly not your hair."

She gave a much more natural giggle. "No, it doesn't." She walked over and nudged the crate with her foot. "It started with this..."

By the time she was finished, the full sunlight of morning was streaming across her windowsill, and Victoria was nodding. "Oh, Great Balance. I thought I had faced dangers in my old career, but you've been drawn into the Great Game at a level even old Bridgebreaker wouldn't care to reach—not that he can stay out of it, really, not when he's playing commander in chief for the Sauran King himself."

"But, Auntie..." Kyri said, and suddenly the weight of her exhaustion was pressing her down and she felt young, frightened, and completely, utterly inadequate to the pledge she'd made. She sank onto her bed and covered her face with her hands. *I will* not *cry. I've cried too much.* "Auntie," she continued, and hated the quaver that had somehow crept into her voice, "I...I just don't know what to *do* now. I want to ride straight back to Evanwyl, tell everyone..." she shook her head, even before Victoria could speak, "...but I know that won't work. Even if everyone would believe me, whatever's behind this couldn't afford to let me talk that obviously. If I did, I'd probably be just getting a lot of people killed." She looked up at her aunt.

"That is almost certainly correct," Victoria concurred with a sigh. "This is a very deep plot, Kyri. Hiding such things from the gods is not an easy task even for another god. There may be a thousand gods or more, but not all of them are equal, and only a very few could manage what we have seen here; Toron said that before, when he completed his investigations into your parents' deaths, and this only reinforces his conclusions."

"It's more than that, too." Kyri leaned her chin on her hands. "What Myrionar said...I have to be just in all my actions. That means that even if I *could* beat all of the Justiciars and their backers in one go, I wouldn't be right to do so without making sure."

"Sure? Are you implying there is any doubt they're behind it?"

"No, no." That much wasn't in doubt. "Myrionar basically confirmed that Itself. But...Myrionar didn't say at what level all of them were responsible. Justice, Auntie. Why didn't Rion just tell us, tell Arbiter Kelsley? Maybe some of the false Justiciars aren't... aren't all bad." *Please. Not all of them.* She remembered their last speech to her. "Maybe there's good to be salvaged within some of them. I have to be willing...willing to see the possibility in anyone for redemption, or I'm not being what Myrionar says I must be."

"I begin to see what a weight Myrionar has placed on you, child. Such fairness could also get you killed." Victoria studied

her niece for several moments. "The one true Justiciar of Myrionar." A smile began to grow on her face.

The smile itself began to lift Kyri's spirits. "Auntie, what are
you thinking?"

"You don't dare confront them directly, Kyri, nor merely kill them
out of hand. But what if you could force *them* to confront *you*?"

She was puzzled. "I'd just have to start speaking—"

"No, no! Not forcing them by apparently threatening them with
the truth." It was a positively *predatory* smile by now. "Threaten
them with a lie. Threaten them with their *own* lie made truth."

"I don't understand."

"Become a Justiciar, and gain the reputation thereof, Kyri. In their
area, in Evanwyl itself. They will *have* to respond to some impostor
running around pretending to their power, wouldn't you think?"

That makes sense. "And they're unlikely to search for me in
a group, given how formidable they are and how much area
they'll have to cover to find me." The plan was making sense.
*And especially since I know Evanwyl at least as well as they do.
I won't be easy to catch.*

"Precisely. And alone, individually, with you having the true
powers of a Justiciar as well as the strength of a Vantage, I do
not think they could overcome you. You would have a chance
to test their true nature."

"Except..."

Victoria nodded again. "Yes. Except for whatever or whoever
it was that killed Rion. I do not think those wounds were the
work of the Justiciars themselves, but of their patron, whatever
monstrous patron is giving them the ability to pretend to be
Justiciars." She frowned. "I would go with you, Kyri, except
someone must stay here, and watch the estate and especially your
sister. But if you are going to attempt that approach—alone or
otherwise—you first need to become a Justiciar in fact."

"Isn't that what Myrionar has done? I mean...I haven't tested
the powers, but I think I sense them within me."

"A Justiciar is not just a set of special abilities, Kyri, and you
should know that as well as I do. The Justiciars of Myrionar have
abilities that are not *that* much greater than those of many other
priests, holy warriors, and so on, let alone the God-Knights of
Aegeia. But the Justiciars have their armor, their weapons, and
their symbolic names. We could give you a name, naturally, but

the power of the Justiciars in reality is that holding that position, along with the ancient armor, not only gives them the symbolism, but the ability to wield and channel the energy of the god directly." Victoria stood, looking out the window. "While Myrionar may be unable to do such a thing often, just having such armor will turn you from Kyri Vantage to ... well, whatever symbolic name you choose. You need to be that symbol, a symbol which will become a question."

Kyri frowned. "Well, I suppose there must be armorers in the First City that could—"

"Absolutely *not*. Do you think for one minute that—even if the armorers there could produce what you need—you could keep that a secret from anyone?" Kyri felt herself flush in embarrassment. "In any event, Kyri, to make your role a true one, you need true Justiciar armor, created in the same way."

"But that was forged by the Spiritsmith, Auntie! Maybe two Chaoswars ago!"

"And rumor is that he still lives." Victoria smiled. "Toron told me that himself, some years ago. Besides, Kyri, you will need experience to prepare yourself. This is a plan that runs centuries deep; taking a few months, or even years, to prepare, is hardly a poor idea. By making the journey yourself, by convincing the Spiritsmith to create the armor you will need, you will come to know what you can do, you will perhaps find the allies you need, and find the name and symbol that suits you, and you will master the skills of a warrior which, right now, you have but a student's experience of."

She thought of her little sister—probably still sleeping even now. "You're ... You're right, Auntie. But ... where would I look?"

"The search is yours," Victoria answered, "but I would say that old Toron is the best bet for a hint. He has long been a friend to me and to our family."

She said something else, but Kyri didn't catch it; to her surprise, she realized she'd faded for a moment. "I'm ... tired, Auntie."

"Hardly a surprise. Thank all the Gods that you're feeling it, actually. You need the rest." She forced Kyri to lie down, at which point Kyri felt her eyes closing almost against her will. "We'll talk about this later ..."

But by the last word, sleep had already dropped its curtain over Kyri's thoughts.

18

"Victoria? Victoria Vantage, you hellsword, why didn't you *tell* me you were in the City?"

The booming voice was intimidating enough, but the fact that its owner—an immense Ancient Sauran—then stepped forward and picked up her usually dignified aunt and swung her around like a child greeted by her favorite uncle left her standing there with her mouth open.

It was especially shocking because her aunt seemed to *enjoy* it, even as her heels barely missed an ornamental statuette on one of the high shelves in this anteroom of the Dragon Palace. Victoria Vantage laughed as the Marshal of Hosts tossed her into the air, and did a complete flip, hair nearly grazing the ceiling, landing with only the slightest stumble. Her silvery hair was in disarray from the gentle violence of the greeting, and her eyes shone with affection for the massive scaled being in front of her. "I just *did*, Bridgebreaker! I hardly had a chance to tell you before now, we only arrived day before yesterday."

"Well, well, I suppose that will have to do, then. I can't expect the Vantage V—"

"Don't you *dare* finish that in front of my niece."

The great creature raised a brow-ridge, eyes twinkling. "Really? Haven't you told them the truth about your rough-and-tumble past?" He looked over and seemed to take note of Kyri for the first time. "I ask your pardon, young Vantage; I have not greeted you." He straightened and did a full Armed Bow, huge sword and axe crossed on his back and clearly visible as he turned a full circle on one foot, to end facing her just as he had been when he began. "T'Oroning'Oltharamnon ʰGHEK R'arshe Ness, Adjudicator and Marshal of the Hosts, greets you in his name and in that of my cousin and lord."

The greeting snapped her out of stunned paralysis and she took a deep breath, bowing, making sure her own sword was visible, performing the spin with at least tolerable smoothness. "Kyrie Victoria Vantage greets you, Adjudicator," she said. *I am not going to even* attempt *his name right now, I'm so nervous I'd choke on it.*

He laughed. "And with the formalities past, call me Toron, as once you did—long ago, as you might measure it, though it seems scarce yesterday to me." The dark eyes studied her. "You *have* grown, little one. Taller than your aunt, and by the Sight of the Dragons I would wager you have at least her strength."

"At least," agreed Victoria. "Toron, it's good of you to see me on such short notice. I know you and the King are always busy—"

"Never so busy," interrupted Toron, "that we would forget a friend and ally such as yourself. But your urgency makes me sad, Victoria. I begin to suspect you have some business in mind, not merely a friendly visit."

"You began to suspect that as soon as I arrived, and you've already made arrangements—or you're far fallen from what I remember."

He rumbled agreement, a huge-fanged smile combining friendliness and danger. "Arrangements, yes—if necessary."

The smile faded from Aunt Victoria's face and she smoothed her hair back, looked about, and took one of the elaborately carved, human-sized chairs, gesturing for Kyri to sit. Toron eased himself into a much larger seat with a split back that accommodated his massive tail. "Oh, I believe you'll find them necessary, old friend. You recall the time I called you up to Evanwyl?"

"I could hardly forget; fifteen hundred miles or more with great swiftness, and then I had to return."

"We now have the answer you could not find; we know who killed my brother, his wife, and—now—my nephew Rion." She gazed at him steadily. "It was the Justiciars."

Kyri saw the news hit the Marshal of Hosts like a blow; his great eyes widened and a grunt escaped him.

She let Victoria sketch the entire situation—how it had happened, how they knew, and what had happened to her afterwards. The Ancient Sauran listened without a word.

When Victoria had fallen silent, Toron turned to Kyri. "And you are now Myrionar's chosen?"

She nodded; even though she knew it was true, she blushed as though telling a lie. *I can hardly believe any of this myself; it must sound insane, even coming from Aunt Victoria! What must Toron think?*

But Toron was not laughing. "I begin to think I was wiser than I had thought in accepting your request here, and *not* bringing you to the Throne."

"What?" Victoria said sharply. "You can't mean you don't trust—"

Toron's offended snort clarified his meaning. "Of course I trust him. My cousin and my King has ruled this land for untold thousands of years, and ruled well, under the guidance of the Diamond and the Sixteen. However..." he trailed off, nodded. "Let me begin another way."

He turned back to Kyri. "Young Vantage, you are now the chosen—the *only* chosen—warrior for a god counted as an ally to Elbon Nomicon, and to his allies Terian, Chromaias, and others. Indeed, with these Myrionar has long had the strongest of alliances, a pact of the gods to aid and support each others' followers in all areas where they do not conflict—and few are the true areas of conflict.

"Thus, I would offer you the support of the Dragon Throne. We shall bring you officially before the King, you shall tell him this terrible tale, and I have no doubt that you will find him willing to give you all support." His smile was fierce. "The T'Teranahm forget not their allies, great or small. Though even conquered Dalthunia lies between, we shall raise a force from the followers of the Dragon God, from the warriors of the Chromaian faith, from those called by the *Nomdas* of Terian, the Spear and Hammer—oh, I believe many will come to aid Myrionar—and with that force we shall go to Evanwyl, unmask these impostors, and bring that justice you—and Myrionar—deserve to your home."

Kyri was dumbstruck, with a rising sense of wonder and joy, and she saw her aunt's gratified expression, the look of someone who sees her hopes fully justified. "Sir... Toron... I don't... don't know what to say."

The rumbling chuckle was like thunder in the distance. "Say only *yes*, and we shall speak to the King himself, yes, within moments, and it shall be done."

We could avenge everyone! *We could restore Evanwyl!* She looked into the Ancient Sauran's eyes, and she knew he meant every word. She still could hardly grasp it. All she needed to do was *agree*, and an army—an army of the Dragon King and his allies!—would march, perhaps even with her at its head alongside the Marshal of Hosts, and even the dark forces holding Dalthunia would surely stand aside and let them pass, and even the false Justiciars would not withstand such a force—nor would any doubt the word of the emissary of the Dragon King along with her own. She would be a leader of a force out of legend, the Army of the Dragon which had stood as a force for peace and justice since before her people had even set foot upon the world of Zarathan.

"So you believe us?" she said, still unable to fully comprehend the offer, even though she knew it was—had to be—in full earnest.

"I do," Toron said emphatically. "As Marshal of the Hosts and an Adjudicator, I have much in the way of truthsensing. And in this I have also the blessing of Arlavala of the Sixteen, Elbon's General. I see that you believe what you say, and I know your aunt well enough to have trusted my life to her a dozen times and more. Yes, I believe you, and will—in the name of your god, and mine, and for the sake of my most-loved friend Victoria Vantage—set the very Armies of the Dragon against your enemies."

Say YES! She opened her mouth to speak, tears of joy trembling at the brink of being shed...

And she found she could not speak.

Why? He's offering everything we could possibly want! He's on our side! I don't—I won't—believe that there's anything wrong with his offer!

And still Kyri could not speak, and the joy receded, turned to a wave of pitiful tragedy and *still* she could not speak. She could see the expressions of the others darken, her aunt staring at her with utter confusion.

But it was not confusion, but grim understanding, on Toron's face. "And so *now* we see why it was wise that I not bring you first to the Throne; for my cousin would—no doubt!—have immediately ordered the mobilization of the Armies for this, for the sake of honor and justice that we all understand, and once begun such an action could not be reasonably recalled. Yet you cannot speak to give me the simple permission to help you."

"I don't know *why!*" Kyri finally burst out, trying to restrain tears that were now of frustration and anger. "It's the *perfect* solution! It could even bring the Balanced Sword back to your own country! You...you might even give a chance to cleanse Rivendream Pass! I *want* to accept your offer..."

"But you cannot. And that tells me a great deal, Kyri Vantage, a great deal indeed, for unlike you I have had to deal with the gods many times." He took her hand with startling gentleness between his two massive clawed hands. "I expected this, as you see. So I ask that you breathe deep, think of the calm of morning and the quiet of night, the eternal light of Sun and stars, and be seated again, and we shall speak of what is, and what *can* be."

She nodded, unable to speak, but took a breath. Then two, and recalled to herself her training and discipline, and by the third breath she felt calm, if not joy, returning. "My...apologies—"

"No need," Toron said, a momentary smile of blades flashing. "I can easily imagine what it must feel like to see the solution before you, and then know you must reject it."

"But it's *insane*," Victoria said in an outraged tone. "Why in the name of Itself would Myrionar refuse—"

"Because It knows many things we do not," Toron said bluntly. "You recounted Myrionar's conversation with Kyri, and it was as clear as the Dragon King's diamonds that there is vastly more going on than we understand, a game of gods and stratagems layered a hundred deep—something even the Dragon Gods do not know for sure, or they would clarify this to me. Myrionar told her the path would be difficult—and this would seem easy. It told her she must have faith in Myrionar—and this is more faith in the might of the Dragon State and our loyalty to a cause."

Kyri nodded. The words made sense to the part of her that had been unable to speak. But still... "I can't imagine the Balanced Sword would not trust your loyalty or strength, or reject you, sir!"

He seemed to attempt a laugh, managed only another smile. "This is not a rejection. I think..." he looked suddenly more serious. "I think...it is a warning. Something even more terrible will happen if we take this course of action. I could imagine many scenarios, but the short of it is simply this: your god Myrionar has told us, in no words but strong actions, that you *must* do this alone, or at least without forces such as I offer."

"Yes," she heard herself say, and knew from that feeling within her that it was true. "Yes, Toron. I may not be always alone, but I have to be the spearhead of any force. I can't walk in with an army."

"Then," he said, settling back in his chair, "what *can* I do for you?"

"We were hoping," Victoria said, having finally accepted that the wonderful offer was not to be, "that you might be able to give us directions. Specifically, directions to the Spiritsmith."

The huge head tilted, the wide-set eyes regarded them, and the mouth suddenly curved up in that fang-edged smile again. "Of course. The Raiment of a Justiciar, forged for the last living Justiciar, Kyri Vantage. And none other could forge such armor, unless it were the Wanderer or the Archmage—and the tradition would be lost, and neither of those is easily reached, either." His gaze suddenly snapped back to Victoria. "Pardon me for a momentary diversion—but what of your other niece? Does she know—"

"The truth?" Victoria shook her head. "Not yet. Oh, I shall tell her—and soon. She is a Vantage, she has the right to know, and she is a wise girl who knows enough to stay silent on these matters. But I have not yet told her, and I will not until after Kyri is well gone."

Kyri nodded. "She'd follow me otherwise."

"Most assuredly—as you would, if it were Rion setting out alone on such a journey."

"That was my concern," Toron said gravely, "and I am glad you have already anticipated this possibility." He rose from his chair and strode over to an ornately carven silver-and-blackwood cabinet. "Now, as to your question..."

The cabinet folded open, became a map of Zarathan—or, at least, of the huge continent on or near which was every country or place Kyri had ever heard of. Toron smiled again at her surprise. "Did you think I had chosen this room idly? One of several meeting places within *T'Teranahm Chendoron*, the Dragon's Palace, meant for strategy and consideration of deep policy. A map is just one of the tools oft-used for such things."

Kyri nodded, moved to join him, as did Victoria.

The cabinet-map swiveled down and moved outward, became

a flat table-like surface. Toron touched a point in the center, towards the lower half, and a glittering white star of light shone out. "Here we stand, in *Fanalam' T' ameris' a' u' Zahr-a-Thana T'ikon*, Zarathanton. North, beyond the Forest Sea, the Ice Peaks, and at their center and apex, the Crystal Mountain." A line of blue traced its way almost due north to the mountain that some said was the seat of Terian himself.

"On this map, then, we look to the west, and slightly north from the Crystal Mountain, for the Spiritsmith works on the border of beauty and destruction, where he might look to the Crystal Mountain with eyes that see past the horizon, and turn precisely around," the line streaked across and stopped at a range of mountans, at a point between two rivers, and Kyri felt a shock of disbelief, even as Toron continued, "and look to the center of *Kuri'shenkildis*."

Victoria shook her head. "Why in the name of the Dragon Gods would he build a forge on Hell's Rim?"

"You—or rather, Kyri—might ask him, when once you have reached him," Toron answered wryly. "There are many reasons one might choose such a place, not the least being the desire to observe that corrupted place that you call, so inaccurately, Hell, and think on what once was."

Kyri did know that the name "Hell" merely reflected the cha-otically deadly conditions within, that produced aberrant mon-strosities, and was not in any way connected to the netherplanes called the Hells, but she didn't know there was a *past* to Hell, or *Kuri'shenkildis* as Toron called it. "What once was?"

Toron nodded slowly, staring at the ring of mountains sur-rounding abomination. "Once it was one of the fairest parts of this world. And we were not blameless in what happened." He shook himself. "But that is not a tale for now. Many reasons the Spiritsmith might have; there are undoubtedly ores and gemstones to be found in those mountains which are rare or unheard of elsewhere. Or perhaps—even most likely—he simply prefers his privacy. Nonetheless, here he makes his home and his forge."

Victoria squinted at the map. "Can you narrow it down a bit? That dot of yours, if I read this scale aright, must cover at least fifty miles of the mountains."

Kyri's heart sank a bit as she saw Toron shake his head. "I am afraid I know it only in this general sense, Victoria," he said.

"Once, true, I visited him...but that was very long ago, before the last Chaoswar, and the details are gone from my mind."

She shook off the momentary doubt. "It doesn't matter, Auntie," she said confidently. "Myrionar said to have faith in It, and what Adjudicator Toron's told us is incredibly useful. I could have searched all the continent from the Empire of the Mountain to Thologondoreave and the White Blade and never have come close in a hundred years of looking. That's a big area, I know—I patrolled parts of Evanwyl, remember, so I know how very large a mile is in the wild—but still, it's not impossible. And if there's anyone there at all, they'll have to know *something.*"

Aunt Victoria looked, for just a moment, like a mother worrying about her children, and Kyri felt a surge of affection. *She'd really rather be doing this* herself *and keep me out of it...but she knows she can't.*

Victoria's head came up and once more she was the sharp-eyed adventurer. "True enough, and there's almost nowhere on the world where there is not *someone.* I would not, however, recommend you follow the route old Bridgebreaker just traced."

Toron snorted. "I wouldn't recommend it either; I was merely following the directions I recalled."

Kyri just shook her head and laughed.

"Is that so amusing?" inquired Toron.

"Oh, no it wasn't that," she answered, and pointed. "It's that the only *reasonable* route...is the one I just *arrived* by, and it's a long, *long* trip." *Close to three thousand miles by the Great Road, I think, fifteen hundred in a straight line.*

"Then," said Aunt Victoria, in her most practical tone, "you'd better get started."

19

"Well?" Poplock asked. "Any luck?"

Tobimar grinned, accompanying the smile with a gesture as though handing something to Poplock that meant things had gone well. "We'll be talking to the Adjudicator and Marshal of Hosts T'Oroning'Oltharamnon ʰGHEK R'arshe Ness by the end of the day. And maybe, if we're lucky, the King himself."

Poplock bounced onto Tobimar's shoulder, which sported solid guards excellent for a Toad his size to perch on. "If you manage his name that well when we meet, he'll probably be impressed. Humans usually don't do that well."

Tobimar nodded. "It's not easy. Some of those sounds aren't *meant* to be pronounced by our voiceboxes, you know." He shook his head with a wry smile. "The Lord of Waters—my mother— was very, very emphatic about getting those sorts of things right, though. I remember when my brother Terimur tried to use an *exhaled* cough for the ʰ*GHEK* sound . . . oh, the Waters were troubled *that* day. A dry day for Terimur."

"Don't suppose you speak much Toad."

Tobimar snorted. "I know enough to know I'd look like a fool trying. Your language includes little hops and face-shapes for the nuances, and some of the sounds! I don't have an air-bladder for a mouth."

"True, you poor humans are crippled that way," Poplock agreed equably. "But I'll give you credit for knowing your limits. And you do seem to have learned something *about* our language, which is more than most of you bipeds bother with. I guess being a prince makes you learn stuff."

"If you're a Silverun of Skysand? Learn or get no water past your ration, that's the way of things." Tobimar emerged from the carved-stone doorway of the Winnower of Speech, the office devoted to ensuring that proper petitioners had their opportunity to speak even with the highest in the land, and looked to his left and up.

The towers of the palace loomed up nearby, the highest reaching more than half a mile into the sky, and it sent a small chill of awe down his back to think that soon he would walk through those gates and speak with one of the Ancient Saurans who might have actually walked his ancestral lands. It was too much to hope that he would *remember* the information Tobimar sought; the damage the unleashed energies of a Chaoswar did to even deific memories left only legends and vague senses of continuity usually. But there was no doubt he stood closer to the past in this place than anywhere else in the world—save, possibly, the peak of Mount Scimitar itself, or the rumored Fortress of the Wanderer.

"By the Rainbow Mountain, that's a big building. Gets me every time I see it this close."

"I don't think you're alone there. Sand and Stone, I think the central tower could hold most of Skysand's entire palace, maybe all of it, the Seven as well as the One."

"What's the meaning of that?" Poplock punctuated his question with a whipcrack of his tongue that snagged a passing beetle. "The Seven and One thing. That was in your story, that poem, too."

"Oh, that." Tobimar saw a flamespice vendor and handed him a pair of silver Glints for a couple of skewers of the seasoned, fire-cooked meat. "It all has to do with Terian." He explained the tradition of his family's connection with the Mortal God. "Eight is his number, but it's also crossed over with Seven—Terian's one of the few gods that is respected in the Empire of the Mountain because somehow the numbers Seven and One are sacred to the God-Emperor himself, or so they say."

"So is there...um, well, a Seven and a One?"

"The Seven Stars and the Single Sun?" Tobimar frowned in thought, taking a bite of the first skewer. "Well...there *should* be. 'Seven Stars and a Single Sun hold the Starlight that I do own.' *Terian* is sort of a derived name—it's from T'Tera a Mion, Greatest Lord of the Stars."

A bounce-nod. "Isn't it Terian Nomicon?"

"You're joking." A glance showed otherwise. "Oh. Well, no, *Nomicon* is ... um ... something like giver or creator or source of good power ... it's a title for any of the great gods of nobility and good."

"Oh. I thought it meant that Elbon Nomicon and Terian Nomicon were related."

Tobimar burst out laughing, then apologized. "I'm sorry, I'm sorry. But the thought of the Father of Dragons being related to the Mortal God ... might as well ask if they were related to your god with the silly name—"

A kick to his ear stung. "Bah. It's you human and lizardy types that have gods with silly names. *Our* god's name *means* something, and not in a language everyone else can't speak either; Blackwart the Great, and you will know him if you meet him, by that name alone."

Tobimar rubbed his ear gingerly and accepted the justified rebuke. "Anyway ... where was I? Oh. Anyway, it's said that the Seven Stars are talismans Terian made that, combined with the Sun of Infinity, become something tremendously powerful."

"Infinity—that's the other name for Terian," Poplock said, pointing at the golden sigil clasping Tobimar's cloak.

"Indirectly, from the Seven Sacred Scrolls which tell parts of his tale, yes, as he is always referred to the same way throughout, as in that verse we were discussing."

"I did wonder," Poplock said, crawling with casual quickness over Tobimar's head to the other shoulder, "why it was that you didn't try that verse. Your mentor said it would be a weapon, right?"

"When nothing else would serve, yes, I guess. Though Khoros' words were never all that simple to interpret. And the power of Terian is really strongest against things of spiritual darkness—much worse than *mazakh*. If they'd summoned one of the *Mazolishta*, well then I might have tried it. But magic isn't really my strong suit."

He saw a towering shadow in the smaller castle doorway (a doorway still large enough for four men to walk through side-by-side) resolve itself into the massive figure of the Marshal of Hosts, accompanied by two human women who, while shorter by far than the immense Sauran, were clearly quite tall themselves. The first was an older woman with hair that had once been black, and still had streaks of midnight within the silver here and there; the other was much younger, maybe his own age, but with hair of mountain-sky blue, tipped it seemed with gold, and a brilliant flash of pure white in the center of her forehead. He'd noticed there was a lot of hair-coloring, skin-tinting, and feature-shaping in Zarathanton. The amount of casual magic, in fact, was staggering.

He stood to see if they would be next, but the Marshal leaned down to the Winnower and said something as the two women continued down the Road past Tobimar; the Winnower nodded and the Marshal disappeared back into the Castle, presumably to take care of some errand. Several other groups in Petitioner's Square, the area of the Great Road that was in front of the castle, had been doing the same thing.

"Where are we in line?" Poplock asked, showing he'd been thinking along the same lines.

"I *think* there's only one more group ahead of us, from what the Winnower said. If they don't take too much time, we'll be in pretty soon." He gestured at a small knot of five very young people standing near the Winnower's doorway, as though afraid to lose their place in line. "Still, 'pretty soon' could be an hour or so," he said. "So let's take a look at what's around the Palace Square. Lots of stores and booths here meant to take advantage of this big flow of petitioners, you know."

"Should we just wander around like that?" Poplock asked, look-ing back at the gate they were planning on eventually entering.

"Don't worry about losing our place," he said, and held up the carved crystal callstone. "The callstone will let us know when it's our time."

Poplock looked at it suspiciously. "How sure are you that it'll work no matter where we go?"

Tobimar laughed. "*Very* sure. This is very similar design to ones I've seen in Skysand, and I can't think of *any* time one failed, unless someone hit it with a negation—and *that* would be sand-blasted *obvious* since the crystal would stop glowing. And they'll work for at least a mile and a half."

"But *that* would take us a long time to get back from."

"True," Tobimar acknowledged, "and while they would be able to tell from the stone that we were responding, they wouldn't want to waste the time waiting, and neither would we. So that's why we'll stay here in the Square. Only a few minutes to cross even from the far side."

Satisfied, Poplock settled back down on Tobimar's shoulder,

and Tobimar walked idly around the perimeter, examining cloth, buying a small crystallized sweetsap treat (and getting a bag of crickets for Poplock), and generally surveying the immense variety of goods to be found here in front of the Castle.

A display of goblets, trays, and other eating utensils caught his eye and he strolled over to the vendor. "Unusual to see a Child of Odin dealing in these wares."

"Hah!" Very humanlike but both too wide and too short for normal humanity, the *Odinsyrnen* vendor looked up with a smile on her broad-featured face. "You mean us dwarves deal more in the military workings. You'd be surprised indeed. But not so surprised, at that. Similar skills, and both requiring a heart for beauty in shaping, even if the one is for killing or preventing killing, while mine is—I like to think—far more practical application for everyday beauty." She watched him as he carefully picked up various pieces and examined them. "You have an eye for symmetry, I see."

"Symmetry is often a foundation for beauty," Tobimar agreed. "This one..." he held up a long serving platter, half of a silvery-blue metal, the other side of gold or a heavily gold alloy, the two halves separated by a filigreed border bar of silver or platinum, "...an excellent *Ya-Shi-Naiga* serving dish."

"Correct—but how do you know? After all, the matebond dishes for *mazakh* bonding feasts are very similar."

"Well, first, I *think* the *mazakh* bond-dishes have two pairs of handles, one pair near each end; they're carried to the table by the bonding couple, facing each other and moving sideways, if I remember right. This tray has two handles only, one large one on each end. Second," he pointed to the handles, "the blue end's handle has what looks to be an eight- to ten-carat Ymir's Blood set in the center, while the gold end sports a Fire Ruby of about the same size."

Poplock hopped onto his hand and poked at the Ymir's Blood, a gem the impossible pure blue of a glacier's heart. "Chilly. Oh, I get it!"

"You are quite correct, young human. The virtues of those stones now fill their respective portions of this dish, so that the hot-and-cold dishes favored in Artanian *Ya-Shi-Naiga* maintain their temperature and freshness during one of their interminable ceremonies. If you were able to identify those gems so certainly, however, you must either be far more perceptive, or perhaps more educated, than many."

Tobimar grinned. "It was the gems that caught my eye, actually."

He noticed the Marshal now emerging from the main castle gate, then striding over to the Winnower; a few moments later the group of five young people followed the Marshal inside. *Almost there.* "I'm Tobimar Silverun."

"Silverun..." she said, seeming to roll the word around in her mouth as though sampling it. Then her eyes lit up with understanding. "Ah, now, of *the* Silverun family? From Skysand itself? That would indeed make sense. Many gems from your country's mines have I used over the years; their magic is powerful and fresh. Well worth the premium." She leaned forward. "You wouldn't happen to have any...trading supplies, would you?"

Tobimar smiled back. "I'm not a miner or a vendor, but I have been carrying some...reserves with me."

"Any you care to sell? I'm looking for materials now as it is."

Tobimar brought out the small pouch he kept hidden in his clothing and handed it to the merchant. She carefully opened it and poured the contents unobtrusively into a nearby table, set slightly below the level of the display stands, with a low ridge running around the outside to prevent anything on it from rolling or falling off.

"Not a bad collection..." the Child of Odin began. "Let's see, now..."

After some considerable haggling (with occasional interjections and heckling by Poplock), Tobimar and Kalma Odinforged arrived at agreement, and she gave over a bag with a satisfying heft of assorted gold and silver coinage in exchange for two Suncores and a decent-sized Vor-nahal whose deep sapphire color echoed the power in it; it caught at the winds and nearly levitated itself through its own magic, even though it had not yet even been cut.

"You aren't working for the money, I see." Poplock said as they walked away.

"Not entirely, no—though I really prefer not to dip into that reserve very often. I just have a feeling I might need a lot of ready money soon, depending on what we find out today. And she'll make good use of the stones." As he spoke, he saw the five young people leaving the castle gate, talking animatedly among themselves.

"Ooo. We should be up next then," said Poplock, following his gaze. "Good timing; you've got your reserve, and we'll be in soon."

"I don't see the Marshal yet, though. He—no, wait, there he is."

The Marshal now emerged from the second door and spoke to

the Winnower; they exchanged a few comments, the Winnower shrugged, and suddenly the callstone in Tobimar's left pocket vibrated and gave off a crystalline chime. "That's us!"

He hurried up to the Winnower's doorway and presented the callstone, which now also flickered with a leaf-green light. "Tobimar Silverun and Poplock Duckweed," he announced.

"Very good. The Marshal will speak with you now, and you have also been granted an audience with the His Majesty." The Ancient Sauran Marshal took the callstone, which changed to a clear white light in his scaled hand, and turned to face Tobimar.

Tobimar bowed, one leg extended, and managed a swept-pivot to the full rear-facing position before turning back around. The Marshal returned the gesture, his motion far more impressive than Tobimar's given that the great Sauran stood over eight feet high and massed ... well, more than Tobimar wanted to guess. "Tobimar of the Silverun, welcome. And to you, Poplock Duckweed ... of Pondsparkle, I would presume?" The deep voice was full of subtle humor, and Tobimar liked it immediately.

"Good presumption. Left home about four years ago though," the Toad answered.

"I thank you for your welcome, T'Oroning'Oltharamnon ʰGHEK R'arshe Ness." He was actually quite pleased by the way he managed the inhaled-choking sound in the middle.

A deep rumble of an approving chuckle rolled out from the Marshal. "I appreciate your kindness in attempting my name— and in truth, you do wonderfully well with it for a human. But please, call me Toron, as my human friends have. Follow me."

"Thank you ... Toron."

This time they were taken in through the main gate, and Tobimar could see just how immense the interior construction was. It was not merely some sort of overly ostentatious entrance hall; instead, the corridor continued, for a good fraction of a mile north it appeared, with a height of four hundred feet and a width of nearly three hundred, ending in a set of doors of pearl-white and jet-black, set with the lightning sunburst of the Dragon King in the center of the double doors.

"No need for thanks; the summary of the intelligence you bring to us was ... quite interesting. Indeed, his Majesty was most insistent on speaking with you directly once we understood the nature of your interest."

"Does he ... know something, then?"

A snort of deep draconic amusement. "He knows many things. About your quest, perhaps not, but then again, perhaps yes. It is your friend's story which we both find of more import—and the possible connection to it which you have discovered within our own city. But we will not ignore your own request, I assure you; Skysand is far away, but a good ally to have in the north of the world." The deep-set black eyes, with a visible faint red glow deep within, shifted to Poplock. "Your news is four years old, as I understand it? How is it that you did not bring it to our attention before?"

Poplock shifted uncomfortably, and Tobimar felt some sympathy, having discussed the issue with him before. "Well ... at first it seemed more our problem. And the problem was *over* when everything went boom, so no reason to worry any more. But a while ago I started thinking it was maybe *not* quite over, since old bugface had made a bunch of threats, and I tried to get an audience a couple of times, but the Winnower ... well, I didn't know how to put it, exactly, and he didn't seem to take me seriously."

The frown of an Ancient Sauran could be pretty intimidating, and Tobimar was relieved when Toron spoke again. "I am afraid that was a failure on our part. Even careful checks of one's moral outlook and diligence will not reveal so subtle a bias as simply not taking Toads seriously ... not when this is a widespread attitude. Fortunately we replaced that Winnower recently."

"And I met Tobimar, who seems to know how to talk to people like that and get their attention," said the Toad.

"Fortunate, that. But unfortunate that your own mistake and our failure have combined to keep such a potentially dangerous situation from our attention. We will of course discuss all of this in detail in the Throne Room."

They were now approaching the black and white double doors, and Tobimar could now see that Elbon Nomicon's symbol apeared to have been carved from a set of impossibly huge diamonds, single crystals fifty to a hundred feet or more in length. "Where in the world did they find such gems to carve?"

"Ah, that *would* be a question to occur to a Skysand, to one of the sands and mines. No ordinary crystal, that, for it was carven entire from a single one of the Dragon King's scales."

Tobimar did not quite catch the next few words, as his mind was suddenly overwhelmed by imagining the size of a Dragon which could have a single scale so huge that it would have clearly served to cover most, if not all, of that entire door. "I beg your pardon?" he said, realizing that he had just been asked a question.

"I said, do you understand the etiquette of the Throne?"

"I've been told it once, but I wouldn't mind you reviewing it."

"It is fairly simple. You will enter, I will announce you to the King. You will then advance near to the base of the throne— about ten human paces back—and perform the Armed Bow. Make sure your weapons are more visible, your cloak hid one of them when you did it for me. It is *imperative* your weapons be very clearly visible; it is a grave insult for there to be appearance of an unarmed guest or petitioner in the presence of the King.

"When you have finished the full turn, the King will rise, advance to the base of the Throne, and return the bow. He will then speak to you to begin the audience, and the rest will go as conversation takes it. When you are dismissed, you must perform the Armed Bow once more and leave the room. The doors will close for a moment, you will wait, then I will emerge after having performed my own bow and received any instructions my King may have for me, and I will lead you back outside." Toron looked at both of them. "Are there any questions?"

"No," Tobimar said, "that seems fairly straightforward." Poplock bounced agreement.

Toron nodded, then raised the callstone in his hand; the doors echoed the light, and swung smoothly and with startling silence inward.

Before them was the Throne of Dragons. It dominated even the immense, egg-shaped room it was in, facing the doors from the far end of the room. It sat upon a circular layered dias of seventeen pure glittering crystal slabs, different colors alternating until the pure diamond at the very top, which seemed to be a single piece with the throne itself a polychromatic jewel carved by a master sculptor. There was no ordinary stone on the throne or its supporting dias. Eight pillars, each of a single massive glittering crystal, supported the room in a pair of long opposed arcs, with the path to the Throne leading between them. In many ways it was impressive in stark simplicity; the floor and walls were pure polished stone, granite or so it appeared, unadorned, unmarked by symbol or painting.

In the throne sat the Sauran King, his dark form silhouetted against the transparent brilliance of the throne, which, along with the dias, seemed filled with light that brought vision to every part of the throneroom. He looked even larger than Toron, and his head was lowered as though gazing down on those entering his domain.

"Your Majesty!" Toron's voice was powerful and formal now. "I present to you Tobimar Silverun of Skysand, Seventh of Seven, Seeker of his people; and with him Poplock Duckweed of Pondsparkle."

Tobimar took a deep breath and advanced steadily forward. The *Sauran King*. The most powerful ruler in the entire world—save, possibly, the God-King of the Mountain—and the holder of the throne which had seen all the history of Zarathan unfold since the very beginning. He hoped he wouldn't screw this up.

When he'd reached what he guessed to be ten paces, he stopped, whipped his cloak off (almost upsetting Poplock, but the little Toad was very nimble) to expose his twin blades' scabbards, and bowed low, extending his foot as far behind as he could. A moment later he completed the ritual pirouette and stood, looking upward.

A moment passed. Two. Still the King did not move.

Toron moved up to them, puzzlement clear on his face. "Majesty?"

There was still no response, and now a deep foreboding came over Tobimar's heart. *Something's badly wrong.*

Toron apparently felt the same way, for suddenly he was moving briskly up the Hundred And One Steps towards his King. Poplock had bounded from Tobimar's shoulder and was hopping his way up faster, outpacing the massive Sauran. Tobimar ran after both.

"Stay *back*, both of you!" Toron bellowed, and even the little Toad stopped dead in his tracks. Toron reached the top and advanced carefully to stand before the King. A few moments passed, and then he whirled suddenly and gave a roar that was amplified to deafening intensity by the empty vastness of the Throne Room.

A glow of light materialized before Toron, and he began speaking quickly into it, mostly in the tongue of his people. Tobimar cautiously advanced to where Poplock stood, on the Hundredth Step, and picked up his friend.

From this range, he was only about twenty feet from the Throne, and he could see the King, head bowed almost to his chest.

And in the chest, showing dark-red against dark gray-green, four perfect holes in a curving line.

The Sauran King was dead.

20

The jungle below was thick and green, breathing with life in the brilliant sunshine. As he watched, a flock of brilliant birds burst from the canopy, pursued for a short distance by a bat-winged shape, a *merinam* or least dragon, before it grew bored and settled down onto the top of a tree like a giant crimson flower.

It's not working.

Usually Aran came here to...well, recover, to let beauty and quiet soak into his soul and alleviate the pain that still sometimes came to him when they were called upon to do something for their patron which was...well...*evil*.

And usually it worked. He'd long since realized that the power of Myrionar had faded, that the Justiciars were one of the few forces of order left in Evanwyl and that keeping that force alive— even through deception—was better than just allowing things to fall apart. He'd managed to erase the roiling in his gut after that terrible night years ago when they'd taken the Vantage estate. A few days here had always managed to bring some peace back to his soul, every time he'd needed it.

Until now. Aran sighed, still gazing at the sea of emerald and flowers that extended from the Khalals all the way to the rampart of Hell's Rim; he sat on a low ridge of the Khalal foothills, and for that reason did not look too far to his left, because if he did, Rivendream Pass would intrude upon the perfect view.

He remembered Kyri's face, shattered and devastated, streaked with tears when they first saw her after...after it happened. Then helping her load the coach...*and of course she was leaving. It makes perfect sense. Why* wouldn't *she leave?*

And he remembered the lies they'd told her. *Not* all *lies. I...I really wish we hadn't killed him. He was a* true *Justiciar. Maybe... maybe if I'd said something to him...*

"Still up here, lad?"

He jumped slightly, then tried to pretend he'd just been stretching. "Shrike? How long have you been there, *sirza?*"

The older man pulled off his silver-gray helm with the short, hooked beak and dropped to the ground next to him, puffing. "Just...got up the Balance-damned hill." Despite the virtues of the Justiciar armor, Shrike's bald head was trickling sweat, which he mopped up with a cloth from his belt. "Never fails that I'll find you here when you've got that look about you."

"Usually makes me feel better. The quiet...the beauty of the world."

Shrike's sharp brown eyes studied him from above a nose that rather resembled the front of his helm. "But not this time, eh?"

As if I could hide it from him. Aran sighed and shook his head. "No. No, not this time."

"Did you think it'd ever work, boy? You and I, we helped finish her parents."

He gritted his teeth and turned away. "That was...before. I didn't know her. Didn't know the family." *Didn't have any real reason to reach* out *beyond the Justiciars.*

Shrike snorted. "You think that'd've leveled any balance for her, Condor? If she knew—"

"There was never any need for her to know. She'd...healed. Her family had healed. I'd...I'd almost managed to forget—"

"*Forget?*" Shrike's voice cut through his protests with icy fury—fury with no small trace of fear. "You can't afford to forget a Balance-damned thing, Condor. You've got too blasted many ideals as it is—"

"Ideals *you* taught me!" He was suddenly shouting, with tears stinging his eyes, pain and anger directed at the man who'd raised him, part of him wanting to blame Shrike for everything.

Shrike met his furious gaze...and then his eyes dropped and he sighed, and drew his knees up to rest his chin on the shining metal of his armor. "Aye. That I did. Taught you the Justiciar's creed, made sure you went to temple...but by the Fallen Balance,

Aran, what choice did I *have*?" He rolled to his feet and stamped a few paces away. "Even now y'r nothing much of a liar, not good at hidin' anything without death hanging over you. Back then..." his face softened for an instant and a smile flickered over the weatherbeaten face, a smile that reminded Aran of long-past times. "Back then, you hadn't a trace o' deceit in you, boy. Eyes as bright as new leaves and a heart about as green and untested, too. You couldn't've kept the secrets if you'd known about them then. You know you couldn't."

"I ..." They'd had this discussion before, though never so intensely—except for the first time, when he'd nearly left in fury, stopping only when his foster father and best friend had literally thrown himself in his path, crying, begging him to stop, for the sake of both their lives. "I know. No, I couldn't."

"So I raised you ... right. Maybe I shouldn't have. Maybe I should've given you to the Temple. But ... you were ..." Shrike stopped, seemed as though he was about to give up, but then set his jaw and plowed on. "You were the last moral decision I got to make for myself, I guess. Last one before I accepted that everything had to follow a plan, be a choice that fit the plan ... or else. Mist Owl warned me there'd be trouble, and there was. If I'd known just how bad trouble could get, maybe I wouldn't have made that decision ... but then I'm glad I didn't know then." He reached out and patted Aran's shoulder awkwardly.

Aran seized Shrike's hand. "*Sirza*, let's just get out of here. Go somewhere else. To ... to Zarathanton, even."

For a moment he thought his head had come off his shoulders. He looked up, dazed, from the ground, to see Shrike glaring down at him, face white as the dead under his dark tan, Condor's own blood smearing the gauntlet on his clenched fist. "Do not say that. Do not even *think* it, boy. You fear *him*, you do, but you don't fear *him* enough, by all the gods and demons you don't. You don't know what *he's* become. You know what happened to Silver Eagle, but you haven't *felt* what happened to him, and that makes all the difference."

He's actually shaking *with fear,* Aran realized with a creeping sense of horror. He knew how formidable his foster father was, and—with no false modesty—knew that he was probably even more dangerous. *Is it really that hopeless? We cannot even flee?*

Shrike's jaw tightened, and he reached down and pulled Condor roughly to his feet. "My mind's made up. It's far past time, and I can see that damned girl's got your mind turned around to the point you'll go do something stupid if someone doesn't set your head straight."

Still groggy from the backhanded blow that had laid him down moments ago, Aran shook his head. "What . . . what are you going to do?"

"What should've been done years ago." Shrike's gaze was unyielding, and his hand hovered near his axe. "You need a talk with our leader. A *private* talk . . . like his master had with me, once.

"Like he had with me, after I'd adopted you."

Though Shrike said nothing else, Aran felt a slow and rising dread as they passed into the shadows beneath the trees.

Beauty was gone, and he was gripped with a sudden conviction that, even if he were to turn around and run, there would be no beauty left to see.

21

Kyri turned and looked back, finally unable to keep herself from doing so as the shadows of morning had shortened, shortened, and then begun to lengthen again as they passed to the afternoon. She had been walking all that time, forcing herself not to look.

But just once...

She had come a very long way; the Great Road here was as smooth as a ballroom floor, with just enough added roughness to be an ideal surface for walking or riding, and she had long strides. Zarathanton was now sinking below the horizon, only the tallest spires visible now, with the rolling hills of the landscape and her distance coming between her and the high walls of the city. She could see the bright lines of the Dragon's Palace shining in the sun, but to the north she could only see the Forest Sea; it was cut back from the Road, a full ten miles on either side, but the road curved and the Forest Sea was high and dark, a bulwark of green that filled the entire center of the continent.

She turned away, feeling as though she was swallowing a ball of ash. *You silly! You've hardly been there a few days!*

But that wasn't it. She was leaving her family behind, leaving Urelle who wouldn't know where she'd gone for days, long enough that she could be convinced not to try and follow. Leaving Aunt Victoria. Leaving *home*, because home really was where your family was, and she realized that *Rion* had left home, but she never had.

That's what you're crying about, isn't it? her sharp inner voice said. *That you're all alone now, the little girl in the dark.*

"It's hardly *dark* now, is it?" she answered the voice aloud. There were few people on the Road now, this far from the great city and not yet approaching Eastern Twin, so no one else was there to hear her talking to herself. "And I'm not a little girl . . . in any sense of the word," she added, looking at her shadow stretching off to her left, exaggerating her already excessive height. *On the other hand, if I wasn't that tall, I wouldn't be able to use a greatsword.*

The greatsword, a small backpack, and a few pouches and common tools—a knife, a flamestick, and such—were the only things she carried visibly. Aunt Victoria had insisted that she take Victoria's adventuring pack—a neverfull model that, while not quite literally never full, could hold more equipment and supplies than she was ever likely to need. *And she shoved what must have been a small fortune in there, when she thought I wasn't looking.*

Which, she had to admit, was just as well. She looked to her right, the west, which was where she was headed—though technically the road led south for the first few dozen miles. *Then the Twin Cities—across the lake from the Eastern to the Western— and keep west until I reach the Dragon's City, then north . . .* She remembered much of the journey, and just how long it had taken. *It will be months before I get to the Spiritsmith, and who knows what I'll need money for on the way.*

No point in musing on it, though. *A bird doesn't fly by looking over the edge, she does it by spreading her wings.*

Eventually the sun *did* begin to go behind the distant hills of trees, and she started looking for a good campsite. *I think I remember . . . Ha!*

There was, in fact, a waystation—a large, open-sided roofed structure, with space for several groups to camp under it, and three firepits. She felt that small satisfaction that comes from having a faint memory vindicated, then reminded herself that the same faint memory said there were a lot fewer waystations maintained along the later parts of the route. *Enjoy it while I can.*

There was another figure already under the waystation, sitting near one of the pits with the fire already going. She approached slowly and obviously—it was unwise to surprise anyone on the road, especially alone.

As she got closer, she noticed that the firepit was burning cleanly with no fuel. *A mage, or he had something with enough magic to run it—fire essence, maybe.* The figure nodded, his strange five-sided hat emphasizing the gesture. "Good evening, young woman," he said in a deep, sonorous voice.

"Good evening, sir," she said. Looking carefully in the dwindling sunlight and firelight, she saw that the long hair streaming from beneath the man's hat was pure white. His hands, partly wrapped in some ritual fashion, were weathered and tanned, the hands of an old but still healthy man.

"Join me, if you wish," he said. "It will save you the trouble of building your own cooking fire."

"I thank you," she said. *He could be dangerous... but most people on the road aren't, and there's no particular reason he would be one of the few that are.* She corrected herself. *Many people are dangerous—myself included, I guess—but most of them aren't hostile.*

A waystation wasn't a good place to plan an ambush anyway; too many people likely to happen along to spoil your fun. She got out some tineroots and, after a hesitation, the racerunner steak Victoria had packed for her. *It won't last long even in the pack, so I might as well eat it now.* The tineroots she wrapped in some of the thick, wet leaves of the hallius that twined up the waystation's supports, and dropped them at the edge of the pit. The pit also included a grill that could be set over it, so she did so and started the steak cooking. "Would you like some?" she asked.

"I thank you for your courtesy," he said, and she saw a white smile flash from beneath the hat. "However, I have already eaten."

As she continued cooking, he spoke again. "You are travelling from Zarathanton?"

She nodded. "Left there this morning."

"This morning!" His tone echoed his respect. "You have long legs and quick strides indeed, Lady..."

"Vantage. Kyri Vantage," she answered, before realizing that perhaps she should have given a different name. *Well, I guess it won't matter this far away. But I'd better figure out how I'm going to hide when I get closer!*

"Lady Vantage, then."

"Oh, gods no. That's my aunt. Just Kyri will do."

"As you wish. You travel impressively fast. Alas, I left the day before yesterday, and as you see you have already caught me."

"Oh, I'll probably slow down after a while," she said cheerfully, turning the steak. "And it's only a few days to the Twin Cities." She said the last with a faint questioning tone.

He laughed and shifted. A chiming sound came from the staff she saw lying near him. *Definitely magician or priest.* "Ah, now, a reasonable guess, but not, I am afraid, accurate. I have much, much farther to go, and aside from the occasional inn at this rate it may be the better part of a year before I sleep indoors again."

She looked at him in surprise. "Where are you *going*?"

He hesitated, and she realized that her question might be intrusive. Then he shrugged. "I suppose there is no great harm in telling you. I travel past T'Tera, the Dragon's City, then north, far north, past Dalthunia, even."

She was stunned. "Are you . . . going to *Evanwyl*?"

"Evanwyl? Hmm . . . no, not there, precisely, but not far from there, either." He sighed. "An old friend of mine lives in that region, one I have not seen in many years. He had been wandering about most of the continent, off and on, but I finally had word he had settled down and was invited to visit."

She could think of several settlements around Evanwyl—and others that, on the scale of *this* journey, would also be "not far."

"That is quite a coincidence, sir; I travelled from there only a short time ago. From Evanwyl, that is."

"Indeed?" For a moment she saw the flash of a surprised eye, blue as an untroubled sky. "Truly that is amazing. Yet, then, where are you going now? Have you travelled so far only to return?"

The steak's appetizing odor now wafted throughout the shelter. "As you said, not to Evanwyl, precisely, but I will be much closer to there than here by the time I am done."

The steak was done, brown and black on the outside with lovely pink inside, and she dug out the tineroots, handing one to the old man. She noticed him make a quick gesture and the wrappings not only came off, but flattened and cooled, making a sort of plate on the ground where the old man sat, cross-legged.

He was quiet for a time while she ate, then he spoke again. "If I might be so intrusive, will your course take you past Dalthunia?"

She considered; she'd already almost told him so already. "At least some distance past its southern border, but not in any area they patrol, I think."

"I see." He rubbed his chin—clean-shaven, she saw, despite the long hair. After another moment, he seemed to reach a decision. "You move like a warrior, though you are young. Has your sword been blooded in combat?"

She thought back to that terrible night when Rion died and shuddered. "Yes, you could say that."

"Then I have, perhaps, a proposition that might benefit us both. I have a...method, let us say, of swift travel. Exceedingly swift travel. But it has certain dangers about it that I would not, myself, assay alone. With someone to guard and protect me along the way, however, I would feel it worthwhile to attempt."

It was a tempting offer. Reducing the travel from what might be half a year to... "When you say 'exceedingly swift,' what do you mean?"

He smiled. "I mean, Kyri, that if tomorrow we set out together, then by the time the sun has set four times we shall be past the borders of Dalthunia and over the Straightcut, on the banks of the Gyre itself."

She felt her jaw sag open and knew how foolish she had to look. *Teleportation? No, that would be instant...and hasn't been reliable at distance for many years, not in that region. Too many wards up. Flying? Maybe, but I don't know much about how to handle myself in the air...* "How?"

The smile sharpened. "I will explain tomorrow...if you have accepted my offer. Otherwise," he looked more serious, "I will have nothing to show you, nor to explain. I will say, however, that it is likely no method you have ever heard of...or ever will again."

The momentary twinkle she saw in his eye, revealed for a fraction of a second again as he raised his head, was maddening. He *obviously* knew how that mystery would nag at her.

Her more stubborn and reactionary side wanted to balk, to just roll over, go to sleep, and let the old man *walk* his way across the continent—far behind her. But...reduce months of walking to a few days?

She gave an exasperated sigh, then smiled. "All right, old man, you win. Tomorrow we'll use this method of yours—if your explanation's good."

"Tomorrow, then," he agreed. "Then we had both best get our rest," he continued, deep voice now with a warning tone that sent a faint chill down her spine, "for while swift, our journey shall be neither easy nor safe."

The words, and their tone, followed her that night, and sleep did not come easily.

22

"Shadestriding," the wizard said, standing on the Great Road, "is a delicate business indeed. For this reason, it is vastly preferred that the one who strides the shades of reality be followed and assisted by those who can watch for the inevitable hazards and both warn of them, and—at least for a time—deal with them."

The head tilted, showing that he was looking at her to verify she understood. Now that he was standing, Kyri realized her new companion was a giant of a man, over a foot taller than she was; it was a disconcerting feeling to be looking so far up at another human being, since usually other people were looking up at *her*. It was also *more* disconcerting to realize that somehow the shadow of that strange hat covered his visage even from below. She could not make out his features, only hints of nose, cheeks, chin, and the occasional brilliant glint of a blue eye.

However, he was waiting for a response; she nodded her understanding. The idea that a wizard might need someone else to watch out for them while performing some difficult operation was an obvious one. "So you must maintain concentration at all times?"

"To an extent, yes. It is, however, also something more like controlling a very fractious mount, or perhaps sewing a length of cloth with a most intricate pattern." He lifted his staff, which Kyri could see was capped with a complex, crystalline design that moved and chimed and was composed of a repeating seven-sided star design with other elements. The staff was bound with four thin pieces of metal joining cap to heel, the wooden sides in between worked with runes and symbols almost entirely unfamiliar to her. The multicolored crystals chimed loudly, and a golden light shone softly out, momentarily overwhelming even the dawning sun. "Follow me. You may leave enough space between us for comfort and close combat, but do not stray more than a few tens of feet away."

They began to move along the road; Kyri was quiet, watching the morning-misted greenery to the side and the small roads leading to nearby farms. There didn't *seem* to be any immediate threats, but she took the magician's words seriously.

After a few moments, the wizard spoke again. "Now we have begun. To clarify, except at certain very crucial stages—such as the beginning of our journey just now—I can converse, walk, and so on, but I cannot simply stop what I am doing to permit the shadestriding; if I do, it would be tantamount to releasing the reins of one's mount when it is in a panic, or leaving the rudder of a ship in a storm. At the least, I must have time to... fix our position and course, one might say."

"I understand. If anything happens, I have to keep whatever it is away from you for long enough to keep a disaster from happening. I've seen a few magicians interrupted at the wrong time—I know what can happen."

He chuckled, the deep voice carrying well through the morning air. "Many things can happen, yes, and most are not good. In this case they would be worse than most. Perhaps not *immediately* fatal...but it is quite possible that even if we lived, we would never reach our destinations." He glanced back. "As you know, I am going to visit an old, old friend. I was wondering—if I am not prying too far—what brings you to leave Evanwyl to travel so far, and then immediately to turn about and travel much of the distance back?"

Kyri hesitated, stepped over a small crack, looked around as she considered. *How much can I afford to tell people—especially a person I don't know? In the long run I'm going to need a completely different name, leave behind my identity entirely.* She continued her surveillance of the area. *Strange. The farmlands and treeline seem closer. Aren't we still in the middle of the Road?*

She felt her brow furrow and a faint, tingling shock of something *wrong.* They were still walking in the center of the Road, yet it couldn't have been more than twenty-five yards to the edge.

But the Great Roads are one hundred yards across, from Hell's Edge to Dragonkill and all places in between!

She stopped in consternation, turned, looked back. They had been only walking for a few minutes, fifteen or so at the most, yet the waystation they had slept in was nowhere to be seen. The road they were on was unfamiliar. Even the greenery nearby has a subtly different cast to its color and shape.

"Do not fall behind, Kyri Vantage," came the deep voice, and she heard amusement that did not comfort her. "No matter what you may see that puzzles or confounds you, do not fall far behind me."

She ran a few steps to get closer to the mysterious man with his staff. "What in the name of the Balance is this, old man?"

"You have noticed quickly, I see. As to what it is...shadestriding, as I said."

"But what *is* shadestriding? What do you mean by it, by the 'shades of reality'?"

"You might come to understand by merely watching," the man said. "Watch, and I shall explain in a while, if you have not come to understand yourself."

She watched, but at first was more mystified—and, she had to admit, *frightened*—than she was enlightened. The road turned, and as they passed the curve it was even smaller, a track half its prior size. Leaves thinned, brightened in their green even as the air cooled, and rustling grasses rippled in a clear cut between the road and the forest which was itself no more than a hundred yards. The surface of the road was cracked and chipped and patched, but in a single turn now was cobblestone and it seemed it had always been so.

Their boots clicked on stone and crunched on gravel, and the pathway led a winding course through a forest that was cool and dim, the sun completely hidden by trees whose needle-thin leaves and aromatic scent she had only seen on the higher slopes of Evanwyl. Small creatures scuttled away, making rattling sounds in the underbrush. Around the next bend and the bark of the trees was a shade darker, the needles longer.

She turned her head and could see that this was the way the whole world looked—but she never actually saw the *change*. They crested a hill, and she looked back, seeing the forest just as it had been, then looked forward, saw scattered trees with broader leaves of lighter green between the needle-trees, cast a glance backward and saw that, indeed, the same few trees were scattered throughout the forest as though they had always been there.

"Do you begin to understand, Kyri?"

She swallowed. *Who...or* what... *is this?* "You...you're chang-ing the world. A little bit here, a little bit there, but each change adds up, so..."

The laugh was hearty, cheerful, and much less threatening than the lowering, gray clouds that she could see now between the branches, in a sky that minutes before had been cloudless blue. "Changing the world? You attribute to me power that is, I am afraid, vastly beyond my capabilities. I suppose I should be flattered.

"I am not creating changes, Kyri. I am...how can I put it... *choosing* what to see. For most, the world simply *is*, and has been, and will be. But that is, to me, something of an illusion. There are some truths eternal...but many others are choice and chance, event and consequence. If one has the knowledge, and the training, and the power, one can guide his steps—and the steps of those nearby—to alternatives, worlds that are the same world yet not the same."

Kyri stared at him, nearly tripped over a branch that lay across the faint trail they were now walking on. "I...I don't understand."

"This world—Zahr-a-thana, Zarathan—is a nexus, a crossroads, a focus. It is not even, strictly speaking, *a* world. It is *many* worlds, touching upon all possible realities, overlaid upon each other with but a few anchors, a few truths that remain in all realms, in all varia-tions. Most of us are set along one dimension, one track of reality, one shade of color on the palette, one single page in the book of all possibility. But magic, and especially the greatest of magics, the magic of the spirit—that touches upon the fabric *of* reality, and one who understands this, and can see beyond what *is* to what *might have been*...such a one can choose to step to that next page, pass from one tale of the world to another, color the world a different shade that never was, but that could have been...and now, is."

She stared around at the leaf-littered ground and the forest with occasional stumps of freshly cut trees. "You're saying...I'm not even on Zarathan any more?"

"Not the Zarathan you knew." The stumps were ancient and overgrown, coated with moss; a farmhouse stood not far away, half-collapsing from age, and the forest was quiet. "This is also Zarathan, but it would be quite likely that if we were to stop here and you set out on your own, you might find no more than a handful of names—of places, of people, of creatures and things—that would be familiar, and even the familiar would be also alien."

She sensed a subtle movement, whirled, saw *things* coming—joint-legged, taloned, armored, like spiders and scorpions and warrior ants but also covered with moss, moving with the whispering, clunking sound of half-rotted wood, eyes flickering in the shadowed gloom with the color of foxfire and glowflies, mandibles showing the gleam of polished wood and shattered crystal. *"Old man—"*

"I see," he said, voice still calm. "You must keep them from me for a time... or if we survive, we may be stuck in this world forever."

I can't let that happen, she told herself, and even though the horrific things before her caused her heart to race and sweat to break out, she whipped out her sword and prepared to meet them.

At least they're a mob, not an organized assault. There were seven of the things, no one of them quite identical. *They seem* created *from deadwood and other things. May not be actually living, and even if they somehow are, no certainty they have the same vital spots...*

She managed a small smile. *Well, except the* obvious.

Most were converging on her—closer to their ambush—but two seemed more intent on catching her companion. *You're first, then.* She kept her mind focused on the targets, and kept her fear leashed. *At least they aren't* people.

The first one tried to pass her, and her greatsword slammed into its leading leg, severing it off, sending the thing skidding sideways. She spun, swinging around and down, and the impact was rewarded with a splintering crunch from within the spider-thing's body; it collapsed like a bridge broken in the center.

A sting whipped into her, the point catching and breaking on her upper armguard but the impact sent her tumbling. She was surrounded with the damp-earth smell of rotting wood and mold and an undertone of festering flesh. *If any of these things cuts me, blood poisoning might kill me before we can find a healer!*

She spun her body on the ground, extending the sword, cutting off the foot of one creature, forcing the others that had swarmed forward to leap back, giving her *just* enough time to roll to her feet. *One's heading for the old man!*

There was only one possible way to deal with the problem, and she took it. She leapt *towards* the nearest of the things, as high and long as she could; a claw smashed into one boot and she tumbled over in midair, managed to come to a landing that only slightly twisted one ankle, but she was outside of the ring of seven-foot-long abominations, and just barely able to chop deep into her target's dead-log abdomen.

The impact didn't seem to hurt it, but it *did* divert the thing's attention; it whirled around, terrifyingly agile on ten legs, and lunged. She parried, but these limbs didn't break easily. *Something like steelwood?* The others were closing in as well. She tried to dodge, but something hit her from behind, the pain sudden and shocking, and she went down, blocking as best she could, but the crystal and rusting-metal mandibles were opening—

A deep voice thundered something in a language she had never heard, and a wave of blazing fire flowed over her, around her, enveloping her attackers in a cloak of red and orange; they convulsed, spun, screeched, and then collapsed, burning swiftly to white and gray powdery, flaky ash.

The old man was kneeling by her. "Are you injured, Kyri?"

"They hit me in the back...don't know if it's anything visible." She was shaking all over from the closeness of death. "S...sir, I—"

"Wait. Let me tend you first." She felt the ragged sting of an open wound as he touched her back gently. "Yes, one cut you deeply. A filthy wound, as well. Can you stay still while I cleanse it?"

She nodded and gritted her teeth.

White flame burned its way down her back, then slowly subsided to a dull throb. "Clean. Now, let us see..." There was some rustling and clinking. "Here." She looked over and saw him extending a bottle. "Drink that."

"A healing infusion?"

"Concentrated, yes. Not useful for disease, but I believe I have addressed that." He looked around. "You did very well."

The draught tasted...like nothing she'd ever had before. She wasn't sure if it was one of the best things she'd tasted, or the worst. But the throbbing in her back began to fade, the bruises in her arms faded. "We'd better get moving, sir. Those things... they weren't natural. Something made them, either some really angry spirit of the forest..."

"...or an extremely hostile magician responsible for this area being uninhabited in this world, yes." His massive hand helped her up; she felt a strength in that hand which might match her own, something that was at least as disquieting as it might have been comforting. "I agree entirely." He smiled as they began to move forward. "But I believe you now understand why I had not wished to use this route alone."

She laughed, feeling a lightheaded euphoria of relief with the things defeated and her injuries fading to nothing. "I think we can say that, yes."

"You wield that blade—an astonishing blade, I will say—with considerable skill for one so young. And you show an amazing coordination and focus. Where did you get such training?"

She smiled. "His name was Lythos; he was *Sho-ka-taida* for Evanwyl, and especially for the Vantages, for quite a long time." The terrain was rougher, hills rising on either side of them, and fewer trees to be seen.

"*Sho-ka-taida*? An *Artan*, then." He nodded and smiled. "Those who take up the blade in the name of the Suntree are often tasked to pass that knowledge on, and do so well...but rarely do they choose to do so outside of the Forest Sea and their own brethren."

"You know a lot about the *Artan*?"

"I suppose that depends on what you mean by 'a lot,'" he said, leading them down a narrow canyon with high limestone walls that made her nervous; an ambush here would be very hard to fight off. "But I have visited them in *Ar-Tan-Nya*, walked the battlements of *Nya-Sharee-Hilya*, and gazed upon *Hali-Shan-Alyin*, the Suntree, in the center of the Forest Sea." He glanced back, even as they passed a curve in the canyon and the great high walls curved away into mere foothills, "But of Evanwyl I have heard little. What is it like?"

She felt almost...embarrassed by the question. "Hardly as grand or inspiring as anywhere you've been, I'd say."

But he seemed genuinely interested, so she tried. She talked first about Vantage Fortress, built into and from the living rock of the foothills of the Khalals, and everyone there—her aunt, Vanstell the Master of House, Treidi and Riderin who cared for the grounds (and chased little girls who pulled up flagstones to look underneath them for arrow-worms and glittercurls), Seeker Nayn who travelled the Eyes' houses—and that led of course into talking about the Eyes and the Arms and the Watchland...

They camped in a small, rounded valley with crater-like walls. The air was cold, much colder than she was used to, and the grass here was tough, short, alien. None of the plants looked familiar. The old man walked around and put down small sticks at intervals on the edge. "That will prevent most things from entering here," he said. "Still, one of us must be on watch. I trust you can endure a night or two with less sleep than normal."

She nodded. "I'll take the first watch, then."

The night was dark, even the stars being dimmed and eventually shut away by encroaching clouds. *Moon's not out tonight.* They had no fire now—and in this moonless blackness, where she couldn't see her hand in front of her face, even the smallest fire would be like a screaming beacon. She decided it was best to simply keep her senses at top pitch. *Lythos would approve of not being bound by any one sense, anyway.*

Something...felt wrong with the night, suddenly, and after a moment, she knew what it was.

Silence.

When even the smallest insects and other creatures made no noise, she knew, there was something else afoot. She moved to awaken the old man.

The air became colder, even as the clouds parted above and starlight shimmered faintly down, and suddenly she saw *something.* It was dark, black as the night; there was a glint of crystal as of teeth and a writhing movement like grasping tendrils about some huge maw, amidst a flowing, amorphous floating ebon substance that glistened and stank like decay and acid.

The wizard awakened at her touch, even as she shouted and dodged from a barely seen slashing movement that carved a line through the dirt, left the short grass fluttering in half-visible silvery motes of severed stalks.

Her sword was in her hand and she swung, but her edge seemed to get no purchase; there was the faintest resistance, as though her blade trailed its tip through an unseen foul swamp, and the dimness receded, arced around, returned, its presence chilling her far more than any of the monsters she'd faced before, radiating an alien hunger, and she saw the stars above flickering, fading, saw outlined more patches of absolute black with hints of bladed diamond within, and the cold that enveloped her was not the night air but shocked horror as she realized there were more of these things, *many* more.

"EÖNAE!"

The shout echoed across the valley like a great bell, and from the upraised staff burst pure golden light; for a moment she could *see* the things and closed her eyes, knowing she dared not look for one second longer on something so alien and monstrous. But alien tentacular mouths could scream, and there was a keening of shock as the light continued, blazed higher, and she felt that *wrongness* weaken, dissipate, flee.

She opened her eyes, to see the staff gently chiming, shimmering now with light of gold and white and green. The mouth beneath its concealing hat was quirked up in a grim smile, and the skin was pale. "I think we should move," he said. "What do you say to continuing on, far from this sheaf of possibilities and nightmares?"

She nodded, mouth too dry to answer.

It seemed a pattern for those few days—conversation, often of Evanwyl or her past, sometimes of places the old man had seen, things he had done, which told her of parts of the world she doubted she would ever visit, punctuated by encounters with things that might roll past them, or attack, or simply regard them curiously. A small flock of glittering spiders, seeming made of glass, that landed and killed everything near where they touched; eyeless black creatures that moved against them in wedges, channeling the power of each into the foremost being with such force that her guide found himself hard-pressed until she began killing them from the rear forward; flat-headed reptilian creatures swimming in a dim and poisonous swamp, who suddenly stopped following them, warning of the immense tentacled monstrosity ahead; in four days she faced nearly a dozen different assaults, and had the old man not also been a healer of considerable skill, she knew she might not have lived through several of them.

But then she realized they walked on a wide road, and around the next turn the road was a hundred yards across, though not quite perfect in its surface, with the clear-cut borders running to the horizon on each side, warm and humid air blowing across them from the direction of the lowering sun, and she laughed. "We're ... home again, yes?"

He chuckled. "Back to the Zarathan from whence we came, yes, we are. Look back, along the road."

She looked, and in the distance she saw a bridge she remembered approaching, what seemed half a lifetime ago, when she and Victoria and Urelle were travelling. "We...we're well over the Dalthunian border!" *And considerably past the Dalthunian border interrogation posts, which I never want to see again.*

"As I said, so I have done. If I understand your intentions, our paths must now part—for you will be following this side of the river Gyre, north and west, while the Straightcut River there," he pointed to the east, where she could see the river the bridge behind them had just crossed, "leads closer to my destination."

She was still stunned. She knew how long that journey had taken her and Victoria and Urelle. Now, five days out from Zarathanton, and she was nearly to Hell's Rim, the Gyre River visible to the west by a smudge of trees along its course. "Yes, I think you're right." She shook herself and bowed. "I thank you."

The mage chuckled and took her hand, shaking it in farewell in a firm grip. "I thank *you*. Such time saved, and would have been impossible otherwise. Good luck to you, Kyri Vantage." He turned, nodded his head, and walked towards the east and the Straightcut.

She looked to the west again, and realized that she was no longer as scared, as lonely, at the thought of the journey in front of her. *Even if I hadn't saved the time...this journey's given me so much experience, in just a few days, of what an Adventurer has to face...of what a* Justiciar *has to face. I owe him more than just thanks for travel!*

At that point it dawned on her, and she turned. "Old man, I never got your name..."

But the grasses before her were empty. Look as she might, there was not a trace of the mysterious old man...not even a footprint in the grass.

23

"My thanks, and those of the city, again, Tobimar," Toron said, sinking into one of the massive split-backed Sauran chairs with the air of one who knows he will soon be forced to rise, and relished the moment of stillness.

Poplock hung on a bit tighter as Tobimar gave an embarrassed wave and shrug. "We've just done what anyone would have," the young Human protested.

"If only it were so. There are those who would not have wished to remain for the inquiry at all, I assure you—and not all of them because they felt they had something to hide. The Lord of Waters would have understood this, and I would be surprised if her son did not."

"Not everyone trusts even the Sauran King and his people," Poplock said bluntly. "At least, not when something like this happens." He bounced side-to-side, a Toadish shrug.

"Indeed. But more than that," Toron continued. "Your testimony was invaluable. We now know how it was done—at least, we know the basic outline of the assassination, though many details—critical details—are missing. But again, your information has given us other clues that may allow us to find out those answers as well."

Poplock smiled and hopped on Tobimar's head, something the black-haired prince tolerated with only occasional complaints. "Because Tobimar's trained to observe, and because at my size you learn to watch everything carefully."

"Don't interrupt the Marshal—"

"—King," corrected Poplock, unable to keep a smug tone out of his voice. He saw the involuntary ripple of the dorsal spines that was Toron's equivalent of a wince.

As Tobimar gaped, the Sauran glanced at Poplock with narrowed eyes. "And just how did you come by *that* little bit of knowledge?"

"I watch," he answered simply. "See how people behave. Bunch of little things. I suppose the key was when I saw Adjudicator Salandaras and the White Robe leave the Throneroom, and they were putting their dustcloaks back on." He could tell by the way Tobimar's head moved suddenly that he'd understood the point of that.

Toron stared at him and then gave a quick, explosive laugh. "Never underestimate a Toad. I've given that advice a thousand times, and it seems I still have failed to learn it myself."

As abruptly as he'd laughed, Toron became serious, even grim, again. "Yes. The Sixteen confirmed that I was Called early this morning, and while I tried to get them to defer that Calling or to select another, they convinced me that—at least at this time—there is no one in a reasonable position to take the position other than myself, and that a new King *had* to be selected before the general announcement. We have managed to delay the announcement thus far—partly because we were fortunate enough that it was just the three of us who discovered..." For an instant there was a deeper, rougher note in the Ancient Sauran's voice, an involuntary pulling back of the scaled lips and a flaring of the deep nostrils, "...discovered the body of my King and cousin. As Marshal I was able to assume direction of all the *T'Teranahm Chendoron*, the Dragon's Palace."

Tobimar nodded, forcing Poplock to hop off the human's shoulder. "I...understand. But you were saying you had figured out what happened...?"

"Yes. I owe you that much, at the least—especially as I'll have another request for you in a few moments." Even on the reptilian face there was no mistaking the serious expression.

"It was terribly well planned and executed—and in essence terribly simple, as many good plans are. It may have been readied for days, weeks perhaps, awaiting precisely the right set of circumstances.

"The culprits were waiting—listening, somehow, to my conversations with the Winnower—until they had a sense of my speech, my rhythms, my characteristics critical for a necessary deception. Following my interview with . . . the two women you noticed, I told the Winnower I would be back shortly; he knew that usually meant I was going to take my day's meal—and so would our unknown enemies. That meant that they knew I would be an hour or so in returning."

"But we *saw* you come back out a few minutes later," Poplock said.

"You saw *someone* come out who *looked* like me, yes." Toron leaned forward. "And I assure you, that is one of the most troublesome of all mysteries. How is it possible that a duplicate of myself was present? How could such an enemy have entered the castle and been present, waiting for this moment, and able to assume a perfect disguise at what would have been very short notice?" The reptilian ruler shook his head. "Understand, there are very powerful magics—summoned watchers, symbols of warding, prayer-screens, and others—to maintain the safety of the castle, and of its people. Most powers or beings capable of such an imposture should have set off half a dozen alerts as soon as it made the attempt." He shrugged in frustration, then continued. "The impostor, your own testimony showed, did not return via the Winnower's Gate, but by the main gate—a necessity, of course, to ensure that the impostor and I did not meet.

"He then went to the Winnower, who was mildly surprised to see me but it was not entirely unheard of for me to change my mind, especially if there was something particularly interesting about the next group."

"And was there?" Tobimar asked.

A flash of a sharp-fanged smile. "That, Tobimar Silverun, you will have to tell me."

Poplock looked at him. "What do you mean?"

"All in due time. As I said, the impostor returned and then escorted the next group—the five young people you described. What makes this particularly disturbing is that while you should have noticed nothing during your visit to the Throne, there are—even more so than in the rest of the castle—powerful, subtle, and—until now—absolutely reliable wards and seals which would not permit any to approach the King without being escorted by myself or one of a very few others."

Poplock understood in a general sense what that meant—after all, he'd been subverting some similar security himself not all that many days ago. But Tobimar reached up, took the Toad off his shoulder with a grip that almost squeezed the air from his body, and set him down. "*Sacred* seals," he said. It was not a question, it was a statement, one filled with grim horror. "This is the capital, this is the castle whose ruler is blessed by the Father of Dragons himself. There is not the faintest possibility that those 'wards and seals' were *not* placed there by Elbon Nomicon and the Sixteen themselves." He held Toron's gaze, and the Sauran nodded, slowly.

It dawned on the little Toad, finally, why this seemed to strike Tobimar so personally. His mother was the ruler of a country of her own, one probably protected by wards very much like those here. And something had apparently walked through them without so much as raising a question, let alone an alarm. "Oh, now that's bad."

Both the human and the Sauran gave a tiny smile. "Yes, one might say that," Toron said. "Now, exactly what happened next... we do not know. Perhaps the group he escorted were innocent, perhaps they were accomplices. If they were innocent—"

"—then the ritual gave him the perfect opportunity to kill, at that point when you have escorted the guests out and close the door to take your own leave and hear anything that the King wants to tell you privately," Tobimar finished, running a hand through his hair absently. "Then he escorted them out and... vanished wherever he came from."

"And we have checked every single person—Sauran, human, *Artan*, even Toad—in the Castle. None of them are our impostor."

Poplock scratched his head with a rear foot. "Um, I'm just a Toad, but that confuses me. If he could walk through god-forged wards, how can you be sure he's not one of the people you're questioning?"

"Because we found the body of one of my guards concealed under one of the floors, so we know what face he's been wearing when he wasn't wearing mine: one of the Heads of Watch, Fureas. We're still working on determining just how and when he died, but it was quite some time ago." Toron stamped his foot suddenly and his next words were very nearly a roar. "And I *spoke* with Fureas myself just three days ago—not two hours before the assassination! The impostor was within my grasp!"

"If he could do that, though," Tobimar said slowly, "why didn't he just...kill the King whenever, maybe when he's sleeping and wouldn't be disturbed for maybe many hours?"

"Could be plenty of reasons," Poplock said quietly, hopping back onto Tobimar's shoulder—and receiving a small, apologetic glance and a pat for the prior rough removal. "Fear and confusion. Maybe get the other people blamed. Maybe get *you* blamed, Toron—then they take out the King *and* his heir in one shot." *Or other reasons.* "Maybe something made it necessary they do it now. I don't know. But the longer they stayed hidden, the more they could learn, right?"

"True enough, *Sylanningathalinde*," Toron acknowledged, using the Ancient Sauran name for Poplock's people. "A perfect spy in the household—and if he—or better, *it*—could be disguised as myself, well enough that the Winnower did not sense the deception, one must presume that at various times it could have been anywhere in the Castle, as anyone."

The door was suddenly flung open; Poplock flipped backwards off Tobimar's shoulder, drawing Steelthorn; he saw the lightning-fast flicker of the Skysand Prince's twin swords being drawn, and Toron was on his feet and in a crouched combat stance.

The Winnower almost screamed in panic, throwing up his hands. "Apologies! Apologies!"

"Tehry," King Toron said, slowly relaxing and straightening up, "this is a poor time to be surprising us. What is it?"

"My Lords...Your Majesty..." The Winnower seemed at a complete loss for words, gesturing outward.

Toron glanced at Poplock and Tobimar, and strode out towards the front gate. They followed, Poplock once more riding in his accustomed position, and all three quickened their stride as they heard an unfamiliar murmuring, a sussuration of unrest that grew to fearful calls and shouts.

They reached the open doors of the Castle, in view of the Gates, and the King staggered to a halt. *"Q' u rr' a Terian khe' Elbon..."*

In the courtyard were dozens of people—some human, a few Iriistiik, a Child of Odin or two, but mostly elves, *Artan*, and all with the haggard, drawn look of those who have been running for their lives. Some were bandaged, stained with blood, injured to a greater or lesser degree.

Poplock spotted a small knot of Toads trying to make their way to the left fountain, and leapt from Tobimar's shoulder, hopping as fast as he could. "People! Hello! What—"

As he got closer, he recognized some of his people—and especially the keg-sized one being carried, bandages ominously dark. "Oh no. No. *Barkboat!*"

The old priest opened one gold-and-black eye. "... Poplock. Is that really you, or—"

"What *happened?*" Even as he asked the question, he felt a terrible cold feeling, like sinking into an icy bog, rising over him from the ground under his feet.

"Duckweed..." It was Padsinker, who he'd never liked, but the wide eyes and scratched, loose hide brought with them an aching empathy. "They... they were everywhere. Armored warriors, wizards, monsters... *mazakh*, humans, fire exploding..."

Oh, no.

He'd been too late. Too late.

"M... Majesty..." an *Artan* warrior was speaking, so exhausted that he did not even attempt a bow. "Majesty, we... we are attacked. *Hali-Shan-Alyin*, the Suntree, is fallen. The Forest Sea... we no longer hold its heart."

Barkboat's eye slid shut, and he was limp. Unconscious, or...

The little Toad hopped a few feet, then stopped and sank to the ground, hearing the tiny peeping noises that were his sobs. He'd had four years.

Four years.

And he'd wasted them all.

24

Tobimar staggered as he placed yet another gasping body—a child, no more than ten in human terms, with delicately pointed ears and long silvery hair smeared with blood—on the altar. *I can't fall now. We aren't even near done.* He called on his meditations, the training Khoros had given him, released the reserves of his soul. Strength flowed back into his body, clarity to his thoughts. *There'll be a price for that, later . . . but not now.*

The *Lurali*, a priestess of Terian, looked even more exhausted than he had felt. She wavered as she laid hands on the girl, invoked the power and prayer. Blue-white light as gentle as gathered starlight flowed from the Lurali, into the little *Artan* girl, knitting the injuries, pulling together sundered sinew and flesh, restoring blood to the flow and pulse of life. Then she collapsed to her knees; Tobimar caught her before she fell forward. "You have done as much as the Light in the Darkness can ask, *Lurali*," he said. The semiconscious priestess tried feebly to argue, but others came to bring her to a place of rest.

Tobimar shoved his sweat-soaked hair back into place and looked around. The Temple of Terian was filled all along the eight walls with refugees, the injured, the homeless, and he could see more being brought in. "Sand and sun . . . how many *are* there?" he whispered.

"A lot." The voice, a very subdued one, spoke from near his feet. Poplock looked up at him, a completely uncharacteristic expression of exhaustion and pathos clear on his amphibian face. "Tobimar . . . it's like this all up and down the Blessed Quarter.

The Hall of the Aesir's practically full—not that the Spear and Hammer will turn any with the courage to make it this far away. You know the Palace courtyard was crowded. The Cavern of Endless Crystals," Tobimar nodded to show he recognized the name of the temples of the Dragon Gods, "the Cavern's full. Hundreds of refugees there. The Triad, the Three Beards, the Lifecross, the Aegeians... even Blackwart's Pond. All of them, it's the same." He seemed to deflate. "The priests are running out of strength, even the greatest of them. There will be people dying in the temples tonight, Tobimar. Dying. In the temples of the gods."

Tobimar bent and picked up his exhausted friend, hearing the grief still in Poplock's voice. "Don't blame yourself. Please."

"How can I *not*?" the little Toad's voice was something between a scream and a croak, a pathetic sound that sent a shiver of sympathy up Tobimar's spine. "I knew they were planning everything... I should have *made* people listen to me!"

The thought of little Poplock—dangerous though Tobimar knew he could be, in the right circumstances—trying to *force* someone like the Winnower to listen brought a faint, sad smile to the exiled Prince's lips. "You know that wouldn't have worked. And Khoros always told me that we must learn from the past, but not let it pain us more than the learning requires. For like any open wound, it will never heal if we do not let it alone."

"Heed the words of your friend, Poplock Duckweed." It was the *Nomdas* herself, highest priest of the mortal god on all Zarathan, the Shading Glory's pearlescent glow blurring her features as all representations of Terian blurred his. She was clearly exhausted as well, but refusing to stop. "You cannot fault yourself for being who you are. Learn, but do not punish yourself. There is too much at stake for those who are already a part of this great game to abandon their places."

"Great game? What are you—"

Yet the *Nomdas* had passed on, was bent over an injured *mazakh*, and Tobimar could tell the time for talk was already past. He saw how few of the priests were still up, still able to act, and realized that Poplock's horrific prediction was all too likely to come true.

Deaths in the Temples. It was a horror story, something to frighten children with. Yes, it could happen in the wilds, in places where there were few priests, but in the greatest city of the world, in the very temples of the Blessed Quarter?

But looking around him, seeing the refugees still trickling in, a slow but relentless flow of need and pain that was overwhelming even the servants of the gods, the alchemists, the sorcerers who practiced the healing arts, Tobimar realized that was going to happen. It *was* happening. And the very fact that it was happening told him that Master Khoros' warning had to be true; somehow, the gods themselves could no longer act, could not step down from their realms and wield their supernal powers directly to stem the relentless tide of the injured and dying.

"I refuse," he muttered.

"What?"

Poplock's confused query shocked him; he hadn't realized he'd actually spoken that aloud. "I refuse to accept this, Poplock. This is...monstrous."

The little Toad looked at him with a wry tilt to his body that seemed at least something more like the old fearless, carefree Poplock Duckweed he'd come to know. "Well, yes, it is, but exactly how can you not accept it? If you close your eyes and put your thumbs in your ears you'll still be tripping over the people."

"I mean that *this* is part of what they—whoever they are—intended."

Poplock narrowed his eyes. "Oh. Oh, my. You mean that the assassination—"

"Has to be part of it. It was all coordinated." He whirled, strode over to the northern wall, picking his way carefully past healers and injured and sleeping, to point to the inlaid map of the continent. "Look. That first group of refugees...came from Pondsparkle. Right?"

"Well...some of them had 'ported or gated from farther in, but they'd come to Pondsparkle, yes. Couldn't pop to Zarathanton for some reason."

"So here...Pondsparkle's about two hundred miles north of Zarathanton—but if you go about this far south you can take the river for a good long distance, which you would if you were refugees in a hurry. If they took that route, when did they start running, to get here when they did?"

Poplock thought for a moment, tongue flicking out absently, and he suddenly sat up. "That's—"

"Exactly. The attack must have started almost precisely when the assassination took place."

The little Toad bobbed slowly. "And the refugees..."

"They're not trying to kill *everyone*. Driving so many people here will overload the Temples, terrify the population, demoralize people... and reduce support, because people will start to worry about protecting their own. Fewer nobility subscriptions because people don't feel the privilege is worth it now, maybe established nobles retract their subscriptions... with the Sixteen not able to intervene and make a show, the State's in trouble."

"The Adjudicators?"

"They'll do what they can, but they can't support the defense of the whole city. If enough people lose faith, the whole system will collapse."

"Oh, drought and quicksand." Despite the grim situation, Tobimar felt his heart lighten a tiny bit. Poplock was sounding more himself, and somehow that made things better. "What can *we* do? I don't think we can defend the city ourselves either."

"No," agreed Tobimar, "but right now we need to make sure the King sees the whole situation, and then..." he gave a weak grin and shrugged. "Then we do the best we can. He can't leave. He's the Sauran King, the living representative of the Dragon Father and the Sixteen. As long as he's here, he might by himself be able to keep the people's confidence. But he'll need all the help he can get.

"Still, *someone* has to find out who did this, track them down, and stop them."

Poplock hopped on his head and then leaned perilously over, looking down into Tobimar's eyes. "That's an awfully tall order for one exiled Prince and a somewhat height-deficient Toad."

"True. But if we can at least find out *who* we need to stop, maybe after that we can figure out that little question of *how*."

Poplock's gaze bored into his own for an eternity of seconds; then the little Toad suddenly bounced off Tobimar's head and onto his shoulder. "Then it's a good thing we registered with the Adventurer's Guild last week!"

"Helped to have Toron as the sponsor. Come on." He turned, bowing to the remaining priests. "My apologies; we have just realized something of grave importance that needs to be told to the King."

The *Nomdas* returned the bow wearily. "You have done much here already. Go, and Light Unto Darkness."

"Light Unto Darkness, *Nomdas*."

Tobimar strode out into the night.

25

Kyri looked up at the looming mountains ahead of her. It wasn't the first mountain range she'd seen since leaving Zarathanton, but it was by far the most forbidding she'd ever faced.

Of course, she admitted to herself, *that might just be because I know what it is.*

Now, for the first time in weeks, she felt uncertain. There was no one near to help her, no one to advise her, and no one to reassure her that she was on the right trail . . . or tell her she had gone terribly wrong.

And when facing the gray-black, knife-edged spires of Hell's Rim, the feeling of something gone terribly wrong was nearly the only sane reaction. Within that almost unbroken circle of mountains was a land of aberration and monstrosity, wracked by magical repercussions of battles and disasters that went back to the very Time of the Fall. The city of Hell's Edge existed for the singular and sole purpose of sealing the only existing pass into—or out of—Hell.

It wasn't, of course, any of the netherplanes that were variously called Hell by any of a dozen dozen religions, but by all accounts it was something maybe worse. It occurred to Kyri that the stories of Hell were very similar to those of Moonshade Hollow, on the other side of Rivendream Pass.

Maybe too *similar.* The thought made her shiver.

The problem before her, of course, was to find the Spiritsmith's forge. Unfortunately, given what Toron hadn't been able to tell her, the best guess she could make was that it was probably somewhere between the Gyre River and the next river flowing from the Rim—a river which didn't even seem to have a *name* on her map!

Kyri took a breath and got a firmer grip on both her pack and her resolve. *Myrionar promised that I simply had to be true to It, and have faith. Not that I had to be right all the time.* There would be small communities along the mountains—though not *too* near. And one of them would have to know *something*. After all, even the Spiritsmith, whoever and whatever he was, would have to get supplies from somewhere, unless he could just conjure them from nowhere. And even then, would he want to stay entirely alone for centuries?

Still, this could take a long time. I should be grateful for that wizard's help. Those few days had been terrifying and nearly fatal, and the old man himself had been disquietingly enigmatic . . . but without him, she'd still be . . . what, maybe not even to Elbon, certainly nowhere near Asgard's Fortress, let alone all the way to the Rim past the Gyrefell Forest.

That's *the part I should be most grateful for,* she thought. Dalthunia—or whatever that country had become—controlled the region between the Ice Peaks and the Gyrefell. No one sane entered the Gyrefell, and when she went through Dalthunia before she'd been in a carriage, with Aunt Vickie, Ingram, and Quester; even then, there'd been some close calls, when she knew Aunt Vickie was afraid they'd be halted, searched, or worse by the soldiers. *I might have been able to sneak through by myself . . . but now I don't have to. Thanks, old man,* she thought to herself.

She paused, then turned, almost expecting to see that figure standing behind her. But there was nothing but forest and hills, wilderness bereft of any sign of civilization. *What did he want with me?*

Despite the eerie and frightening nature of the encounter, now that she truly understood how very strange that part of her travels had been, she found herself certain that whatever the old man really was, he wasn't an enemy. He'd certainly had the power to kill her at any time, especially now that she understood that the entire sequence of events must have been nothing more than his excuse to . . . what? Study her? Interrogate her? Place some unknown spell on her? Help her reach her goal, even though he shouldn't have known anything about it?

She gave a little laugh—somewhat shaky—and shrugged. *I suppose I will only know if I ever meet him again. Or—*

She topped a low ridge, and her train of thought was interrupted as she saw below her a village, wood and stone houses surrounded by fields with a reasonably well-defined center visible. It was close enough to make before nightfall, which was a definite plus. *And maybe they'll have some answers for me.*

But as she got closer, she heard the shouts, the screams, and realized, *It's never quite that easy.*

Drawing her sword, she broke into a run.

Kyri skidded to a halt in the rough center of the village. It was easy to tell where the trouble was coming from, since most people were running *away* from that direction. A few figures, apparently the people who served as guards or sherriffs, were advancing a little ways ahead of her. A hissing, rattling shriek came from that direction, and the guards hesitated.

She took advantage of the hesitation to catch up. "Anything I can do to help?" she said to the leader, who jumped slightly as she spoke.

The short, brown-haired man in metal-scaled leather glanced up at her, taking in her stance. "Adventurer?"

"Zarathanton Guilded," she said, uncovering the patch on her shoulder that glittered with the symbol of the Dragon King. *Thank Myrionar Aunt Victoria was able to convince the Guild to take me on short notice.*

He looked back up the street, to where one of the houses seemed to squat threateningly, broken door like a gaping mouth, then sketched a complex symbol in the air which glowed slightly and settled on the patch; the crystal starburst-bolt glowed white. "Genuine, I see. Thank Chromaias, I don't like this one at all."

"What have you got?"

One of the other men, about the same height as the leader but wider, with a black beard and one brown eye—the other missing, a scar across the face showing what had happened—spoke up. "Not sure yet, ma'am. That's Borshseth's place. She's still inside, think her husband is too. That," he pointed to a body lying in the dirt in front of the house, "looks like Kimsha. Dunno what *he* was doing there, thought he was out on patrol these last couple days."

Seeing her expression, the leader gave a wry grin. "I'll run it down for you quick. I'm Varji, that's Menka, these other two are

Terrek and Fejri. Borshseth is Tinna Borshseth, she's one of our healers; alchemist mostly, a little regular magic of some kind. Kimsha's an *ayr-kin*." Kyri nodded, showing she recognized the word; it meant roughly "sweeper" and was an *Artan* word for a person who was a sort of hunter, outrider, and scout for a village. Not necessarily an official post, but one that could be very dangerous but also very lucrative. "People running by said they saw *something* in the doorway that cut Kimsha down, something with a lot of legs and fangs."

"Yeah, but not much past that," Menka grumbled "And you *know* scared people ain't much on seein' what's there, better at seein what they *think* is there."

"What's Borshseth's husband do? And do they have any children there?"

"Mostly he does whatever she says, but to answer your meaning, old Quil's a sage. He's a researcher, used to be Guild but that was *way* back."

Another screech, slightly softer this time. "So they're old?"

"No, Tinna's pretty young, actually. She's always picked 'em for their brains more than anything else. Quil's her third husband, see, since she came here 'bout ten years ago."

That's going through them pretty quickly. She saw Varji's raised eyebrow. He knew what she was thinking. "And...?"

"Actually, no. Not as far as I can tell. Tinna's tough and focused, but she's not that type. Wouldn't have gained anything from their deaths, as far as I could tell."

Time's passing fast. "Have you ever heard that...cry before?"

Varji shook his head; the others followed suit. "There's some things out there, especially right on the Rim, that sound sort of like that, but none that really sound the same."

Kyri took a deep breath. "Well, I guess I'd better go take a look."

She gave a quick prayer to Myrionar and focused; she could feel the faint tingle as she was bathed in protective power, energies that would stop or at least blunt any assaults.

Slowly she approached the house. Kimsha's body lay face-down, about five feet from the broken doorway. She studied the location, remembering how the Sauran Adjudicator, Toron, had acted when he arrived to investigate her parents' murders, and how she'd been taught by the Temple and others. The door had been broken open violently from the inside; fragments scattered as far as ten feet away confirmed this. There was a scuffed-looking section of Kimsha's leather armor with what looked like wood splinters in it; from that it appeared that he'd actually been what broke the door, which would indicate he'd been shoved or thrown into the door with tremendous force. Kimsha the Sweeper's left hand was in a half-closed position; a short-bladed sword lay not far off. He'd clearly kept hold of it as he passed through the door but dropped when he hit. There was a large pool of blood under him; Kyri slid her sword under and levered the body up gingerly, keeping a wary eye on the dark doorway.

Kimsha's chest was torn half-open; it looked almost *shredded*, and there looked to be another wound, a puncture, in his gut. Kyri let the body fall back, noting in passing that his right hand had a slight yellowish stain on it, and looked like it had also recently been burned.

She moved forward slowly, sword held so that she could cut or block quickly—and so that it would impede just about anything charging her. As her eyes adapted, she could see the inside of the large house was in chaos; furniture broken, blood on the floor and the walls, mingled with something that looked dark blue-green in the dim light.

Now a rising screech-hiss came from in front of her, and she saw something move away from her. She did not run forward, however; instead she stopped and surveyed the whole room. An upward glance caused another something that had been squatting on the ceiling to dart down and away through the same archway the first had. She had an impression of something long and low with many jointed legs, glinting with crystal and silver. *Tried to catch me unawares from above, but I'm not* quite *that naïve.*

"Is someone there? Kimsha? Help us, please!"

The voice was shaking, a woman's voice, and it came from the archway the creatures had fled down. Now that Kyri's eyes were fully adjusted, she could see that there would be no point in making the standard gesture for light; something had torn down the brackets and shattered the lightglobes that had been here. A very faint light, occasionally with a swift flicker as of something crossing between it and her, was visible through the archway. Cautiously, Kyri moved forward. *Myrionar, help me see through Darkness to the Truth.*

A soft light surrounded her at her prayer and gave her the

ability to pick her way carefully through the wreckage and pass through the archway. A hallway ran at right angles to the archway, but there was also a set of wide stairs going down, clearly the direction the creatures had gone and the pleading voice had come from. Making sure there was nothing above her, Kyri made her way down the stairs.

The stairway opened up into a very large room—a modified cavern, it appeared—with multiple shelves and workbenches around it, the shelves filled with a myriad books, scrolls, tablets, and bottles and packets of various materials. At the far end of the room a lightglobe still glowed, but the scene revealed was far from comforting.

A mass of creatures—low, sinuous, large, perhaps twelve feet or more from end to end, intertwining so as to make counting them difficult—squirmed and clawed around what seemed an insubstantial barrier in the air. As she entered, two separated themselves from the mass and ran at her, scuttling on multiple pairs of legs, sideways-opening mandibles wide and showing a horrifying assembly of grasping, ripping appendages within. *That's what tore Kimsha apart, no doubt about it.*

She braced herself to meet the charge, but to her surprise the creatures simply lunged at her a few times, but well short of actual attack distance, as though they were trying to just drive her back, and then retreated to sit about a quarter of the way from the main group. Kyri could see another figure near the very end of the room. "Hello!" she called. "Healer Tinna Borshseth?"

"Yes!" called back the shaky voice. Kyri could see the speaker was a petite red-haired woman—even younger than Kyri had expected, though very pale and drawn looking. "Kill these monsters, please! I can't keep the barrier up much longer—it's an improvised ward!"

"I'll have you out of there as soon as I can. Is your husband with you?"

"They stung poor Quil, he's poisoned! I can't get to my antidotes, either, they're on the other side of the room. Please hurry!"

As Kyri advanced, Myrionar's light showed a broken area of the wall on one side; it was clear that this was where the creatures had come from. "Do you know what these creatures are, Healer?"

"What?" she sounded understandably distracted. "Tinna, please, you're trying to help me," she said, an automated courtesy in the

midst of disaster. "These things...oh...I think so, but," she gave
a ragged laugh, "I've never been quite this close. I think they're
vrytrills, sort of a giant centipede that's native to the Rim. Very
hard to find, they usually avoid contact with people."

Kyri, being taller than anyone or anything else in the room,
could now see over the vrytrills and into the area Tinna was in.
It was a rough circle about thirty feet across, defined by six stones
glowing with a faint blue radiance; the stones had clearly been
hastily placed, almost scattered. Inside the circle were Tinna, a
tall slender man with short white hair who was collapsed against
the wall, and three tables with equipment and odd materials
on them—distillation devices, a small bookshelf, a set of twelve
different-colored crystals, a box of silver-and-crimson spheres, a
rack of tubes and bottles...

The two vrytrills made another run for her, but again stopped
short of actual attack—though they were closer, now, than the
first time.

Her first impulse was to take advantage of this hesitation, and
the focus of the other five or six of the creatures on the barrier,
and start cutting them down. That the things were dangerous
wasn't in doubt; Kimsha's body proved it. Yet something didn't
seem right about the whole thing. The rest of Tinna's workshop
was an odd mixture of the untouched and destroyed. Most of the
damage seemed along a line coming from Tinna's location towards
the stairway, and she saw a vrytrill body lying, half cut apart, just
off to one side. There was a crunch underfoot; she looked down
to see a silvery-red shard and a thick liquid mixed; a sharp smell
warned her and she moved quickly away, scraping the boot to get
the viscous material off it. *Some kind of acid in those things.*

She saw the wardstones dim slightly. The force of the pressing
bodies caused them to move inward; the wardstones rebrightened
as the perimeter contracted, but that just showed clearly how they
were weakening. It would keep shrinking slowly until it reached
a breaking point, or the vrytrills could reach their goal...

Something about that rang a faint bell of warning in her.
"Tinna, these things came through the wall?"

"Yes! I'd walled off the small caverns back there years ago,
nothing there before."

"And were all three of you here then?"

"Yes, yes—why are you *talking*? I can tell you all this later, please, please get them *away!*" The healer-alchemist's voice was nearing the edge of hysteria, and Kyri couldn't really blame her.

She heard a low humming noise, barely audible over the screeching hisses. "What is that noise, that hum?"

"Hum?" Tinna seemed utterly at a loss, then gave an exasperated curse. "That's the Rimchimes." She indicated the silver-crimson spheres.

Just maybe . . . "And was Kimsha holding a Rimchime when they broke in?"

"Well, yes, he'd brought them in for me and—" She broke off, staring. "Oh, no."

"*Could* it be true?" She could tell that Tinna had come to the same tentative conclusion she had.

Even as the perimeter contracted slightly again, Tinna was standing, staring at the box and its contents. "Rimchimes hum for only a few weeks . . . it fades after a while . . . I was going to try to figure out how to stabilize it . . . And I've never actually had any in here before . . . they're usually shipped out, curiosities . . ."

It could be. And if it is . . .

Kyri lunged forward, slashing with her sword—but with the flat, and with choppy strokes that could be avoided and were clearly being pulled. The vrytrills leapt aside, screeching and chittering and snapping at her, but only one mandible actually contacted her, and glanced off her armor. "The vrytrills aren't seen often. They avoid you. Maybe they're smart. Maybe very smart. And they're things of earth . . . tunnel using acid?"

Tinna nodded wordlessly, pale as she realized what had been happening. "Yes, they do, that much is known . . . Oh, Chromaias and Terian . . ."

"Is there a speaking charm anywhere in here?"

She shook her head. "I . . . no, I've never had a reason to work on that. Besides, it has to be tailored for the target."

Have to try the clumsy way. She was now against the barrier, the vrytrills closing in. She bent down, face now perilously near the hissing maws, and picked up one of the Rimchime fragments, holding it up. The screeching increased, and she winced as some of the yellowish goo—the same shade as had been on Kimsha's hand—began to eat into her gauntlet. She stood, holding the fragment out, then gesturing to the box. She made a gesture of turning and giving the box, several times.

Slowly the screeching hisses diminished. The creatures seemed to be warily settling. She made a broader gesture, sweeping, trying to say *back away*. After a few more repetitions, the vrytrills gave ground, moving backwards a few feet.

Now or never. "Tinna, please drop the barrier."

The alchemist hesitated. Then, with shaking fingers, she picked up a central stone and passed her hand over it.

The glow of the wardstones went out. There was a rustle among the massed vrytrills, a movement to lunge forward—but one, marginally larger than the rest, gave a single screech and the others froze.

Kyri walked to the table and very slowly and carefully picked up the box of Rimchimes. She walked over and placed it with exquisite care on the floor in front of the largest vrytrill, then backed away.

The vrytrill reached out and took one of the spheres between its mandibles—mandibles which she knew could cut through armor—and raise it with the delicacy of a jeweller examining a gem. The low humming seemed to rise in volume. The other centipedal-like creatures came forward, each taking one sphere. One by one, they moved sinuously out of the room, through the hole they had made. The largest was the last to leave. It lowered itself in an unmistakable bow, then turned and left.

Tinna ran on shaky legs to one of the other tables, pulled down a bottle and ran back, tipping the contents into Quil's mouth. Almost instantly Kyri could see color returning to the old man's complexion. Tinna looked up. "How terrible. They were *eggs*."

"Of a thinking species." Kyri shook her head. "It happens too often. How many hundreds, maybe thousands, of types of thinking creatures are there? New ones born from random magic every few centuries, others wiped out by accident or design...perhaps the vrytrills themselves have only recently become intelligent."

Tinna Borshseth nodded. "It...makes sense. When they came in, Kimsha was holding a Rimchime—oh, by the Four I was going to open it!—and he moved off to get room to maneuver, they all came at him, I think his hand must have contracted and it cracked...then he threw it down when it burned his hand, and they seemed to go berserk. Kimsha backed up, fighting...I saw him get up the stairs, so...?" Her look was hopeful.

Kyri sighed and shook her head. "No. He made it as far as the door, and that was it." She shifted her glance. "And you, Quil? How did you end up hurt?"

The old man answered, laughing slightly. "Me? Heh. I charged them when they started circling and they lunged back. Thinking on it, I think the sting was more accident than anything—they were threatening, not trying to attack, you can tell that, that hole in the wall shows what would have become of me if they wanted me dead." He looked at Kyri with respect. "Good work, young woman. You solved this without killing that would have, it seems, been terribly unjust."

The words made her realize the peril she had avoided, and how very close she had come.

But Myrionar had been merciful, and perhaps her feelings had been born, not merely of her own caution, but of the subtle guidance of the Balanced Sword. She closed her eyes, smiled, and gave her heartfelt thanks that she had followed the True Path.

Justice before Vengeance.

26

"Good travels to you, *ayr-kin*," Tinna said quietly, as she lit the apex point of the Five-Fire under Kimsha's body, the point to the east and the rising sun. "May the One and the Four receive you well, and forgive you the missteps along the path and the misfortunes that led you to this end. Chromaias, receive Kimsha of Waycross in your House of the Five Ways; as he wished, so we have done."

Kimsha's body was arranged with his head to the point, the terrible wound left by the *vrytrill* hidden, covered by a thick ceremonial robe. Getting that robe on had been a nasty business, which Kyri had volunteered for; in a village this small, all of these people would have been his friends or close acquaintances. *No reason to force any of them to do it when I'm here.* She still kept her eyes mostly averted from that area, because she could still see the savaged, ripped flesh all too clearly in her mind's eye.

Varji came forward, placing Kimsha's sword at High North, to the right of the Sun. "Your weapon is returned to your hand, Kimsha. May your blade sunder all bonds in service of the Mistress of Music, in her name, Stymira Thanamion."

Quil was next, and on the upper left point he placed the broken fragments of the Rimchime, the vrytrill egg. "The cause of your death was tragedy and accident. Take both with you, and may the Queen of Power burn away all such dark comedies of the world, in her name, Kharianda."

Mangar, the local Watchland, was next, but Kyri missed the

exact dedication and prayer to the Lady of Light, because she knew she was next, and was at a loss as to what she could say. She knew the structure of the Chromaian ritual, and she certainly paid her respects to the One and Four, but she'd never actually *met* Kimsha...

It was quiet, and she realized her time had come. She swallowed and stepped forward, reaching out and placing her hand on the final point of the Five-Fire, even as the flame reached her. The sharp, hot pain seemed to clear her mind, and Kyri understood what she could offer the dead. She endured the flame's touch for a moment and then lifted her hand enough to prevent the burn from becoming too great. "My thanks go with you, Kimsha, *ayr-kin*. Through you I was tested, and perhaps your spirit saw through me and guided me through the perils to Justice. Though we never met, you did me great service, and you will be remembered in my prayers as well. May peace come to you and may the Guardian of Command embrace your spirit, in her name, Amanora, and," she continued, "may you be welcome, too, in the House of the Balanced Sword, in Its name, Myrionar."

The fire leapt up, all five sides blazing a different color, the blue fire of Amanora enveloping Kyri before she could move. Then the Five-Fire was gone, and all that remained of Kimsha was a black outline that began to blow away on the winds. Kyri blinked, then looked down at her hand.

It was completely unmarked, even the redness and blisters of the earlier burn wiped away. Varji touched her shoulder and bowed when she looked down. "That was well done, Lady Vantage," he said with respect. "Especially for one who had never been a part of a Chromaian funeral before. Your heart's offering was well received."

"Thank you. I...I wasn't sure if I should add that last, but I felt I had to."

Mangar, a grizzled, middle-aged man with a bit of thickening about his middle and the look of someone used to quiet politics more than ritual, smiled. "Chromaias is not terribly jealous of other gods, as long as they respect him. You have told us you serve the Balance of Justice, and at such solemn ritual it is only to be expected you might call upon Her...er, I am sorry, *It*." He touched hands with the others in the five-fingered open manner of Chromaians. "Now that Kimsha is on his way, I have a small dinner of thanks prepared in your honor, milady, for your fortuitous arrival in our moment of need."

Kyri couldn't restrain the blush. *I suppose I should get used to this sort of thing. It's one of the things a Justiciar would expect to encounter after a successful mission, and part of my point will be to be* obvious *about being a Justiciar.* "I... only did as anyone would have."

"Perhaps almost anyone would have tried to *help*," Tinna conceded, "but how many would have realized the truth before more—either of us, or of the poor vrytrill—died? Not many, I would wager."

"I... well, perhaps not. But I am sure that was Myrionar's guidance, not my wisdom, of which I have little." *If I was wise, I don't think I'd be here in the first place.*

The "small dinner" was, perhaps, small by the standard of Aunt Victoria's parties, but from Kyri's point of view it was far too large for comfort, with almost 40 people present, most of them talking to her, looking at her, or talking *about* her. But she drew a deep breath, remembered her aunt's lessons, and tried to be as charming and bright in conversation as her nervousness would let her.

The numbers dwindled as the night drew on, fortunately, and by the time the second dessert, a surprising frozen confection of fruit ices surrounding a flavored cream ice, was served, there were only a few people at the table with her—Tinna, Quil, Varji, and Varji's one-eyed lieutenant Menka; Mangar himself had excused himself to go to bed shortly before. Tinna turned to Kyri and leaned forward. "So, Kyri, you've done very well diverting certain questions, but you didn't just happen to wander by Waycross. What brings you here?"

She realized this was actually the ideal time to ask. "Well... I'm looking for something—someone, actually. I know he's around here *somewhere*, but that 'somewhere' could be anyplace along a hundred miles or more of Hell's Rim."

Quil nodded, leaning forward himself with a professional air of interest. "So it's information you're after! My speciality! So who is this person you seek? And details, mind you; any details you know may help us remember him, or connect him to someone we *do* know."

"Don't laugh," she said, realizing what her request might end up sounding like.

"Lady Vantage—" Menka began.

"Kyri, *please.* 'Lady Vantage' is my aunt."

"Kyri, then. Kyri, no one's going to laugh at you no matter what you're questin' for. Believe us."

"Thank you, Menka." She nodded. "All right, then. I'm looking for the Spiritsmith."

The table went silent for a moment, all the others looking at her with almost unreadable expressions. This was not the laughter she'd feared, nor the incomprehension she'd rather expected; this was something else, and much more unsettling.

Quil was the first to break the silence, with a snort of self-deprecating laughter. "Well, now. I suppose that little dead moment rather limits our ability to claim we know nothing."

"Only now that you've drawn *attention* to it, Quil! What in the name of—"

"Never mind, love, never mind. Likely neither of us would be here to argue, if she hadn't been on quest. We owe her, and it's according to the Law, I think."

Varji rubbed his chin. "Yes...Yes, I guess so. It's just been so long."

Kyri looked from one to the other. "So I just *happen* to find the right place the very first time I ask?"

"Not quite *that* great a coincidence, girl," said Quil with a sharp smile drawing lines on his face into clear relief. "You wouldn't have been in *this* area if someone hadn't already given you some good hints, and we're not the only village that knows; far from it! No, the Spiritsmith's got his arrangements with every village along that little arc you mentioned. All of us know about him, and every so often we have to do something for him—clean up some monsters, bring him supplies, whatever. In return, we occasionally get little gifts. Little for him, of course."

"You've *seen* the Spiritsmith?"

"What?" Quil looked shocked, then laughed again. "Oh, no, no, not me, nor any I've ever spoken with. But when we bring our supplies to certain points, they disappear shortly afterwards. And every once in a while, something else is left; a weapon, a piece of armor, a set of tools, a plowshare or a digging tool, all mystical and of incredible quality and performance, and almost always something we really have need of."

"So...will you tell me..."

"Exactly where to go? With pleasure." He gestured to the now-black windows. "Go to the place where the road exits our village to the west, where the Rim lies. Look to the west and north, and see the Sundered Peak. There, between the two fangs of heaven, the Spiritsmith has his forge."

Wonderful! I'm almost there!

"But be warned," Tinna said, "it will not be easy."

"Yeah," Varji continued, "there's rules he set up ages back, and he means them. Means them a lot, if you know what I mean. In any case, here they are.

"First, if you are planning to see him, you need to set out tomorrow morning; within one day of learning his location.

"Second, you must go alone. No one can guide you, no one can accompany you.

"And finally, you can buy no more equipment than you already carry. You may leave material behind, but you can neither make nor buy anything new before departing on your journey. You will climb the Sundered Peak on your own...or you will never reach the summit."

Kyri remembered the incredibly steep, forbidding slopes that seemed the entirety of Hell's Rim, and swallowed. *I have to climb that with nothing more than I have on me?*

She shook her head. "I suppose I should have expected another test."

"That," corrected Tinna, "is not the test."

"What?"

"That is just the method he uses to prevent people from bothering him too often. The real test will begin if and when you reach his forge; and if you fail that," Tinna's face was grave, "yours will be the next Farewell that we must give."

27

The door to the meeting room crashed open, rebounding from the wall and being caught again by the massive scaled arm that had flung it wide.

Poplock was the first to speak, as Tobimar found himself momentarily speechless at King Toron's fearsome snarl of anger. "Oh. Bad news again."

The casual tone breached the armor of grimness, and the huge Sauran shook his head with a weak, rumbling chuckle. "Yes. What should surprise me about this?" He placed a cubic crystal on the table and waved a hand over it.

The air above the crystal shimmered, thickened as with pearlescent fog, and the fog solidified into the image of an exhausted-looking human with brown hair and eyes, a partially healed wound across his forehead. "No time for a full report, scaleface. The depth-cursed bastard made his move; I barely made it out of Nya-Sharee-Hilya before the first wave hit, and they've been on my ass ever since. Ditched 'em for long enough to give me a breathing space."

The little visible background showed a shattered, rugged landscape with little growing, and shifting mists drifting across it; the man glanced hurriedly around, eyes narrow, listening for sounds that might—or might not—be approaching him. "It's been...six weeks since the attack. Took me that long to make my way to land, I practically had to circumnavigate Artania ahead of the invaders. Landed somewhere to the south-southeast, think I'm just south of the Great Abyss. Can't go north if that's the case; the Lone Lord's patrols'd get me sure. Gonna try to head south, but you know what that might get me." He looked over his shoulder. "Think they might be back on my trail. I'm gonna send this straight to you, hope it gets through; it's my last linkstone, broke the others in the escape." For the first time, the expression shifted from casual grim to painfully serious. "Toron, if you can—this isn't a skirmish like the others. Bal's forces hit all the coast I could see. The *Artan* need our help, and they need it now." He bent closer, and passed his hand across the field of view, and the air was suddenly empty above the little crystal.

Tobimar looked at Toron. "And that arrived just now. Six weeks."

"The same timing," the King confirmed. "Artania, the homeland the *Artan* claimed for themselves, struck at the same time as my brother, as the Forest Sea. Communications with the Empire of the Mountain have been cut off. I have yet to hear anything from Aegeia, the White Blade, or," he nodded apologetically to Tobimar, "Skysand, but even if they have thus far been spared I must assume this will not continue."

Poplock swayed in stunned awe. "But Artania's . . . what, two thousand miles north of the Khalals?"

"This is a vast and organized conspiracy. Which narrows our pool of suspects greatly—the Great Wolves, terrible though they are, are loners and work not with other creatures for any plans other than their own—and *many* other creatures are involved in this, from the highest to the lowest." He paused, rubbing his crest with an absent-minded air. "'Suspects' . . . why does that—"

Abruptly, one of the great scaled fists crashed down on the table. "*S'lurl khe' mbar!* Darkness and death, but I am an idiot!"

"What?" Tobimar asked, but King Toron was already heading for the door, the clawed hand gesturing for them to follow. "What is it, Majesty?"

"*Suspects*, Tobimar. With the complete chaos that began when the refugees arrived, I first put off, and then forgot completely, something I had been about to discuss with you that very day." The Sauran King was leading the way through passageways heading downward, into the living bedrock beneath Zarathanton.

Tobimar cast his mind back to that terrible day, trying to recall what possible detail of their conversation could be associated with that word. And then he had it. "The five who were in the group before you discovered the murder." He stumbled as the import of Toron's words caught up with him. "They've been down in the holding cells for *six weeks*?"

"Unforgivable. Reprehensible. Abominable. Even if they were involved in my cousin's murder, still would I owe them an apology." The King's strides were so long and quick that Tobimar found he nearly had to run to keep up; Poplock was holding tightly to the young Prince's shoulder. "Oh, they will not have starved or been unduly uncomfortable, that is all taken care of, but in no way should it have been even *possible* for this to have happened."

"Don't get *too* hard on yourself, Toron," Poplock said. "What's happened in the last month or two isn't something you would have thought possible either."

"Perhaps...but still, I cannot easily forgive this. I can only hope they will be more lenient than I."

The sealed doors of the Prison of the Dragon opened as Toron approached, and the guards on the other side began the Armed Bow, stopping as they realized the King was in far too great a hurry. "What is it, Majesty?" said the one on the left—a Child of Odin with salt-and-pepper hair, a scar on her left hand, and a warstaff slung over her shoulders. "Most of the cells have been already converted to house refugees, as you ordered, except the secure holding area—"

"It is the holding area that concerns me, Telga. I must see the five prisoners in the Star Cell immediately."

"At once, Majesty." Telga glanced at her companion. "You remain on guard." She then followed the King to a nearby vault which opened only when both she and the King placed their hands on the door, and removed from the vault a crystal star, which Tobimar realized must be the key to the "Star Cell."

They made their way through three successive gateways, each deeper, more massive, and more secure than the last, worked through with spells and alchemy to make them proof against any attempt to breach this nearly impregnable fortress of security. Despite the emptiness and quiet, Tobimar somehow had the feeling of being watched, followed, but glancing around he couldn't *see* anything. *Some kind of monitor, watchspell, bound spirit?* Finally, ahead Tobimar could see a large door with a glittering hollow star in its center.

Telga stepped to the door and passed her hand over a patch

of blue-green metal to one side. "We are about to open the door. Do not make any sudden moves," she said to apparently empty air. "Stay back from the door until you are told otherwise. The enchantments of warding will automatically fire upon any who do not obey these directions."

She paused, but there was no reply. Shrugging, she said, "You have been warned; I will assume by your silence that you understand."

She handed the Key to Toron, who passed his hand over it and then gave it back; the five-pointed star now had a slight but definite glow. Telga inserted the star into the hollow in the door, and to Tobimar's considerable astonishment, the door literally simply faded away, to the sound of a distant bell-chime.

The "Star Cell" was actually a connected set of rooms—no actual interior doors, but doorways, with sleeping cots, a fixed table and chairs, and reasonable comfort and cheerful design. It was, however, missing something.

Poplock regarded the scene with professional curiosity. "Pardon my saying so, Majesty … but there appears to be a distinct lack of prisoners in your cell."

28

Poplock hopped up on the table. "So they got out by themselves?"

Having been around the Sauran King for several weeks now, Tobimar had come to be able to read the draconic expressions; Toron wore a complex look of chagrin, amusement, and consternation. "So it would appear," the King said slowly.

"How is that *possible?*" Tobimar demanded. "The prisoners are watched, are they not?"

"By sight and sound crystals built into the very walls," agreed Toron. "But recent events made this observation less . . . assiduous than normal. In particular, it was Fureas who was in charge of the Secure Holding area—"

Tobimar winced. "—and he was of course dead some weeks before, when the assassin had infiltrated. So after the assassination, he left, and then all the other things happened—"

"—and no real replacement was set," Poplock finished. "Still, there must be many things securing those 'secure holding' areas. You must have taken any weapons they had on them—"

"According to the records, they were unarmed. The only weapons they should have had were those kept before the Throne Room door, so that visitors will be armed and not disgrace themselves or the King. They did have strong mystical auras," Toron continued, "but there are powerful suppression spells woven into the walls which would prevent the operation of almost any form of magic—elemental, symbolist, essentialism, even suppressing the channel between priests and their gods or the powers of the mind itself. It is said that at least once, a lesser god was held securely in these cells."

"So how *did* they get out? What did the crystal records show?"

"That is the problem. They don't, exactly." Toron gestured for them to follow. "At least one or two of them possessed powerful magic which could manage to function to some small extent—and which they were able to use to excellent effect, blurring imagery and sound alike. I have brought in a specialist in the magic of the elements and nature who has been working on extracting as much sense from what remains as can be managed, but," he opened the door to another room, "even he has been quite impressed."

"Astounded would be the better word," corrected a voice even deeper than Toron's, and Tobimar stopped, startled. A truly immense Toad squatted before a large polished table, with faceted hexagons of crystal four feet wide on the wall in front of him, showing various angles of view of the Star Cell.

"Willowwind Forestfist," Toron said, "please meet Tobimar Silverun and Poplock Duckweed."

Tobimar bowed deeply, recognizing who this was. "The Guardian of Eonae and Shargamor's Chosen. Warden of Nature for the Forest Sea. It is a great honor."

The giant Toad looked embarassed, in the exaggerated hangdog manner that only his people could manage. "Less an honor now that I have failed to foresee and stop such an abominable invasion. But what talent I have gained and what I have been granted are certainly the ones appropriate to this conundrum." He waved a gray-brown webbed hand at the crystals. "When our visitors first entered, all the pictures were clear, as was the sound."

The image that appeared was sharp and bright, showing five young people—younger even than Tobimar—as they entered the room and turned, almost as one, to look at the door as it materialized, sealing them inside.

The first thing that struck Tobimar was the beauty of the five. There were three boys: one taller than everyone else in the room, with golden hair that fell in a smooth wave over one deep violet eye; he was slender and moving with an elegant economy of motion. Both of the other boys were black-haired; in that, the two could have been twins, the hair long and perfectly straight, thick and polished as ebony. One, however, had bright blue-green eyes that seemed almost slanted, almond-shaped, their gaze edged as razors, and a faint almost reddish undertone to the skin; his face was delicate, heart-shaped; his companion's face was dark, almost olive in color, a study in sharp planes, a hawklike face with large, direct-looking eyes of steel-storm gray.

Of the two girls, one was nearly as tall as the first boy, with long tresses of a startling emerald color and eyes as brown as oak; the other was much more diminuitive, the smallest of the five, hair as pale as moonlight, eyes blue as sapphires; her face seemed at turns as hard as marble and as soft as clouds, and Tobimar thought she moved like a soldier—watching, even without seeming to watch, every part of the room. The same, he realized, was true of the golden-haired boy and the dark-skinned one. *Most of these people have been trained to fight, and to watch.* The other boy didn't—quite—have the same implication of combative skill that the others exuded, but his gaze was if anything more observant, scanning everything almost simultaneously and constantly. The green-haired girl...*she moves like a storm on a leash. Not very subtle, but don't get in her way, either.*

All five of them showed no blemishes—scars, unsightly wrinkles, unevenness of skin or lack of symmetry. They seemed something that must have been produced by perfection of art, not of nature. This made the fierce expression of the green-haired girl all the more terrible for its distortion of perfection.

"So much for *that* idea!" she said. "We—"

The green-eyed boy made a cutting gesture with one hand. "Say *nothing.*"

His gray-eyed companion glanced around the room. "I don't think they've got security cameras in *this* place, Toshi."

"Cameras, no. Something else...you want to bet against it, Xavier?"

The gray eyes widened slightly, and the boy smacked himself on the forehead. "*Duh!* Magic."

"Magic."

"We can't stay quiet and say nothing the whole time we're here," the blonde girl said reasonably. "And we really need to discuss things."

"Well..." The boy named Toshi seemed to consider, then turned to the golden-haired boy. "What do you see, Gabe?"

"Something's definitely repressing...us," Gabe answered after a moment, clearly avoiding saying anything that might give a listener details. "But..." He closed his eyes, opened them again, turned slowly in place. At one point, it seemed to Tobimar that Gabe looked straight at him.

Gabe stopped, looked at Toshi, nodded.

"Right. Look, Nike, you're right that we need to talk, but not until I figure out how to deal with this. We need to be able to talk in privacy, and obviously our jailers don't want that. And they've got something that's shutting us way down. So I have to think. *Nobody else*," he caught the eye of the green-haired girl, whose mouth tightened, and he also seemed to flicker another glance at Xavier, "do *anything*."

Willowwind waved his hand again, and the image dissolved to shadows. "So they did sit there very quietly not moving for quite a while—about two hours—while this Toshi wandered around the room, looking at things and thinking. In itself, that is rather extraordinary; five young humans staying so quiet for so long. We hear some occasional shuffling noises, see a couple of them get up and get drinks from the basin, and a few noises that we can't identify, but for the most part nothing of significance until about three hours later. And then this happens."

The crystal lit up again, with the five young people changed in their positions but otherwise pretty much as they'd been before. Toshi sat down on a chair, turned towards the others, and said something.

Tobimar blinked. "What was that?"

Willowwind chuckled, gestured, and caused the scene to repeat.

Poplock bounced forward. "Again."

After the third repetition, the little Toad and Tobimar looked at each other in equal confusion. "You know, it *sounds* like it makes sense, somehow. Yet when I think about trying to understand it, I get nothing."

"It's one of the most drought-damned brilliant and subtle tricks I've ever seen," the Guardian of Eonae said with real admiration in his voice. "The boy's using elemental magic—in a suppression pentagram, no less!—to effectively cloak their speech with some absolutely inspired...well, I guess you would have to call it sound encoding. He's overlaying the sound waves with another sound he's generating that ends up leaving it sounding like you're hearing conversation, but reducing the actual sounds to nonsense words. And he's *changing* the pattern fairly frequently, so I can't easily compensate for it without knowing what's being said—and of course if I knew that, I wouldn't need to compensate."

"What about the lips?" Poplock asked. "The human types can be pretty easily read that way."

A deep Toad-chuckle. "Indeed. Watch."

They saw Toshi sit down and say his now-nonsense phrase. Xavier replied. After a few moments, Tobimar shook his head. "The lips are...off. Blurred and distorted."

"How can he do *that?*" demanded Poplock. "That's not sound!"

"No, indeed. But if I assume he's an elementalist whose domain is air, that's a different thing entirely. The air itself is the source of both problems; he's distorting the perceived lip movements in the same way heat waves produce a mirage."

"Well, do we at least see how they *leave?*"

"Alas, no. When that day comes, the whole room fills up with impenetrable mist for a few minutes, and it's empty afterwards."

Toron walked up to the crystal, as though to get a better look at Toshi. "Can you get *anything* from the recordings?"

"I believe so. He is clever, resourceful, and he is vastly more powerful than anyone his age should be. But a sledgehammer— even a very skillfully wielded one—remains a sledgehammer, and after a hundred and fifty years I'm a bit better than our little sledgehammer. *But...*" the Toad conceded, "it will take me some time longer to get whatever sense I can from this."

"I don't think these people are part of the plot," Tobimar said finally. "They didn't talk like they had just assassinated someone, or even seen it done."

"I am inclined to agree," Toron said, "but they were present and may have vital clues to the actual assassin, without even knowing it. And to escape from the Star Cell—!" He gave a rippling shrug of incredulity. "They are an unknown quantity; the way they *spoke* is alien, as though magic were something almost unknown to them; but if that were the case, how could they wield so much of it?"

Willowwind sat up higher. "You have hit upon it, Majesty. Not elementalists; *Elementals.* They do not *wield* magic, they *are* magic, their spirits are bound to one of the essential elements. This explains both why they sensed as powerful mages and yet the suppression pentacle did not fully succeed; the cells are designed to keep all prisoners healthy, and thus cannot suppress a being of essential magic below a certain threshold. To do more would injure or kill without judgment or justice, anathema to your people and any of the State of the Dragon God." He bobbed a nod. "Yes, yes! And thus the five, for Earth, Air, Fire, Water, Spirit."

"But those are nothing like ordinary elementals which are either summoned manifestations, representations of the symbols of their elements, or avatars of gods or demons of those powers," Toron pointed out. "Which means they are almost certainly creations of tremendously powerful magic—creations made for some purpose. A purpose we do not know and without information cannot guess." He gestured to the others. "Willowwind, I will leave you to this. Get us some answers."

He looked at Tobimar. "I owe you some answers as well, Prince of Skysand; answers which may aid you in your quest, and ones you should have had from my brother. But indulge me a few days more; I would know first what I can of this unknown force, and whether they are friend or foe, before I speak to you of things which may send you far from this city, because," he gave an apologetic bow, "in this time of crisis, I have come to rely on you, an outsider drawn within. We were fortunate in your presence, and your absence will be noticed."

Tobimar could not restrain a slight laugh. "I'm sorry, Majesty, I'm not laughing at you. I just...well, don't worry, Majesty; I can hardly deny you a few more days, when you ask with such extravagant praise."

"I thank you, Tobimar. We shall know in those few days, I promise. Whatever Willowwind can do, will be done by then, and then we shall know...and so shall you."

29

"Come on, Poplock! The King says Willowwind is ready!"

"Mmmph!" It was difficult to reply with a struggling hornbeetle in your mouth, especially when it was trying to poke you in the eye. Poplock bit down harder and bashed the beetle against the nearby wall a couple of times; stunned, the insect went limp and the little Toad was able to cram it down. "Coming!"

It's odd, he thought as he leaped up to Tobimar's shoulder, *how . . . comfortable this is. It's not exactly like that "familiar spirit" bond that I hear some of our people have indulged in, but there's something like a connection between me and Tobimar.* The thought firmed his resolve to stick with the exiled Prince. *I'll keep this extra set of eyes out for him, and maybe the two of us will live through the messes we keep getting into!*

Willowwind was in the same room where they had first met him, but . . . *well, he has been working here for a week!* Shelves which—upon their first visit—had been essentially empty, to the point of being unnoticed, were now filled to overflowing with notebooks, vials of sands and metals, packets of herbs, random assortments of small gems and other objects that were less immediately identifiable. Scribbled symbols, half-erased and then written over, were all over the room—pentacles on tabletops, the Seven-Star on one area of the floor, the four-pointed device that Poplock irreverently thought of as "Chromaias' Caltrop," and endless repetitions of variants of the elemental symbols—Earth and Air most prevalent among them. Over much of the floor, like a drift of leaves, were wrappings and boxes showing that the huge Toad had been taking most of his meals here as well.

"You've succeeded?" Tobimar asked as they entered, clearly doing his best to ignore the startling clutter.

Willowwind's deep chuckle echoed around the room and into the corridor before Toron shut and locked the door behind him. "I have done as much as can be done by any mortal agency, I think." He bobbed side to side uncertainly.

Toron looked at the hexagonal crystal viewmirrors. "Are you saying you have not retrieved all of the information?"

"All?" The Guardian of Eonae made a rude noise with his throat-sac and tongue that made Tobimar jump, almost upsetting Poplock. "Far less than I might have imagined. This... 'Toshi'... wielded his mystical sledgehammer with far more cunning than even I had suspected. I have more information, yes, but it falls very much short of what I had hoped."

"He was *that* powerful... or that good?"

"Both, young Tobimar. Were he not powerful, he could have done nothing at all in those cells; were he not astonishingly adept at making use of his reduced powers, I would have had no difficulty reconstructing that which he sought to obscure. As it is," Willowwind made some gestures and images began to materialize in the crystals, "I have been able to retrieve a select and very limited set of additional information. Most of it is in fact Toshi's own words; when he spoke, I deduce that he had to at least to some extent reduce his mental focus on the techniques he was using to obscure the conversation."

As the events in the Star Cell from weeks in the past began to replay, Poplock found the effect quite eerie; five young people were having a conversation, but mostly in what was reasonable-sounding gibberish... with one voice often suddenly coming clear. It was... it was like hearing only one side of a conversation in a crowded room, but as though the person was talking to someone *not* in the same room. Unsettling.

"All right, I think... that... does it."

A mumble that almost made sense from the moonlight-haired girl. "I think so, Nike." Toshi glanced at the others. "I'm scrambling... the air. They can't use active magic... inside the cell."

It was clear that even when he was talking, Toshi was concentrating on something else; the slow speech and off-timed hesitations showed that. The others began speaking, and he raised his hand. "Slow down! I have to...keep this working. No, the suppression field...seems to work on everything. Almost. So their bugs... have to be listening just like us, seeing like us."

"Um...'bugs'?" Poplock asked.

"Appears to be a term they use for covert observation magics," Willowwind answered, pausing the images. "They have a number of such...unique phrases and idioms."

The boy called Gabe asked something, raising an eyebrow; Toshi gave a sharp, almost smug grin. "Mess with the air...enough, it'll work. Impressing an encryption frequency...on the noises... distorting the images just enough...Guards already busy. If no one comes busting in on us...in the next few minutes...should be safe to talk for a while."

"So let's skip those minutes—they just waited—and then..." Willowwind made a pointing-dragging gesture and the images whipped forward in time, stopped when the Toad stopped his pulling gesture. "There we go."

"Okay. Think it's good enough. Nike, why don't you start?"

More half-comprehensible mumbles. Toron grimaced. "And he goes around the group that way, doesn't he?"

"You begin to see the problem," agreed Willowwind. "For the next hour or so, he orchestrated a conversation among the other four, which I cannot interpret, and his only contributions were almost meaningless; all that I derived from that hour that was of any use was confirmation of all the names of our subjects. The one called Gabe is named Gabriel; the green-haired girl is Aurora; the smaller girl is Nike; and the other black-haired boy is Xavier. I believe Xavier's family name is Ross, and Nike's is Engelshand, but the other familial names have not yet been mentioned." Once more the images sped forward. Poplock felt Tobimar's shoulders tighten, saw the head turn. *Something's bothering him. Maybe more than one something.*

The five had shifted around; Toshi was leaning against the wall casually, while Gabriel had seated himself near the two girls, and Xavier was sitting in a strange cross-legged position on the floor. The discussion seemed to be getting energetic, possibly even acrimonious, judging from the expressions. Finally Toshi's voice cut through the incomprehensible babble. "*Yamero!* Stop it! We can... go around forever on that line. We aren't *on* Earth any more."

Toron glanced at Willowwind, who nodded.

"What's this Earth?" Poplock asked.

The great Toad and the Ancient Sauran both looked grave. "The word 'Earth,' used in that context," King Toron said, slowly, "is one of the names for the world we call *Zahralandar*."

Even Poplock found himself momentarily stunned; one of the most ancient of legends, suddenly come to life? "Zarathan's sister world? The one cut off from us, they say, during the Fall?" Too late he remembered he shouldn't refer to it *that* way around a Sauran.

Fortunately Toron either did not notice, or was unbothered by, the unspoken "of the Saurans" that trailed, unvoiced yet ominously present, after the naked words "the Fall."

"The very one. And by that speech, it would seem that these five are *from* Zahralandar, something that I should have said was impossible."

"So how did they get here, then?" Tobimar asked. Still his eyes shifted, as though he was not entirely paying attention to the conversation.

"Indeed, that *is* the question. One of many to which—as yet— we have no answers."

Poplock edged closer and whispered, "What's wrong? You look like you have a bug buzzing your ears just out of tongue-reach."

Tobimar gave a small snort of laughter. "Ugh," he whispered, responding to the simile with typically human disgust. "Just... a feeling. Off and on I've had it for a while, but now...I keep getting a feeling of being watched, even though there's nothing here." He took a deep breath, forced himself to sit down and relax as the images restarted.

Toshi was continuing after other dialogue. "We can...look at it that way, yes. But...we've been here a while. No one's come to see...us. And what little we've heard...sounds like they have even more problems."

He looked grimly at his friends. "We were the last group present before their king was killed. That kind of thing means it was an insider's job. And the best insider to do it? That talking T-Rex that was the major-domo, captain of the guard, whatever, the one that brought us in, and then left us outside in the hall alone before he came back out and let us go. And then sent people out to catch us." Toshi paused, both to regather his concentration and apparently to let that sink in.

"He's got a point," Poplock said, looking at Toron. "From where they sit, you're the top suspect."

"I can hardly deny it. Especially when in a way they are absolutely correct; the 'Toron' who was with them in the Throne Room was, in fact, the murderer of my cousin."

"So think about that," Toshi said finally. "What if he's the killer? We make a perfect set of scapegoats. Especially if we don't get to talk to anyone else." The small pale-haired girl spoke, followed by Gabriel and Aurora. Toshi's smile was cynical. "Yes, they *could* be perfectly fair, but just because it's all a sparkly magical kingdom doesn't make this a Disney adventure. Or it could be, and he's the Grand Vizier. They've got advanced magic, but they've got a monarchy—maybe a dictatorship, I don't know. This could be... as bad as any banana republic." The others said something. "Yes, exactly. Sure, they've treated us okay—even if isolated—so far, but that means nothing. Remember what we were told..." Toshi's brow furrowed even more, and now his voice blurred out as well.

Toron turned to Willowwind. "I don't think we can keep taking the time to watch all of this. They don't leave immediately, correct?"

"No. They remain for another week and a half," Willowwind confirmed.

"Great Sixteen!" the King said involuntarily. "Are you saying that the cell was empty for more than *two weeks*—nearly three—without anyone recognizing this?"

"I am saying exactly that. I cannot say exactly *how* that is possible. I do know that they discussed methods as to how they would leave—but the details are always obscured by his clever tactics; he is clearly aware that *if* anyone could read through his tricks, they would be hearing his voice, and therefore he avoids, for the most part, saying anything that means anything out of the context of his conversation."

"It would seem, however," Toron said finally, "that they are definitely not involved in the overall plot; they were intended as distractions. Yet... they are also unique; they must be part of something far greater in and of themselves. They were 'told' something by someone—"

"Ah, yes. There were some other similarly cryptic references," Willowwind said, "but taken together... yes. They were assembled together and given some sort of instruction. By someone known to at least the one named Aurora, who does not hold this unknown in great esteem, and possibly by the one named Nike, who, conversely, does."

Toron sighed heavily and sat down. "A terrible mess, and a mystery. I wish I had a chance to speak with them—any of them."

With the viewmirrors no longer showing anything of interest, Poplock was looking idly around for any leftover bugs or flies, not that someone like Willowwind was likely to have missed anything. But because of that, it just happened that he was looking directly behind Tobimar when the boy named Xavier simply... *appeared* from thin air.

The little Toad had no time to voice a warning or even surprise, for Tobimar Silverun leapt to his feet, spinning and drawing his swords in the same motion, sending Poplock tumbling to the floor.

A clear double chime resounded through the room as both of Tobimar's blades were met in perfect counter by a pair of leaf-green swords. The two youths seemed frozen for an immeasurably short second, eyes of sapphire blue locked in furious glare into eyes of stormcloud gray.

And then the tableau dissolved into a whirlwind of blades.

30

Upon that nebulous sense of unease becoming absolute certainty of something behind him, Tobimar had struck, instinctively, as quickly as his years of training allowed. He was stunned by the other boy's speed of reaction. *He's at least as fast as I am. And he read my strike* perfectly!

Tobimar was vaguely aware that Poplock was gone from his shoulder, Willowwind had bounced halfway across the huge laboratory behind a table, and Toron was standing back near the entrance, watching like a man trying to decide if he really wanted to try to separate two fighting dogs. But almost all of his concentration was focused on the level gray eyes across from his.

He's using the twin-blades too! Dual-sword combat was not common, not using matched blades, and usually that gave its practitioners a small advantage. Three more cuts, both blocking perfectly, almost identical strikes parried in nigh-indistinguishable ways, and Tobimar leapt backwards, flipping in midair, gaining distance . . . and realizing to his astonishment that Xavier had performed the exact same maneuver, at the precise same moment. He landed, swords held in perfect parallel across his body in the guard stance he had been taught . . . and saw Xavier standing in the identical pose, as though Tobimar looked into a mirror; with a start he realized that there was even an eerie similarity to their appearance, both with long black hair and dark skin and features sharply cut, though differing in detail.

He opened his mouth to speak, but Xavier Ross spoke first. "Who was your sensei?" he demanded.

"What?" It wasn't the most brilliant of rejoinders, but Tobimar wasn't sure what that last word, sensei, meant.

The others straightened slightly, seeing that the two had changed from fighting with swords to testing each other with words.

"Your sensei! Your... master, teacher. Who taught you how to fight like that?" Xavier's stance was tense, and now Tobimar could see lines of exhaustion, circles of even-darker skin under his opposite number's eyes, and the other boy's voice was filled with confusion and worry.

Tobimar considered. He'd never been told in so many words not to discuss it... but the old sage/wizard had always been close-mouthed, and he had been surprised over the years to discover that quite a number, even in the court, had never actually *met* his advisor and teacher, did not know his name, were not even sure of his existence. Still, there were too many mysteries here, and if this would keep Xavier talking... "I was trained by many people, but the one who taught me most of that style, and other things, was Master Khoros."

"Khoros?!"

To the Skysand Prince's surprise, that expression of startled revelation didn't come just from Xavier Ross, but from Toron and Willowwind as well. Xavier also glanced in startlement at the Sauran and Toad, then sheathed his leaf-green blades and sank into a chair, the exhaustion Tobimar had seen emphasized in the heaviness with which the other boy sat. A faint whiff of sweat told him that Xavier probably hadn't been able to bathe very often in the last few weeks, either.

Tobimar looked over at Toron, who was now regarding both him and Xavier with a look of extreme wariness and understanding; glancing to Willowwind, he saw a similar expression in the huge golden eyes, mingled perhaps with what might even be pity.

"Well, *that* name seems to strike deep and pull hard," Poplock said, settling back onto Tobimar's shoulder. "Any of you want to say more about what's so surprising about the name of Tobimar's old teacher?"

Toron did not answer immediately. Instead, he turned to Xavier. "You were trained by Khoros?"

"No. Well, not in that fighting style. I wasn't sure he knew that...though I guess I should have figured he did." Xavier shook his head. "But yeah, he taught me some things. Taught all of us something, more time with some of us than others."

The deep black gaze of the Sauran transferred to Tobimar. "And your mentor and teacher was Khoros?"

Puzzled by the serious inquiry, Tobimar nodded. "That was the name he used. Konstantin Khoros."

"An extremely tall human?" Willowwind put in. "In light yet elaborate robes of unique design, with a hat that somehow concealed much of his face no matter the angle from which you viewed him?"

"Yes, that was Master Khoros."

Toron growled something in Ancient Sauran that Tobimar couldn't quite catch, but seemed to insult the Dragon Gods themselves for putting Toron in some untenable position, and Willowwind sat with an unreadable expression on his broad, brown-warted face.

Xavier gave a tired chuckle. "I see you guys like him almost as much as Aurora does."

"Like?" Willowwind said, and took a deep breath, letting it out with a rippling rumble like rocks tumbling underwater. "The one named Khoros is not someone that one *likes*...or *dis*likes, precisely. Those who are, or who are close to, the great Powers know *of* him, and they may hate him, or fear him, or admire him from a great distance. He is said to be many things; warrior, sage, alchemist, symbolist, master of the elements, even a spirit mage of power undreamed of. He has been seen walking *down* from Mount Scimitar, striding out of the Great Abyss, passing through the Forest Sea without a trace."

"Most importantly," Toron said, "he is a manipulator and meddler of the highest order, one who has made the Dragons dance to his tune and tricked gods of light and darkness into doing his will."

Tobimar's first reaction was to protest that Khoros wasn't *anything* like that; he had absolute faith in his old master. Yet, as he thought back on how he had been taught...how Khoros had left that frighteningly accurate message, how he left so many things unsaid, while saying what forced Tobimar to certain choices... he realized that the description was all too accurate. "But...I think he's really on our side."

Poplock had been quiet; now he suddenly sat up. "Hey, this Khoros—his hat, was it like, um, five-sided? And his hair was white?"

Tobimar glanced at him, almost crossing his eyes to focus on the little Toad. "Yes, that's him. Why?"

"That's the old mage that pointed me here! I was...a little off course." He held up his blade. "He also put a blessing on Steelthorn, too. Said if I was going to wander around on my own, I'd better be able to hurt just about anything."

"Black night and no stars!" Toron cursed. "So this *entire* sequence of events, even your presence, little Toad, is part of one of his plans. Or more than one." He paced back and forth for a moment, claws scratching loudly on the stone. "I am very much tempted to have you all leave immediately and say not another word. But then," he said with a snort, "I would wonder if I was simply doing what he expected me to do. And I can't afford to throw away more information at this point." He dropped into the chair available for his use, with the tail-split back. "Where are your companions, Xavier...Ross?"

Xavier shrugged. "Don't know, exactly. That was part of Toshi's plan. We couldn't afford to all get captured again, so everyone was supposed to split up; something Khoros had said had implied something like this would probably happen." He acknowledged this confirmation of Khoros' methods with an ironic smile that looked too old for his youthful face. "So I stayed behind because I could go pretty much anywhere and watch anything, and decide if I could risk talking to you people, and the others scattered. I could make guesses about where they'd go," he admitted, "but I'm not going to."

"And do you know anything about your purpose here?"

The younger boy grimaced, then yawned. "Ugh. Look, I'm about done in. Can you at least get me something to eat if you're going to keep questioning me?"

Toron sighed, then managed a toothy smile. "I suppose we can arrange that."

Poplock bounced to the floor. "I'll go order something for everyone." He scuttled out the door.

"To answer your question, not exactly. And he warned us to be very, very careful about telling anyone anything about what we were doing."

Toron's eyes narrowed. "Xavier Ross, you have been—somehow—walking unseen inside *T'Teranahm Chendoron* for nigh on three weeks, and that with the entire castle on high alert, seeking for spies. You have heard, undoubtedly, many counsels meant not for your ears. If you do not know that I am the Sauran King and bound by tradition, my training, and my heart to protect and serve the people of my country, then you have seen nothing in all your time here. You owe me, at the least, an explanation of your presence and your purpose."

Xavier studied him, then stood and gave an odd, but very formal-looking, bow. "You are right, sir. I've been a spy in your house long enough to know what you—and these other people—are like. And I do owe you for that.

"All Khoros told us—once he gave us what was, really, just a sort of bare-bones summary of what we were—was that if we wanted to get home, we had to break some kind of seal between this world and our own, and that there were a lot of forces that wouldn't want that to happen."

Toron stared at him in silence for a long time, looking after a few moments more like a statue than a living creature; Poplock came hopping back in and stopped, looking at the frozen tableau in puzzlement before finally climbing back onto Tobimar's shoulder.

"You need...to break the seal between Zarathan and Zahralandar." Toron said finally, as though he was trying to make sense of words that had no meaning. Or that had meaning that was so impossible that it was difficult to even grasp enough to speak of the impossibility. "Do you have any idea what you are saying?"

"Not really," Xavier admitted, "though I guess from what you're saying it's not going to be easy."

"Easy!" repeated Willowwind with a humorless laugh. "The seal has been there half a million years, or so it is said, ever since the Blackstar placed it there during the Cataclysm." The Toad used the more formal (and less offensive) term for the most ancient and devastating of the Chaoswars.

"This 'Blackstar' is a demon or something?"

Tobimar blinked at that. It was hard to imagine someone could be unaware of something so pervasively terrible and feared as the King of all Hells.

Toron shook his head slowly in disbelief. "A god of demons.

The god of demons, ruler of the Hells, one of the most powerful beings of this or any world, one of the few before which even Elbon Nomicon would not care to stand. The thought that five children could even hope to stand against his lieutenants is laughable; to be able to break the barrier he forged from uncountable sacrifices and treacheries five thousand centuries ago? I *would* laugh. Yet... Konstantin Khoros is never to be laughed at. Somehow he believes it is possible that either you shall be able to destroy the seal, or that in some wise your attempt to do so shall enable another to succeed at that task."

"You mean," Xavier said, "we might just be... well, a distraction to let someone else get the job done?"

"Something of that nature, yes," agreed Willowwind reluctantly. Tobimar kept himself from objecting; while he found it hard to imagine Khoros being *that* coldly calculating, he couldn't say for certain that it wasn't true.

The gray-eyed boy shrugged. "Well... maybe. But he promised me that I'd have a chance to finish... something I started back on Earth, something that brought me here, and I don't think he makes promises he doesn't think he can keep."

Toron frowned, mulling that statement over; two servants came in with a large two-level float-tray filled with food for everyone, then left at a gesture from the King. "I admit that I have always heard that he keeps his promises," Toron conceded. "If he did indeed make a statement that straightforward to you, then he intends that you, at least, would be able to survive whatever this task requires of you." He reached out and took a three-foot section of meatroll, began chewing thoughtfully. "If you split up, how are you supposed to rejoin?"

"Well, Khoros said that we'd each have... dunno what you'd call it, a sort of individual journey or adventure where we'd find... how'd he put it..." Xavier thought a moment and then continued, with a fair imitation of the measured cadence and timbre of Khoros' voice, "I think it was 'answers to the tasks before you, the powers within you, and the doubts that surround you.'" He grinned and shrugged. "From my point of view, I think I need to find out where this seal would *be*. I mean, it's got to be focused somewhere, and if I know where the target is, then that's at least a start." He took some food for himself.

Tobimar realized he was hungry as well, it being past lunchtime, and grabbed an assortment of food from the floating trays. For a few moments all of the people present ate in silence.

Then Toron nodded ponderously. "I have decided. I do not wish to become further entangled in Khoros' machinations, but I also am not so much a fool as to believe I can escape without playing my part. So I, T'Oroning'Oltharamnon ʰGHEK R'arshe Ness, will give all three of you direction, as best I can, while trying to guess what it is that Khoros wished revealed and what he intended to conceal." He looked over to Tobimar, who straightened. "Young Skysand, you were awaiting direction even before this day, and indeed I should have given you that, and my hopes and directives, before now. Perhaps even this event is not fortuitious, but another subtle evidence of Khoros' work, forcing me to allow you to continue rather than keeping you here as a trustworthy and little-known ally."

"Don't apologize, Majesty." Tobimar said. "I wanted to help."

"And you have. And you still shall, I feel certain." He looked back to Xavier Ross. "Son of Zahralandar, you may stay and rest here for a few days, for I can see it has cost you much to maintain that incomprehensible invisibility of yours. But then you have a great journey ahead of you, for I can think of only two beings who would both have the knowledge of where the key weakness of the greatest magical barrier ever wrought might be, and who—unlike most of the gods—are not sealed away from this world and sworn not to interfere. One is the Wanderer, the Unbound and Unborn, wizard, sage, trickster of a thousand faces... if he still exists. But if he does not, only one choice remains: the Archmage, the greatest of magic-wielders to ever live upon this world, the God-Emperor of the Empire of the Mountain, Idinus of Scimitar."

"Terian's *Light*, Majesty!" Tobimar heard himself say, before he could stop.

"I know, Tobimar Silverun. Yet if he and his companions are to have any chance, they must have powers and capabilities beyond easy imagining, and perhaps they can seek the Wanderer's Fortress and pierce its veil of confusion and enchantment, or even, like Khoros himself, be able to reach the highest mountaintop and stand face to face with the Archmage himself."

"Okay, go find some guy who might not be there, and then climb a mountain and talk to the wise man at the top. Works for me." Xavier grinned at Tobimar's half-stunned, half-scandalized expression. "Relax, people, I know it won't be that easy, but if these are the best wizards in this whacko world, then the King's probably right; they're the only ones who'll be able to tell us where to go. And with what *my* sensei taught me..." he was suddenly deadly serious and terribly proud, "well, if I can't get right up to their faces, through anything they've got in the way, then there isn't any one of us that's got a chance in hell. I could walk around your castle for weeks without anyone knowing I was here. You," he nodded towards Tobimar, "were the only one who even sometimes seemed to get an idea I was around... and who trained you?"

Tobimar laughed, and bowed. "You're right. So," he turned to King Toron, "where would you send me?"

"I thought upon the story of your people long and well, in the past few weeks; it was a sad story, but a distant one, and less filled with pain than the reality we must face each day." Toron went to the main viewmirror table and gestured; instead of showing the Star Cell, a great map of Zarathan materialized on the centermost crystal.

"Here, of course, is Mount Scimitar, your second destination, Xavier Ross, the heart of the Empire. Far to the south and west are we, here, in *Fanalam' T' ameris' a' u' Zahr-a-Thana T'ikon*, Zarathanton. Many are the lands, large and small, which have had their being on this great continent and those islands nearby. Yet as I thought upon all of them, one stood out in my mind as perhaps holding your answers—one that has recently had other reasons to be called to my attention." He pointed to the opposite end of the Khalal mountains, to a tiny country outlined in pale green, so far to the west of Mount Scimitar that it lay outside of the reach of the Empire, so far to the north that even conquered Dalthunia lay hundreds of miles below it, beyond the *Kerla*—the Black River. "Evanwyl, once wealthy and famed for its position before the only pass through the Khalal Mountains; now the lone and weakened guard sealing off that pass, for their ally beyond that pass became enemy in the past Chaoswar."

That would fit! Tobimar studied the little country closely; the image suddenly swelled and he could see more detail, rivers and hills and towns and fortresses. "What else? Is there anything else important about Evanwyl?"

Toron seemed to be weighing exactly what to say. "Evanwyl is perhaps the last place where the god Myrionar, whose attributes are Justice and Vengeance, has a stronghold, and from which its Justiciars have—"

"Yes!" he shouted suddenly. "That's it! The oldest stories often began, 'Long ago, when justice and vengeance lay just beyond the mountains...' I always wondered why they started that way!" He felt a burst of joy that washed like cool water from his heart through his veins. "Thank you, Majesty!"

"It is only what I owe you—a small part indeed of what you are owed. But I will add one other final point. You see, here would be your *first* destination, Xavier Ross, for it is said that the Wanderer's Fortress lies within the Broken Hills, near their very center."

Xavier looked, as did Tobimar, and the two suddenly glanced at each other and grinned. "Not so far apart, are they?" Xavier said.

"No, not much at all."

Xavier yawned, showing his exhaustion, but looked back at him seriously. "If you'd be willing to wait a couple days...I'd really appreciate it if we could take part of this trip together. I still haven't seen much of this place, and having someone around who knows the ropes..."

"Consider it done. I'd be glad of the additional company. It *is* a long, long trip."

"Great! Then, I think..." he yawned again. "Yeah. I need to get some rest now."

Toron's chuckle echoed around the room. "Follow me, Xavier Ross; I shall see to your having a room where you need not spend the night invisible." The two left, Xavier's feet obviously dragging slightly.

Tobimar picked up Poplock and held the little Toad up before him. "So, Poplock—you want to go on a long trip north?"

The Toad bounced on his hand. "I suppose I'd better." He chewed on one of the large spiky beetles that seemed to be a favorite, then gave an exaggerated expression of resignation. "*Someone* has to keep you two out of trouble."

31

A faint vibration and movement beneath her boot was the only warning Kyri had as the tiny ledge she'd thought a secure foothold crumbled. Pebbles and gravel chattered down the gray cliff-face, bouncing in miniature foreshadowing of what would happen if her handholds failed as well. Hanging desperately on, she found her gaze drawn involuntarily down along with the debris, forbidding basalt cliffs below her vanishing into swirling clouds that concealed another three thousand feet of terrible steep stone slopes.

Above her, another layer of cloud, a few hundred feet above, streamed by like an insubstantial river, dark and threatening, the motion giving Kyri momentary vertigo. She closed her eyes, took a breath, looked slightly down. Left and right. Up and down, but only short distances. *There. That's another foothold. I can make it.*

Her right hand loosened its grip the tiniest bit, then flicked over to another slight knob of rock. Her dangling foot moved a few inches closer. She slid her foot over, closer, stretching...

Her toe touched the ledge. She put more pressure on it; *Myrionar, please, no more repeats of that scare.*

This time the stone held. She sidled over, inches at a time, upward and sideways towards the point where the mountain peaks began to converge. *There's a flat spot there, a real ledge, something I might even be able to lie down on.*

Finally she had one hand on real flat stone. The other. Then she was up and over the side.

Chromaias and Terian, that was hard. Her hands and arms

and shoulders, her back—*truth, my whole body!*—ached. Lifting her own weight wasn't all that hard. Once. Twice. Even ten times. She'd *carried* those stonesculpt hangings herself, and they weighed more than twice what she did. But this was something of a completely different scale. Lythos had forced her and Rion to climb trees, hills, small cliffs during their training, but nothing like this.

I must be almost a mile up...and I've got a long way to go.

The clouds had descended as she had climbed, and now they dropped the last hundred feet and she was enveloped in clinging, chill grayness. Drizzle, rain, and then a rumble of thunder, and suddenly the winds rose to a howl.

Myrionar's BALANCE! She fought to find a safe position on the ledge, pushing herself back against the cliff face on the narrow stone shelf—barely three feet wide—as the storm lashed the mountain with a random, drunken gale that nearly lifted her from the ground, tore at her clothing from every side. *By the Four, even below!*

Kyri focused, remembering the training and discipline Lythos had instilled into her, and the legends of the Justiciars. *I've been given Myrionar's blessing. If I can only find my own center, I can pray for balance about me.*

The driven rain was now mingled with sleet, something Kyri had never encountered before; truth be told, she had hardly even imagined such cold as this. She'd heard of places where water froze naturally, but she'd never *been* to one before. *Focus! Only the calm of balance can save me!* She was aware that water was starting to stream down the cliff face; in a few minutes—or less—the flow might be enough to unseat her, wash her down to a bone-shattering death as she tumbled down a mile of jagged stone slopes.

But that thought was directly counter to the calmness she needed. Despite the increasing stream of icy water, she took a deep breath, concentrated, tried to blot out the storm, the sleet, the wind, everything, and remember the calmness of home, of herself and Rion sitting side by side...breathing...breathing...

For a moment it *felt* like Rion was next to her, and that almost made her lose the chance; but at the same time it added a warmth she desperately needed. She balanced for that instant between fear and peace, between warmth of heart and chill of air, between terror of failure and determination to survive. And in that moment she was able to shape her desire to a prayer. *Myrionar, please, as you are balance in all things, bring balance to this point, a place of calm and peace and safety.*

The winds faded to a distant howl; the water, which had become a small waterfall pushing against her, began to diminish. She opened her eyes, hardly able to believe her prayer had been granted, even though Myrionar had called her a Justiciar.

But there was no denying the faint-shimmering barrier that now surrounded her, visible by the futile battering rain and sleet, by the rippling of the thundering freshet that divided around her, leaving the water draining slowly away from her ledge. The air, too, was warmer, still and comforting. She leaned back, smiling in sheer relief. *Thank you, Myrionar! Thank you!*

There was no reply, but she needed none. Perhaps It would never speak to her directly again, but by answering such prayers in the time and place they were needed, Myrionar was saying all that needed to be said.

In relief, with the howling wind now a more distant moan, Kyri closed her eyes and took a deep breath. Then another. Somewhere between the second and the third, she fell asleep.

Morning sun blazing into her eyes awakened her. *By the Balance, I've slept the whole night!*

Every muscle in her body screamed at her as soon as she attempted to move. *Stiff! Move slowly!* She knew that if she wasn't careful, the stiffness could lead to a very fatal misstep. So she focused on carefully stretching and loosening her limbs and back, then getting out some of the pressed fruit and dried meat and eating that for breakfast. *And I was too busy staying alive last night to remember to refill my water. Still probably have enough, but how ironic that I almost got killed by too much water last night.*

Finally she was ready to move on. *The place where the peaks divide.* She was nearly to the great, deep seam where both mountains met; that would be somewhat easier to climb, but she couldn't see what lay nearer the top.

No point wondering. Let's get moving.

She became aware, some hours later, that even breathing was harder. *That's right... air becomes thinner, that's what Father said. I'll be able to breathe... but I'll have to take things slower.*

The clouds fully enveloped this part of the mountains, making everything more than a few dozen yards away fade to indistinct gray. Kyri squinted. Both mountains seemed to be looming more steeply above her. She took a few more breaths and advanced upward. *One step at a time. One hand up, one foot up. Just keep going.*

The V-shaped seam she'd been following abruptly darkened above, just as it seemed the mountains were closing in. A few more feet and she could see what lay beyond: the seam between the mountains became a chimney-like tunnel continuing upward. *At least I'll be out of the wind ... but a storm like last night's would turn this into nothing but a giant drain.*

But there wasn't any alternative. The cliffs rose up completely sheer around her. *Into darkness, I bring light. Light reveals truth. Truth and Justice, Myrionar.*

Light shimmered just above her, a gentle light that revealed without dazzling. She could see into the chimney, rough rocks with a coating of drying mud that would make them fatally slick if she was not careful. *So I'll be careful.*

Some way inside it wasn't so bad. Wind rose up through the chimney-tunnel, drying the stones, which were—mostly—solid enough to climb on. Having learned her lesson earlier, Kyri did not come near to falling again. How long that climb through darkness lasted, though, she could not say. Finally she looked up and saw a pale circle of light silhouetted against the dark stone. With a burst of energy she clambered up the final twenty feet and emerged at one side of a small plateau, a few hundred yards across, with the twin peaks looming above. There were no structures visible, and almost no sign of life ... but then she spotted the smoke, issuing from somewhere amidst a tumble of rocks near the midpoint of the plateau. Cautiously, on slightly wobbly legs, she approached. As she got nearer, she could see a large tunnel at the edge of the rocky pile, the smoke she had seen apparently coming from some hole farther back. The tunnel was over ten feet high and slanted sharply down into the heart of the mountains.

"Halt, seeker, and speak your name and purpose."

The voice echoed across the plateau and drummed in the mountains, deep as the ocean, powerful as thunder. Kyri was brought up short by the sheer force of that voice. She took another deep breath, both out of habit and to clear her head, and answered. "I am Kyri Victoria Vantage, and I seek the Spiritsmith."

A rumble of laughter like an approaching avalanche. "Of course you seek the Spiritsmith," the unseen creature said, moderating its voice so it was no longer deafening, merely deep and rumbling, resonant from within the earth, and—somehow—almost familiar. "None come here but that they seek me; and so I say again, speak to me your *purpose.*"

So be it. "I seek armor that none but you can forge, a sword the like of which no other would even attempt, for only you have ever done so. I come to you to ask that you make for me the armor of a Justiciar of Myrionar."

The great voice was silent, but now she heard movement, a scraping and a stirring below. "The Raiment of a Justiciar?" it said finally, slowly. "Long ago was I charged with that task, by the God Itself, and I completed that work, and it is done. Who are you to ask me to take up again the work of the gods?"

"The Justiciars who wear that which you forged have turned, have become false; I alone remain, I who have no armor have been chosen to be the last and only Justiciar of Myrionar." Though she had thought these words many times, speaking them to this unknown being brought the truth back full force, and her voice trembled and nearly broke. "I must drive back the falsehoods with the strength of a Justiciar, with the power of truth, that there be justice for the betrayed and vengeance against the betrayers. Will you help me? You *are* the Spiritsmith, are you not?"

"Help you?" The movement was louder now, something walking with ponderous steps, a massive, vague shadow becoming visible. "If you can prove yourself I shall help you, little would-be Justiciar, yes, for it is not to be tolerated that the Armor that I forged, the Condor and the Shrike, the Thornfalcon and the Silver Eagle, Mist Owl and Bolthawk, the swift Skyharrier, be worn in defiance of their purpose and true nature. It is an insult never to be borne. For indeed I am T'anavhioroniath'Tela'k'Helianatalacalabal, the Spiritsmith, and my work is my soul, and the souls of its wielders, and the steel of my soul is not to be sullied by treachery."

As the Spiritsmith spoke, he emerged fully into view, and even before then Kyri realized with awe and dismay what sort of a being the Spiritsmith must be, for that impossible *name* left no doubt: towering nearly nine feet from scale-crested head to taloned feet, eyes glinting with power and incalculable age, lashing behind him a massive armored tail, the Spiritsmith was an Ancient Sauran, larger than Toron, with an aura of ancient wisdom and strength almost beyond belief.

The Spiritsmith brandished a sword of his own, a blade nearly as wide as Kyri's body and longer still, and with a fearsome flourish pointed it directly at her. "And so now you will prove with your blade and your body that you are worthy of the name of Justiciar... or never will you leave this mountain alive."

32

Kyri stood openmouthed, unable for a moment to accept this. To fight one of the Children of the Dragons was something almost unthinkable; to duel one so ancient that he had forged the armor that was eternal legend in Evanwyl?

But at the same time she felt her spirit rising, even to this impossible challenge. *I would face a power that could undo Myrionar Itself. I go to throw lies in the faces of false Justiciars who killed my brother, took from us our mother and father in our own home. It is little enough that the Spiritsmith asks, that I prove to him that I am what I claim to be, that I have the strength and the will and the power of a Justiciar.*

That I am a Vantage, child of my mother and my father, descended of those who have stood sentry on Rivendream Pass since the last Chaoswar.

She reached back and drew her sword, the two-handed blade looking slender yet sharp as a rapier before the immense weapon of the Spiritsmith. "So I will, then. For I shall leave this mountain alive, armed and arrayed as a Justiciar of Myrionar. This I have sworn to the Balanced Sword, to Terian of the Infinite, to Chromaias and the Four." Despite the pounding in her heart, she extended her arm and lowered the blade to point at the Spiritsmith, all five feet of the sword as rigid as her purpose. "So I have sworn to the memory of my mother and my father, to the spirit of my brother, and to those who yet live. Come."

The fanged mouth smiled, and he came on, a rush of scales

and muscle and claws preceded by a sword that loomed like a mountain. *Fast—faster than I thought!* She dove to the side, straining every muscle. The impact of the monstrous sword resounded through the ground like a hammerblow, and she realized that the Spiritsmith's words had contained not a bit of exaggeration. If she did not meet whatever standards he had set, he would kill her without hesitation.

That giant blade was up, out of the gouge in the stone already, arcing over and down again. *Roll!* One cut on one side, one on the other, both nearly cutting her in half, one striking the armored cloth she wore so hard that even the deflected blow felt like a mace. She swung from the ground, a flat, swift swing for the Sauran's ankle, forcing the creature to retreat with an astonishing leap backwards. She had just enough time to roll to her feet before the Spiritsmith lunged back to the attack.

This time she did not underestimate his speed. Despite his mass—which might be close to a ton—the Spiritsmith moved like someone her own size. But he had the strength of Dragons and thousands of years of experience. She whirled her blade as fast as possible, deflecting blows like falling oaks by the narrowest margin. *I have to find a tactic . . . something . . . anything!*

She focused on the giant sword. *I don't care how strong he is, that weapon's larger compared to him than mine is to me. It has to slow him somehow.*

It was horrifically difficult to watch the movements of the weapon dispassionately, analytically, while its mighty wielder was using it to rain down blows on her that could shatter bones and break limbs with a glancing blow. Her own blade was showing its quality by the fact that it was bending, rather than breaking, under the punishment . . . but that couldn't continue forever.

There!

After every heavy, long swing, there was just the tiniest fractional hesitation before the great sword finished reversing its direction.

For a moment she stood in a different place, facing Rion, on a day when both of them were praised . . .

And her sword was up and moving, just as the Spiritsmith began another swing, down like an avalanche, but her blade had switched sides, was *behind* the gigantic sword of the Spiritsmith, pressing on, matching the creature's own swing and amplifying it, shifting even as the Spiritsmith realized what she was doing, increasing the speed and twist of rotation, faster, all her strength behind it, and suddenly he gave a low *grunt* of pain and the titanic weapon was arcing up, somersaulting through the air, ten, fifteen, nearly twenty feet high and much farther away, to clatter away and over the cliff edge.

Just as Rion's had, years before, so did her blade finish its sparkling arc directly at her opponent's throat. "Yield."

The black eyes, with a faint glow behind them, narrowed, and the fanged mouth smiled. With the speed of a striking serpent, the Spiritsmith's hand closed on her razor-sharp sword, heedless of the steel biting deep into scales and muscle, and *ripped* the sword from her hands as though taking a riding crop from a child. "One little trick will not suffice against your enemies, Kyri Vantage!"

To her dismay, she saw the cuts closing even as she backed away, trying to devise some way of fighting this monster now that she was unarmed. *I am here to prove myself; Myrionar has nothing to prove save that It has selected me.* And that could be after the battle, by healing her wounds. She had to assume she was on her own here; praying for Myrionar's assistance against the Spiritsmith would almost certainly avail her nothing.

Sizing up the creature as the Spiritsmith advanced with a measured, unhurried stride, she decided she really wasn't any worse off than before. *That sword gave him incredible reach; he's still got arms slightly longer than mine, but not all that much.*

She ducked and jabbed. The impact stung her knuckles, even through her gloves, and she winced; the Spiritsmith, on the other hand, seemed almost not to feel it, and his return strike nearly gutted her. She rolled to the side, trying to get behind him—

For a moment she could not remember where she was or what she was doing; her head, her whole body, ached, but there was a terrible sense of urgency... she rolled away and up by instinct as something pounded its way towards her, evading... *the Spiritsmith, yes, that's it... I was trying to get away...*

The creature's armored tail had nearly killed her. *He is not human, or anything like it. He is child of Dragons, and nearer them than anything I have ever fought. One more mistake like that and I'm dead, as he's promised.*

Obviously the Spiritsmith was not fighting her to his full capabilities; a being so old yet timeless who had practiced with weapons for longer than her country had existed would surely be able to defeat her in moments if it took her seriously. No, he was simply waiting to see if she could reach some minimum standard of capability—of skill, of strength, of training, of sheer unbending will, perhaps. But if she failed to meet that standard, she'd die.

All I have left is what my Sho-ka-taida taught me. She focused on Lythos' teachings, of sharpening her perceptions, increasing speed and strength through the Living Will, what he sometimes called the Ninth Wind, letting the power of the spirit do that which the body could not. She could see, now, the pattern of movement, the double step forward and then one sideways, trying to drive her in a particular direction. She dove and rolled again, immediately doing a handspring that took her over the thrashing tail and to the side, her booted foot lashing out and cracking with precision against the side of the knee joint.

A real roar of pain accompanied that blow, and she tumbled away, trying to shake off a frightening dizziness. *That... tail strike I took. Hit my head. Might have real damage. No time now!*

As she came to her feet again, she blinked, trying to will away a dark fogginess in her sight. The Spiritsmith was coming for her again, this time with a limp—though the limp was already improving. *Anything I do has to at least incapacitate him long enough for a convincing possibility of something killing him.*

She knew better than to try the same maneuver again, but her options were limited. One of the armor-scaled fists caught her on a backhand, and she staggered back, feeling more dizziness assailing her, tasting blood in her mouth as she fell against part of the heap of boulders and rubble near the center of the plateau.

That gave her a minor inspiration, and she suddenly turned, grasped a boulder the size of her head, and *hurled* it at the advancing Sauran.

The creature barely blocked it, but failed to block the second rock which had followed a split-second later. The Spiritsmith was momentarily stunned, and Kyri battered him with a short shower of boulders, smashing the Spiritsmith's head, legs, and chest with granite and basalt missiles thrown by the full strength of a Vantage.

But even *that* wasn't enough; the draconic monster hunkered down, taking a couple more blows, and *charged*.

She tried to dodge, but her choice to try to beat him to death

with stones had backfired; she had in effect built herself a miniature dead-end alley with no safe dodging directions.

Immense arms caught her up and began to squeeze. She had
one arm free, and tried to reach the Spiritsmith's face; but he
was just a bit too large, able to tilt his head enough to deny her
the ability to reach the eyes—the only clearly vulnerable spot.

Her ribs creaked, even as she struggled desperately, and she
realized this was the end of the battle. *If I have nothing left...
it ends here.*

But there *was* something. The Living Will. The Dragon's Claw,
the Claw of Stone.

Her vision began to fog with red, but she called up the discipline once more. "Focus your strength into the hand," she heard
Lythos saying in that cool, dispassionate voice. "Let it flow from
heart to hand, tensing muscles here, arching there, building like
a bowstring being drawn back. Feel your spirit concentrating,
rising like a wave, cresting..."

An agonizing pain as a rib cracked, and yet it seemed so distant. Only Lythos' voice was clear. "Cresting higher, the bowstring
drawn, the tension of your hand hard as iron, hard as granite,
hard as mountains, and now moving, an avalanche released as
an arrow! Strike!"

Her hand sledgehammered into the Ancient Sauran's throat,
just where it was exposed by the creature pulling back its head
to shield the eyes. The shock of impact resounded through the
Spiritsmith's entire body, and she felt bone and cartilage snap
and crumple.

The great creature dropped her instantly, hands going to its
throat, gagging, going for its knees. Black and red spots danced
before her vision, and the whole plateau seemed to be tilting, but
she saw her sword, lunged, grabbed it up, swung the glittering
blade high. "And is there mercy, or only death, Spiritsmith?"

She began the downward swing, aborting it as the Spiritsmith
threw up a scaly hand in a clear gesture of surrender. She let
the blade drop from her hand and found herself sagging to
the ground, head whirling and a smell of iron that tasted like
blood. "If that's...not enough...I'll forge the Balance-Damned
armor...myself."

The creature coughed, managed a pain-wracked chuckle, fell
back in a coughing fit; its regenerative powers were rebuilding the

throat, but it was far from instantaneous. She heard its breathing slowing, but it was as from a great distance; it seemed as though she viewed everything through water.

The Spiritsmith coughed once more, and then spoke. "That will do well enough, little Justiciar," it rasped, and then the voice smoothed out, regaining its old resonance. "You have the spirit, the strength, the will, and—though still far from realized—the potential for greatness. All I need see now is proof of your blessing. Myrionar, show to me that this is your chosen emissary, that she is, in truth, the last and only true Justiciar of Justice and Vengeance, and then shall I forge for her as I forged for you long ago."

There was a moment's pause, and then the golden light shone out, the same awe-inspiring light she had seen first with tears streaming down her face in the Forest Sea. The light touched her and lifted her up, wiping away pain and confusion and exhaustion, sharpening the senses, and she found herself standing straight and unbowed before the Spiritsmith, as though the battle had never happened—as though, indeed, she had not climbed a mountain to reach here, but merely stepped from Aunt Victoria's receiving room to the outer hall to greet this strange visitor.

As the light faded, the Spiritsmith bowed low before her, baring twin daggers at his sides, and pivoted in the full Armed Bow. "And so you *are* the final Justiciar, Kyri Victoria Vantage, and I, the Spiritsmith, shall forge for you that armor and those weapons which only the chosen of the Gods may wield, as I have done since first the Dragon King and the Sixteen placed the tools and fire in my hands."

She stared at him, for a moment unable to believe that she had triumphed, even though it was something so necessary for all she hoped to do.

"But nothing can I forge unless you give to me one more thing, Kyri Vantage," the ageless draconic smith continued. "To become a Justiciar is to become a symbol; a symbol requires its own name. What shall be your name, your symbol, which will go before you, bringing hope of justice to the helpless, striking fear of vengeance into the guilty?"

She had touched upon those thoughts many times, yet—until now—she hadn't dared to dwell on that question. It seemed to presume too much.

She could not use the old names; the old names, like their armor, were tainted, must be cleansed first before any could bear them again. And she would not use them anyway, for she needed to stand apart and beyond them, not be confused for one of them. Yet there was the basic essence of their names to preserve, swift wings of justice, claws of vengeance...

What was it he had just said?... *and so you* are *the final Justiciar*...

"No," she said. "I am the *first* Justiciar." It was suddenly clear to her, as though she had known it all through her journey, had known it since she was a child. "The old Justiciars ended for me when they destroyed my family, sending my home up in flames, though I knew it not then.

"In those flames I died, and they died. And now... now they must be reborn, through me." She had gripped her sword again, without even being aware of it, and raised it towards the deep-indigo sky, where the first faint sparks of stars, and where the Balanced Sword, glinted back at her.

"Through me, in the golden fire of the heavens, in Myrionar's flames of Justice and Vengeance, they must be reborn, and for that there is no name—there *can* be no name—other than the legend of death and rebirth, the red-gold fire of the soul, the wings that heal and destroy, no name other than *Phoenix*."

The Spiritsmith bowed even lower, the great head scraping the stone, and above she thought—for just an instant—the stars of the Balanced Sword blazed with red-gold fire.

33

"We cannot transport you terribly far," Toron said apologetically, "but I believe we can at least send you to the lakeside area of the East Twin."

Poplock glanced at Tobimar, whose grin reflected his own feelings. "Oh, don't apologize for *that*, Majesty," Poplock said. "That's at least a few hundred miles we won't have to hop on our own."

Xavier snickered. "Yeah, I can just see me and Tobimar hopping that far. Not."

He looked over at the older woman who was checking various symbols around the circle carven atop the small tower. "So, we just stand in this circle and then *poof*, we'll be at this lake?"

Wyneth Aurin looked at Xavier with a raised eyebrow, tucking a strand of brown hair back behind her ear. "Yes, that is the essence of it. You seem surprised."

"Well...I guess I *shouldn't* be, with everything else I've seen here. But why can't you just zap us over to the Broken Hills or this Evanwyl in one shot?"

"If we knew the answer to that question, we might well be able to solve the problem," Toron answered, while Wyneth went back to her preparations. "Once it *was* possible to go such distances. Since Dalthunia was conquered, there has been increasing interference or diversion of the various means of fast travel."

"So someone or something in Dalthunia is messing it up for everyone?"

"That was, indeed, the initial assumption; however, some of the few communications we have received from Dalthunia indicate that they are just as frustrated by this turn of events as we are, and in fact originally believed it was some attempt by either the Dragon King or the Archmage to cripple *their* capabilities."

Poplock rocked pensively. "So that means either the timing's a coincidence, or whatever force is doing that is hidden inside Dalthunia and hasn't told the new owners."

"Yes."

Wyneth straightened. "All preparations are complete. Please stand in the center."

Tobimar and Xavier walked to the center; as he was sitting on Tobimar's shoulder, Poplock was saved the effort of doing so.

"Farewell, and may your quests be successful, Xavier Ross, Tobimar Silverun, Poplock Duckweed," Toron said with a bow.

"Thank you, Toron. And good luck to you too," Tobimar said; Xavier echoed him, as did Poplock.

Toron nodded, and Poplock saw Wyneth reach her hand over one of the symbols—

Before them lay a vast expanse of pure blue water, surface ruffled by waves, with huge wooden piers extending a seemingly impossible distance; Poplock guessed it was half a mile from the shore to the end of the East Pier.

"Holy sh...er, crap," Xavier said, staring. "It *worked*."

While a few of the nearer people had glanced at them in mild surprise, their arrival hadn't apparently startled anyone, despite the crowds on the waterfront this morning. Looking down, Poplock could see the reason; they had been transported to a smaller pentacle which was roped off from the main dock, and he could see a sign reserving this for quick transport from the Castle.

Tobimar didn't look exactly *surprised*, and neither was Poplock, but the instant transformation of the world around them *was* impressive. "Worked perfectly. We've saved like a couple weeks of walking right there!"

A Malasand—an amphibious semi-humanoid person, common in waterside towns—jogged up to them as they exited the pentagram. He gave a quick turn-salute, and Poplock noticed that he wore a uniform with the matching-pier symbol of the guardsmen of the Lake Twins. "Welcome to East Twin, sirs," he said. "Is there...new news from the Castle?"

Poplock turned around and reached into the top side pocket

of Tobimar's pack. "Here," he said, dragging out a heavy, thick green envelope with tiny symbols written along the edges. "The King gave this to us—you should take it to the Lord of the Eastern Lake, he said."

"Thank you." The guard took the envelope and put it in a small case at his side that had a lock on it. "Are you returning?"

"No, we've got a long trip ahead of us," Xavier said, still staring at the waves and the almost countless ships and boats of every size.

The Malasand saluted again and trotted off farther inland—presumably, Poplock guessed, to wherever the Lord was.

"Okay," Xavier said, "I guess we have to cross here, right?"

"Right," Poplock said. "Across to the West Twin, then we've got a lot of walking on the Great Roads, all the way to Dalthunia."

"Is this really a *lake*?" Xavier asked after a few moments as they walked up the huge pier. "I mean, this smells almost oceany, and those waves aren't small."

"The largest lake I know of on the continent, although there are rumors of an even larger one to the far north, somewhere very far west of Skysand," Tobimar answered, as he led them to a point on the dock where several people were waiting in a line.

"Skysand's where you're from, right?" At Tobimar's nod, Xavier looked over to Poplock. "What about you?"

"My home?" He tried to keep from looking too sad. "It was called Pondsparkle. You heard about the attacks, must have seen—"

"Yeah. Didn't know your hometown was in the middle of that, though. I'm sorry."

"We'll go back and fix things up one day," Poplock said with certainty, gripping Tobimar's shoulder a bit tighter as the Prince paid for two full-size and one small fare on *Circle*, a large lake ferry. "Blackwart told us that was our special place, and he won't let us lose it forever."

He saw Xavier's mouth twitch, restraining a familiar smile. "Blackwart? Who's that, one of the kings or something?"

He's from a completely different world, Poplock reminded himself, warding off his usual annoyance at the ignorance of the bigger people. "Um, no, he's our god. God and patron of the Toads and anyone else who wants to follow him. A lot of elementalists, Forestals, those kinds of people follow him. And Shargamor and Eonae, of course." They made their way up *Circle*'s long deck and stood near the prow.

Xavier looked up. "They're taking in the sails—I guess they'll use magic to go against the wind?"

"Most ships on Heart of Water have magic to help do that, yes, and the regular ferries would all have to if they want to have anything like a schedule," Tobimar said.

"So, um," Xavier went on, looking oddly... embarrassed? Confused? Poplock couldn't quite figure it out... "Do you... I mean, what's your god, Tobimar?"

"The Skysands have followed Terian, the Light in the Darkness, for as long as we've been in Skysand, maybe before," Tobimar said proudly. "What about you?"

"Um," and now the nervous look was strong enough for Poplock to recognize it. *It's that look humans get when talking about something that they think is really delicate or maybe crazy.* "Well, I don't have one. I don't believe in gods."

For a moment Poplock couldn't quite wring *meaning* out of the words. The words themselves were familiar, but put together... "What do you *mean* you don't believe in gods? That's... that's like saying you don't believe in this boat we're standing on!" He could see Tobimar was equally dumbfounded.

Xavier, meanwhile, was obviously trying to look apologetic in the face of something he couldn't quite accept. "Look, Pop, Toby, I can *see* this deck, but I've never seen a god, or ever seen them *do* anything."

"*Never?*" Poplock was astounded. "Don't you have temples and holy emissaries in your world?"

"Well, sure, but all they do is *talk*, you know."

Tobimar had finally found his voice. "I... begin to realize that we have not yet fully understood just how very different your world is from ours, Xavier. Let me clarify, just to be sure: in your world, your priests do not heal the wounded and the sick, or seek out the truth for the rulers, or use the powers of the gods to hold back and destroy evil?"

"No, not really," Xavier said, his tone that of a man picking his way through a nest of snares. "I mean... well, there's some that *claim* to do a lot of that, but I've never seen it and there's never been any good evidence. The best stories of that come from a long time ago when there wasn't much idea of *proving* anything." A pause. "So... yours do?"

The discussion of the different worlds continued as *Circle* crossed the huge lake Heart of Water, all the way through dinner in the West Gate Inn, and resumed the next morning as they set out on the long walking part of their journey.

Poplock found himself alternately pitying the people of Earth, envying them, and being completely baffled by them. The feelings were obviously mirrored by Xavier's reactions to Zarathan.

"So everything in your world seems to run on these 'electronics' you say aren't magic, but certainly *sound* like magic to me," Tobimar was saying the next day, as the sun was dropping away before them and the shadows were starting to lengthen. "I wish I could see some of this. We can show you magic, and the gods will reveal themselves to you sooner or later, but your world remains on the other side of the Great Seal . . . unless by some chance your mission succeeds."

Xavier looked thoughtful. "You know, I *could* show you something." He brought out a strange object, like a stretched oval, mostly black with silver highlights. A large rectangular area in the center was black, shiny, but without feature; on each end were some raised areas with various symbols on them. "This is my LTP—LumiTainment Portable. It's a videogame handheld console."

The last words might as well have been in Ancient Sauran for all the meaning they carried. "What does *that* mean?"

"It means I can play games on this thing without having to be at home. Games made for it, that is."

Tobimar took the LTP gently, turned it over, passed his right hand over it with a look of concentration, then let Poplock look at it. Poplock studied it for a few moments and did the usual mumbled scans. There wasn't a sign of magic on it anywhere. "Well, then, can you show us? As far as I can tell, it's a really funny-looking and not very good mirror, and that's it."

The young man from Zaralandar hesitated. "Well . . . I guess so. I just hate to use up the last of the batteries. But I suppose this is as good a time as any." He took the LTP back and touched a barely noticeable stud on one side. To Poplock's startlement, light suddenly glowed from the formerly black central region, and a chime of music echoed out. More music—sounding like an orchestra heard from a distance—streamed from the LTP and brilliant scenes of moving images appeared, showing landscapes of fantastic design and people performing momentary feats of combat and magic of surprising skill and versatility.

Poplock bounced over to Xavier's shoulder and down, mumbling the scans again. Still there was no sign of magic of any type. *And it's active now, so even things like gemcalling or hidden symbols would be sensed.* "It really *isn't* magic!"

"Told you."

"This is...a game?" Tobimar said, looking at it more closely.

"Yeah—this is Chrono Victory, one of my favorites so far—I haven't finished it yet. I could start a new game and show you how it works when we camp."

"That would be...very interesting, I think," Tobimar said.

Poplock bounced his agreement. "I'm *really* fascinated by this. I know, to you our magic and things must be really exciting, but this is something new to us!"

Xavier laughed. "Sure, I understand."

A few hours later they set up camp, using the self-anchoring tents Tobimar had picked out with Poplock's help before they left Zarathanton. The Skysand prince brought out some of the packed meals Toron had given them. "We'll have to either buy food along the way, or do some hunting and picking," he said, "but no reason we can't relax tonight."

"Yeah, no big rush."

Once the dinner was finished, Xavier brought out the LTP. "Here we go. I'll start it running and give us a new game start. It's got a tutorial—a teaching sequence, you know?—at the beginning, but I'll bet it makes all kinds of assumptions about what you know." He spent a few minutes telling them about what the raised areas on the sides did; they controlled the performance of various actions in the moving world of the game, something that Poplock thought was very ingenious. *I wonder...I could see something like this being a lot of fun. Have to see if there's some easy way to do this with the right magic. Alchemy or symbolism, maybe with some illusion-shapers, maybe?*

The game finished a pretty introduction sequence and they began selecting aspects of a character to play. Xavier glanced down. "Well, we've got started and to the first save point. But I don't know how long it'll run." He pointed to something blinking red in a corner of the LTP. "Batteries are almost dead."

"There's something *alive* in there?" Poplock backed away from the LTP.

"What? No, no!" Xavier laughed. "That's just an expression, you know, like when you're finished with a discussion or something and you say the topic's dead?" He pushed the little stud on the side and the LTP shimmered and went dark again; the boy then flipped the LTP over and opened a hidden compartment underneath, removing a flat, rectangular silvery object with writing on it. "That's a battery. It holds electricity, stores it, you know, and then gives it to the LTP when it's on."

"And it's almost out of electricity?" Any elementalist worth *anything* knew about electricity—lightning, the little sparks from rubbing some things together, stuff like that—but this was something new, something that used electricity to work.

"Yeah. My guess is there's maybe twenty, thirty minutes left of play before it goes dark."

Poplock turned the little object over, flicked his tongue over various points. *Ooch. That* sour *taste. Definitely a little electricity across those areas.*

"Hey!" Xavier said with concern. "Don't, like, bite it or anything. It's the only battery I have."

The Toad looked thoughtfully down. "I might be able to make it work better."

"What?" The boy stared at him. "Are you serious? You don't even know how it's *built*. Honestly, I don't either."

"Well . . . would it really hurt to try? You said it will last only a short time more."

Xavier looked reluctant, then shrugged. "I . . . guess not. Just be careful, I've heard doing the wrong thing with batteries can make them blow up. And I know that you have to have the right, um, voltages or whatever to run a gadget like this."

With permission given, Poplock focused on the battery-thing. *Okay, it's giving enough power to operate that LTP now. So if I can keep* that *taste about the same, maybe just a* little *more intense, but find a way to keep a little power flowing in . . .*

He took the battery and pushed it into place. *Spring-loaded clips. That leaves a little space here and here.*

"Hey, Tobimar. You got any Zeus' Rains in your 'reserves' over there?"

"I think I've got a few . . . not very big, though."

"I don't need big ones."

Tobimar opened up the small bag, rummaged around in it as Xavier watched. "Um . . . yeah, there's a couple . . . three. That's it, though."

Two of them were too big, but the third was a deep blue-black oval that was small enough to fit on one side without crowding.

Now, let's see. This is sort of like that trap I ran across back in the mazakh *stronghold. I want to channel the energy out of the Rain into this battery-thingie, and just enough to keep the taste the same—not sharper, not sweeter.*

He took out his notebook and riffled to the section with runes and symbols. A lot of them were still way out of his comfort zone, but just a simple guide-and-drop channel... "Hey, do you just get new batteries when they run out?"

"No, you recharge them."

There were several shiny gold-colored parts of the battery. "Can you tell me if these are the parts that 'recharge,' or the parts that give the power out?"

"I don't think..." Xavier blinked, then grinned. "Maybe I can!" He dug around in his backpack and came up with a small battered printed booklet with a picture of the LTP on it. "Here, I still have the manual, never can bring myself to throw them away...um..."

After a few moments of looking at pictures in the manual and arguing, they were able to conclude that two of the "contacts," as the book called them, were for recharging the battery.

"Okay, here goes." He first fit the battery back in carefully and then pulled it back out after marking the right spot. On that spot he put the Zeus' Rain, sticking it fast with a drop of hawkspinner's glue. Then he took out a thin engraving stylus and drew two lines, one from each end of the Zeus' Rain and each going to one of the two contacts in question.

Elemental magic...here, this page. He focused as old Watersparker had taught him and began to channel his own strength into the symbols, copying each precisely along the lines graven on the battery. It took a while, during which Xavier and Tobimar started talking about their fighting styles. *That'd be interesting, but not time to get distracted...There!*

He felt a tingle along his fingers which were still touching the Zeus' Rain, and he was sure he could see a very faint blue-violet glow.

"Hey," he said, as the two were both reaching for their scabbards. "Instead of comparing your swords, let's see if this worked."

This time Xavier *and* Tobimar looked at him suspiciously. "I don't think you chose those words by accident," Xavier said.

Poplock grinned inside, but just blinked innocently. "I don't know what you mean by *that*. But here, put your battery back in."

The gray-eyed boy studied the modifications for a moment, shrugged, and put it back in. "Doesn't look like you did anything that would damage it, anyway. Well, here goes nothing."

The screen lit back up, and Xavier's jaw dropped slightly. "Damn! Look at that!" The little corner symbol was now a full green. "Thanks, Poplock! That's great! I mean...maybe I won't get lots of chances to play it, but it's like a kind of, you know, comfort reminder from home."

Poplock felt a warm swell of pride and some mingled surprise. *It worked!* "I guess practice pays off. I'm not much of a mage... not really a mage at all, mostly more into sneaking *past* mages, and sometimes you have to know how they work to get away with that."

"You sound like a couple other people I know, which means I bet you can do more than you admit. But thanks again." He handed the device over to the Skysand prince. "So here you go, Tobimar!"

Several hours later Poplock kicked the little device almost out of Tobimar's hands. "Time for you to go to sleep, Tobimar."

"But I'm almost through this challenge! Just another few minutes and I'm sure I'll figure it—"

Poplock just *looked* at him, and Tobimar sighed and shut the strange device off. The little Toad then dragged it over to Xavier, who was already asleep.

Maybe fixing that "battery" thing wasn't the best idea I've had.

34

"Ha," said Xavier, looking at Tobimar. "Got sucked in, didn't you?"

The expression wasn't hard to figure out, and neither was the knowing grin. Tobimar rolled his eyes and nodded. "Yes. I suppose that's not uncommon?"

"Depends on the person, but no. Especially if it's new and exciting. First time I played, my mom came into my room and I wondered what she was doing up so late... and that's when I looked up and saw that the sun was *rising* and I had to get ready for school. Didn't learn much *that* day." He started packing up his sleeping roll. "So where'd you get to?"

"Trying to cross the river."

"Oh, that one stopped me *dead* for a while."

As they prepared a quick breakfast, Poplock spoke up. "Hey, Xavier, I was wondering—have you known the rest of your group a long time?"

"Long time? Ha. No, Khoros yanked us all together and then dumped us in your world with some old mysterious wizard handwavy advice maybe six weeks before we got grabbed by the city on suspicion of regicide."

That makes sense. "I rather thought so," Tobimar said aloud. "The way you stood and talked with each other; you knew each other somewhat, and you'd been through at least enough to feel like a group... but you weren't friends, really."

"Yeah. Though they're all pretty nice people, really, even Toshi. Who can be such a dick, without meaning to, if you know what I mean."

Tobimar was breathing in when Xavier said that, so the laugh came out more as a snort. "Your precise meaning is lost in sand, yet I think I still understand you perfectly." There was a short pause as they continued walking. "But one thing does puzzle me, a great deal. There's no magic in your world, right?"

"Right." Xavier suddenly blinked, as though he'd caught himself in a lie. "Um...lemme change that. There *wasn't* any as far as I knew, up until a little while before Khoros got us together."

"Ohhh," Poplock said with an enlightened tone. "Of course, if he'd just been brought over by Khoros, how'd he learn those magic tricks from his sensei?"

"Those aren't magic. At least, I don't think so," Xavier protested. "If they were, I'd have been detected, right?"

That *did* stop Tobimar, and from his suddenly wrinkled expression, Poplock too. "I...I think I would have to agree, yes," Tobimar said after a moment. "Yet you wandered around the Dragon's Castle for weeks without anyone noticing."

"Still," Poplock said, "from the way you act, that's got to at least *seem* like magic to you, so how'd you end up learning what you know before you *got* here?"

Xavier's sharp-edged face showed expression clearly, and now it was suddenly downcast. "I did something inexcusably stupid, that's what. And didn't *quite* pay the full price for it." He sighed, looked up into the sky, then back at them. "My...my brother died. Killed, while I was talking to him on the phone."

Tobimar restrained himself from asking what a "phone" was, and his glance kept Poplock from doing more than opening his mouth.

"It really messed up our family bad. And the cops, the police, they couldn't find who it was—eventually pinned it on some guy I *know* hadn't done it, because I'd heard the killer myself, and it wasn't a man, it was a woman, sounded almost like a little girl, and she'd *laughed*. So...I decided I'd go find the killer myself. And so I got less than halfway there, cut through the wrong alley, and got ambushed by a gang that didn't like some kid walking through their turf. They'd stabbed me in the gut and were going to finish me off when this old man shows up and tells them to back off—and then beats the heck out of all of them when they don't."

"Khoros?" asked Poplock.

Xavier managed a cynical grin. "Oh, no, *that* wasn't Khoros. *Khoros* was the bastard who'd told me to take *that* alley as a shortcut, I found out later. No, the old man ended up being my sensei. I knew some fighting stuff, martial arts, before I met him, but by the time he was done I knew how to do things I didn't think were possible. This after he told me how much of an idiot I was and got me to realize how much I was hurting my family by disappearing."

"So why didn't you go back *home* instead of staying to learn with this sensei?"

The smile grew bitter. "Because he also recognized...I recognized...that I'd probably end up breaking myself if I didn't finish what I started. Knowing she was still out there would eat away at me every day. So he taught me, and a year later I came out, went down the alley another fifty feet, and Khoros showed up and dragged me off to fairyland." He managed a better smile. "So that's *my* story. What about you guys? What brought both of you all the way out here?"

Tobimar looked at Poplock and grinned. The Toad gave a little hop-bow. "After you, O Prince."

Talking made the miles flow by quickly, and Tobimar came to know Xavier much better. That didn't mean he—or Poplock— really *understood* Xavier, because the boy and his world were so very *alien* that even what seemed simple assumptions turned out to be very incorrect. But he had the same courage, loyalty, and toughness that any adventuring companion should have, and a sense of humor and curiosity that fit well with both the exiled Prince and his Toad friend. He was glad that Xavier was able to travel with them for at least a while.

Over the next two weeks they crossed a few hundred miles, partly by catching rides on caravans that moved on through the night. Tobimar's fascination with Xavier's little machine didn't completely go away, but the immediate obsession dimmed quickly; the LTP's games were amazing, but the world around them was even more so.

The three were now looking up the road where hills rose higher, the farthest piercing the lowering gray clouds, covered with the thick greenery of the jungle and showing the wavering line of the cleared perimeter narrowing. "We coming to a mountain range?"

Poplock glanced at a miniature map in one tiny paw-hand. "Um...Not really *mountains*, but that's the Fallenstone Jumble. We'll be going up a little, but the Great Road stays pretty level."

"Still, we'd better be alert," Tobimar said, feeling nervous for the first time in a while. "The Fallenstone's the most dangerous part of this leg of our trip. The clearcut narrows in this area down to a few hundred yards, so bandits, monsters, that kind of thing have a better chance of catching people unawares."

"Can we get through that part today?" Xavier asked.

"Not a chance," Poplock answered promptly. "More than a hundred miles through, maybe two."

Xavier studied the Jumble as they approached. "You know, I didn't ask about that. Why this huge clear-cut area most places?"

"Gives room and security to build farms, little villages, things like that. If you let the jungle come in, well, gets too dangerous." Poplock nodded sagely.

"But your people live...*lived*, sorry...in the jungle. So did the *Artan*, right? So..."

"Special people, special places, but it's never safe or civilized. People like us—adventurers—go in, but it's always a mystery."

"Huh. Where I come from, the whole continent's pretty much explored and safe. I mean, there's some preserved wilderness areas and all, but I think there's a lot more chopped down, turned to cities and fields and such, than there is wild. And no one's *afraid* to go into the woods, really."

Another huge difference, Tobimar mused. *His world truly is completely different.*

The hills became higher, until Xavier said that he didn't care what *they* thought, these were mountains as far as he was concerned. Tobimar didn't feel inclined to argue; the highest peaks might not be more than seven or eight thousand feet overhead, puny compared to the Firewalls or, of course, the Khalals, but they were steep and forbidding.

"Why didn't they just build the road *around* these mountains?" Xavier said after a while, with the mist now descending on them and reducing sight to only half a mile.

"Oh, that's easy," Poplock answered. "The mountains weren't *here* then."

Xavier goggled at them both, looking momentarily like a Toad himself. "*What?*"

"It's true."

"*Oooohhh*," Tobimar said, feeling revelation and surprise. *This is the place!* "That was *here*?"

"I think so. They said he fell from the sky across the Great Road and nearly broke his back, right?"

"That's how I remember it." *What was it Khoros called it? "Chains of the Mind," that was it...*

Xavier was watching them as they talked, and his incredulity hadn't faded. "You people can't be serious. What could possibly fall down and make a hundred-plus miles of mountains?"

"A Dragon, obviously."

Xavier was apparently still trying to decide whether they were pranking him or telling the truth when Tobimar noticed something. He pointed up the road. "Look—someone's stopped up ahead."

The darker shadow resolved slowly to a cart, parked slightly to one side. But as they got closer...

"He's pulled in funny," Poplock said.

Tobimar slowed, stopped, Xavier following suit. The Skysand Prince looked for a few moments, trying to figure out what bothered him. "You're right. The way he's diagonal down there, he'd have a demon's own time trying to get back out." The three were quiet a moment, studying the cart ahead.

"I'm not hearing *anything* up there," Poplock said. "No voices, no movement. No animals or insects, either."

Tobimar drew his swords, heard Xavier's two leaf-green blades whisper from their scabbards, and even saw Poplock checking his own little Steelthorn.

The Toad looked over at him. "Could be an accident. Might need help."

"But it's a classic highwayman gambit, too."

"I'll go check it out," Xavier said. He closed his eyes and a moment later...just *faded*.

Tobimar couldn't sense anything from where he *knew* Xavier still had to be. He and Poplock studied the ground carefully, but nothing moved, even the dust on the road. *It's like he doesn't exist when he does that.*

Something's wrong. Tobimar trusted that sense, when he was able to feel it at all. This was not just an accident. He felt Poplock shift, turning so he faced backwards; if something tried to ambush them, he'd be able to give Tobimar warning.

A few minutes later Xavier rematerialized. His dark-tinted skin had a pale hue. "It's . . . bad."

The two followed Xavier up. A faintly metallic, nauseating smell with a somehow sweetish undertone touched their nostrils.

"Ugh," said Poplock.

The cart had run off the side of the road and down a slight embankment; one wheel was broken on the lefthand side and the axle was bent, showing the effect of a high-speed collision with the granite outcropping on that side.

But it wasn't collision that had beheaded the Sithigorn harness birds, or ripped the entrails out of the two women and one man lying broken on the ground.

"We *could* just move on," Xavier suggested slowly, but he didn't sound convinced.

"Perhaps *you* could." Tobimar heard the iron-cold tone in his voice, the sound of his mother's upbringing, of a Skysand of Skysand. "You have your own journey to complete and your own honor. But a Guild Adventurer?"

"Nope," Poplock said. "We can't pass this by. Part of what we're Guilded *for.*"

"Good," Xavier said, and managed a smile. "I didn't want to leave it, either. Anyway, whatever did this might be farther down the road. Who knows what it was or where it went?"

"That," Poplock said, "is something we're going to find out. How good are you at tracking?"

"*Me?*" Xavier asked. "My master taught me a lot of cool tricks, but it was all in this underground dojo; I don't know anything about tracking."

"I know some," Tobimar said. Khoros had required he be able to read some tracks, make his way through a mystery by the traces left behind. "Let's see what we can do."

Poplock dropped to the ground. Seeming unfazed by the stomach-turning odor, he moved to the bodies. "Cut through with a single sharp-bladed strike. Mostly vertical—cut from top to bottom."

Tobimar nodded, studying the riding birds' corpses. *Clean cut, too.* "More horizontal on the Sithigorns. But still it's got a top to bottom slant."

"Could be scythefeet, I guess." The semi-reptilian, feathered creatures could deliver devastating, leaping blows with the large foot-claws.

"Hm ... I'd say more doomlock spiders. Scythefeet have about eight-inch claws."

"You're right," Poplock conceded, examining the bodies more closely. "This woman you could do that to with eight-inch blades, but those animals, you'd need at least a foot and a half." He scuttled around the area, peering. "More than one something... two ... no, I'm guessing at least four, maybe five. Ground's awfully hard, mostly rock here with a little soil scattered here and there."

Tobimar ran up the hill and back the direction they came, looking along the side of the road, trying to read the traces in the dust and mud on the road surface. "There's marks along the side here. I think whatever it was tried an ambush from this side, drove them down this way so they'd run off the road."

"Makes sense. What marks I see show the somethings came up around the crashed wagon on both sides. Guess they panicked the Sithigorns, then came up and killed everyone when the crash happened. Don't see any sign of struggle, really, they didn't get to fight. Then ..." He bounced over, looked up. "Marks on the wagon. Went inside, came back out, left. Whatever it was probably wasn't just predators."

Xavier went in and confirmed. "Boxes and stuff were torn open here, but not like the bodies. Like you were looking for things you wanted."

Tobimar followed the traces he could see ... but the tracks seemed all muddled, and he had to at least momentarily admit defeat. "Poplock, can you get a direction for our culprits? I'm not clear, myself."

The little Toad circled the camp three times, checking the faint scratchmarks, scuffs, indentations. "It's really hard. Marks all over. They could have gone back to the road. I'll have to widen the search." Poplock bounced out farther and ran a long curve around the site.

A few minutes later he found something. "Thicker soil out in this area, and I've got marks heading out this way. Several of them. Not doomlocks, though."

Tobimar nodded. "Already figured that; doomlocks are nasty, but not very bright, and don't care about looting anything."

"Bipedal, I think ... hopping, too." The three moved into the woods, the ground now rising into the higher reaches. "Hopping *long* distances. Some of my cousins could jump that far, but these aren't Toad marks."

Tobimar suddenly shivered.

"What is it?"

He felt his eyes shifting rapidly, searching shadows for movement that wasn't there. An oppressive, heavy feeling settled over him. "I'm...not sure," he said finally, hearing his own voice tense and nervous. "But I feel something...dark. Evil. We're not dealing with anything ordinary."

"Don't sense anything myself...but you've got good instincts, I'll bet." They moved farther along. "Okay, now I'm wondering if my eyes are going. Was my count wrong? Just three here, now that I've got clearer marks. They're hopping in a pretty organized group..."

"Hold on," Xavier said, pointing.

The marks were on a tree trunk about nine feet up. *Oh, smart. Very smart.* Tobimar said, "Some of them are in the trees."

Xavier frowned. "I dunno about you guys, but I'm not thinking of too many things that do most of their locomotion by hopping, and most of those would look stupid trying to climb up trees."

Tobimar paused and looked down at Poplock. "He has a point. Your people hop, but they're four-legged. These...things seem two-legged, and there aren't very many...Hm. Iriistiik?"

Poplock studied the tracks again. "Could be." The Toad sniffed at the tracks. "Smells...funny. Like...like thunderstorms and heat, if that makes any sense."

Tobimar felt a cold shock in his gut, remembering the most ancient tales, of storms from the quiet desert when no storms had been seen. "It...might." He glanced over at Xavier, then at Poplock. "I think we should turn back."

Xavier hadn't missed the conversation. "What is—"

Dust and sand erupted from the ground, howled from the trees, blinding and stinging and sapping strength with blasting, oven-strong heat whose bone-dry savagery was doubly shocking in what had a moment before been a wet, warm rainforest. Tobimar lost track of his little Toad friend in the maelstrom, even as figures began to materialize from the haze. Xavier and he were coughing almost in unison, blinking eyes clear, trying to be on guard, but words in a rough, hissing language echoed out and the sand itself coalesced from the air onto both of them, weighing them down. *No! I can't be caught like this...have to move...* But there were hundreds of pounds of sand clinging to them, and they collapsed under its weight, pinned to the ground.

The air cleared slowly, and the tallest figure gestured; the others moved forward, weapons at the ready, and he could see that he had been right. *Demons! The curse of the Skysand has followed me!* There were *mazakh,* too, the snake-demon hybrids being smart and deadly servants for many things of evil. *And other things, stick-figure skeletons on springing legs. They're the ones surrounded by this sand-stuff.*

The commanding figure was now close enough to see; it hovered in the air, its body trailing away in swirling dust that left nothing but dust behind it, shrubs and underbrush withered and crumbling in its wake. From that indistinct base rose the torso of a woman, armored in polished bone, with decorations of gems and mother-of-pearl inlaid across its surface. The face was that of a woman too, but something subtly *wrong* with the features, a little too long, too sharp and narrow, beautiful yet alien, and the eyes were blank, dark holes with red sparks dancing within. A mace dangled from her waist, just above the point where fading into dust began, but she had no weapon in hand.

"Lady Misuuma," one of the *mazakh* said, "there are two youths."

"I can see that," the one named Misuuma answered, with just a hint of impatience that made the assemblage twitch backwards.

"Then which must we take?"

"The one with *his* eyes, of course."

One of the demonic, skeletal things raised a hand, and the sand blew away from the heads of the youths before them. Lady Misuuma drifted forward, studying both of them; Tobimar tried not to show any reaction.

With the speed of the whipping wind, her hand grasped Tobimar's chin with painful strength, forced his head up. Her dark-well eyes with crimson sparks bored into his, and she gave an alien, chilling smile.

"Ahh. We have found you at last. You have forced us to wait long, child. Not in Zarathanton is it wise to attempt an attack; nor, indeed, on a vessel of the Ancient Ones. But finally you have left the safety and journeyed here, and the trap has served its purpose."

"*You* are the demons who follow my family." It was not a question.

"As the Queen directs, so it is. And today another Seeker dies, as they always have." She drew back her hand, and the fingers lengthened to claws.

I have to move!

But in the moment he gathered all his strength to try to break free, something else distracted the demons and their servants.

Next to Tobimar, the other figure bound in sand vanished... and the sand collapsed.

35

Ooo, thought Poplock gleefully. *That's my signal!*

He had no idea how Xavier did what he did, but his *timing* was superb, and the little Toad knew exactly how to exploit timing. From the vantage point in a tree that he'd reached while everyone else was focused on the two eerily similar young men, he took careful aim and put a silver-coated needle right through the nearest *mazakh*'s eye.

The tiny, carefully inscribed runes etched on that needle exploded into ice and fire and the reptilian creature shrieked, clawing at its face. The others spun around, seeking the source of the attack, one returning fire with a quick incantation and a gesture.

Even before the gesture was completed, Poplock hurled himself from the tree. *Down down down got to get* DOWN!

Fire detonated against the tree, centered almost where he had been sitting, and the concussion knocked him another several feet. The impact wasn't too bad—when you were as small as he was, falling actually wasn't nearly as dangerous as it was to the big people. Much worse was the fact that three of the skeletal hopping things seemed to have caught sight of his desperate leap. They bounded towards him, sand howling outwards, blotting out sight, stinging his skin.

Nictitating membranes wiping furiously, Poplock dove between two rocks, but the wind howled louder and blasted him straight through and out the other side. There was another shout from behind and he thought it was Tobimar's voice, but he couldn't tell if it was the sort of shout that means you're free, or about to die. *Gotta worry about me first, can't help anyone if I'm skewered.*

Two clawed, bone-white legs slammed down into the earth scant inches away. *This stuff doesn't impede their vision!*

He still had an advantage of size, and the thing being so close gave him an inspiration. With a bound of his own he was on the thing, scurrying up through its ribcage. The other demons hesitated, obviously not willing to chop their companion down; the one he was inside grabbed and snatched, trying to get him as he clambered swiftly upward. *Whups! Missed me! Ha, now I'm on your spine! Hard to scratch back here isn't it? Hey, now, getting out a weapon is cheating. Back on the other side, yipe, look out, that was close, got to get farther up, up I said, stop running a sword through your own ribcage, it looks silly and you're not hitting anything.*

But now he was at the top, and skeletal hands hovered to pluck him off as soon as he was clear of the cage of bone. But he had no intention of actually emerging *yet*. Steelthorn was in his one hand now. *Okay, Khoros, let's see if that blessing you put on was good enough!*

He swung the slender blade, directly between the vertebrae, as he leapt up the last few inches. There was a flash of white light as Steelthorn struck, and the spinal column was not merely severed, but *cleaved*, as though Steelthorn had been a bastard blade wielded by a full-grown human warrior. The sand-bone demon collapsed in a heap, the animating spirit gone; Poplock bounced from the pile, heading for cover.

His victory enraged the other two demons, who *howled*, sending a blisteringly hot, achingly dry storm of sand after him. Instantly he felt slower, more sluggish, and in horror he saw the plants nearby collapsing, withering, going through hours of dehydration in seconds. *My will's holding off some . . . but I'm a Toad, I can't handle this for long!*

And then there was a chiming double *clang*, and the heads of both demons were spinning through the air. Xavier Ross stood behind the collapsing bodies, both blades extended fully.

"Good timing!" Poplock croaked.

Xavier flashed him a smile and paused for just long enough to allow Poplock to hop on his shoulder. "Let's go help Tobimar!"

In the short time they'd been gone, Tobimar had managed to break free. But as the focus of this trap, most of the forces had concentrated on him, and Poplock had a sort of *deja-vu* moment, seeing the young Prince of Skysand surrounded by monsters, including *mazakh*, in what seemed an untenable position.

This time, however, he had *two* allies. Xavier made a tremendous jump as he approached, and Poplock jumped from his shoulder at the peak, bounding into the branches above for a better, and safer, vantage point. *They had some allies in the trees before, but I think those were the* mazakh, *and most or all of them are down* there *now.*

Xavier Uriel Ross landed precisely, back-to-back with Tobimar Silverun, and for a moment the two black-haired, dark-skinned young men stood in identical poses, dual swords held parallel before them.

Something about that caused the demons, especially the leader, to draw back. To Poplock, it looked as though she was staring in shock at Xavier, at his swords and then at his face, perhaps his eyes.

But the *mazakh* were not so intimidated, and they lunged forward, clubs and blades raised.

Tobimar cut high and low; Xavier, low and high. Two bodies fell in unison, and then the boys leapt apart as though signaled by the same mind, into the mob pressing in on them.

Poplock sent a well-placed bolt or two into the *mazakh*, but the fact that the demon called Lady Misuuma was edging away seemed *much* more significant. He scuttled through the trees and bounced towards a location above her.

"...retreat to the extraction circle," she was saying. "Those blades and eyes...it is worse than she believes. If this new ally is truly what we think—*c'arich!* We must retreat. Let the snakes buy us time." Even as she spoke, two more *mazakh* fell, and Poplock agreed with Misuuma's evaluation; unless the two boys messed up *bad* in the next few minutes, they'd be both standing and none of the snake-demon things would be.

From higher up, Poplock could look ahead and could see the destination—a glowing mystic circle, made of twisted, woven dead plants in runic shapes he could read *just* enough of to know how bad news that was. *Gotta move!*

He leapt from branch to branch, trying to keep ahead, get *farther* ahead, and he only had seconds at best. *Only gonna get one chance at this! Have to distract them!*

He focused, extended his throat pouch for maximum resonance. "You're running from the wrong threat," he said, his voice far more hollow, echoing slightly around the mountain clearing they were entering. "Your doom is already *ahead* of you."

As he spoke, he stopped on a forking branch at the edge of the clearing, reaching back into his pack. *Hesitate, please, just a moment...*

Lady Misuuma halted, looking up, searching, finding. "You threaten *us*?" Her laughter slithered through the air like a hiss of sand. "You should run in fear for your own life!"

"I'm not the one who needs to run," he said, pulling what he'd searched for out of his pack. Even as two of the sand-bone demons bounded through the air, he hooked the *nynyal* strap across the forked branch and pulled back with both legs on the slingshot, holding the marble-sized sphere in the pocket. *Aim, up, up...* there!

"You should fear *me*," he said, and let go.

The tiny glowing sphere bulleted away, streaking through the air and detonating on impact—right in the middle of the mystic circle. Fire essence blasted the runic creations to shattered ash, consumed the structure, and with a blazing blue-black flare an implosion shook the mountainside; a crater yawned where the circle had been moments before.

"*No!*" Misuuma shrieked.

Well, that was satisfying. Glad I salvaged a few of those things from the cave. The sand-bone demons had paused only momentarily as the escape circle had collapsed, but that gave Poplock enough time to jump to the next tree. *Can't keep ahead of them forever, but at least I kept them from just running off to tell whatever it was to whoever it was. Which is probably a victory.*

"I will *destroy* you, Toad," Lady Misuuma hissed. She tore a glittering crystal from a harness about her body and raised it. "Come forth, Phy—"

Brilliant green blades suddenly grew from between Misuuma's shoulders, one striking and shattering the crystal, which exploded in crackling flame and buzzing smoke that circled the clearing once and then flew off into the sky. At the same time, the sand-bone demons collapsed, clattering apart like poorly made toys. Misuuma herself coughed, looked horrified, and then literally began to disintegrate, turning into a dark, noisome cloud that slowly dispersed in the sun.

"Ancient magical blades, I choose you!" Xavier said enigmatically.

36

Kyri watched, fascinated, as the Spiritsmith hammered layers of metals together, producing an iridescent shimmering pattern across the armor, a shimmering like that seen on a bird's feathers. The immense hands were startling in their delicate precision, the usual claws chipped and roughly trimmed to keep them out of the way. As his claws grew quickly, she'd already seen the Sauran performing his manicure a couple of times in the past week—grabbing some handy metal shear and chopping the claw back until it no longer protruded. "That's beautiful," she said, nodding to the feathery pattern.

The draconic head bobbed in acknowledgement. "Armor itself can be plain and solely for protection. The Raiment of a Justiciar is far more than that. It is defense, yes, but also a weapon—a symbol of fear to the enemy, a rallying cry to your allies, a flag or standard. It is your touchstone when you are in the darkness, something to remind you of who you are and what you have chosen to become." He took the armor and tapped once on the inside with the hammer, and to her surprise the feather-patterned metal dropped off in a single layer, a gossamer-thin iridescence that floated down into a tank of some dark liquid the Sauran armorer had placed nearby. At her glance, the Spiritsmith explained, "That, too, has its use, and must also be reinforced to withstand the use to which you will put the armor; it will remain there for three days."

Kyri bent down to the liquid; the smell was sharp, metallic, and her skin tingled from some immense power held within; at this range, with the fire nearby, it seemed to have a tinge of red in the dark color. "What is it? It smells almost like blood."

"It is. Dragon's blood, to be precise," the Spiritsmith confirmed.

She straightened, startled, nearly banging her head into one of the anvils. "Dragon's blood? But you're—"

"—A T'Teranahm as are they, yes." He shook his head. "I did not kill any of my brethren for this, nor even injure them. Such materials are freely given me by Elbon and the Sixteen, from time to time, so that I may fully ply my trade."

She looked with awe at the tank, whose contents now showed sparkles of other colors deep within it. "That . . . is the blood of one of the Dragon-Gods?"

"It is. T'Eless'a of the Amethysts, the Traveller Between. Appropriate for your symbolic wings. I am, as you know, not a magician of any sort. Yet my armor must at least equal, if not surpass, that made by any of the modern enchanter-smiths. To that end I have learned all the techniques ever conceived to make such armor. I walked to Asgard's Fortress in ages past and in Thologondoreave, the Cavern of a Thousand Hammers, I learned the skills of the Children of Odin that can bring forth the power of an image and a name in steel; at the Suntree I watched the ways in which the essence of the Forest Sea might be guided into the very heart of a weapon; I have spoken long with the Wanderer on the ways of metal and lightning-power in a world where magic is seen not at all; to the Great Abyss I travelled in the dawn of the world, when Erherveria sat for a moment in dominion over the Demons, and learned the powers that lie beneath the foundation of the world; and I have sat in the Great Archives and studied the meaning of symbols and sigils, the alchemical secrets of power locked within blood and bone and crystal, leaf and stone and living hearts."

He opened up the armor and spread it out upon an anvil larger than a banquet table. "And I have studied at the feet of the gods themselves, to understand what it is that they would ask of their servants, to know what it will be for you to become the instrument of Justice and Vengeance, what it would mean for one to train from infancy in the Crucible of Athena and become a God-Warrior, one of the Chosen of Chromaias or an Einherkyn of Odin."

He's studied under everything from the Gods to the Wanderer; no wonder there is no one to compete with him. She watched him laying down a pattern of metal the color of summer sky with an undersheen of gold, placing strands of delicate thinness in a pattern like veins throughout the armor: layered metal cuirass, arms all the way through the gauntlets, and legs from the mail-and-layered-plate that would cover her from the waist to mid-thigh, down all the way to the toes of her new armored boots, the wire-thin metal held in place by some adhesive liquid he painted across the surfaces. "What is it that you are doing now, if I might ask?"

"This is thyrium. A rare metal, a magical variant of copper, with unique properties. It is perhaps the perfect channel for power, especially for that of the gods, when properly prepared. If you confront enemies such as you must in your quest, one day you may need to call upon the power of Myrionar and become a vessel for Its power; your armor should contain and guide that power with you, supporting you in your union with the god, not be a hindrance; without careful design, such power could simply destroy your armor, and without containment your other equipment would likely be destroyed by the power of the gods."

Kyri blinked at that. It hadn't occurred to her that there would be such... mundane yet crucial problems associated with being a god's representative. This triggered another thought. "So my sword—"

"Oh, indeed. That is an alloy of krellin, iron, silver, thyrium, and valatra, with a single strand of *terianing* as the core." He gave a savage smile. "No strength will break that blade, and few the powers that it cannot withstand."

She picked up a strand of the thyrium that lay near. "You say this is a variant of copper? They look nothing alike."

"No, they do not," agreed the Spiritsmith with a shrug. "Yet the Wanderer says they are the same base material, with thyrium having magic infused into it; the alchemists with whom I have worked agree. Many are the things for which it is true that a bit of magical essence utterly transforms them. Diamond becomes adamant, looking much the same but hard enough to scratch even a krellin breastplate; amber becomes suncore, holder of holy light, capturer of the essence of souls; sapphire transforms to Vor-nahal, and dances upon the wind."

"But if that's what they become with magic, how do magicians manage to make, well, ordinary things? I've heard of alchemists making gold, and there was a wandering wizard who used to conjure up little silver toys as part of his act."

The Spiritsmith chuckled as he carefully moved the armor over a large firepit and pulled a lever, releasing a blaze of blue flame that was cold enough to put frost on his scales and make Kyri shiver even ten feet away. "There is a great difference between that which magic creates, and that which already exists. In some cases the magician is actually creating nothing, merely building it from materials he has summoned thence; in others, they may indeed be creating something, but it remains magic in its essence. For many years it may last, but unlike that which was built from the true material, a single dispelling or negation or counterspell gone awry may cause it to vanish into nothingness." The hammer came down through the blue fire, driving the thyrium threads into the chilled metal, somehow neither shattering the threads nor cracking the armor. "It is not just that there is magic with the copper that makes it into thyrium; it is that the magic is *bound* to the copper's essence. One could make thyrium from magic—create magical copper and bind more magic to it to create thyrium—but it would be potentially evanescent. In the true material, the magic bound to the heart, or essence . . . what did the Wanderer call it . . . *nucleus*, that was it . . . of the copper cannot be removed without shattering the material itself into nothingness."

That did make some sense. "So that's one reason your armor is used by the gods, rather than—for example—them creating it from pure power?"

"An excellent deduction, Kyri Vantage. There are a few—a very few—ways to make armor that can be, in effect, summoned or created into existence without need for a material structure, but almost all of those will have a terrible vulnerability to being countered by a power like unto that which made them." He drew back and leaned for a few moments against one of the other firepits, this one glowing with the warmth of ordinary flame, letting the ice and frost that had accumulated melt away. "And so they come to me for my weapons and armor which are forged by my hands from steel and krellin and gold, from dragonhide and demon sinew and crystals dug by long labor from the heart of the mountains, and into those I forge the attunement of the armor and weapon to a purpose that lies beyond them and within them, with a piece of my own soul as the price."

Her head snapped up and she stared with horror at the Ancient Sauran. "A piece of your *soul*?"

The booming laugh rolled out again, as the Spiritsmith reached out and took up his hammer again. "Yes, Kyri Vantage. An artist places a part of his soul into all his works. In my case, this is simply a more literal truth than it might be in others. I thank you for your concern, but this is not black necromancy, no terrible demon's price; a soul can recover from such a loss, if it be not too great, and it has been a long time indeed since I forged something so worthy and so well; my spirit has long since recovered, and I have much to give without it being a grave danger."

"But I had heard that soul-wounds..." she remembered Rion's death, "...soul-wounds are almost impossible to heal."

The Spiritsmith frowned, but his eyes were gentle. "Something close to you, I perceive. But here we speak not of soul-wounds in the same way. I place my soul into my work slowly and carefully as the work proceeds, and it is less a wound than merely a reduction, a sacrifice of current strength, which will rebuild in time. What you speak of are the results of attacks upon the very core of existence, the powers of the highest of the Undead, the weapons of the *mazakh* assassin-cult Ssivilisstass, the Hunger of the Great Wolves, the spirit-destroying powers of the most powerful and fearsome demons. From those, indeed, recovery is slow, perhaps impossible for some, and for those of magical or spiritual powers they are more terribly dangerous, for you may feel physically fine; yet make any attempt to use your powers, to channel magic through your soul, and your soul shatters as though it were cracked glass."

She swallowed, remembering what had happened to Rion, and how Arbiter Kelsley had nearly followed him by trying to bind a soul together that was too damaged to save. "So the cost...isn't the same. That's a relief."

"I am weakened, yes. But not to the same extent, and not in a way that makes me fragile; merely unable to do certain things until I have recovered. And by doing this," he smiled again, with the razor-sharp teeth giving the smile its predatory edge, "I make the armor and weapons themselves become a part of the living will of the person who wears them, of the one who has the *right* to wear them and wield them."

"You mean," she said slowly, "that the armor, that my sword... will be alive?"

"Not ... precisely." The Spiritsmith pulled the armor from the coldfire and dropped it into a quench tank; the enchanted water hissed as though struck by red-hot steel, and vapors boiled out— but instead of rising like ordinary steam, the mist cascaded to the floor and flowed out. "Yet in a sense, yes. It will resonate with your will, support your soul and senses, impose itself between threats that lie beyond the physical, give you the ability, if you are strong enough in mind and body, to strike down even those things that are not of this world. The power is still dependent on you—your mind, your skill, your will and dedication—but a true Justiciar can cleave through spells, deflect or split demonfire, even break curses and ancient seals with a stroke of a blade, if their will and courage be enough."

She looked at the armor with new respect as he lifted it from the tank, small shards of ice falling from it to tinkle on the stone beneath. "I thought that was either, well, exaggeration or the doing of Myrionar's power itself."

A smile of blades. "No exaggeration; and some of those feats can, in fact, be achieved by a warrior sufficiently trained that she can pit her own will against powers sent against her. As to the others, Myrionar—and the other gods—could of course achieve such ends, but they do not provide such protection at all times. That is, after all, the point of the gods appointing their champions, their Justiciars and paladins and high heroes; to have these be their eyes and ears and hands without the god having to directly perform all of the deeds." The Spiritsmith examined the inlaid thyrium pattern carefully. "The gods support us, but even they cannot watch us all the time—and there are the other gods who oppose us. Thus, in the end, it oft-times is not the power of the gods, but the power of the mortals—Adventurers and champions, priests and sorcerers, rogues and skalds and sometimes simple farmers—and that which lies within them which will decide the day. And for those days, for those battles, you will find no finer weapons and no stronger armor than mine, forged with my soul and my arm and my will ... and by your own."

"Mine?"

"Why, do you think, you have stayed here, rather than being kept to the guest quarters and told, otherwise, to stay away from my work? You are no smith. You are quick of hand and eye, but scarce as useful as the greenest apprentice. But your hands

I have asked to steady the ingots as I forged them, your eyes I have asked to help judge the angle and the choices of metal and design, your strength I have had deliver blows, your mind and will I have called upon to remember what it is we forge here and why. To you, the first Phoenix of Myrionar, I am binding this armor and this sword, and they shall be born, as are all children of our races, of two parents." He nodded again, slowly, approving both of the dawning realization on her face and, it seemed, of the condition of the armor after this latest work.

"We shall complete this work, you and I; and in a few more weeks you shall give to your sword a name, and then," he held her gaze, "and then—only then—shall the Phoenix Herself be truly born."

"Not quite," Kyri said slowly, as the nearness of her departure began to sink in. She looked to the northeast, where Evanwyl lay, not far off at all, no, much closer than she might have thought when she first began this quest. Though here she could only see the mist and smoke and stone of the Spiritsmith's forge, still she could envision the houses and shops and Vantage Fortress as though they were before her. "Here the Phoenix was conceived, but the bird must hatch from its egg.

"And that will happen when I leave, when I return home... and when the Phoenix first speaks her name as a Justiciar.

"Only then will I have been truly reborn."

37

Once more, the argent and auric mirror-scroll showed the night-black throneroom of the even darker King of All Hells. "A few more weeks," the black-glowing figure said. "The alignment of the forces required could not quite be achieved yet." A night-glinting smile. "Fortunately this was not necessary for the first stages."

Normally the man was very happy—indeed, thrilled—to be a part of these conferences. A *small* part at this point, true, but with a slowly increasing importance as Evanwyl became more significant to his patron and, in the greater game, to Kerlamion Blackstar himself.

But today I must be concerned for myself. Yet I must not fear, nor allow fear to drive my decisions. I must trust that...my patron... will continue his policy of listening to even bad news fairly.

His patron was replying to the King of All Hells: "Indeed, Majesty." It nodded, gesturing to place maps upon the mirrors. The other panels were dark, this being a conference solely between ruler and master planner—and the master planner's most favored servant. "Without Voorith's misfortune, the attacks would have been launched long since. I have become convinced, however, that this was a stroke of good fortune in disguise."

"Perhaps. Show to me the way of things now."

It pointed. "The Forest Sea is almost entirely emptied of the *Artan*. The only remaining stronghold—as one might have suspected—is Pondsparkle. Many were driven from it, but a surprisingly stubborn core of the Toads and some of their allies remain, and have found the Temple a particularly strong fortress." The human-seeming figure glanced at Kerlamion's image, seeking counsel.

"Well enough," the Demon King said after a pause. "We shall destroy Pondsparkle...*and* its patron...in time. But for now we shall not challenge even so small a god as that directly, as long as the Golden-Eyed meddles no more. Go on, then."

"Artania is mostly ours, but Nya-Sharee-Hilya resists."

The darkness thickened, the cold blue fire of eyes flared. "Balgoltha promised a swift and final victory."

"It appears," it said with a sideways smile, "the Master of the Sea has promised more than he could deliver. I *did* warn you that I thought he was neglecting some aspects of their defenses."

A subliminal pulse of pure darkness showed Kerlamion's displeasure, but all the great Demonlord said was, "Do you believe he will fail in the end?"

"Oh, no. The swiftness has failed to some extent, yes, but without aid from outside, or some other threat to draw off the forces of Balgoltha, the seige cannot help but end in the total destruction of the *Artan* city, and thus their last hope of a homeland."

"And is there chance of such aid?"

It laughed, a sound that seemed to make the very lightglobes flicker in fear. "I think not, Majesty." It pointed, and the maps blackened. "The White Blade is assailed on all sides by your brother's forces; I am sure he is most distressed by his success."

The man could not quite restrain a smile at that thought. *Speaking professionally, I would say that the Curse of Blackness is one of the most artistic of Kerlamion's creations—perhaps his greatest in a way, despite the undeniable power and symmetry of the Great Sealing.* He recalled the terrible simplicity of the curse that Kerlamion had placed upon his brother Erherveria, one of the few Demons who had chosen a lighter path: "Always shall you remain who you are, good and just and kind *in your thoughts*, while in actions and words and deeds you shall do the opposite, unmaking that which you once sought to build, slaying those you would protect, destroying that you sought to preserve." *A positively inspired way of dealing with a traitor; making him useful, and punishing him at the same time.* He thought he detected a similar half-smile on his patron's face. *We do share...certain tastes.*

His patron turned, pointed again. "We could not act directly against the Mountain yet—that, I am afraid, must wait until we can devote our full attention to that problem. However, our forces in Dalthunia launched a simultaneous set of raids into the Empire's territory, keeping the Archmage and his forces distracted, while the passage of magic across the borders is being severely interfered with."

"And Aegeia?" This was of course one of the most crucial areas, as the Lady of Wisdom was incarnate.

It chuckled. "As I promised you, Aegeia is no longer a concern. Your other spies have undoubtedly noted the chaos of their pantheon, the . . . private little war that they're having. With some fortune, it may result in that entire odious little country becoming a godswar-torn battlefield, in which case we shall have little to fear from them for a long time indeed."

The black-on-black figure studied it for several moments. "And how was this achieved?"

It smiled. "My private secret, Majesty. We all have our own."

It took most of his control to prevent *that* from triggering any sort of shift of expression. *You are practically* daring *the King of All Hells to suspect you? Who and what* are *you, really, my patron?* Despite that, he felt now more than ever that he had chosen his ally very wisely . . . or perhaps that his patron had been most wise in choosing him.

Kerlamion's blank fiery gaze regarded the figure narrowly, but did not press the issue. "And Evanwyl?"

Oh no.

He dared not interrupt, though, as his patron replied easily, "Remains entirely secure. A peaceful refuge," it said, with ironic humor, "in the midst of other countries at war. My Justiciars have seen no sign of any significant efforts in this area in all this time."

"It is well, then. You believe that our forces will hold for the time being?"

"For some time, yes. But you do realize that they will mobilize soon enough; a new Sauran King has been selected, and he is already beginning to bring things under control in his own city. The Archmage of the Mountain will also not long remain on the defensive, and when *he* moves—"

Kerlamion smiled his light-destroying grin again. "Oh, indeed. But the time shortens apace, Viedraverion."

A name! At last, I know its name!

He could see the momentary grimace of annoyance, but despite its apparently privileged position, Viedraverion obviously did not dare to chastise Kerlamion for mentioning his name in front of his servant. "The forces are aligning well, yes. When can we expect...?"

"Unless something interferes...one month. Perhaps two."

That inhumanly glittering smile from his patron. "Oh, *most* satisfactory, Majesty. I assure you we can hold things for that long, even if I must go and act myself to make it so."

"It is well." The head shifted. "I have other reports. We will speak again." The mirror went blank instantly; the King of All Hells had no need of courtesy.

Only his patron's image remained, looking at him. "Hm. Gained more than you expected today, did you not, my friend?"

Time to tread most *carefully.* "I admit to having curiosity satisfied, though the name itself tells me little."

A tiny smile. "At the moment. But I would be disappointed if you had no intention of researching it."

"I will do so, of course. Unless you care to make it easier and simply tell me."

"Ah, now, that *would* be far easier. But I did not choose you for your tendency to take the easier path. Now," and the face grew serious, "tell me what bothers you."

He swallowed, took a breath. "You are *most* perceptive...my patron."

"Dear me. As bad as all that?" It studied him, leaning back in a carven chair. "You are rarely so hesitant. Out with it, then."

"A thousand apologies," he said. "Understand, if you allowed us to...approach you in any other fashion...but your rules are absolute, and I have not forgotten your lessons."

The lethal smile, glittering below warm blue eyes. "I would think not. What was so urgent, then, that you would even have considered violating that rule?"

"We have a real problem. There is...another Justiciar."

All of its lazy, genteel demeanor vanished instantly; it was on its feet and glaring down. "What do you *mean*, another Justiciar?"

He bowed, placatingly. "Patron, I am devastated to be unable to clarify it all that much. But rumors began...oh, a couple of months ago. At first we thought it was just confused retellings of things we'd been doing, but pretty soon we heard about a Justiciar driving out a haunting in Vardant."

"The Twilight House?" Its expression was a tremendous relief. *It's taking this seriously ... and not blaming me, at least not yet.*

Of course, his patron *should* take this seriously. While it, naturally, didn't care a bit about clearing away taints of supernatural evil, the Twilight House was a local legend and center of dangerous happenings that normally confined its destructiveness to those stupid enough to enter the grounds of the old madman's mansion.

"I see," his patron said finally. "Due to ... certain events, it might have been spreading its influence ... and anything that could destroy or drive out those influences is not an ordinary warrior; a very powerful adventurer at the least." It slowly seated itself. "And few indeed are the adventurers seen in *this* remote region of the world."

"Exactly." He felt the tension on his face relaxing. "It hasn't ended there. He or she—the reports aren't clear on this—hasn't come to Evanwyl's center, the city itself, yet, or at least not that we know, but this so called ... Phoenix Justiciar ... has been sighted all around the area otherwise."

It leaned forward. "Phoenix?" it repeated. A pause. "Have there been any reports of ... healing?" it said, slowly.

He nodded. "Man and his daughter, ambushed by leafaxes, he was taken down, then this Phoenix shows up, kills the whole swarm single-handed, then heals the man with a prayer."

"And what have you done?"

"I have had those I could spare out looking. But the other ... projects ..."

"Understood." There was new tension in the humanoid figure now. "But this now takes absolute priority. I want you to drop the other projects. I want you to find this new Justiciar. If you can, find out his—or her—purpose. But above all," it said in a low, hissing tone, "this new Justiciar needs to *die*."

He was somewhat surprised. "Of course he, or she, does, but you seem ... much more upset than you were—"

It snarled, and he stopped in midsentence. "I will not call you *stupid*, my friend, for you are not, but you do not see the entirety of the picture. Even so, you *should* realize how different this is. Silver Eagle was *ours*. We could watch him, divert him, see where he was going, what he planned to do ... and be prepared to counter any move he made.

"We do *not* control *this* Justiciar if indeed that is what he is! And that, my friend, means that he or she may do *anything*. Including, I will point out, becoming a new *focus* for Myrionar, and that would be *most* unfortunate for you and all your brother Justiciars, I assure you."

He bowed low. "I . . . I will gather the others immediately. We will begin the searches at once." *My patron is right. I should have seen this* instantly. *If the true God of Justice and Vengeance begins to regain Its power . . .* "My apologies again. With your permission . . . ?"

"Go. And . . ." It smiled again. "This is not *all* bad news, my friend."

"It . . . isn't?"

A chilling laugh. "To risk this, so close to your center of power? This is the move of desperation, the god's last fading hope, a single thrust to the heart of its enemy before the god itself passes. Now," the smile widened, and he felt his own smile return, hungry and dangerous, "now, my friend, the fun can *truly* begin."

38

"Halt and turn, stranger!" The shout echoed through the twilight-gloomy clearing.

Kyri heard the sharp, clear voice and her heart seemed at once to both leap and sink. *Of all the Justiciars it could have been...*

She turned slowly, until she faced Mist Owl fully. The other Justiciar was fully arrayed, as was she, with his broadsword drawn and shield partially raised. She knew that he could see only a tall figure in similar armor, the predatory "beak" serving to cover her features, the molded breastplate and loose armored skirt serving to confuse many as to whether she was man or woman.

The *Artan* Justiciar pointed his sword at her. "I am Mist Owl, Justiciar of Myrionar; I seek one not of our number, who has claimed to be a Justiciar, and I believe you are that one, that has been called Phoenix."

She gave a short bow, heart pounding. *Please, Myrionar... if ever I needed your help, I need it now.* Mist Owl, nearly as old as Lythos, oldest and possibly the most dangerous of the Justiciars. *But maybe I won't have to fight him.* Gathering her courage, she answered.

"I am the Phoenix Justiciar of Myrionar, Mist Owl." She spoke in a low, measured tone, not wishing to give away anything of who or what she was until the time was right. "Your eyes are still sharp, I see."

"You do not deny it. Well enough. Then perhaps—just perhaps, I say—this can be resolved without your death, 'Phoenix.'" Mist

Owl advanced a few more paces, but was still very cautious. "Cast your weapons upon the ground and remove your armor, and submit yourself to the justice of the Justiciars and Myrionar. I have heard no tales of your doing wrong—other than using a name and title to which you have no right—and perhaps you have no evil within you."

"I make you a counteroffer, Mist Owl," she said, trying to keep her voice calm and level, and show no sign of the tension or, yes, fear that she kept within. "*You* disarm and take off that armor, and submit yourself to *my* justice. For you know, as I do, that to submit to Myrionar's justice you can no longer accept that of the Justiciars."

There was the barest hesitation before Mist Owl responded. "What nonsense are you speaking? We are Myrionar's chosen representatives, Its Sword and Balance on this world."

"Then tell me, Mist Owl, what justice of Myrionar directed the Justiciars to attack and destroy the Vantage estate?"

Now the other was silent, and stood immobile for several moments. "If you know *that*, then you must know that I cannot permit you to leave here alive," Mist Owl said finally.

"It is not too late for you, Mist Owl." Her voice was more urgent now. *Please let him listen.* "I am Vengeance, but I am also Justice. If you would turn from whatever your true master is, and join the one you have claimed to serve, then you may be redeemed, for you have much knowledge of the enemy and can help us to defeat him in turn."

"You claim to be a true Justiciar? You expect me to believe that a single new Justiciar has been sent, to try us all?" Despite his grim and mocking tone, Kyri thought she heard a faint trace of hope—or fear—that this impossible thing could be true.

"I do, and I am, and I have. Myrionar answered my call, and I answered Its; a Justiciar I am, with armor new-forged by the Spiritsmith himself, and it is within my power to save you."

Mist Owl laughed, a bitter laugh and cold, cold enough to send a chill down her spine. "Myrionar could not save the Justiciars before. For a hundred years and more It did nothing, and It can do nothing against the powers that have moved against it. You are either deluded—though with knowledge deadly enough to require your death—or you are the last pathetic throw of the dice that Myrionar can muster. In either case, how can you offer me anything?"

She pulled off her helm and glared at him, letting her hair cascade down. "I can offer you *redemption* for your crimes, Mist Owl—or by the Balanced Sword, I'll have to give you death, for all that I used to trust you!"

That startled him; he stepped back a pace, and his voice was touched for a moment with emotion more gentle than contempt or resignation. "*Kyri Vantage* . . . of course it would have to be you." The sword and shield sagged down slowly. Then they rose up as his face hardened. "Once more your sister will be bereaved, I fear."

She reached back for her own sword, but her voice was pleading. "Please, Mist Owl, *don't make me do this!* Let Myrionar protect—"

"Myrionar cannot protect Its own *temples*, you stupid little girl!" the *Artan* Justiciar snarled, coming to full guard position. "And the *worst* you can offer me is death; what *he* threatens—and can do—is far, far worse, as Silver Eagle found out all too late." His voice dropped back to the cold-iron of a warrior prepared for battle. "Draw your sword, Phoenix Kyri, or die a pathetic death trying to argue with my blade." His sword, Cloudweaver, came up in the ritual salute.

She felt tears sting her eyes as she slammed the helm back on her head and pulled Flamewing free. *Blink them clear now! No time for blurred vision!* The great two-handed weapon glowed faintly in the falling night, showing the red-gold pattern that looked like ascending flame, and she brought it up in salute.

No sooner had she finished than Mist Owl was moving, circling. She had watched him fight on two occasions and understood his tactics; use the terrain, use the lighting, maneuver and confuse the enemy, make him believe one tactic while unleashing another. Now he circled, watching, looking to see where *her* weak spots were, and formulate a plan to take advantage of them.

Don't play his game. She remembered Rion saying those words when they trained, and Lythos, too, though in terms more flowery than Rion's blunt description: "Mist Owl's a thinker and a planner. Give him enough time, he'll beat the living hells out of you."

She charged forward, whipping Flamewing in a circular arc that made it difficult to parry, forcing Mist Owl to leap aside. *Keep him moving, off balance. Force him to improvise.*

The problem, of course, was that even if Mist Owl didn't have time, he was still old and yet unaged, an *Artan* deadly and savage. *An* Artan . . . *maybe* . . .

She focused on the speed within, praying that Myrionar would support her here. Warmth rewarded her, warmth that drove heaviness from her limbs, lightened Flamewing in her hands, and she suddenly parried and cut as though she were wielding a dagger, not a greatsword; her opponent was taken aback, driven entirely on the defensive as a storm of metal edges seemed to descend upon him. "Lythos trained me for most of my life, Mist Owl. I am a Vantage. You know what that means."

She could see Mist Owl's mouth tighten; he had known her brother, too. "Myrionar is with me. You can *see* that, Mist Owl. Maybe whatever monster you serve could withstand It, but you cannot."

The lips compressed even more, then spat out a curse in *Artan* that she did not recognize. "Do you think we are able to play the part of Justiciars without the *power?*"

And now it was *her* turn to be driven backwards by a hail of blows that flicked out and back like lightning. A stinging on her cheek from one barely deflected, another shock of pain in her upper arm as Cloudweaver tried to bite deep; but the Raiment of the Phoenix, the newest work of the Spiritsmith, was far too strong to be cut even by Mist Owl's blade—at least with a single stroke. Even so, the impact staggered her and left her arm half numb.

Mist Owl stepped back a half pace and spun Cloudweaver three times; gray mist flowed from the blade like water from a fountain, and Mist Owl's next series of cuts sent cold, clinging fog in all directions, shrouding the area in almost impenetrable gloom.

I'm an idiot. Of course they have all the powers. The charade would never have lasted. Rion would have seen through them immediately.

Mist Owl had disappeared; his armor had been designed for this, just as his namesake would appear from night fogs and strike its prey. *And he's very quiet. Fast and silent.*

Cloudweaver tore through its mists, the Mist Owl's talons outstretched. Something, perhaps only the sound of wind on steel, warned her with not a single fraction of a second to spare. Even as she dove aside, Cloudweaver sheared through her hair as it trailed behind, and then he was gone again.

I can't play this game his way, she reminded herself. *But the mist is everywhere . . .*

She grinned suddenly. *Not quite, I think!*

With a leap, she was in the trees edging the clearing, climbing the ancient oak, climbing... and at only twenty feet she came into clear air. At the next branch she stopped, waiting.

A low, hard chuckle came from below. "Ah. Well played, Kyri Vantage."

She concentrated. *As I am balanced, so you balance me. These trees are no more to me than the ground below. You are my guide and balance, Myrionar!*

The sound of boots on bark, *running up the tree.* She sprang aside, landing with the surety that proved that the Balanced Sword had heard and answered her prayer, just as Mist Owl streaked through the space she had been. Her return stroke, however, nearly cleaved him in half, rebounding from his armor with an impact that sent him skidding off the branch and plummeting towards the ground below; he somersaulted and landed with an impact that shook the tree slightly. She was sliding down just behind him, trying to follow up on the attack before Mist Owl recovered.

She found she was once more in balance, strangely so, with herself. Half of her was filled with a fierce joy in this battle, the first blow she had been able to strike against the people who had slain her family, betrayed everything she believed in; the other part was crying in pain and aching sympathy, for one thing she had heard in Mist Owl's voice: a moment of longing, of wishing for what she offered, and a fear that would never let him accept it.

And with that balance of vengeance and justice—or even mercy—came the renewed determination to finish this. *I accept the pain and the responsibility, Myrionar. They are yours, now they are mine as well.*

And even as Mist Owl's sword rebounded from her helm with an impact that made her ears ring and the world go momentarily dim, she realized the path to that ending, at least for this duel. Mist Owl was better than she was, but—surprisingly—not by nearly as much as she had feared.

And he was *Artan*, not Vantage.

Now she attacked with her full strength. *That* was something that he could not counter easily. Oh, he might pray to whatever dark god was providing false Justiciars their powers, but she could be strengthened in the same way—and the differential would still be in her favor. Skill could negate strength...sometimes. But she was not that unskilled, and Mist Owl's mouth was set in a grim line so narrow that his lips were all but gone. "Surrender, Va-Nye-Kimda," she said, using finally his name, a name all but forgotten in the years since he had become a Justiciar. "You never wanted this. You are *Artan*, a protector, not a killer and a false friend!"

Mist Owl redoubled his attacks, suddenly putting her back on the defensive, forcing her to retreat, until she managed a parry-block that made him stagger back; her riposte struck his helm on the side, tearing it from his head, sending the owl-helm flying into darkness.

The twilight-gold eyes held hers for a moment, and she read the truth there; that she was right, that he regretted every moment.

And that he had no hope.

Even as she saw that, he was charging, Cloudweaver tearing through the air. She leapt aside, deflected his blow, swung her own blade.

He did not dodge, and his block was slow. Flamewing cut cleanly through muscle and cartilage and bone, and the head that rolled on the night-shadowed grass wore a strangely peaceful expression.

As Mist Owl's body fell, Kyri felt as though she had struck herself as well. The eldest Justiciar had never been a family *friend*, but a trusted advisor, a defender, a local legend. And now she had slain a legend.

"No," she said after a moment. "No, *Artan* Justiciar, I didn't slay you. *You* did, didn't you?" The half-smile on the still face answered her, and once more the tears threatened to overflow. *But I shouldn't feel that is wrong. We need to be able to cry for the loss as well as be strong in the quest for justice and vengeance.*

She stood and looked down. "You decided that you couldn't live the lie any more...but you feared your secret master too much to ever fight against him. And so...with that...the worst I could offer became the best you could hope for."

She sighed. *This wasn't what I dreamed it might be. I wanted to save them or kill the wicked, not...not find they were neither so foul they had to die, nor brave enough to turn against their master.*

She went to her pack, which she had dropped when the combat began, and took out a cloth to clean Flamewing. Once that was done and the sword returned to its sheath, she went back to Mist Owl's body. "I'm sorry, Mist Owl. You have paid the price for your crimes, and vengeance is satisfied. But there will be justice, too. I will make sure your death was not in vain. And if any of the Justiciars be not beyond redemption, I will reach them . . . somehow."

That left the question of the body. She couldn't take it to the traditional burial ground (*and there's* another *problem. How many false Justiciars are buried there? There'll have to be a complete purification when this is all over!*) and she didn't have any shovel worthy of the name, so burying him here was out of the question.

But as with the Chromaians, there was another way.

Smoke looks very like mist as it rises.

39

"Well," Xavier said, looking at the faint trail leading to the east, "I guess this is where we split."

Poplock felt somewhat depressed at the thought. Not only had Xavier been a useful companion, he'd been *fun*. And constantly surprising, what with his strange attitudes from his native world.

Tobimar seemed to feel even more strongly. He stepped forward and gripped Xavier's hand. "It's been an honor and a pleasure to travel with you, Xavier Ross."

Poplock noted again how the two seemed, in many ways, similar—the hair, the dark-tinted skin, and of course the twin swords. Xavier looked slightly disconcerted—not by the emotion, Poplock guessed, but the formality. "Well, likewise. I mean, I really appreciate your help, Tobimar, Poplock. I might have made it on my own, but it sure wouldn't have been as easy . . . or nearly as much fun, even if we did almost get killed several times along the way."

"When you're stopping off to investigate reported monster trouble in one town, bodyguarding a family to their village, and spending three days trying to find the entrance to Thologondo-reave along the way? We were lucky things didn't try to jump us more often." Poplock observed. "Though, as the saying goes, the failure isn't in the jump but in the landing, and we've gotten very good at giving nasty people very, very painful landings."

Both Xavier and Tobimar laughed. "I suppose we have, at that," Tobimar said. "But I don't think we regret any of it; none

of us seemed inclined to ignore people in trouble, for which I
am glad. And it appears that—at least for now—our extremely
sound defeat of the Demons has thrown them off the track, or at
least caused them to reevaluate their strategy." He bowed quickly
to Xavier. "And with your ability to go unseen, you were able to
get us past the Dalthunian border without trouble, something I
am not at all sure we would have managed on our own."

Xavier nodded. "Maybe not; they sure had a buttload of guards
on that border, and a lot of 'em weren't human or anything like
it. I think we've made real good time, too; we've actually made
it most of the way in three months."

Good thing, too, Poplock thought. *Rainy season's going to start
in a couple more months and while I won't mind at all,* they
certainly will.

Xavier had gotten out his own copy of the map Toron had
given them. "So you guys continue pretty much along the north-
northwest path here, and I go east and a little north along this
path until I hit the Broken Hills, right?"

Tobimar nodded. "If legend is at all correct, the Wanderer's
Fortress should be somewhere near the center—and not easy to
get to. He's supposed to put all sorts of tricks and challenges for
people to get past."

"I'll bet. But I've got a few tricks of my own to show him."
He looked at the map again. "Still, whether I find him or not,
I'm still gonna be *awfully* close to Evanwyl. Let's see if we can
meet up there, okay? I mean, who knows where you're going to
have to go next."

"I think we'd both like that a lot," Poplock said, and Tobimar
added his agreement.

After a few minutes of measuring distances and making guesses
as to time, they settled that they would stay in the Evanwyl area,
checking in periodically, for at least the next month. "If I'm not
there in a month, either something bad's happened or, more likely,
I had to get moving somewhere fast and couldn't afford the side
trip. But where would I check? It may be a small country, but
it's still a *country.*"

"The capital, which is also named Evanwyl. We will leave mes-
sages at the local temple—they're sure to have a main temple to
some deity, probably this Myrionar that Toron mentioned—and
at whatever the local inn is."

"Sounds workable." Xavier turned and used thumb and fore-finger to shake Poplock's hand. "You keep watching out for both of you, Toad."

"I always do. *You* watch out for yourself. You're going to be alone."

Xavier looked uncertain for a moment, staring into the distance where the rough, rolling tree-dotted plains began to merge with jungle again. "Yeah, I know." He shook himself, then straightened. "But there's no other real choice. You've got your things to do, too." He did a stiff bow. "We'll meet again—I promise!"

"We'll be there," Tobimar said. "You have our word on it."

Xavier turned and strode off down the eastern pathway. "Later!"

Tobimar and Poplock watched him for a moment, pushing through the grasses almost effortlessly, and then Tobimar turned northward and started on the final leg of their journey.

The departure of Xavier cast something of a damper over the rest of the day; they made camp and slept, but their conversation just seemed...empty, as though an essential element was missing. For three months and more he'd been there, a constant presence with strange alien expressions but a familiar courage and will, and now he wasn't.

Still, the next morning dawned bright, and Poplock felt cheery. Tobimar seemed more positive too, and they set out early, moving quickly down the remains of what had once, before the last Chaoswar, been part of the Great Roads. Despite cataclysm and many millennia of neglect, parts were still intact, but it was a far, far cry from the perfect maintained smoothness of the road they had traveled from Zarathanton to the Dalthunian border.

A darterfly came just a little too close and Poplock snagged it, chewed appreciatively. "That one had a nice crunch and a sort of smoky flavor to it."

Tobimar looked sideways at him. "Poplock, I suspect our taste experiences would be rather different. For one thing," he brushed at his shoulder, making the little Toad hop over the fingers, and sent several long glittery wings flying off into the breeze, "if—and I must strongly emphasize the *if*—I were to eat bugs, I'd have to cook them first."

"Go ahead, ruin the meal. Though steamed or deep-fried armorfang is pretty tasty according to a lot of humans I know."

"Point. I've eaten those myself, and they *are* good. Giant

water-beetles, yes?" Poplock bounce-nodded. "Thought so. Dart-erflies, though..." Poplock held on and rotated slightly, check-ing behind them as Tobimar continued his steady walk up the roadway—a road much more like a trail than the Great Roads they'd been able to follow for much of their trip. Nothing there at the moment, but it paid to keep an eye to the rear.

Of course, the other part of this sort of travel was spotting *big* trouble in time to avoid it. Tobimar was good, especially with that not-magic magic stuff he could do in battle, but even with a Toad's help there were some things you didn't want to mess around with.

Poplock had scuttled up onto Tobimar's head *en route* to the opposite shoulder—he tended to alternate sides every half-hour—when something caught his eye. "Hey, what's that?"

"What's *what?* Your eyes are higher than mine right now." Tobimar walked forward a few more steps, finally reaching the crest of a small hill. "Oh, now *that* looks more hopeful."

Ahead, the road and small river they had been following passed through a small ridge, the river having cut a miniature canyon through the rock. Across this natural choke point was a solid, blocky wall, a guardpost with a gateway that closed off the road and extended not merely to the river's edge, but well into it, precluding any easy passage; the water ran swiftly here and was quite deep, and Poplock knew that a lot of very nasty things indeed would likely be found in that water, waiting for anything dumb enough to try to swim around or across. There wasn't much of a shoreline on the other side... and, squinting up, the little Toad was pretty sure he could make out arrow and spell slits. Try climbing ashore there and you'd just be target practice... and there were watchtowers on each side of the ridge, too, so if you tried to go the long way around, you might get spotted; the forest wasn't nearly as thick here. *Probably they burn it back every couple of years,* Poplock guessed, looking at a blackened stump nearby.

He could tell his human friend had spotted most of the same things; Tobimar had a good eye. As the two approached the guardhouse, a man in uniform stepped into view, holding up his hand. "Stop, please, and state your name and business." A glance upward revealed faint movement behind the nearer slits—crossbows or spells being readied, Poplock figured—that gave the guard's polite request a great deal of force.

"Tobimar Silverun of Skysand." Tobimar deliberately didn't mention Poplock; the two had agreed that there were definite advantages to people not noticing the little Toad, and Poplock didn't feel bothered at all when being ignored was part of his plan. He sat in the shadow of Tobimar's long hair; if they saw him at all, people would likely consider him to be a pet or familiar spirit or something similar. And while some familiar spirits were pretty tough, Poplock knew they had some pretty strict limits—limits he didn't share.

"Your business?"

"Guild Adventurer." Tobimar displayed his shoulder patch, and the guard's eyebrows rose.

"Zarathanton Guild, too." He verified the patch and saluted. "Well, sir, I can't say there's no work for you here. Been all sorts of goings-on in the past month or so."

"Well, I'm glad to hear there might be some interesting adventures; sorry to hear of the trouble that leads into them, though." *Tobimar's walking that stretched rope between sounding like a problem-solving adventurer and, well, what some people accuse us of, being like carrion birds.*

They began passing through the guard post and the relatively short, high-walled gantlet that could be sealed off in the case of attack. Something on the wall caught Poplock's eye, and he tugged slightly on Tobimar's hair.

It was a notice on the wall, carefully written and spelled against weather, defacement, or unauthorized removal (well, Poplock couldn't be *sure* about the last one, but he'd have bet three darterflies on it). It was a simple request for any qualified bounty-hunters and adventurers to inquire at the Temple of Myrionar in Evanwyl—the capital city of the country itself.

"That *does* look promising," Tobimar agreed. They were still following the "look without looking" strategy to some extent, which worked for Poplock since he figured that since they now knew there *were* monstrous forces trying to keep secrets from Tobimar's family, they'd be more confused by his actions if he wasn't apparently *trying* to find out stuff. And this way Poplock would get to see more places and do more fun things, which was, after all, the point of adventuring.

Evanwyl—the city—was still about a hundred miles away, and it looked like there wasn't all that much population here. A small village right near the guardpost, probably *because* of the guardpost, and a few farms around it, and that was it. By evening, there wasn't a trace of human habitation other than the road itself.

"Where will we camp tonight?"

Tobimar frowned. "I hate to get in the way of anyone...but it's never a good idea to get far off the road."

Poplock bounced off his shoulder to the ground. "Well, they don't seem to get much traffic through here, do they?" He scuttled around, checking the markings. "I don't see anything very fresh. Maybe a few walking through, but this isn't one of the Great Roads."

Tobimar glanced down at him. "You can read that on this hard-packed stuff?"

"I spend an awful lot of time down here. You learn to tell that kind of thing really fast, especially when missing little details might get you killed."

"I guess so. You certainly showed what you could do back with the demon ambush. So on the road it is."

Nothing bothered them that night, which was a pleasant surprise. *Maybe not so surprising; this* is *just down the road from a permanent guardpost.*

That seemed to be the case; the next couple of days did have some "exciting" incidents. Well, one actually exciting one, when their sleep was interrupted by a very hungry striped worm—about twenty feet long and a ton or more of land-crawling eating machine. *That* was a good five minutes of serious running, stabbing, slashing near-death experiences. The one the next night *could* have been pretty exciting, but the three flame-ant scouts turned tail and ran when he bounced into view. It was rather odd that even very large insects seemed to have an instinctive fear of his people. Tobimar was not very sympathetic to his disappointment, pointing out that they no longer had Xavier with them and that flame-ant *scouts* often meant a lot more flame-ant *warriors* not too far away. They'd moved another mile or two down the road before camping again.

The fourth day, just as the shadows were getting long and Tobimar was starting to cast uneasy looks at the trees around them, they suddenly emerged into a cleared area.

The foothills of the Khalals rose in deep blue-and-purple majesty in the distance, and in the twilight shadows lights were starting to appear. The clearing around them showed areas of cultivation. Far ahead, a much larger collection of buildings was visible, straddling the shores of the Evaryll River.

"That *must* be the city."

Poplock bounce-nodded. Evanwyl didn't compare with Zarathanton, of course, but it was a lot bigger than Pondsparkle—more than big enough to call it a city. The thought made him curious about how his friend viewed it. "So how's that compare to your home?"

"Hm? Oh, you mean compared to Skysand? It's ... not much, actually." He pointed to a fortress-home perched on a ridge not far off. "Things like that look like their biggest buildings, and they wouldn't be a dust-devil next to a sandstorm compared to the Towers. But it's still a good-sized town, and for a small country ... well, I wouldn't expect anything bigger."

Tobimar quickened his footsteps, which Poplock had rather expected; while *he* wasn't really bothered much by sleeping outdoors, he knew his friend very much preferred comfortable beds when they could be found, and where there were large towns, there would be comfortable inns.

The road widened and occasional patches of crushed stone, packed rubble, and such gave way to carefully maintained pourstone; not nearly as tough and enduring as the ancient god-spelled Great Roads, but still a far better surface for travel than even the hardest-packed dirt. For the first time in many weeks, Tobimar's boots clicked out a sharp and energetic rhythm along a real road.

People stopped and studied them—sometimes covertly, sometimes openly staring. Apparently strangers were rare here. *Not surprising, considering how much of a pain in the feet it was to get here.*

Ahead, a bright lightglobe hung above a wide sign that showed a somewhat irreverent symbol: a sword impaling a roast, with the pans of a set of scales balanced on its point holding a tankard on one side and a mess of vegetables on the other. The predictable name was emblazoned below: "The Balanced Meal."

"Obviously the seat of the faith," Tobimar murmured with a slight smile.

"I like a sense of humor in a religion. But that isn't the temple, I'd guess."

The Prince couldn't quite restrain a snort of laughter. "Ha! No, I don't think so."

The building was more solidly built than the homes surrounding it, and taller, at least two stories; the aged look of the timbers and slight rounding of the granite showed the inn had been there for many, many years. Tobimar pushed open the door and entered. The Balanced Meal was a well-lit inn, with an actual dining hall off to one side, a watch and registrar station just in front, and stairs to what Poplock presumed were rooms for rent ascending on the other side. *Must be the place the locals come to eat and chat, too; they sure aren't making their living from travellers!*

"Welcome to the Balanced Meal, sir." The man behind the desk was much older than Tobimar, with gray hair shot through with a few remaining black strands; the width of shoulder showed he had probably been either a warrior or heavy laborer when young, but the width of his gut told a tale of many more years of heavy eating. "My name's Kell; how can I be of help this evening?"

"Thank you for the welcome, Kell. A meal and a room, in that order; I've been traveling a long time."

Kell nodded, with a surprised smile. "If I know my accents, a longer time than most. That's a Skysand lilt, or my ear's gone bad."

Poplock could tell that surprised his friend. "You're exactly right, Kell, but that's . . . amazing. You can't have had many visitors from my country *here*."

"No, indeed, not many." Kell rose with a grunt and escorted them into the dining hall, seating Tobimar at a corner table and calling over a server. "But years back, I was a wanderer, adventuring—never guilded, but never dishonored the name, I like to think—and I stopped in Skysand for two years. Went to the mines, did a few weeks helping there, found myself a handful of sparklies, circled the whole desert back to the coast and its cities."

"Well, it makes me feel a little more welcome. Thanks. I'm Tobimar, by the way."

"Nice to meet you, Tobimar. Room and meal's one Scale."

Tobimar nodded, dug into his belt pouch and pulled out a small gold coin. "Here's five Scale, keep it; I'll probably be here a few days anyway."

The inn owner (the way the other employees reacted to him confirmed it for Poplock) grinned in the manner of any businessmen being paid in advance. "Well, thank you and the Balance be in your favor, Tobimar." Kell's gaze rested for a moment on

Poplock, who blinked back, looking as stupid as possible; the man glanced down and noticed the patch on Tobimar's shoulder. "Guilded. So you'll be wanting the Temple tomorrow morning."

"You know anything about that?"

Kell frowned. "Might. But it's not my place to say, not now. Let them tell you. If you have questions after that, I'll tell what I know, or what I think." He gave a quick nod and headed back to the front hall.

Tobimar ordered and ate; Poplock, maintaining his cover, simply snagged any small insect that flew by and stayed quiet. They could talk when they got to the room; in the meantime, Poplock listened carefully.

Some of the conversations were interesting.

Once in the room—corner room, windows with locking shutters, the sort an adventurer would prefer—Tobimar went around carefully, pausing and closing his eyes, casting out his senses in the way the old mage Khoros had taught him. Poplock waited patiently, having seen this several times before. He'd already done *his* check while Tobimar was unpacking.

Finally Tobimar opened his eyes and nodded. "All clear. No scrying or prying magics active."

"Good. You know how hard it is for me to keep quiet!" He bounced up onto the bed as Tobimar sat down. "You catch what everyone was saying down there?"

"Not much of it; I was eating, and that tends to make sound through your head, you know."

"Yeah. Well, sounds like something's got them worried, and it's connected with Myrionar's champions, those, um, Justiciars. Sounds like people have gotten killed or something."

"Fits. That's why the temple's the one calling for adventurers. And I did think the dining hall was pretty empty for a place like this."

Poplock bounced his assent. "And that means it's an ugly problem ... and it's got something to do with the gods."

"Which is just the kind of thing we've been wondering about, ever since everything started coming apart when we were in Zarathanton. It can't be coincidence. We're following a trail and a pattern. If something's causing all these disasters, it's probably not overlooking Evanwyl ... and if Evanwyl was connected to our homeland, then maybe—just maybe—whatever's here is connected to our enemies."

"And if not," Poplock observed, "at least it's the kind of problem we should be looking at anyway."

Tobimar laughed. "Yes." He started to prepare the bed. "Maybe we'll find out tomorrow what we're looking at."

"Maybe." The Toad moved under the bed; he preferred sleeping under things closer to his head than human-sized rooms, which felt uncomfortably like open air. "But my guess is we'll just get ourselves in someone *else's* mess again."

"Are you complaining?"

"No. That's what we're really out here for, isn't it?"

A pause. Then another low chuckle. "You know, I think it really is. I mean ... I haven't given up on my search—you know I won't, ever—but I've been doing this for years now, and it ... feels *right*. Mother knew I never really wanted to sit in the Throne, or even be a Ruling Prince in one of the other cities. That old Khoros, I guess he knew that too."

Poplock scuttled back out from under; the tone of Tobimar's voice showed he wasn't really sleepy, and—truth be told—neither was the little Toad. He bounced up to the bed. "So what do you think about him, anyway?"

"Khoros?" Tobimar sat up and frowned, then shook his head, looking out the window to where the last purpling of the sky was fading to black. "I did some poking around into that before we left—well, you know some of it—"

"But not all. I was running around town doing some preparations of my own. And visiting old Barkboat."

Tobimar's smile was sympathetic, and Poplock shuffled uncomfortably; he'd spent a long time making that carefree exterior and doing things like giving all his money away to the refugees—Toads and others—endangered that reputation. Not that it *bothered* him, exactly, but he preferred to be approved of for his more spectacular actions, not charities.

"And," Tobimar said, letting him off that hook, "we've done a lot of talking with Xavier. That's given me perspective on the old mage."

"Oh?" Poplock knew some of those conversations had taken place when he was doing other things—scouting the area, or sleeping while the others were on watch. "I heard part of it, but what'd you learn?"

"Khoros apparently has spent a lot of time on *Zaralandar* as well as on Zarathan, and manages to get his power to work there as well. According to Xavier, the two girls in their group—Nike and Aurora—had both met, or heard of, Khoros before they arrived here."

"The one girl didn't seem to like him much."

"No—Xavier says he had tampered with her family somehow, made sure she was raised a certain way, and it made things very hard for her. In fact, he said that he's pretty sure Khoros didn't just watch their lives, but made sure their lives went in a certain direction." Tobimar looked pensive. "I really don't like some of what I'm hearing. I liked Master Khoros. He seemed very wise, and skilled, and very much sympathetic to people's needs. It's hard to imagine he could be capable of something that coldly calculating, even if I accept that he needed these people to do something for him."

"I wouldn't know, really. He was nice enough to me, but I was already going in the right direction, I guess." Poplock heard a faint scuttling noise, bounded off the bed and snapped out his tongue, snaring a beetle. "Mmm. But you know, the scary thing about this is that if they're right, he somehow either knew we'd bump into each other ... or he was able to *arrange* that, without anyone knowing."

Tobimar was silent for a while—a long while, so long that Poplock started to think his friend might have fallen asleep. "That ... is frightening. But ... it's possible. I can sometimes see— sometimes sense—where sword blows are about to fall, when a branch is going to give way, that kind of thing. And sometimes I can extend my soul and push, and *change* what's going to happen. It's very crude, but legends of Khoros go back a *long* way, Poplock. I found references to him, with Toron's help, in stories surviving at least three Chaoswars."

Three? Snakes and quicksand! That's ... "That's ... that means he's, what, forty thousand years old?"

"Or older. If I can do this kind of thing when I'm not even twenty, I suppose someone like him might be able to sense or guide results of events that are days, weeks, even months or years in the future."

"And would be playing a game up on the level of the gods, if he could manage that." Poplock climbed back up onto the bed, thinking. "So we're connected with whatever Xavier's group is. If that's all true, anyway."

Tobimar winced. "You mean that this is all *one* plan?"

"Maybe with a lot of pieces, but doesn't that make sense?"

"Too much sense," the Skysand Prince said after a moment. "He wants to break the Great Seal, reopen the connection between the World of Magic and the World of Knowledge, and if Kerlamion were to guess what he was up to, I'd bet that the King of the Hells could stop it now. So whatever Khoros' plan is, it has to be not just subtle but almost unrecognizable until it all comes together. And he's probably fighting against whatever's doing all these attacks, too. So he's trying to take care of all those events with some huge, overarching plan that involves getting a lot of different people to do things in a precise order." He made a face. "But that *really* bothers me. It's like I don't have any choice, that everything's preordained."

"Not quite that bad, though. He can *try* to get people to follow his plans, but he can't have contact with the enemy, and any choices they make...well, he still has to hope the choices made work for his plan, no matter how good he is at predicting, because anything *they* do may change what *we* do."

Tobimar nodded after a moment. "I...I guess, yes." His tone grew firmer. "Yes, I'm sure you're right. I can foresee a blade strike, but if my opponent has the right skills, he can counter that. My predictions, my senses, are based on what is, and what could be, and what I could do. If I'm against someone with equal or greater powers, they can change that prediction. And Khoros isn't greater than Kerlamion or the other gods, I don't think, so it's still a..."

He broke off and suddenly smacked himself in the head. Poplock looked up with concern. "What's wrong?"

"The *Nomdas!*" Tobimar shouted, remembering the cryptic words of the High Priestess of Terian in Zarathanton. "She practically *told* us!" His brow wrinkled as he concentrated. "What was it... she said, '*There is too much at stake for those who are already a part of this great game to abandon their places.*' That was it."

"A game. Like...like battlesquares?" Poplock asked, thinking of the strategy game he knew a lot of the older warriors played, with different pieces on a large carven board representing different types of combat units.

"*Exactly* like battlesquares," Tobimar said, excited yet grim at the same time. "Exactly like it, except the pieces are real people..."

"...and losing the game costs you a lot more," Poplock finished. The two looked at each other through the gloom for several minutes.

Then Tobimar shrugged. "And I guess there isn't much we can do about it."

Nothing we can do... Poplock suddenly laughed.

"What's so funny?"

"It's *not* exactly like battlesquares at all," he said, and the amused excitement rose in his voice. "Don't you see? This is what the gods are doing all the time, right? But the gods are playing each other, and using each other! If it's a game, it's a game where the *pieces* get to play too!"

Tobimar sat still for a moment, and then a slow smile crossed his face. "So *that* is what he meant. 'All else is but your choice.' It was his way of telling me that at the same time he was giving me directions...I still had to make the moves. That's why he needs people, the *right* people, not just automatons—because we can make decisions, choices, take actions when we see it's needed. We aren't simply inert pieces on the game board. We're players—beginners, amateurs, but we can play."

"And sometimes a beginner can make a move that no one expects."

Tobimar nodded. "If there's a lot of big players—like Khoros, like the Demons, the Gods—they'll all be mostly against each other. They need us because we make the difference. That's why the gods care. And why we're important."

"Good!" Poplock bounced twice. "And tomorrow we'll get back into the game!"

"And on the side of Justice and Vengeance," Tobimar confirmed. "Which sounds like the right side to be on for what's happening right now."

Poplock agreed, and settled back under the bed; he could tell his friend was now ready to go to sleep. *Tomorrow we'll see if we can help find out what nasty thing is killing off Justiciars!*

40

"A *false Justiciar?*" Tobimar was appalled.

Arbiter Kelsley nodded, his expression showing he understood. "So it would appear, sir."

"Tobimar will do, I'm not here for the formality. How's that *possible?*"

Kelsley shook his head. "I have prayed for enlightenment, as have others—some, not even of the Faith, but of other faiths allied to ours—and no clear answers have we gained."

Tobimar could feel Poplock shifting slightly on his shoulder; the revelation was so stunning that his little friend had nearly broken his cover, and clearly wanted to say something. *I'll have to hope I ask all the right questions; otherwise he'll make me come back here and ask them later as though I'd thought of them afterwards, which would look terribly sloppy, especially for a Prince of Skysand.* "It would have to be another god, wouldn't it?"

"I cannot think of another force that could reasonably do this without Myrionar being able to speak directly and tell us all that is passing. But even so...I am mystified. A few words only and we would know the answer to this mystery. Something of terrible, of overarching importance, must be involved to prevent the Balanced Sword from revealing unto me the truth behind this, something which—if It were to speak now—would result in a terrible miscarriage of Justice and Vengeance." The Arbiter looked across the hall of the Temple at the Balanced Sword, glittering in the morning light, with pained confusion.

Time to get to business. "Well, obviously the point of such a thing must be to confuse the people in Evanwyl—which is the seat of Myrionar's faith—and perhaps cast doubt on the true Justiciars."

"That is our presumption, yes," said Skyharrier. Tobimar had studied the silver-and-green armored Justiciar with what he suspected was very poorly disguised curiosity, because Skyharrier was the first of the Saelar—the Winged Folk, often called *Valkyrnen* by the Children of Odin and something unpronounceable by the Dragons—he had ever seen up close, and Skyharrier's armor allowed his wings to be extended outward; they were currently pulled in a tight pair of arches behind him as he stood nearby. "If we are slain and our killer claims to be a Justiciar, then we appear at the least to be weak and, by extension, Myrionar is weak as well."

He looked undecided, glanced at Kelsley; the priest nodded after a moment, and Skyharrier bit his lip, gaze flicking from Tobimar to the priest to the Balance like a bird watching its surroundings, before finally taking a breath and continuing. "We...we have looked over much of the past, sir—Tobimar—and at this time we have begun to wonder..." He shook his head. "Downdraft! That wasn't the way to start. Let me approach again. Have you seen the Temple of the Balanced Sword in Zarathanton?"

"Well..." Tobimar hesitated, but realized that the truth could hardly be unknown here. "I did pass it, but it seems to be no longer a temple; it is empty, and there are those seeking to have another building built there."

The Justiciar's startlingly crimson eyes, contrasting with the brown of his feathery hair and complexion, looked at him sadly. "And that is a tale told far too often. Once, you could alight in any city across the continent and find the Balanced Sword awaiting your need; now, only here in Evanwyl and a few small cities and towns immediately beyond our borders. We now wonder... is this not mere accident, but instead a campaign on the scale of the gods, hundreds of years spent whittling away at the very foundations of the Faith? And then this false Justiciar would be the beginning of the end, the final attack upon the Sword that Balances Justice and Vengeance."

Poplock's little feet dug hard into his shoulder, and Tobimar guessed they'd both had the same thought. *Hundreds of years of planning to bring something down... coordinated attacks...* "The rumors of this false Justiciar—does he have a name?"

"He—or, to be fair, she, for there have been reports of both—calls himself Phoenix."

Another bird, but a mystical one, where all the real Justiciars are named after ordinary birds. Appropriately confusing. "The rumors, did they start about five months ago?"

Arbiter Kelsley glanced in surprise at Skyharrier. "I... I believe that could be, yes."

Skyharrier frowned. "It *might* have been a few weeks later... but the so-called Phoenix may have been present before then, simply watching. Why?"

"Just a thought." *Near the same time as all the rest of this. Coincidence seems... unlikely.* He felt Poplock scuttle down his back; he had no idea what the little Toad was up to, but didn't dare look. "I will need all the information you have on this Phoenix—where he or she or it has been seen, what they've been said to do, how often he's sighted, full description, weapons, anything else. If I'm going to try to track him down and he's dangerous enough to have killed a Justiciar—"

"Not merely *a* Justiciar." Skyharrier looked grim and worried. "Mist Owl, the oldest and wisest of us, an *Artan* warrior."

Tobimar winced. *Artan* could live for many hundreds, maybe thousands of years (they were close-mouthed about that, and of course it was hard to be absolutely sure that the *Artan* you met yesterday was the same one mentioned in ancient texts and not just someone named after him or her). *Artan* weren't generally warlike—that was their sundered clansmen, the *Rohila*—but those that *did* take up the sword had a very long time to master it. *This could be... interesting.*

For a moment he considered backing out. Smart Adventurers lived longer lives because they were good at figuring out which jobs would get them killed *before* they actually took the jobs. But his research had pointed him to this country and this was *exactly* the kind of problem that might—that almost *had* to—have a connection with his own goals. "Anyway, if I'm going after this killer, I need all the information I can get."

"Quite so, sir." Kelsley looked relieved; Tobimar guessed that his indecision might have been visible. "I have here a package summarizing everything we know, locations, people, all that you will need."

Tobimar noticed they had several such packages nearby; *at least the local Symbolist is getting something from this disaster; making packets like this in duplicate isn't cheap.* He took the package and stood, feeling Poplock scurrying up his back and back into place. He bowed, then looked at Skyharrier. "This must be very hard for you and the other Justiciars."

The *Saelar* Justiciar understood what he meant. "Obviously we would like to take care of this problem ourselves—and we are trying, do not doubt that! But between the Arbiter and our own discussions, we have had to—with great reluctance—accept that any being playing a false Justiciar may well have studied us long and well, and knows every feather of our wings; he may well know how to defeat us all. A Guild Adventurer..." He smiled faintly. "Well, even the gods recognize that worlds can be changed by such heroes."

"You do me far too much honor, but by the Sands and the Sea, I will do what I can to resolve this for you." He bowed again and left the Temple.

Back in their room at the Balanced Meal, Tobimar checked again to make sure they were in privacy before nodding to Poplock.

"Mud and *drought* that was hard to keep quiet for!" the Toad burst out, bouncing around the room to work off frustrated energy.

"You did a good job." He broke the seal on the packet and started going through it. "It looks like a terrible situation."

"Very bad. But maybe connected." Poplock hopped to the table and from there to his shoulder so he could read along.

"Hm," the little Toad said about a half hour later, now sitting on the table on top of some of the papers, shuffling them back and forth. "This Phoenix has been pretty sneaky. Even the description's kind of vague."

"We know he's tall—almost certainly taller than me—but probably human."

"You say 'he,' but some of the witnesses think it's a woman."

"True, but more say they thought it was a man. Plus, there *are* no female Justiciars, haven't been for at least a few centuries, and if you were trying to fake up a Justiciar, wouldn't you avoid doing something that completely clashed with the truth?"

"Good point." Several more minutes went by in silence. "You know, Tobimar, this stuff bothers me."

He glanced over and saw the reports Poplock was indicating.

"Oh, those. You mean because he's doing all the heroic work? But wouldn't that be necessary to manage the whole confusion trick?"

"Maybe, but...oh, *drought*, I can't figure out what it is. Part of it's that it's so...random. As though he's just moving around the area..." The little Toad suddenly straightened, then bounced. "I just thought of something. Here, look at this." He dragged out the map of the surrounding area.

"First he showed up here," a little foot poked at one spot on the map. "Then he went over *there*. Next time he was sighted, he'd moved *all* the way over here, but then popped up in *this* little town just a half-day later...you see what I mean?"

Tobimar studied the pattern. "He's all over Evanwyl. It's like he deliberately moves all the way across the country in between most of his appearances. He's trying to make himself look ubiquitous? But he's *missing* some areas where he could have been needed, if he's trying to play the part of a true Justiciar."

"That's only part of it. It's the *timing*. No one's mentioned a sithigorn, riding wolf, horse, or any other mount, Tobimar, so he's almost certainly on foot. He's making it to these places just about as fast as you possibly could on foot—and faster, if like us you didn't know which routes to take. Look, there isn't a single road indicated between any of those three routes—from the Twilight House he'd have to go up here, then take this road south for at least ten miles before he started going in the direction he wanted."

Light dawned. "By Terian's Stars. You're saying he's *familiar* with this area."

"He's not an outsider, he's a home-grown problem, Tobimar. He didn't just get here six months ago, or even a year or two. This is the way a *native* would work. He knows this place like the back of his hand."

That makes sense. "If the enemy's smart, that's what they'd choose. Someone who knows the territory as well as their enemy." He ran a hand through his hair. "That does make it a little harder, though. If he knows the area that much better, he's going to be *hard* for us to catch."

"If we play the game his way." The little Toad looked smug. "But we know what he's up to..."

"And maybe if we can predict his next move, we'll be able to be there before he is. What's your little secret?"

"I thought I'd take a look around the Temple's back room. There was a chart on the wall showing the general search areas the Justiciars are using."

Tobimar instantly caught on. "Since he's directly opposed to the Justiciars, he has to keep confronting them. Looking at how he usually shifts a long distance, we'll be able to tell the next attack by checking which Justiciar or Justiciars will be in the likely areas."

A few minutes were spent going over the schedule and comparing it with the map. "I think that's pretty conclusive."

"But," Poplock pointed out, even as Tobimar began to pack his things, "it's already been quite a while since his last appearance. He might already *be* there."

"He might not, too. Plus he might take a bit longer scoping out each victim." He let his twin swords settle into place, then lifted the Toad to his shoulder. "Besides, we need to try if it's at all possible. Sure, the Justiciars can take care of themselves, but one of them is dead already. At the very least," he said as he packed the information away with a last glance at the entry, "we can make sure that Shrike is warned in time."

41

The sound of a footstep behind her had been just a split second too late to warn her as a tremendous blow struck her back, sent her sprawling, and before she could recover something very heavy was on her back, and a sharp, cold metal edge resting on her neck below the helm. "Now, you Balance-cursed imposter," the deep, Shipton-accented voice growled, "I give you a few minutes to explain yourself, not that it be likely any explanation will save your body and soul from the Justiciars' judgment."

Outflanked. I thought I was stalking Shrike, but somehow he caught on. She knew she wasn't the best at this sort of thing, though she wasn't bad. Still, the older Justiciar was clearly a lot better. She thought fast. *He's got the advantage. I have to find a way to get the upper hand.* "And which imposter was it that hewed the head from Kyril Vantage—Shrike or Condor?"

The edge on her neck shifted the tiniest bit as her question struck home, and she heaved upward and to the side, escaping the squat Justiciar's trap. Shrike, realizing this as soon as she moved, rolled to his feet even as she did, raising his axe to find her sword already clearing its sheath.

For a moment they stood, staring at each other, and then Shrike's eyes narrowed, widened, and he gave a grunted sigh. "I know that voice, disguised though it is. That was my axe, lass. And your mother's neck was mine, too, though Condor fought both well; I struck the last blow to both."

"And how was it that you could manage to walk into our house and still be able to look yourself in the mirror, traitor?"

The mouth behind the gray-streaked mustache tightened and the eyes narrowed. "You understand nothing, girl, or you'd be a lot less quick with your judgment. Me, I learned to take what good I could get; better that than what waits for any who try to turn their back on *him*."

"Quick with judgment?" She barely kept herself from starting the fight then and there. *I need to understand. Killing Shrike... part of me screams at me to do it now. He killed Mother. He killed Father.*

And somewhere inside there was a tiny sigh of relief that, somehow, though he had been there, it was not Condor who had slain either of them.

But I can't kill Shrike if I can get him to talk. "You *dare* call me 'quick to judgment'? You killed my parents! You *orphaned* us, all three, and your false Justiciars killed Rion too, and you have the undiluted poisonous *arrogance* to say I am quick to judge you?"

The axehead made an abortive twitch, but stopped. *He wants to get information from* me *just as much.* "I suppose you'd see it that way. Can't argue that, not much, but you're wrong about one thing. *We* didn't kill your brother. Truth be told? None of us were sure we *could* kill him. No, Silver Eagle, he got the direct treatment. And maybe, if you remember that, you'll be a little less certain about what a man should be doing in our position."

The soul-wounding. That's the doing of whatever they're working for. She'd suspected that, of course, but it was a great deal different to actually have those suspicions confirmed. "You could have just *left*, even if you didn't have the courage to right the Balance."

"Hellfire and curses, girl, you sound just like the damn boy. He almost—" Shrike stopped himself, but maybe too late.

Condor? Wanted to leave? "And why didn't he leave?" She let her sword drop a tiny bit. "Because he couldn't leave *you*?"

Shrike spat on the ground. "He didn't *want* to, no, but believe me, he would have if he'd thought there were any way to talk to *you*. Damn near got us both killed, mooning over you and your justice-ridden family—I finally had to drag him in, make him see the *real* truth, before he gave it up."

Condor almost left... because of me? She grappled with the thought, then pushed it aside. *Later. Later. I've spent so much time brooding on their treachery I don't know what to feel. But this means that Condor might not be beyond reason. Whatever*

Shrike did, whatever he showed Condor, it scared *Condor into following their shadow. Maybe I can reach him...somehow.*

It wasn't the time for a duel. If she could catch up with Condor, who was patrolling the Varheyn area—just a little ways over—if she could catch up with him, it might even be worth Shrike knowing who she was. He spoke gruffly, hard and cold, but somehow she thought there was still some sense of decency, or at least old guilt, in him.

She started to back away, towards the thickets of the jungle that she knew well from years of rambling through every part of Evanwyl.

Shrike's eyes widened, and he suddenly lunged for her, axe held high. "You'll not get to him, you Dragon-spelled witch!"

As she parried, her heart sank. *It wasn't an act. He really cares about Condor—maybe the only thing he* does *care about—and this thing that's behind them, he's so afraid of it...*

The copper-colored axe whipped around again, and she saw a shimmer of sharp claws in the air. Just in time she ducked aside; the axe cleaved air where she had been, but not one, but THREE deep furrows scored the ground, one no more than three inches from her foot. *Claws of the Shrike...*

She evaded the next strike, and the next, reading his movements, looking for an opening to flee. He was too methodical, too well guarded to give her an easy strike to stun. Any cut or jab she tried had to be serious, had to be driven home as if she truly meant to kill him, or it would never get through at all. She offered Myrionar another prayer, pulled speed and strength from the Balanced Sword, and matched the older man strike for strike, her new-forged Flamewing catching the metal Claw and holding back the shimmering magical ones at the same time. *No. I'm not getting away from him. I'm better than he is, I think, despite age and experience...but not enough better to just dump him and run.*

She straightened then, bringing her sword up higher, and she saw Shrike come on full guard. *He's seen it.*

"So, lass. You're ready to kill me?" he said, and his mouth quirked up in a bitter smile. "Then prove to me you're a better woman than your mother, or Windclaw'll take your head to lay next t' hers!"

Decision made, she suddenly felt the fury flare up within her. *You killed Mommy and Daddy! You left us alone, and then you came into my house, spoke as a friend while knowing all along—*

And Flamewing suddenly *blazed*, flaming with red-gold fire, as she swung it again, and again, and *again*, three blows so fast that not even Shrike's speed was enough to parry all of them, and she felt Flamewing bite deep into the false Justiciar's armor, shearing off the shoulder-guard as though it were thick bread before a flaming knife, and Shrike gave a low snarl of pain at the burning cut in his shoulder.

But it was far from a disabling blow, and the return stroke of the axe rebounded from her armor only after delivering such impact that she felt a rib crack and every breath was suddenly fixed and circumscribed with agony. Now it was her turn to back up, on the defensive, as she tried to concentrate enough to heal, or at least drive back the pain, without losing the concentration on the fight that was allowing her to keep her head.

Shrike was *hammering* her now, a rhythmic controlled cycle of swift, hard strokes jolting her body, ramming pain through her arms with every impact. *He knows I might beat him if I recover. So he's not giving me a chance.*

But Shrike wasn't Mist Owl; he was stronger than the *Artan* warrior, but not stronger than she was, and not as skilled. Lythos' training, plus whatever instincts and blessings were in the Vantage family, and perhaps whatever gifts Myrionar had seen fit to offer—these outmatched Shrike in every way. She felt the pain in her chest ebb—a bit, a tiny bit, but enough to ease the tightness of sympathetic contractions in her arms, the instinct to curl in and shield, loosen her stance just that critical bit. Her sword caught the next blow, turned it, and she struck, driving Shrike back a step, struck again, two steps, and as Flamewing awakened again, burning brighter, Shrike was backpedaling furiously, trying to get enough distance, had it, bracing himself, and a howling arose from his axe, the Wind backing his swing as the Fire drove hers, and the two weapons met in pure and complete opposition.

The concussion blew her off her feet, nearly ripped Flamewing from her grasp, left her dazed, not even sure of direction, just knowing she had to get up, *up!*

But when she was up, wavering but with her sword on guard, she saw nothing moving, just drifting smoke and mist from the meeting of Wind and Fire. *Where is he?*

The haze cleared, and now she saw Shrike, lying on his back, unmoving. She edged closer, and as a light breeze blew the last of the smoke away, realized that the false Justiciar would never move again.

Windclaw had failed against the newest blade of the Spiritsmith, against a true Justiciar's weapon, and shattered in the conflict. One great edged shard had plunged full-length through Shrike's throat; his own axe had finished him.

She felt, for a moment, vaguely cheated. By the end, she'd *wanted* to take Shrike's head herself.

But...maybe Shrike's own words had had some truth in them, after all. *Maybe I can't completely judge him when I don't know what he feared. He was fighting to protect...his son, I guess.*

She rested a moment, let Myrionar's power heal her in a flow of star-touched light. *Now to find Condor!*

But almost as she thought that, she realized it was the wrong idea. *How was I just feeling about Shrike? If Aran...Condor... was anything like he seemed, Shrike was his father. I can't go to him fresh from killing Shrike and act as though I might be his friend. That would make me just like them.*

She put the conundrum of Condor aside. *Still, I have to try a different way. On another Justiciar. Both of these I've killed, but maybe...maybe I did this wrongly. Perhaps the ones who have some trace of good, some hope in them, perhaps they need to first see a friendly face, not start out facing a stern and unknown figure that fills them with guilt that pushes them to fight.*

She thought about that as she made her way carefully through the woods. *But who? Four left of the false Justiciars, if they haven't replaced Eagle yet—and I haven't heard that they have. I can't go to Condor yet.* She pictured the others: the overly loud, boisterous Bolthawk, now here, now there, as erratic as the flight of his namesake; Skyharrier, with his cool white wings and gentle even temper. And Thornfalcon...

As soon as she thought of his name, she felt a smile. *Of course. If any of them can be reached, it has to be Thornfalcon—the half-clown, the would-be bard and minstrel.*

The smile broadened. *I'll find him. I'll have to be careful, find out which patrol area he has, figure out how to approach him... but I'll find him.*

And maybe...just maybe...I'll find one I can save.

42

"Oooh, *that* doesn't look good."

The comment was involuntary, and probably not very respectful of the scene. But on reflection, Poplock felt it pretty much covered the ground.

Rather like Shrike.

"Gods be damned...too late." He heard the frustration in the Skysand Prince's voice, and Poplock gripped tighter as Tobimar raced to the body that lay in the clearing and dropped to one knee, hoping against hope that...but one good look at the body, even in the moonlit dark, sent that hope to nothingness. "Stars and sand...not a chance. But what in the Dragons' Names is this that killed him?"

Poplock looked around. It was clear that the jagged shard of metal sticking out of the now-dead Justiciar's throat was a piece of something. As Tobimar continued his cautious examination of the body, Poplock's eyes focused on the heavy, ornate metal shaft not far away, and, on one end... "I revise my opinion. It's worse than not good, it's really, really bad. Tobimar, it's a *piece* of his axe."

The head with its long black hair came up and the startling blue eyes followed his own gold gaze. "By Terian's Light...but you're right." He looked down at the body. "And look, his armor's cut through at the shoulder."

For the first time, Poplock *really* felt uncertain. "Those Justiciar armors and weapons...they're magical."

"More than just ordinary magic. I heard it said they were made by the Spiritsmith, which means they use whatever techniques he knew, and maybe were also infused with some of the god's power in their creation as well. To break that..." Tobimar's face reflected the same indecision.

"You want to back out?" Poplock asked quietly, after a moment of silence.

Tobimar didn't answer immediately; he continued walking cautiously around the clearing. "Poplock, can you help me figure out the battle here?"

"Sure."

For the next hour, the two companions worked on reconstructing the way Shrike had been killed. More than once Poplock found himself wishing Willowwind was there; *he* would probably have figured it all out in minutes. But eventually they came to fairly close agreement.

"First...um, we weren't the first here," Poplock said.

"No. Someone else. Either that, or the survivor came back."

"Hm. Hadn't thought of that. Could be. Boots are about the same size...anyway, how do you read it?"

"Shrike actually made the first move; came up and wrestled the Phoenix—we assume it was Phoenix—to the ground. Then somehow Phoenix got free—hard to imagine, given how well-trained the Justiciars are—and the two of them talked for a while, moving a bit to get in position for attack."

"Maybe." Poplock said. "But these marks here are the Phoenix's, and it looks to me like he or she was trying to leave. Over there, Shrike suddenly charges, as though to stop him from getting away."

Tobimar squinted. "I guess I can see that. But judging by the way the battle goes...it wasn't because Phoenix was *afraid* of Shrike. Shrike seems to have gotten in maybe one or two good shots, but most of the time the battle was going to Phoenix—and there's no trace of pieces of either the Phoenix's weapon or armor."

Then Tobimar looked at him. "Part of me wants to back out. But...no, I can't. Not just pride—although there's a lot of that involved. He hasn't been dead more than a day. If we'd just been a little faster, he wouldn't be dead now."

"Or maybe he would, and we'd be dead with him," Poplock pointed out.

"I don't think so. If we're right about the battle, Shrike wasn't quite this Phoenix's equal, but it wasn't completely one-sided, either. Adding the two of us into the fray—especially when one of us would probably not be noticed until the right minute—would almost certainly have either defeated Phoenix, or forced him to retreat." He studied the ground again, paced out a few of the moves. "Tall indeed. I'm guessing six foot three, maybe six foot four."

"You know, that would argue for a woman as this Phoenix."

"What? Most women are shorter than that."

"True," Poplock agreed, "but if this Phoenix is over six feet tall, he still didn't weigh as much as Shrike, who's a lot shorter. Look at the footprint depth in similar soil. Total burdened weight—because this Phoenix is travelling light, not leaving possessions behind—around two hundred ten, two-twenty."

Tobimar shrugged. "I bow to your superior expertise at this sort of thing. But it still doesn't make much difference.

"The real point is still that this almost has to be part of the whole...tapestry of events, the battlesquares game that Khoros is trying to direct through us and those other five...and maybe others. And it's right where my quest takes me. I can't back out. This is...what he trained me for."

Poplock bounced a subdued nod. "And what I'm already mixed up in. We're only a day or so behind this Phoenix. I think we can get a read on his direction pretty quick and then figure out who his next target is."

"The number of choices is getting narrowed fast, Poplock."

"Don't I know it. Seven Justiciars total, one died a while back, now two more, there's four possibilities left." Poplock scuttled along the forest floor. "C'mon, Tobimar, carry the lightglobe over here. I need to read our quarry's footsteps." As they moved along, he checked each impression. *Okay, after that last clash, both of 'em were knocked down—Shrike permanently. Phoenix gets up... looks like he was still a little shaken, staggers a bit here, trying to get his bearings, probably not sure if Shrike's finished or about to finish him. Moves in carefully, sees his target's down for good. Kneels beside him, maybe just to make sure. Doesn't touch him as far as I can tell. Then...sits there for a minute or two.*

Something about what Tobimar said struck a chord. "You know, Tobimar...I just had a thought."

"That's a dangerous thing for a Toad," his friend said, trying to keep some humor. "What have you thought up this time?"

"Well...look at the picture we have of this guy now. He—or she—is really familiar with this area." *Gets up, moves away a bit...hmm, much* much *steadier now—healing concoction? Meditation? Actual healing gifts?—but no clear direction...* "He's calling himself a Justiciar; he either has similar powers or he's good at faking them. The god's not telling them what's going on." *Hmm. Takes two, three steps in this direction with force, made a decision...stops...thinks again...starts moving off again.* "He knows the area—and the people—well enough to get where he wants, how he wants, and for them not to question him. He fits in."

"And? We know this."

"Well, try *this* mud out for feel: ever hear the term 'inside job'?"

Tobimar stopped in his tracks, and stared at Poplock so long that he started to get uncomfortable. Finally he let out his breath in a *whoosh.* "You have a nasty imagination, my amphibious friend."

"And by that you mean it makes sense."

"A lot of sense in some ways. No need to fake the powers if they *are* your powers. You'll know where the Justiciars are going to search...because you *are* one. Maybe the first victim of the Phoenix wasn't Mist Owl; might've been Silver Eagle himself. That armor isn't in use now, is it?"

"Oooo. That's one I hadn't looked at. You'd need some really good armor to fake up being a Justiciar, and if you made something with a design that silly—I mean, silly if you weren't a Justiciar or God-Warrior or other type where the armor's a symbol, anyway— people'd remember it." *Walking in this direction, quickens pace a bit. Yes, he's made a decision. Shifts course here, I'm betting to throw off pursuit. Need to track a little farther.* "But what if you could just, oh, dress up one of the real Justiciar armors a little? Using your own, there's risks with that, but if you had *another* Raiment set...why, you could put a real glamour on that, make it permanent...no, better, you make it conditional, so it's only going to look like this Phoenix when *you* wear it."

"Might be. And it explains how you can also be good enough to *kill* these Justiciars. You've worked with them. You've fought and sparred with them. You could have figured out a strategy against each one." A thought seemed to strike Tobimar now. "You know, that makes sense. You'd also know what you could use *against* them—with words—to confuse them, throw them off. That's how Shrike lost his grip on Phoenix."

"And now we know who our likely culprit is," Poplock said. *Yes, he's changed direction a couple of times...but this time he's got a line and he's holding to it. It's definitely this way.* "Six foot four, said to be one of the strongest of the Justiciars."

"*Condor.*" Tobimar nodded slowly. "And it explains that little circling, talking bit. Shrike and Condor are direct partners; from what I've heard around they're very close. So Shrike's trying to figure out what's going on, and maybe Condor's trying to explain it to him. But that doesn't work out, and Condor finishes it."

"Our Phoenix was definitely flying off in that direction. If I haven't gotten all turned around, that's the Gharis region?"

"I think so." Tobimar put the lightglobe in a nearby tree fork so he could riffle through their notes.

Poplock was still thinking. "Of course, none of this gives us a *reason* for what he's doing, if we're right. Unless..." *That's it!*

"Unless what?" Tobimar supplied the obvious question, while still searching.

"Unless Silver Eagle wasn't *his* victim, but someone else's. Maybe it's...a power play, a, a, what do you call it, a *schism*, a conflict in the faith itself, being played out inside the Justiciars!"

Tobimar winced. "Terian and Chromaias, you like to think of the worst possible... But it explains why Myrionar can't answer. The motivations are internal; justice can't be served either way, and both sides need or want vengeance." He looked down at the paper in his hand. "And our next target is...probably Thornfalcon. I hear he's the most popular of the Justiciars—and the one most people suspect is the weakest, though he's got tales of unlikely heroism to amuse at any moment." He shook his head. "If we don't get to him before Phoenix does, it's going to be ugly."

"Twice as bad," Poplock observed with grim humor as he bounced back to his accustomed position, "if this theory's right. Nothing's so ugly as getting involved in a family fight."

43

Kyri let out her breath in a silent sigh of relief. Through the window of the Southern View (which mysteriously faced north) she could see the soft brown hair and long profile of Thornfalcon, nodding with a faint smile on his face to the rhythm of the entertainer of the evening, a girl about her own age who was singing and playing the winged harp. *He's there, and—for the moment—alone. With his reputation, that's some luck right there.*

It had taken her longer than she'd hoped—almost two days; she'd found the right region after realizing that the first town she was in was Skyharrier's patrol area, and remembering that Thornfalcon was supposed to have a house just a little farther to the west.

She pulled the cloak up over her head to make her hair unnoticeable and hide her face from casual recognition; the heavy mist of this evening, from chill air coming off the Khalals, made this ploy reasonable. The Phoenix Raiment and Flamewing were packed away for now in the neverfull pack; she now wore the same armor and weapons she'd worn when she began her quest.

Myrionar and Terian, I hope I'm doing the right thing. On the one hand, she knew she had to give the Justiciars every chance, and her prior approach had been confrontational—almost calculated to bring things to a bladed end. But on the other hand, this was far more risky in that it inherently revealed her identity, and might leave enough clues for the other Justiciars and their unseen master to figure it out ahead of time, even if she killed Thornfalcon (and what a horrid thought *that* was).

She took a deep breath and moved, pushed the door and entered the inn.

The air was not that much warmer than outdoors—having experienced real cold now in faraway climes, she found this night much less chilling than she would have before—but the warmth was filled with the smell of baking rolls and bread, cooked meat and roasting vegetables, beers and wines and juices of a dozen types, a welcoming smell echoed by the double-chiming ring of the winged harp and the light songs of the entertainer.

She saw Thornfalcon's gaze flicker in her direction when she entered. *I'd expect no less. A Justiciar—or a false Justiciar—has to be aware of danger, even in a place that should be safe. But I'm not a threat to him right now, and he should be able to see that . . . good, he's looked away, almost as fast as he looked at me. Saw me, categorized me as a traveller, decided I was of no immediate importance. Not enough to look away from the singer, anyway.*

She walked up the side aisle as though headed for the far corner, then slid smoothly onto the carved bench that faced Thornfalcon across his booth's table.

He instantly focused on her. "Sir, if you'll pardon me, I was—"

Thornfalcon broke off as he identified the face under the hood, and she found that—despite the tension and deadly seriousness of the situation—she was barely able to stifle a laugh at the way his jaw sagged and eyes widened in an expression of dumbfounded shock that was only exaggerated by his long, mournful minstrel's face. It was a tribute to his control that the shocked expression lasted only an instant—so brief that only someone else who had been watching him closely would have seen it.

"*Kyri?*" he murmured finally, barely loud enough to hear over the music and subdued conversations around them. "By the Balance, what are you *doing* here?"

"Looking for you, actually," she answered. "I need to talk to you, Thornfalcon."

He gave her one of his famous smiles. "Ahh, now, if only I could believe that you came all this way merely to profess your adoration. But I suspect it's something much more serious."

She tried to match his lightness. "Oh, now, I would never dare;

you've so many other choices, from what I've heard, that a girl like me would be wasting her time. But yes, serious enough."

"As I always told your aunt, you insist on underestimating yourself. But this is not at all a good time, Kyri. There's a—"

This time he managed to keep his expression mostly under control, but his face went nearly white. "*You?*"

"Yes. But please, we need to talk, that's why I came here, like this, please, Thornfalcon!"

She saw his expression go through several shifts. A flash of understanding first, when he broke off, with simultaneous disbelief that it could be true. A deeper understanding, and at her words she saw what she thought was a flash of the same fear that had driven Mist Owl and Shrike. But he glanced at her again, and she thought that—because she had come in ordinary clothes, not the armor of an avenger—he was seeing, not someone judging him, threatening him, but the girl he'd watched grow up, and that made him hesitate.

Finally he nodded, his face back to its normal color and humorous expression. "Of course, Kyri. But not here."

"Where, then?"

He looked undecided, then resigned. "This is my normal patrol area. I have a small estate of my own...well, that is far too grand a description, really, a house in the forest that protects the people from my caterwaulings that might charitably be described as practice by those with tolerance in such things."

She smiled under the hood as he rose, and she followed, noting that he placed three coins on the table—vastly overpaying for the meal she saw before him. As they exited, she asked, "Why so much?"

He clearly knew what she meant. "Firstly, most lovely and mysterious lady, because he would normally expect my custom there to last all the night, and thus I am signifying that I did not leave due to a displeasure with the food or the entertainment; and second, because we do not wish him to speak of anything he may have noticed, and money is an excellent lever in this sort of game."

He gestured as she opened her mouth again. "No more, please. We both have...innumerable questions, but until we are inside and safe, I cannot be sure *what* ears are listening, what eyes are watching."

She nodded, and followed.

Thornfalcon was good. Better than she had thought. He moved smoothly, now that he had a goal and was not playing the clown to a crowd—which, now that she thought of it, was the way she had always seen him. She'd never actually had any significant time alone with him. *But of course Rion had, and he told me just how formidable Thornfalcon was. Not that I ever really doubted it—he'd passed all the tests to become a Justiciar, after all.* Thornfalcon led her quickly and silently through a back alley, down a narrow path, then reversed direction, took a few more turns, all maneuvers clearly meant to throw off any possible followers.

The final path he followed had branchings and twists enough so that no one who didn't know where they were going was ever likely to follow the right route, and wound through the jungle for a straight-line distance of nearly half a mile—certainly enough to keep the privacy he wanted, she decided. The house itself was somewhat larger than Thornfalcon had implied, but still was, as he had said, nowhere near grand enough to be called an estate.

She did note, however, that it had a very strong and serviceable fence, with guard spikes, a sense of warding magic, and a formidable lock which he opened with a key hung about his neck. Finally the white-painted door was opened and she stepped in. "It's quite nice."

The hallway was polished brown wood, with a few lightsculpt paintings on the wall in carefully chosen locations. Thornfalcon smiled, though the tension in his face robbed it of its usual easy charm, made it look almost sinister for a moment. "Not quite the den of seduction and sensuality one might have imagined?"

She tried to laugh, and found her own tension turned it into a rough snort. "Well, no."

He seemed about to respond, then shook his head. "Neither of us has time or mind, now, for the pleasantries." He gestured to the next room, a small dining room, and offered her a chair. "Kyri...*you* are this 'Phoenix' we have heard about? The one who has been claiming miracles in our name, who has slain one of us already?"

She nodded, sitting down. "Two, now."

"*Two?*" He shook his head again, then selected a bottle from the shelf and placed two glasses in front of them. "I abandoned my meal and you have had none, and most surely I need a drink if we are to...discuss what I think we are. Kyri..." He opened the bottle and poured a blue-and-gold stream into each glass. She recognized it; an *Artan* flower-and-fruit liqueur, called Goldsea. Auntie Victoria had some, but very rarely served it because it was so expensive. She'd tried it, and it was very good. But she didn't feel very thirsty right now.

"Kyri," Thornfalcon continued, "why?"

She looked him steadily in the eye. "You know very well why."

He dropped his gaze. "But...then you know...that I have to kill you. Or, at the least, give the word to my brothers so all of us can do so," he said slowly, sounding as though each word were being dragged from him.

"I know you don't *have* to do that at all," she said softly. She was trying to pitch her voice carefully, not to confront him with his evils, but offer him hope. "I am not called for only Vengeance, Thornfalcon, but Justice, and tempered always with Mercy. You know these words, now understand that they are *true*."

His head came up slowly, and his expression was much like that which had touched Mist Owl's for a moment, hope and disbelief at war. "Kyri...are you saying...are you really saying what you seem to be?" His facile words and banter were gone, too much emotion roiling within to allow him the face of the clown or minstrel. He took a large swallow from the glass in front of him, yet his eyes now never left her face.

"I am saying that just as you are no longer merely Wollin Venpa but Thornfalcon, I am more truly named Phoenix. I am saying that Myrionar Itself spoke to me, and named me the last and first of Justiciars, and has given me the charge to redeem Its name and Its temples and Its Justiciars—by Justice and Wisdom and Mercy, if possible, or by terrible and final Vengeance if not."

A suspicion of a sparkle, a hint of a tear, showed at the corner of the older man's eyes, and his smile and the faint tremor in his voice confirmed it. "Well...well, Kyri...I have no words! What a...an occasion that is, eh? But..." He raised his glass to her. "However this ends...Kyri Vantage, the Phoenix, I salute you. It is...a miracle."

A burst of relief washed through her. *He can be reached!* She took up her own glass and returned his salute. She still wasn't really thirsty, so she just wet her lips and put the glass down, but it was the gesture that mattered here.

After that burst of sentiment, Thornfalcon's shoulders slumped. "But Kyri... Phoenix, I suppose I should say... You must know I don't dare. I can't. Didn't you try to talk to Mist Owl or... which of us was your second?"

"Shrike." The single word was surprisingly hard to say. It was only now sinking in that she'd really killed a man who'd been like an uncle to her.

"Ah."

"Yes... I did, I did try, Thornfalcon, I tried to talk to them, but they were too scared. I know Mist Owl wanted to, I could never have beaten him by myself; he died because he didn't want to kill me but was too afraid to join me. Shrike... had other reasons, I think. But I thought that maybe I was doing it wrong, facing and accusing..."

"... instead of coming to us like our little lost sister," he finished, "asking her brothers for help. My dear, I am startled by your insight. An entirely correct judgment on your part; a shame it had to come after the first two... but few of us have made no mistakes in our lives. And you likely give yourself too little credit. Mist Owl *and* Shrike? You truly are your brother's mirror. He would be proud, I think." He rose from the table, strode to the window, looking out for a moment. "But I am much less a man than either of them. You look to me for courage that I fear I do not have, for you do not know what it is we serve."

"Then at least *tell* me, Thornfalcon! Please! Even if we must come to blows..." she couldn't keep the pain from her voice or the stinging from her eyes at the thought, "... even if it must happen again, do at least that much more than the others, and Myrionar will keep your soul safe in the Balance, out of even your master's reach." She felt suddenly terribly weary. It had been a long trek to reach Gharis, and not a short one to follow Thornfalcon here, but more, the thought that she might have to draw Flamewing against Thornfalcon weighed upon her.

"Ah, now, that's the problem, is it not? Can a god who's been so weakened, so tricked—or, on the other hand, who is beset by a power so great that the god *could not* oppose it openly—promise any such salvation, unless it has learned some new and key truth, or gained some power or ally that heretofore was lacking?" Thornfalcon stood tensely, seeming to fight an inner battle. "A part of me would very much like to at least tell you the truth—as much of it as I know. Very much indeed. Yet...where will I find assurance of even my soul's existence? You must know how your brother met his end and what that meant."

"I know that Myrionar swore me an oath—on the powers of all the Gods—that if I were true that I would see both Justice *and* Vengeance, in full measure, for all that I and my family have lost." *I really* am *tired,* she realized. *Too many nights of worry... and not sleeping very well...catching up with me.* Still, she could see the import of that news strike him.

"A Gods-Oath?" he said, as thought trying to grasp the immensity of the implications. "Such a promise goes far beyond the one god, Kyri. That would extend..."

"...to those known to be allied in the heavens with Myrionar, especially to Chromaias and Terian of the Infinite, yes." She barely restrained a jawcracking yawn; this would be a bad time to break the mood. "Thornfalcon, is even your master so great that he might disregard the Light in the Darkness with impunity?"

A long hesitation. "No. No, I would not say that. I have heard... it says things which would make me believe even it would be cautious about confronting any of the high gods directly."

Now the yawn came despite her best efforts, and she felt herself sway. *Now...wait a moment. I cannot be that tired.*

Even as she thought that, she realized the only possible explanation. "But...I didn't drink..."

Thornfalcon turned, and the long face was drawn in a smile so thin and cold that the sheer horror of the transformation momentarily shocked the rising mists of unconsciousness away. "Naturally, my dear, but I would hardly rely on *that.* Alchemical glass made with a number of sleep and paralysis venoms—my own creation, I'm quite proud of it. And by now, though you still have—surprisingly—some ability to move and speak, not enough to achieve the balance necessary for the gifts of a true Justiciar."

Her horror rose as she realized the implications of those glasses. *He did not make those for me; they were simply one convenient tool at hand!* He strode forward, even as she fumbled to draw her sword, and picked up the goblet. "Activated by the touch of female lips, not male, as I see you understand. Thus no danger to me of choosing the wrong glass."

She was desperately clinging to consciousness with terror and fury. "You...monstrous..."

"I take that as a compliment—and allow me to return that compliment; your family's inhuman stamina is as freakish as ever I might have guessed. I've felled ogres with the same concoction as made that glass, and in less time." He reached down, gently eased her hand down, forcing the sword back the few inches she'd managed to draw it. His hand drew back with a slow caress that sent a shudder down her spine. "Monstrous, exactly. You see, my patron has promised me that—if I do well enough—I shall become one of its people; it has already brought me far along that path. I have no intention of remaining human, even if there are certain human... amusements that I expect to enjoy for the rest of my immortal life."

Following Mercy, did I fail to have Wisdom? Myrionar, help me! Horror, as well as unconsciousness, claimed her.

44

Kyri came slowly awake, aware of lingering traces of horror that, at first, had no clear source. She could not quite remember...

Balance and Sword! Thornfalcon!

As though the thought had summoned him, she heard the false Justiciar's humorous, yet acid-toned, voice say "Ahh, my Lady, I see you are awakening. Welcome to my...boudoir."

Her eyes snapped open.

The room she was in was of moderate size, elaborately decorated with paintings, tapestries, stone and lightsculpt hangings, with soft lighting and a warm, almost rosy glow over everything. The artworks were all romantic scenes, and the overall effect was of the lover, poet, dreamer that was Thornfalcon's face to most of the world.

But she herself was bound to an articulated framework of metal, crystal, and wood, cushioned softly on every edge, which lay somehow suspended upon a very large bed. To one side of her was a beautiful and elaborate keepsake chest...but the devices and tools within glinted cold and sharp, arrayed like wizards' material and formulae, not what any would expect in such a sentimental container. On her other side, Thornfalcon lay, his shirt already open, his hair unbound, and his smile sharp and eager.

To her surprise, she was still fully dressed. This did not comfort her at all. It took surprising effort to speak; the paralysis of the alchemical glass seemed to have worn off, but the shock and horror of her position was almost impossible to overcome.

She knew, though, that if she did not speak—did not distract him—any chance she had (and her chances did not look good) would be gone. "Your...reputation."

He raised an eyebrow. "Not the initial reaction I expected." His smile looked almost genuine for a moment. "Marvelous. I really find the raging 'what have you done, you'll pay for this,' et cetera, almost as predictable and unimaginative as the screaming and pleading. They all certainly have their pleasures, I admit," and there was a brittle, shaking edge to his voice that made her feel as though something long dead were crawling down her spine, "but new reactions are new thrills.

"And such a compact opening!" He sprang from the bed and walked to the chest, examining the blades, needles, shears, and other devices carefully and with deliberate, cruel ostentation. "You mean, now you understand aspects of my reputation in a new light than before."

"You've always been known as a ladies' man..." she said, trying to keep her voice under control, "but especially for the travellers, the adventurers. The most beautiful you'd entertain—if they were willing—at your house, perhaps for days, before sending them on their way.

"But they never actually left this house, did they?"

"Quite precisely right, my dear." He put down the tools, and with a gesture caused the suspending framework to rise up. He began—with exquisite delicacy, almost never touching her—to unlace and unfasten the exterior armor. His pale complexion was now touched with a hint of rose, and he ran a hand through his hair at one point, disarranging it. "Naturally, I enjoy the quite ordinary pleasures of womens' company, but for the more... unusual of my appetites, I must carefully choose individuals who won't be missed. A string of disappearing women in my own neighborhood, or even throughout Evanwyl, would cause talk."

"I suppose your...master approves of this sort of thing, too."

He laughed. "In truth? Not at all. Well, I don't think it disapproves of the actions in and of themselves, and surely it approves of most deeds dark and savage in some way, but it finds my interests...oh, juvenile, probably a potential weakness, not something that interests *it*, certainly. It *does* approve of the fact that I do not waste the material, however." He continued the slow, sensuously blood-chilling operation as he spoke. "Your words do seem to indicate you labor under one misapprehension. My patron is not, precisely, my master. We are ... partners. And while I am, admittedly, a junior partner in the greater enterprise, here it is *my* domain, to do with as I will so long as I do not forget its purposes as well."

Her body armor was being laid gently, piece by piece, on the floor as he spoke, and his smile grew slightly wider, the tone of his voice subtly more excited, as he removed each one. Inlaid in expensive woods and metals in elaborate form on the floor—revealed only in pieces, even now that his words and actions had drawn attention to it, because many soft rugs were scattered here and there—was a mystic circle, perhaps a pentagram, and some of the symbols she saw brought an even deeper chill to her heart. *I knew he was going to torture me to death.* The fact that the structure that held her was meant to hold her in various positions on the bed told her that he would be doing ... other things, as well. *But it's worse, even worse than I thought. This is not just a place to satisfy appetites I can't even begin to imagine ... it's a ritual circle. He'll use my pain, my fear, my soul in the end, for something even worse!*

Myrionar, help me! she thought. Fully awake and undrugged, she knew she had her Balance now, at least for a few moments. But at the same time, she didn't know exactly what to pray for. She did not have the Phoenix Raiment on—it was within her neverfull pack, up against the far wall, so no true godspower could be sent through her without possibly killing her outright. And even if she had the strength to break free, it would take too long; Thornfalcon's rapier was still on his hip, and she suspected that even ... later, he would never be without a weapon close to hand.

He shook his head. "The Balanced Sword is weak, Kyri. And remembering the magnificent strength you showed off to us when moving, I've reinforced the bindings."

"So you'd target adventurers—the women among them, anyway—and especially those who were alone or known to go off on their own." She returned to the prior subject, trying to buy herself time. "And I'll bet you'd do it *after* they'd done whatever they were here to do, so everyone expected them to leave anyway."

"Or before, sometimes, if they had the mad ambition to enter, say, Rivendream Pass. In that case, I might have been actually more kind to them than they were planning for themselves." The irony of the word *kind* was emphasized with another smile. "I know more of what lies beyond that pass then you, or any other in Evanwyl, I assure you. Now, I—"

Faintly, from below, came a sound of someone hammering on the door, and for a moment Kyri's heart leapt in hope. But then the shouted words came through: "Thornfalcon! *Justiciar Thornfalcon! Answer! Are you there? Thornfalcon!*"

Thornfalcon closed his eyes for a moment, struggling to wipe away the savage snarl of frustration, and the whipcord-slender, perfectly sculpted muscles tensed and twitched. As the pounding and shouting continued, he opened his eyes, gave a smile as gentle and welcoming as ever he had.

"Tsk, what a shame, my Lady, our private moment is interrupted. Yet...momentary reprieves, solitude in anticipation of what is to come, these have their place in the entertainment as well. Fear not...or fear greatly, but I shall return...shortly."

45

Gharis, in light, warm evening rain, was a faint misty glow ahead, that resolved into a village of several houses, at least one large smithy, a wide-fronted building that probably combined warehousing and labor resources for several local businesses, and the lightglobe-illuminated sign of the local inn, the Southern View.

"Looks quiet," Poplock said as they walked down the street.

"Phoenix is neither stupid nor impulsive," Tobimar answered, glancing around. *Unfortunately, we don't really know what we're looking for.* "Neither of the first two fights occurred anywhere that witnesses were possible, and unless he's just a madkiller, he's not going to get sloppy now." People who killed for the sake of killing, he knew, usually grew more bold as they succeeded, but he doubted that the unknown Phoenix was anything like that. "If anything, he's going to get more careful, now that the Justiciars have started hunting for him and put up adventurer contracts."

"You're probably right," agreed Poplock, turning around on his shoulder and looking behind them as he often did, "but then what do we do now?"

"Luckily our information bundles included summaries of all the Justiciars—since they were clearly potential targets of our quarry. So we know what Thornfalcon looks like and something of his personality."

"Noticed there's aspects about *that* which weren't emphasized in the packet, though. They talk a lot in there about his acting and performance talents, but not so much about his hopping from one pond to another, if you know what I mean."

Tobimar shook his head. "They seem a lot more sensitive about that kind of thing here in Evanwyl." He shifted course slightly. "This is his regular patrol area; he's got to be known at the inn."

"And you want to get in out of this nice rain. What about in Skysand, what do *they* think about that kind of thing?"

"Yes, I do. In Skysand?" He grinned. "You don't even want me to *start* on that. The Way of Sacred Waters is pretty complicated."

As they reached the doorway, Poplock turned up his warty head in a manner that somehow conveyed a snort of disbelief. "You're just evading the subject. So your people *are* pretty tight on that kind of thing."

"Yes, and no, and still it's complicated. Now shut up." He pushed the door and went in.

No one really took notice of the entry, though there were a few who looked mildly surprised after a moment, recognizing that he was a stranger. *On the job now. Focus.*

He extended his senses as Khoros had taught him. *When seeking among others, there are always lies,* the old man had said with a cynical smile. *You need to be able to steer your course around them.*

So I'll be able to sense lies?

Khoros had shrugged. *That is possible, but that is an ability that is often overrated. It is not the* lie *that is your enemy, for people lie about many things, especially when questioned; they may believe you are seeking some secret they hold which, in truth, matters not at all to you. More, they may say something that they* believe *to be true, when in fact it is false or a misleading portion of the truth. What you need to sense is when something is wrong with your course, when something is sending you astray. That is what I will teach you.*

I... don't understand.

Many people sometimes have a sense of danger that warns them just in time of some terrible event about to happen. It is unreliable, and for most people it works but once or twice in their lives. But it is a part of becoming one *with the universe around us—or, more truthfully, of making the universe attuned and one with us. I will show you how to extend that sense. It is not easy, it is not—at the level you shall reach in ordinary time—foolproof or a panacea—but it will serve you well.*

Tobimar could feel it now, as though all the people—all the

elements around him—were connected and connecting at levels most of those present could not even imagine. And through those connections, maybe, just maybe, he could get to Thornfalcon in time. A quick look around, however, did not reveal anyone with the gangling frame or long features that the images of Thornfalcon showed.

Smaller than the Balanced Meal, the Southern View combined the welcome desk with the main counter, so Tobimar headed there. A dark-haired woman with a streak of gray down the center of her head looked up from a plate she was preparing. "Yes, sir?"

"Excuse my interruption, please, but have you seen the Justiciar Thornfalcon?"

"Frequently, sir." She smiled at his momentary blink. "But I'm guessing you mean if I have seen him this evening. And indeed, he was here, earlier." She nodded to a booth now occupied by what Tobimar assumed was a local couple.

"I have an urgent need to find him, ma'am."

"Vlay was on then. *Vlay!*" she called over to the far end of the counter with unnecessary volume, and the large, somewhat tired-looking man with brown hair at the other end turned.

"Cinders, Gam, you don't need to screech like a raven. What?"

She nodded to Tobimar as she finished filling the plate in front of her and started off across the room with it. "This boy, looking for Thornfalcon!"

Vlay came over, wiping his hands off on his apron and leaving streaks of the sauces he'd been working on. "You missed him, youngster."

"When did he leave?"

"A while ago."

"Do you know where I can find him?"

He rolled his eyes. "Usually it's the ladies asking that question, but I'll give you the same answer: even if I knew, I wouldn't tell you. Not my place."

A sense of urgency was rising in Tobimar, even though he couldn't put a name or reason to it. "It's very important I find him, as fast as possible."

"He'll be on patrol tomorrow, I'm sure. Sorry." Vlay began to turn away.

"Wait, sir!" Tobimar bared the patch on his shoulder. "Tobimar Silverun. Adventurer, Zarathanton Guilded."

Vlay looked mildly impressed, but not nearly as much as others often were. "Young to be an Adventurer, but all right. If I see him, I'll pass on your name."

He doesn't expect to see him again tonight, though. And he's not telling me where...

Suddenly it hit him, and he caught Vlay's arm as he turned away.

"Let go my arm or I'll break it, boy!"

He let go, since he once more had the man's attention. "Thornfalcon—he didn't leave alone, did he?"

Vlay laughed. "Never does, eh?"

That stopped him for a moment. "You mean he left with a woman?"

"That's his type, yes. Not you, if that's what you're after."

Tobimar restrained a roll of his eyes, and suddenly it hit him, as Poplock's grip on his shoulder suddenly grew painful. "No! Listen, the person he left with—tall, very tall, six foot three, six foot four, moved like a fighter?"

Now he really had Vlay's attention—and part of him felt there was something sinister in the man's gaze, but that wasn't important now. "Might be, 'Venturer."

"And you're sure it was a woman?"

His eyes narrowed. "What are you saying?"

"I'm saying that by Sand and Sea you'll tell me where I can find Thornfalcon or you might never see him again!" Tobimar hissed, trying to keep his voice down. *No point starting a panic or too many rumors, even if I might be too late now.* "I've been *hired* by the Justiciars and the Temple to find the false Justiciar that's already killed two of the others."

"Two? I heard 'twas one—"

"Two, and you may be the first one other than me to know, because I've been tracking him since I found Shrike's *body*. And what you've just told me means he *left with the person who means to kill him!*"

"Great Balance." The man's gaze shifted, then came back. "All right, but if you're having me on, boy, I'll send word all the way back to the Guild and have you stripped and hounded." He gave quick, precise directions on how to find Thornfalcon's home. "Luck to you."

"Thank you, Vlay. Pray to your Balance that I won't be late."

Outside now, he focused, drawing on his reserves. *Time to move.*

"He might be dead already." Poplock observed cheerfully.

"Let's hope not. If our mystery Phoenix really is a woman and she's taken *this* tactic, well, there will be dinner first before he's in the most vulnerable position."

"Hmm. Yes, he's known as setting quite a table, I hear."

The dark, wet jungle streamed by on either side as Tobimar ran, enhanced senses guiding him more surely than ordinary sight would have. *Please let us be in time, let us be in time...*

And then they were through, into a wide clearing with a large house, surrounded by a high and solid fence of slatewood, in the center. The gate to the house was closed and locked. Tobimar looked around. "He's got guard spikes all around and I'm not sure I can jump that. It's warded too. Just breaking through is not going to work. And his callcharm's showing a privacy seal— even if we send a call, it's not going to signal inside the house. Drought and Death! So close—"

"No need for cursing, not yet." Poplock hopped up to the gateway. "Hmm. Yes, looks tough. Wards are panel-and-post wards, though. Not perimeter. Except for verminseal—which still is pretty expensive, and slow going—perimeter's very hard to do, very expensive, takes a lot of work. Easier to do panel-and-post, and lots cheaper usually, even if you have to have the panels and support posts shipped all the way from Zarathanton." He indicated the massive pillars supporting the sections of solid wood fencing.

"So?"

"So that means he only has verminseal perimeter wards *here*."

And Poplock squeezed himself straight through the three-inch gap between the gateway posts and the main fence, getting only momentarily hung up when Steelthorn tried to turn sideways. His voice came back through the hole. "And verminseal isn't all that strong, and anyway doesn't stop anything that's thinking much."

A pause. "Urk. He needs to oil the inner latch. Why do you..." a Toadish grunt, "...humanoids...always make things hard... to...*turn?*"

There was a click, and suddenly the gateway popped open. Tobimar ran through and caught up Poplock, dashing up the path to the front door. "You know, you're more dangerous than I thought. And I thought you were pretty dangerous before."

"Fear me," the little Toad agreed, with a self-satisfied smile on his face.

The callcharm on the door was showing privacy as well. "Darkness and Death."

"Not hearing anything much from inside right now. Maybe a little movement upstairs. Want me to—"

"No, no time for subtlety." Tobimar raised his fist and pounded on the door. "Thornfalcon! *Justiciar Thornfalcon! Answer! Are you there? Thornfalcon!*"

For several moments he was sure he was too late, but then he heard an answering voice—one filled with annoyance. "Very well, very well, *enough!*"

The door was yanked open and Thornfalcon stood there, bare to the waist but with a long, keen rapier in his hand. "I know not how you've come past my wards and wall, boy, but if you have no explanation that pleases me, I'll cut the clothes from your back and leave you with scars you'll have to explain for all the rest of your life. And if it displeases me enough, you'll never leave."

It was clear, from the faint sheen of sweat already visible on the Justiciar's face and the somewhat disordered hair—not to mention the state of semi-dress—that they were just barely in time. "Sir, I'm sorry, very sorry." He reached to his shoulder, and saw that the rapier twitched at that sudden move, but was restrained. He pulled down the patch covering. "Tobimar Silverun. Hired by the Justiciars and Temple to chase that false Justiciar."

"What of it? That does not give you authority to enter my estate."

"No, sir, but this does: the woman you brought home with you tonight is, almost certainly, the Phoenix, and she intends to kill you." *Why is it that my sense of unease is not gone? It almost feels* worse.

Thornfalcon's long face only emphasized the comical drop of his jaw. "*What?*"

"She's very tall, six foot three, slender-looking, maybe two hundred pounds or less soaking wet, and I've just tracked her from Shrike's body. Sir, you have to believe me!" The sense of imminent peril grew even as Thornfalcon slowly backed away and let them enter. *What is it? What is wrong? Has the Phoenix recognized that the interruption means her disguise has been penetrated? Are we all at risk now?*

That thought made *sense . . .* and yet there was no sense of rightness about it; indeed, it seemed completely against the connections of past and future.

But Thornfalcon's expression had slowly shifted to unwilling acceptance of possibility. "You speak with conviction, and while I am loath indeed to imagine the young lady—indeed, *any* young lady—could harbor such dark designs against me, I would be foolish to ignore a warning so earnestly given." Thornfalcon turned and reached out, and Tobimar saw that his Raiment was on a stand nearby. The mystical and symbolic armor seemed to *flow* from its resting place and garb its owner in a smooth combined motion that ended with Thornfalcon's arms stretched above his head.

Thornfalcon lowered his arms, tugging at the gauntlets as though adjusting their fit *just so*. "Well, then, let us proceed to discuss this with the lady who awaits us. But you shall owe her an apology of *staggering* dimensions if you prove wrong in this, I assure you!" He gestured to a wide stairway farther down the hall. "Shall we?"

As Tobimar turned, three things happened almost at once:

One: A tiny weight disappeared from his shoulder with an inarticulate croak.

Two: Points and connections drew infinitely tight, an array of meaning and possibility frozen in crystal, and he saw horror and dropped, rolling aside in the same instant.

Three: A streak of cold light, steel and sorcery intertwined, speared through the point his skull had occupied in the infinitesimal past; the steel withdrew, the magic continued, shattering a hole in the carven-wood staircase.

Tobimar continued his roll, coming to his feet, drawing the twin blades even as the shock of understanding and the nearness of death sent nausea and terror through him.

Thornfalcon regarded him from beneath the upraised helm, one eyebrow quirked high, a cruel smile on the face that before had been so welcoming. "Oh, well *done*, Adventurer. The Guild has not lowered its standards, I see. And I must say, it is rather appropriate that the young lady have someone arrive at the very proverbial last minute." The shimmering rapier came up in an ironic salute. "Yet I fear that the ending of this play would not please the crowd. Fortunate, is it not, that I play now only to an audience of one?"

"You...you're a Justiciar! How...why?"

The other man shook his head slowly, smile broadening.

Oh.

"It's the other way around, isn't it?"

"Very good, Tobimar Silverun." He could sense more power now, something that made his skin crawl, a power that was not mere magic and energy, but born of darkness, and he no longer saw—exactly—a man before him, but something else, something more—or less. "You have found the true solution to the riddle. But that, I am afraid, will be the final—and never-known—victory of your tragically short life."

46

The room was now empty except for Kyri and waiting horror.
This is my only chance.

Kyri looked at the bindings; they were light, wide straps of
some soft, pearlescent material, but the softness did not mean
lack of strength. When she tried to pull, they gave hardly at all.
Might be shadespider silk. I could break about half *that much.
Maybe. On a good day.* The material was ideal for bindings;
wouldn't cut into the person's arms or legs—*or head, now that
I notice*—or cut off circulation as long as they didn't struggle,
and it was very hard to hurt yourself struggling against it...but
it was also stronger than the best ordinary rope by a great deal.

I will not fail. I will not! *I will find* some *way out of this.*

She cast desperately around, her glance falling on the open
keepsake box. The blades glittered back at her.

He's not here controlling everything. Maybe...

She stretched her body, threw it to one side as far as she
could flex.

The floating platform moved slightly, tilted a bit.

Yes! She tried to gauge the way the unseen, immaterial supports shifted. *Meant to allow him to position his victim in any
way he wants, and do it easily. He can probably lock it down
if he likes, but he didn't before he left.* The keepsake chest was
near her head. *Have to tilt and spin so my one hand can reach
into the chest.*

She raised her chest, arching her back slowly, then slammed

down and to the right. *There!* The platform shifted, tilted just a little more. Again. And again!

Suddenly, through the partially open door, she heard a shout, and a clash of blades. *Whoever it is might have found out too much. Maybe they're good enough... but maybe not. Got to get out of... here!*

The last slam of her body forced the strange suspended structure past a minor tipping point, and it revolved sideways and down, perfectly lined up. Kyri felt a savage grin starting across her face as she saw the chest getting closer, and stretched her fingers out, out. *I just need one thing,* anything, *with a sharp edge—*

But as her fingers were within an inch of the chest and still dropping, the glittering trays of blades and needles *retreated*, the elaborate carven lid slid shut, and her fingers struck only solid wood.

"No!" For a moment she wanted to curse and cry at the same time. *Of* course *he'd spelled it against anyone else touching his toybox.*

A tremendous shattering crash echoed from below, and she realized someone or something had gone through one of Thornfalcon's huge picture windows. She wanted to believe it was the false Justiciar, but she remembered Rion's description of fighting Thornfalcon and her hope faded. *Whoever that is, they're fighting my battle... and they're about to get killed for it.*

A terrible cold fury rose up, but she controlled it, balanced it. *Myrionar, give me strength. Give me all the strength my mortal body may handle. I have sought Justice, offered Mercy, tried to follow Wisdom.*

Now there is only Vengeance.

Smoke suddenly rose from the floor, but the spell-wards of Thornfalcon—though they must have been strong—were not equal to stopping the blessing of a god. She felt strength flowing into her, filling her with power, and she threw her entire body against the bindings that held her.

The elaborate frame itself creaked and seemed to bend slightly under the strain. The webbing tightened, pulled in soft yet imperative resistance, stretched perhaps... but did not break.

No good, she thought, horror starting to return. *Even twice my strength isn't enough to break those bonds. He knew I was a Justiciar. He knows how much I can hope to gain from Myrionar, so he's made the bindings that much stronger.*

But even in incipient despair, something hovered, nagged at her. *Made the bindings stronger . . .*

Creaked . . . seemed to bend . . .

Made the bindings *stronger . . .*

And despair was gone in a rising tide of furious hope. "There's two things you didn't think of, Thornfalcon," she said as she took deep breaths, preparing herself.

"The bindings are stronger . . . but did you make this prisoning *frame* stronger?

"And do you really know everything Lythos taught us?"

First the meditations. I can't afford mistakes. She ran through the Winds of Direction and Winds of Seasons, the Eight Winds, and she felt her mind becoming focused, calm, certain; behind that, the strength of Myrionar waited, patient, eternal, for her to call it forth again.

Her whole body tensed once more, but this time in a smooth, controlled, focused effort, building, building, the power of the Living Will, not merely the Claw of Stone, the *Body* of Stone. For a moment she thought she could see Lythos, with that single tiny smile, nodding to her, as she pit her strength, and the strength of Myrionar, and finally the strength of the human soul, of her living and unbreakable will, against the silken-steel prison of abomination she was bound within.

Thornfalcon's bindings of shadespider silk held softly firm, but the structure itself creaked again, seemed to bend . . . and now there was no seeming about it, a bend, a screeching of metal, and suddenly something broke, and the framework fell, no longer intact, no longer supported. She grunted in pain as she hit the ground, but now the structure was weakened. Pull and bend again. And again!

With abruptness that startled her, one arm came entirely free, remnants of metal and wood suspension still bound to her. She rolled, added that arm's pull to the other, and *that* one came free, and she sat up, the remaining pieces of that grisly horrific trap falling away as the structure's integrity completely failed. Trailing the sound of the pathetic remnants, she leapt to her pack and yanked it open. Flamewing first, and the huge blade made short work of the shadespider bindings.

And then she reached in again, and pulled forth the Raiment of the Phoenix.

47

Tobimar's twin blades flickered back and forth, following the sense of motion, flick of eye and intent, and even with two weapons it was all he could do to keep that terrible rapier from impaling him or cutting him to ribbons with its double-edged blade. The exiled prince leapt backwards, a midair reversed somersault barely clearing another stroke of Thornfalcon's weapon, landing with a skid atop a display table.

"You've marred a near-priceless Imperial table, you barbarian," Thornfalcon said, still smiling, showing none of the tension Tobimar felt. "I'm tempted to take that price out in pain, but I also," the smile widened, "hate to keep a lady waiting."

He unleashed a flurry of blows that backed Tobimar up a step, and suddenly cut lower, much lower.

The slender rapier cut *through* the solid silverwood legs of the table as though they had been reeds, and Tobimar leapt up and over the false Justiciar as the table collapsed, parrying a weak and surprised stroke in midair, taking a cut at Thornfalcon's back with the other blade; unfortunately it rebounded from the Raiment armor.

"You complain about *me* marring your table?" he said, as his senses and mind tried desperately to figure out a way to finish this without dying. Poplock was nowhere to be seen, at least not at a sideways casual glance, but then, he was very, very good at hiding.

"My compliments on your agility; you have already evaded

Lightning longer than many. As to my table, once marred, the value is gone. No point in trying to repair perfection; finish its destruction when the time is right." The long face which made him a perfect choice to play the sad and lost also stretched other expressions, emphasized Thornfalcon's malice.

And that must be the way he views everything. All or nothing, his to keep or throw away. Terian's Light, what sort of a monster is he? Tobimar focused, reaching for what Master Khoros had once called the *High Center*, where he could touch again the web of possibility and certainty. The focus cost him in accuracy and speed, perhaps lethally, but he had little choice. He could not win against the Justiciar as things stood.

The rapier smashed against his defending blades like a bludgeon. One part of Tobimar registered this, was astounded by the force. *This weapon ... it gives up nothing against heavier blades. He has all the speed and maneuverability of a rapier, but none of its weaknesses. I* must *separate him from that blade.*

The other part of him was rising higher, extending outward, touching the essence of the world around him again. The course of the world was now his course ... if only he could chart it.

The next strike of Lightning he met with a perfect cross-parry and twist—and the lethal blade flew from Thornfalcon's grasp.

To Tobimar's shock and dismay, the slender Thornfalcon stepped forward as dark possibility and darker power enveloped him, blocking Tobimar's own swords with his armored forearms and then *hammering* a blow into Tobimar's gut that staggered him, only the realization that to yield to pain would mean death keeping him from doubling over.

"*Where,*" an elbow smashed across his face, bringing a flare of pain and salt-iron taste of blood, "are *all,*" a kick to the ribs that tumbled him over the wreckage of the table, "these overtalented children *coming* from?"

He felt himself lifted up by completely inhuman strength and *hurled* through one of the great windows. *Must not ... let the pain distract me.*

He rolled over and over on the grass, absorbing the force of that tremendous throw. *This ... false Justiciar has powers like nothing I've fought before. He's at least two, three times as strong as anything his size ought to be.*

Even as Tobimar dragged himself upright, Thornfalcon appeared,

silhouetted against the shattered window, the rapier Lightning
back in his hand. "First it was Rion Vantage, then his lovely sister, and now *you*, and somehow I feel this is but the beginning."

The same desperation and pride that had come upon him
in the *mazakh* stronghold rose up, even as he brought up his
swords again. "I know not that family, but I am a Silverun of
the Silverun, Seventh Prince of Skysand."

For just a moment Thornfalcon halted. "Of *Skysand* . . . Ah, now
there is a piece of information most useful."

That halt was crucial; Tobimar had those few seconds to reach
deep within and draw forth the reserves that waited there. Though
the night was dark, now he could sense all that lay about him.
He did not doubt that the vicious false Justiciar was able to see
as well, but perhaps his opponent would think him half-blind in
the dark. With the vision, he gained also the strength and speed.
It might not be enough . . . but it's what I have.

But now Thornfalcon came on, and it was clear that what
he had was *not* enough. The deadly blade was slipping its way
through his defenses, a nick here, a trickling cut there, and suddenly Tobimar sensed a stone, too late, stumbling, and Thornfalcon's smile widening, the arm drawn back for that shattering
thunderous strike—

And Thornfalcon screamed in shock and pain, stumbling
himself as something lanced straight through his calf. "What in
Blackstar's name—?"

Some inhuman sense must have warned him just in time, because
something *leaped* from another direction even as Tobimar rose
and started his own charge, but Thornfalcon whipped Lightning
around with speed to match its name and batted away Poplock like
a pebble from a stick. Even limping, the false Justiciar was able to
block and parry most of Tobimar's attack, but not all; a brilliant
red streak was laid open on the long cheek, and his right arm's
defenses were pierced, as was the flesh below.

Thornfalcon switched Lightning to his left hand and a small
shield *grew* from the armor of his right. "So you had an ally,
one of those mud-hopping lazy creatures that actually gained
enough of a spirit to leave his home puddle. How very interesting." Pale light flickered, and with dismay Tobimar saw the cut
on the false Justiciar's cheek just . . . fade away. "Still, that could
be somewhat awkward; if my little strike there hasn't killed him,

he will be *quite* hard to keep track of and might interfere at a crucial moment."

"What a shame that would be," Tobimar said, drawing once more on his reserves.

Thornfalcon chuckled, circling somewhat more cautiously now. "And I see you have found something within yourself... a strength and speed that you did not have earlier. And it is still growing." He drew himself up. "So I believe it is time to stop the play."

That dark power Tobimar had sensed... *came forward.* Thornfalcon's eyes glowed; for a moment, they seemed to have no pupils at all, just glowing soulless yellow light, and a huge looming shape was all about him, obscuring the human Thornfalcon in a cloak of malice and hunger.

And then it moved.

Tobimar parried, and the blow nearly knocked the blade from his grasp, even held as carefully and well as it was. Another massive strike, and another, each one so powerful that it felt like blocking the strikes of a mountain. The exiled Prince tried to return blows, riposte in a way that would make the monstrous Thornfalcon back off, but none of his blows went home.

Lightning flicked out and touched his cheek with cold fire again; but this time the coldness *spread*, and for a moment he weakened before he could call up his strength again. *Terian and Chromaias... he's somehow able to* drain *my very soul's power!*

"And so you now sense the way of your ending, little Prince." Even Thornfalcon's voice was different, more powerful, less light and ironic. "I will cut from you what you are, and leave nothing but an empty husk."

Is this *the moment Master Khoros spoke of? To pit a child's prayer against... that?*

Tobimar felt his knees trembling, knew Thornfalcon's power was still at work, and began to draw his breath for that last, forlorn hope.

And then another voice spoke, the voice of a woman, a voice of cold purpose and yet burning with fury.

"THORNFALCON."

48

The False Justiciar whirled, stepping back and to the side so as to keep Tobimar in his field of view, but even in the darkness Tobimar had seen the sudden shock and—perhaps—even a trace of fear when that clear, cold voice had spoken.

Just beyond stood...the Phoenix.

She had the hawk-beak visor pushed back, and in the brilliant light of Sathan, the Moon, he could see the sharp planes of her face, beautiful, not pretty, the glint of iron-chilled eyes that warmed for just a moment as they met his; that gaze said, as clearly as if she had said it, *Thank you.* Her armor shone red-gold, perhaps not merely from reflection but from its own power.

Framing her face was a tumble of dark hair with a pure white flash at the precise center, and Tobimar realized: *I've seen that before, somewhere.*

But Thornfalcon had already recovered from his shock. "Phoenix. What a...surprise. How did you...?"

"No answers for you, monster. But," she continued with a humorous smile, "I'll give you my thanks."

Thornfalcon's eyes narrowed, still trying to watch them both. *As far as I'm concerned, they can both wait a moment longer. I'm recovering... but not quite ready for a fight like that, not against that power.* "Thanks? For...what, precisely, my Lady?"

The smile turned icy, and she reached over her shoulder, drawing a blade that was long, longer, just kept *coming* out of its sheath until Tobimar realized with awe that it was a *teracabal*, Great Sword, like

341

none he'd seen any man or woman wield, and she was holding it now in one hand as though it weighed nothing. "For finally giving me a target worthy of all of Myrionar's Vengeance, as I found no joy in the deaths of Mist Owl or, even, Shrike. *You*, murderer, betrayer, liar and false friend, I will most certainly enjoy killing."

"Always happy to please a lady," Thornfalcon said thinly; his tone was less than pleased, and Tobimar found himself wondering if the false Justiciar's rapier would fare so well against what he now realized *must* be a true Justiciar of Myrionar.

"He's a soul-cutter, Phoenix!" Tobimar said in warning, as both Justiciars—true and false—came to a ritual guard pose.

"*Is* he?" If anything, this made her smile more widely. "Oh, now I will have no regrets except that you were not what you seemed, Thornfalcon."

"I regret only that we were not able to continue our . . . conversation, Kyri." The darkness about him gathered itself.

The Phoenix moved first, and Tobimar was once more astounded. That monster blade whipped down and around as though it were no heavier that Tobimar's own twin weapons, blazing a path of red-silver-gold through the night air. Thornfalcon's parry was quicker, but—Tobimar thought—not so smooth, not so easy, and the jolt that went through the false Justiciar's slender frame showed that the Phoenix's weapon had striking power that even Thornfalcon could feel.

I had thought myself well-equipped, some of the finest weapons of Skysand in my hands, yet these Justiciars *wield weapons and powers far greater.*

Lightning flashed its namesake power and a nimbus of blue-white surrounded the blade, only to be met by a flare of golden fire around the Phoenix's, and for several moments the two traded blows nearly too fast to be seen, with thunderbolts and flame splashing from each impact like water.

Tobimar, now fully and firmly in the High Center, could sense the course of possibility, perceive the inhuman power within Thornfalcon brushing the edges of the Phoenix's soul, blunting the force of her fire, eating away at her defenses in subtle and nigh-indetectable ways, like wood-borers eating away the center of a beam. He grasped both blades tightly, pulled the sense of combat about him like a net woven of instinct and prophecy, reached out as well as in for strength and speed to match Thornfalcon's.

Out of the corner of his eye, he saw a tiny movement across the clearing. *Good. I think Poplock's still alive. We might need him.*

Striking a foe from behind would normally be pretty dishonorable, but as a bounty hunter—even one with strict limits on what he'd do and not do—he'd somewhat gotten over that. And Thornfalcon had proven he didn't deserve the honor of a Prince. So Tobimar waited a few more desperate seconds, as Kyri Vantage, the Phoenix, began to slowly give way before her adversary, and then lunged, twin-swords extending at the final moment like the fangs of a great snake.

That pall of darkness about Thornfalcon warned him at the last possible second, and he *leapt* away with immense strength and speed. But even so, he was neither so quick nor so skilled that he could afford such a sudden change of tactics, and that fiery sword cut across his side even as he evaded Tobimar's attack.

Thornfalcon staggered as he landed, dropped and rolled to get even greater distance, and Tobimar's glance met Kyri's. She nodded, and together they charged.

It was the false Justiciar's turn to back up, even the combination of the shield growing from his Raiment and his terrible sword not quite sufficient to holding off both the grim Phoenix and the flashing, slashing blades of Tobimar Silverun, Seventh of Seven. Tobimar's will and the strength of his spirit warded off the crackling, sparking lightnings from Thornfalcon's weapon, and the flame of Phoenix's sword simply consumed the other's power. Even the dark hunger that clawed at their spirits was weaker, unable to mount a clear offense in the face of two diverging assaults.

But Thornfalcon was far from finished, and he proved it with his next evading leap. In the moment he was in the air, he produced from within his armor a small sphere and flung it down.

Black-and-gray vapor billowed from the ground, enveloping both attackers and vanishing. Tobimar felt his limbs slowing down, paralysis beginning to set in. *No! If I can't move—I'll be dead!*

Phoenix merely laughed. "You think the same formula will work on me twice, Thornfalcon? Myrionar is not so weak as you believe. And as this man has tilted the balance for me, so shall I for him." One of her hands released the sword and tapped Tobimar's shoulder, and the red-gold light raced along his form, banishing both paralysis and weakness, with a distant sound like the call of the trumpets at dawn in Skysand.

The false Justiciar did not laugh, but he did not look afraid, either. "It was worth a try. Do you believe that is the end of my arsenal? We have only begun this little dance, girl, and I have danced it many times before."

"Were *you* the one who slew my brother, Thornfalcon? You who cut his soul so it could not be saved, so Arbiter Kelsley nearly died trying to do so?"

Thornfalcon did laugh this time. "Ah, hoping for some truly poetic justice, I see." He circled slowly sideways, and Tobimar and Kyri followeed suit. "Let it not be said I would disappoint a lady. Yes, it was my hand that took your brother's life, who saw him running in terror when he realized I was no longer the mere human he had thought me." The dark power rose again, and once more that terrible shape half-appeared, of glowing eyes and hulking, shaggy hunger, a smile of ice-crystal death.

The young woman smiled herself, more broadly than before. "Oh, that makes me *so* much happier, Thornfalcon." She whirled her sword around, a fiery wheel in the night. "Because now I *know* you speak the truth, for I *saw* you that night, saw this inhuman shadow you wear." Thornfalcon's eyes widened momentarily at the realization he had been seen, had been *that* close to discovery. But Kyri was continuing, "And because you should know this, as well." The greatsword suddenly arced upward, a mighty comet reaching nearly thirteen feet. "By the power of *all* the gods—" The blazing blade came down, and a shockwave of golden fire streaked out, carving ground and air alike. "—Myrionar promised me *Vengeance!*"

Thornfalcon cursed in surprise and shock; too late for him to jump aside, he tried to parry the flamestrike with Lightning; there was an explosion of thunder and flame and Thornfalcon disappeared in a cloud of smoke.

That won't have finished him... where...

And possibilities narrowed to a tension, something touching the web of intuition, *above!*

The twin swords of Skysand intercepted Lightning perfectly, and had Thornfalcon not kept a deathgrip on his weapon he would have been disarmed for a second time. As it was, Tobimar's crystal-flawless parry stopped the false Justiciar despite his inhuman strength and speed, held him for one tiny fraction of a second. Phoenix's mighty sword was already coming and the arrogant look was gone, gone from Thornfalcon's eyes as he twisted aside in desperation, disengaging his blade from Tobimar's, trying to parry the Phoenix Justiciar's strike, unable to entirely evade either the fiery strike or Tobimar's own dual-sword riposte. He was sent tumbling, blood now visible on two sides, and—it seemed to Tobimar—the abominable power about him weakened, no longer as hungry and terrible.

He found himself charging step-for-step with Kyri Vantage, the two in perfect rhythmic accord as they tried to follow up on that strike. Fire now blazing in half a dozen places lit the clearing almost as though it were day, and Tobimar saw Thornfalcon white with pain, fear, and fury as he saw his two opponents nearly upon him again.

He sprang up and away, into the branches of a nearby tree, then lunged across a gap to the next. Kyri startled Tobimar by following suit. While Tobimar thought he could probably do the same, he chose to charge flat out across the clearing, keeping parallel with and below the false Justiciar. He could see in Thornfalcon's narrowed gaze that his adversary understood perfectly. There was no refuge in either direction, no place to flee.

He might, of course, try to fly away—it was said that at least some of the Justiciars could do so—but it was almost certain that the Phoenix could follow, were that the case, and in some ways that would make him more vulnerable.

If he could fly, apparently he didn't dare risk it. Thornfalcon, closely pursued by the Phoenix, suddenly stopped and dove upon Tobimar; the passing exchange of cuts left a temporarily cold-aching slash on his arm, but not so bad as the last, and he thought he might even have cut Thornfalcon again. Thornfalcon's other wounds did seem to be healing...but not so fast as before.

The Phoenix followed the battle to the ground, rejoining with Tobimar as Thornfalcon recovered, and the two charged again, separating slightly to force the false Justiciar to have to deal with more than one direction of facing.

But now the narrow gaze became a sneer, and Thornfalcon abruptly plunged Lightning into the ground, so hard that the false Justiciar was lifted from the earth, balancing for a moment on the hilt of his weapon.

Bolts of lightning snaked out across and through the grass, covering the ground, clawing at the sky. There was no time or

way to evade the wave of electricity, and Tobimar heard Phoenix's scream echo his own as they both convulsed and collapsed,
muscles twitching, weapons skittering from their hands. Another
blast of thunder through the ground and Tobimar grunted, holding desperately onto consciousness but unable to regain control
of his body.

"Perhaps . . . *this* . . . will quiet you unruly children." Thornfalcon returned to his feet, pulled Lightning from the ground and
strode forward. "Not the honorable ending for a Justiciar, no, but
not quite as bad as you feared, Lady, for I will not risk another
escape. Just death, first for your would-be savior and then for—"

The same inhuman senses warned him at the last minute, and
as he had before, Thornfalcon whipped Lightning around in a
flat arc to stop an incoming attack.

But this time it was not Poplock coming through the air.
Thornfalcon's blade struck one of two incoming missiles the size
of sewing needles, and actinic white fire suddenly burned across
the blade. The second bolt struck his armor and the same intense
white flame was hissing, clinging, trying to eat its way through
the Raiment of Thornfalcon.

"Beetle-eating *kloq!*" Thornfalcon cursed, trying desperately to
beat out the hungry flames with one hand and moving in the
direction of his assailant.

But Poplock wasn't waiting quietly. The miniature clockwork
crossbow was rewinding itself and spitting out more of the vicious
alchemical bolts, clinging fire, acid, poison, shock, as the tiny
Toad bounced from one clump of weed to another, racing away
and ahead of Thornfalcon. Many bolts missed, but others hit,
and the false Justiciar could not afford to ignore any of them.

Tobimar clung to High Center and remembered Khoros' words:
"*It is a part of becoming* one *with the universe around us—or,
more truthfully, of making the universe attuned and one with us.*"

*If I am a part of the world, and the world a part of me, I
have the strength of the world. This should not stop me. It cannot stop me.*

His hand stopped twitching. The leaden weight still seemed to
sit upon his limbs, but it was weight, not uncontrollable movement,
and he forced himself upward. *There is no pain. Pain is merely
a warning, and for now I have no need of it.* Pain receded, and
stiffly, but quickly, he stooped and picked up his twin blades. He

thought he also heard movement from the Phoenix's direction, but dared not look.

The miniature crossbow ran down, but now the hopping Toad was scattering things behind him, caltrops, exploding balls, oil-slick spheres, and Thornfalcon was still unable to catch him. *Hold on, Poplock!*

Tobimar forced his body into motion, charged.

Thornfalcon whirled as he approached, parried the slightly clumsy attack, but his riposte was spoiled as a small jar of pickled beetles burst on his forehead, spilling acidic preservative into his eyes. "Kerlamion *take* you all!"

Tobimar didn't waste time talking, just pressed his attack, driving his arms beyond their limits in speed and hammering, driving power.

Thornfalcon was still managing a defense in his desperation, a defense that was starting to solidify. *If I can't get him in the next few seconds...*

But another sound, more footsteps, Thornfalcon turning, one last parry, a diving lunge with the point of Lightning as Phoenix charged, Tobimar's lefthand sword smashing the lunge down, out of line—

And the great sword of the Phoenix impaled false Justiciar Thornfalcon clean through his chest.

The brown eyes went wide in shock; Lightning dropped from suddenly nerveless fingers, and Thornfalcon went to his knees as Kyri withdrew the sword. He looked down in disbelief, futilely trying to staunch the blood, and looked up. "You...have not won, girl," he managed to say, a faint hiss and bubble showing how the sword of the Phoenix must have pierced his lungs. "I am...not alone...and you will not escape..."

"Perhaps not. But for myself, and the Justiciars, all the women you have killed, and my brother—I at least *will* have Vengeance."

The sword flamed gold again, and Thornfalcon's head flew from his body, rolling over and over and disappearing in the tall grass.

Tobimar could sense the dark presence trying to cling to the body, perhaps somehow bring life back even after such terrible damage...but it was a futile effort, one that echoed desperation, like a man caught on a crumbling cliff, scrabbling at something, anything to hold onto, and coming away with nothing. It twisted and grasped and faded, like mist before the sun, fading, fading, gone save for the faintest lingering echo, like the smoke of a fire a dozen years past.

The Phoenix turned to him, sheathing her sword as the fire burned away the last trace of blood and dirt. She bowed deeply, spreading her arms so that for a moment he wondered if she was planning to do the Armed Bow.

And it was that thought that triggered a memory. Before he could stop himself, he said, "Why, *that's* where I saw you! You were with Toron!"

49

Kyri had been about to thank the strange young man, but his exclamation drove all her manners out of her head. She pushed back the helm and stared. "You know Toron?"

He nodded, long black hair falling over his face for a moment. "Quite well now, I should say." He blinked suddenly. "Oh, I'm terribly sorry, I haven't introduced myself."

"Neither have I," she pointed out with a faint, tired smile. The strain and horrors of the day were starting to close in on her, and a part of her just wanted to sit down and cry, or fall unconscious. The other part of her, though, was actually eager to talk to someone who would understand.

He gave an elaborate bow, a flourish of arms and a knee to the ground. "Tobimar Silverun of the Silverun, Prince of Skysand in exile—and," he indicated his shoulder with a grin "Guild Adventurer." She could see the exhaustion in his eyes—and the same eagerness to understand. His face had the same darkness of some of her own family—like Urelle—and features not all that dissimilar, but with eyes a piercing, startling blue contrasting with the midnight hair.

He then bent down and picked up . . . a Toad. "And this," he continued, proudly, "is Poplock Duckweed, who probably saved both our lives. He's saved mine more than once."

The little Toad gave a hop-bow that made her giggle—a sound that she would have blushed at, except it was so light that it made the whole grim scene feel better. "Pleased to meet you, Phoenix.

And he's saved my life a few times too, so I'm sure we'll even things up."

"Well, I am *very* pleased to meet you both," she said, and did her best bow. "Kyri Victoria Vantage, the one true living Justiciar of Myrionar, the Phoenix... and," she gave the same gesture as Tobimar, "Guild Adventurer."

"There's a lot of that going around," the Toad observed dryly.

She smiled again, but noticed how Poplock seemed to favor one side, and Tobimar showed multiple cuts, bleeding from his face, arms, and was not moving smoothly. "Here, let me help you."

She touched both of her new-found companions. *Myrionar, these two saved my life, perhaps my soul, and helped me on the path to Justice and Vengeance. Grant them back their full strength and health.*

The golden light that sang now always within her somewhere emerged, sparkled along the little Toad and his Skysand friend, wiping away injury and pain in a way she remembered well... and one she now felt again, as Myrionar added the same blessing to her, for accomplishing one of the greater parts of her task.

Tobimar looked at her with respect and perhaps a touch of awe that made her uncomfortable. "My thanks, Lady Phoenix."

She shook her head with a smile. "Please, just Kyri. If it wasn't for you, I'd be dead, or much worse."

"And if you hadn't somehow got free from where he'd left you," Poplock said, "*we* would've been buried right next to you, so we're all even there. Why don't we go inside? There's lots to talk about, and looked to me like Thorny there had lots of valuable stuff."

"You're going to *loot* his..." Kyri trailed off, not sure what to think. Initially the idea was repellent, but given the prior owner...

But at that moment, she saw Tobimar stiffen.

"What is it?"

The twin blades whispered back out of their sheaths. "Something's wrong."

She turned, looking, listening.

Rustling. Sounds of movement. Vibrations in the ground.

The little Toad had bounced down, poking around the leaves, looking for something on his own; he suddenly scrambled back up Tobimar. "Back! Back *now!*"

Kyri didn't hesitate, but leapt backwards, backpedaling away—

And the ground where they had been standing suddenly collapsed down, sickly yellowish light emerging from below.

That wasn't a cave-in, she realized, even as she saw shadows moving against the light, moving closer, *That was something deliberate, something* designed *to happen*. Even as she thought that, she was reaching over her shoulder, drawing Flamewing again, and remembering Thornfalcon's last words: *I am not alone... and you will not escape*. She had thought he was referring to the other Justiciars, but...

A movement in the guttering fire-lit clearing, and something emerged from the hole, climbing up what must be a ramp leading down into the ground. Something that seemed humanoid in silhouette, but there was something wrong, wrong with the way it moved, wrong and very familiar, something that sent an instant chill down her back.

And then it emerged fully, with other shapes crowding up behind it, and she understood, seeing the high forehead, the caterpillar-like body, the lamprey mouth. *Of course. The attack on Evanwyl could not have been an accident. He arranged it all. He* controlled *these things!*

The monster charged, three more behind it; she saw Poplock, holding a tiny glittering blade in one hand, drop to the ground, disappearing into the underbrush. *Good luck, little Toad*, she thought, and then braced herself and swung.

Flamewing sheared through the entire upper torso of the creature charging her as though it were a tuft of grass and not something the size and toughness of a man. She felt a spurt of triumph and confidence. *I'm not the scared girl that faced these things the first time. I'm the Phoenix Justiciar of Myrionar, wielding the weapon of the Spiritsmith, and these things are no more a threat to me than they would have been to Rion.*

Tobimar Silverun's blades flashed twice, and the next creature fell; the Skysand Prince leapt high, cut low; another collapsed, bleeding.

But there were *more* coming, a scuttling tide of hunger and death, and there were *other* things mixed with them. A hissing, chittering squeal came from a face of working mandibles and six glittering eyes, and the doomlock spider lashed out with metallic-edged talons the length of longswords on jointed, powerful forelegs. The claws rebounded from the Raiment of the Phoenix, but staggered her backwards, even as she cut and severed one claw from the body.

A *bilarel* suddenly loomed up over Tobimar, eight feet of gray-skinned humanoid rage made solid, club upraised to crush, but it roared and dropped the bludgeon, clutching at one of its lower legs; Tobimar thrust one sword through its eye, and a flicker of motion dashed away from the falling ogre, rippling grass the only trace of Poplock's presence.

Too many! Myrionar—I call upon the power that is mine by right. She whirled her blade again. *"FLAMEWING!"*

The red-gold flame flared outward in a deadly arc, flowing around and past Tobimar but washing in fearsome waves over the mob of monsters, who writhed, screamed, and died.

It was a momentary pause, but only momentary, for already she heard other sounds from below. Tobimar looked up at her. "Thanks for the assist. Shouldn't we be running about now?"

She shook her head grimly. "We can't. Gharis is only half a mile away; there's other farms and houses not far away. We're giving them a focus, they're obviously directed to kill anyone they see. If we run, they'll just spread out from here." She took a better grip on Flamewing. "Every one we kill before we die is one less to kill someone else."

Two more *bilarel* strode out, clad in thick armor, tugging it into place, and these two planted themselves on either side of the ramp. *One of them...has armored claws for arms. The other... something wrong with his shape, too wide, twisted somehow.*

"Sand and storm," Tobimar muttered. "They're getting organized." Even as he spoke, she could see him focusing, bringing forth that unique speed and strength he'd shown in the earlier battle. "But how many of these things could he possibly *have* under that house? If he was feeding that many creatures, people would have *noticed*!"

She was having the same thoughts, but she had no answer. *Obviously he did have that many, somehow. And we have to kill everything that comes up, or the rest of Evanwyl will be under attack.*

She knew the Arms and Eyes would eventually sound the alarm and deal with such monsters...but how many people would die in the meantime? *No, we can't run. Here we stand, even if the ghost of Thornfalcon laughs at me for being caught in his final trap.*

Yet with that decision, she couldn't repress another shudder of horror. The new fires burning from Flamewing's last strike showed the creatures clearly, and none of them were quite normal, each one distorted, showing some monstrous change even for creatures normally monstrous. A doomlock with four clawed arms instead of two, a sinuous draconic thing with the head of a flame ant, an oozing, shapeless blob that manifested human mouths and eyes at random, these and more were emerging, arranging themselves in abominable and unnatural formation at the roared exhortations of the ogre-things.

She glanced at Tobimar, and he nodded. *No point in letting* them *choose the moment.*

The Prince of Skysand and the Phoenix Justiciar charged directly for the center of the assembled ranks, Flamewing blazing anew and a pearlescent aura shimmering around Tobimar's blades.

Shrieks and roars and hisses, the thudding wet sounds of blades on flesh, the jolt of striking bone, smell of scorched flesh, a shout of pain from herself or her ally, the occasional growl or grinding cry of shock from an enemy as Poplock's blade Steelthorn found its mark. She whirled and cut and spun and blocked, severing legs, smashing the pommel into lamprey-mouths, kicking into vital areas, taking impacts that could have broken her before and shrugging them off. At her side, Tobimar Silverun carved a path of devastation through the monsters, twin swords dancing back and forth and leaving death in their wake.

Still, cuts appeared on his arms and face as if by malign magic, and she felt the dull fire-ache of poison trying to work past her defenses, knew the sun-bright shock of a broken rib that tried to blind her with pain, encircle her breath with agony. *Won't be...* *much longer...now...*

She knew they had killed many, and perhaps would kill those around them now, but there were *more*, impossibly more, and she knew there was something else they had missed, some secret Thornfalcon had taken with him, and that Evanwyl would pay the price for her failure.

A monstrous thing loomed suddenly up before her, tall as a *bilarel* but more like an armored crab on two legs with the brown eyes of a faithful dog and the fanged mouth of a gigantic lizard. She was yanking Flamewing free of its last victim but slowly, too slowly, she'd never get it up in time—

Two leaf-green blades exploded from the thing's chest and it gave a gurgling wail, collapsing, falling forward, inert.

A face was revealed, a face and figure of a young man standing behind the fallen body, a boy somehow familiar, with hair and dark-tinted skin the mirror of Tobimar's, and eyes her own shade of steel-pearl gray.

50

"*Xavier!*" Tobimar shouted triumphantly, and he heard the same shout in a smaller size from somewhere in the grass. "By the Seven and One, you've got the *best* timing!"

"Thanks, guys! Now that I'm here, let's kick some *real* ass!"

Tobimar redoubled his efforts, and saw Kyri also swinging with renewed strength. With the addition of Xavier Ross, the tide had at least momentarily turned, and in a few moments, Kyri had a chance to deliver another tremendous flame-strike that temporarily cleared the surface.

"Kyri Vantage, Phoenix Justiciar of Myrionar, meet Xavier Uriel Ross, traveller from Zaralandar itself."

She gave a quick bow. "Thanks and well come," she said. "And I'll have more thanks later. But now we have this problem to deal with. Tobimar, there's something terribly wrong here. Those things can't all be coming from some underground of the mansion."

"No, you're right." The shadows were milling about, probably waiting for another set of creatures to become the leaders. *Won't be long.* "And most would normally live aboveground, so I doubt it's from some unexplored caverns beneath. We need to know where the source is."

"On it," Xavier said. "I'll be back as fast as I can. You guys just stay alive, okay?"

He nodded, and grinned as he saw the momentary puzzled expression on Kyri's face...puzzlement that turned to enlightenment as Xavier vanished.

A new surge of monsters, some the same, but now, others even more bizarre and alien, erupted from the underground. Kyri sent a blaze of flame against them, but this time a small reptilian thing sent a column of ice against the flame and an explosion of steam clouded the area in mist. "Can he really get past this mob?" she asked.

"I'm pretty sure he can," Tobimar answered. "If we can hold out."

"Charge forward," she said.

The two did so. "What is your plan?"

"The corridor they are coming from looks narrower, as though we might be able to hold it—if we can clear out those that we are passing. If we can do that—"

"I understand. Of course, it could get us both killed."

Tobimar almost stopped as they reached the edge. Looking down he saw what appeared an endless river of foes of monstrous shapes, twisted bodies, distorted features, and it was like a waking nightmare, or an entry into one of the Hells themselves. Some looked almost human, others like a malformed and debased *Artan*, or a monstrous centipede with taloned arms and the face of a madman.

But he did not stop, and his swords struck in unison with Flamewing. *My reserves are running out,* he realized, drawing upon them for strength and finding there was almost nothing left to give. A glance at Kyri showed her face was pale and the fire on her sword flickered momentarily. *And she is new to this, channeling the power of the gods, and it has to be wearing on her as well.*

Xavier, you'd better hurry!

Swing, chop, block, take another blow, leap over a falling body, parry and return-strike. His whole existence was blood and monsters and aching arms, leaden with exhaustion and pain, that he pushed to deliver just one more stroke, block just a single attack, then start the cycle again. Time seemed to be running faster, more creatures trying to surround them, to kill, from all directions, yet it was ticking by slower than the fall of congealing blood.

Kyri cursed and stumbled, nearly went down. He didn't know *how* he did it, but somehow he was at her side, supporting her, beating back a half-dozen creatures with one sword as she recovered, and for a moment they stood back to back, and the bodies were piling around them like obscene cordwood.

"Found it! Get *out* of there, people!"

Xavier's silver-green blades joined theirs and led them upward and out. "They're coming through . . . I guess you'd say a portal, or something, in the basement of this place. There's a way down to it from the mansion—a lot easier than fighting back against *this* tide!"

A scramble, tentacles grasping at his legs and Kyri's, a quick slash of swords, *up*, and they were on the scorched earth of the clearing, rolling to their feet, running, a rustling, rattling, slithering horde behind them.

Through the front door of the mansion, skidding on the rugs and slick polished floors, but Xavier was leading them, swiftly, an open door with a lamprey-mouthed monster, cut down, then the three were running down a stairway, killing as they went, but here the mob had not begun to press. She saw why as they burst into an underground chamber, through a door which had obviously been opened by Xavier in his investigation.

The monsters marched out of an archway sixteen feet high, standing in the middle of a circle of symbols that made Poplock, now riding precariously on his shoulder, croak in consternation. "Oh, that's bad *bad* news there."

"No," said Kyri, drawing herself up, even as the creatures noticed their presence. "That's *good* news. Because now, no matter the cost, I know I can *stop* this. Keep them from me, and it will be over."

"Do what she says!" Tobimar shouted to Xavier. "Believe me, she knows what she's saying!"

His friend nodded, and they intercepted the things together. Behind, he heard the girl's clear, certain voice.

"Myrionar, God of Justice and Vengeance, I, the Phoenix, last and first true Justiciar, call one last time this day on your power. To my sword and body give the strength, to my blade the power, to sunder stone and shatter spells that bring forth monsters against my homeland and yours." Brilliant gold light shone from behind them, casting their shadows towering and dark over the monstrosities before, and for the first time he saw uncertainty and hesitation in those creatures, a drawing back.

"I take unto myself all the power you can give," Kyri said,

and her voice was louder, more powerful, and filled with iron faith, though there was the tone of pain and exhaustion, someone pushed to her very limits, "and I shall release it, to protect my allies, to destroy our enemies, and in the name of my brother I call for it—*RION'S VENGEANCE!*"

A blade of unbearable brilliance smashed outward, precisely between Tobimar and Xavier. The Vengeance Blade did not pause or dim or slow as it passed through body after body of the monsters. It struck the mystical circle about the gate and for an instant that circle flared green and black, as though to defend what lay behind, but that magic, powerful though it must have been, could not withstand the absolute force of a god's power, and the circle shattered in poisonous emerald shards of power. Vengeance Blade and summoning Archway met in a cataclysmic flare of opposition, a detonation that blew Tobimar from his feet, blinded him, sent Poplock tumbling away.

He dragged himself to his feet, blinking furiously. Shapes and mist slowly came into focus, as he came to full guard. But then he slowly lowered his blades.

The archway lay in shattered, almost unrecognizable pieces; ash and scattered limbs were all that remained of the monsters, and scorchmarks were visible up the tunnel, as far as he could see, showing that Myrionar's Vengeance was complete and total; none of the creatures had escaped.

"Whoa," Xavier said in a tone of awe.

51

Kyri sagged to her knees, trying to support herself on her sword, feeling utter exhaustion weighing her down like a leaden cloak. Tobimar ran to her, his friend Xavier reaching her at the same time. Together they helped her stand. "Are you all right, Kyri?" Tobimar asked.

She smiled, and through the exhaustion she felt a different weight, one of guilt and doubt and self-hatred, lifting, fading away. "I am . . . I think more 'all right' than I've been in a long time, Tobimar Silverun," she said. "With all of your help," her gaze took in Tobimar, Xavier, and little Poplock who was just now making his way back to them, "I've . . . I've just finished avenging my brother. Thank you." She heard her voice break, felt tears of relief and gratitude stinging her eyes. "Thank you *all*, more than I can say in just words."

"You are very welcome, Kyri," Tobimar said, and his blue eyes were smiling at her. "Believe me when I say it was an honor to be part of such magnificent justice and vengeance."

"He talks prettier than I do, I think," Xavier said, "but helping you kill off those things and save everyone around? I'm all for that. You're welcome."

"Same here," Poplock said. "Glad we ended up on the right side. And I'd guess there's a lot more work to come, if one of the Justiciars was gone totally bad, eh?"

She smiled again wryly. "I am very much afraid so. But," she said as she managed a wobbly step forward, "I'm not ready to do anything else quite yet."

She looked over at the little Toad. "I seem to recall, just before things took another turn for the worse, that you were suggesting looting my fallen enemy's house."

"Look," Poplock said reasonably, as they all started towards the stairs, "we'll have to get moving pretty quick anyway—none of us want to get caught explaining this, right? And if you're fighting the Justiciars like this, you'll need help, you'll need resources, you'll need money. This—" he used a Toadish grunt-bounce that conveyed complete disgust, "he didn't have any family except the false Justiciars, so where are all his valuables going?"

She had to admit the little Toad had a point. A large point. Why leave her enemies with resources she could deprive them of? It was . . . only just that she take what she could use and deprive them of the rest, as this was a war. She nodded slowly. "I . . . can't argue. But afterwards . . . we set it to the torch." She looked at Tobimar as they entered.

He looked serious. "He *was* a monster, and I would guess that he'd done things we don't want to know about."

"You're right."

"Done. First pillage, *then* burn. Remember to get the order right." Poplock dropped off of Tobimar's shoulder and started to examine the cases around the room.

"I'm starved," Xavier said. "Dunno about *you* people, but I've been moving pretty constantly for the last day or so."

"Well," Tobimar said, glancing at Poplock, "we've got at least a few hours before we have to go, and everyone knows Thornfalcon had gourmet tastes."

Kyri looked at the one table and shuddered. "Not in *this* room. And you'd better be very, very careful what silverware, glasses, and so on you use. Those," she pointed to the shattered remains of some glassware on the floor, "almost got me killed."

Poplock bounced over to them, squinted sideways at the pieces, pulled out a strange greenish lens, and examined the material. After a few moments he sat back. "Whoo. That's good work. But don't worry, I'll check stuff out for you. It's something I'm good at."

With Poplock's help, the four of them soon assembled a feast on Thornfalcon's kitchen counters and the three humans sat at a small table near the counter, while the little Toad continued his exploration and accounting of the useful materials available in the house. "Don't worry about me, I'll be listening to you. I've got good hearing."

"How in Terian's name did you *find* us?" Tobimar asked Xavier.

"Well," Xavier said, studying the assorted foods as though intimidated by the choices, "I'd been told I had to find you quick, and so when I came to that one village I was going to ask about where to go. And so I hear this guy getting on his horse, saying 'That Adventurer says Thornfalcon may be in trouble.'

"So I remembered that you guys were officially 'Adventurers' and asked him quick if it was you, and he said yes and said you'd gone off to help Thornfalcon. He then rode off to warn people, he said, but he'd pointed off to the south so I started running in that direction."

"But I was *down* that path," Kyri said, puzzled. "Without directions you just *couldn't* have found the right one."

"You're probably right," Xavier said with a grin, taking a leg from a roast brushhen, "but once you guys started fighting this Thornfalcon guy? Lights *all* over. It was like following a lightning storm that sat in one place. The lights went down for a while, but by then I had a line on the direction, and by the time you started in on the monsters I could *hear* you."

"Good luck for us," Tobimar said, and Kyri nodded her agreement.

She looked over at Tobimar. *This Xavier's a different matter, I think, but...* "So," she said, cutting a slice of coilserpent, "did Toron send you after me?"

"No," Tobimar answered, filling his own plate, "King Toron didn't mention you d—"

"*King* Toron?"

He blinked in surprise, then closed his eyes as though realizing something painful. "Oh, Terian and Chromaias. You don't *know.*"

"Know *what?*"

He sighed, "The news will only just be getting here anyway. I have no idea how you got here so fast—I saw you the day I had my first audience with the King. If you'd stayed just a few more days—"

"I had...reasons to move as fast as I could. And I got lucky, met an old man along the way who—"

"Had a funny five-sided hat," the Toad and Xavier said at the exact same time. Poplock's voice was slightly muffled, as it was coming from one of the cupboards.

Kyri stared in that direction. "How did you know?"

"Khoros," sighed Tobimar.

"Who is this 'Khoros'?"

"Look, we need to all figure out what's going on here," Poplock said. "Tobimar, you tell her your story, I'll tell mine, Xavier tells his, and she tells hers. *Then* if we have any questions left, we ask them."

The black-haired Skysand Prince grinned. "Oh, I'm *sure* we'll have questions left. But you're right, we should stop asking random questions and getting confused." He bowed across the table to Kyri, then looked abstracted for a moment, as though trying to put his thoughts in order. Finally he began speaking.

"I am the Seventh of Seven—the Seventh child of my mother, the Lord of Waters, ruler of Skysand, as she was the Seventh child of her mother. In the normal way of things, I would have lived there and become a ruler in my own right—likely of one of the Seven Cities, or—perhaps—become Lord of Waters myself, if my siblings had died or chose not to take the burden, or my mother chose me above them.

"But we have an ancient history, and a tradition that goes beyond family or rulership..."

As he talked, Kyri began to get an impression of the young man before her, and found herself slightly intimidated. *I spent most of my time waiting for other people to save my world. He was exiled to gain the chance of saving his people... more than four years ago. He's been travelling and adventuring all that time, and I've just been praying and studying.*

A new horror came over her as she heard of the disasters that had befallen Zarathan, one after the other, after she left; the death of the King, the slaughter of the *Artan* and others of the Forest Sea, attacks on others... *And if this is all connected... Myrionar, what is* happening *to the world?*

At one point, Tobimar broke off—it was while he was describing his first sudden confrontation with Xavier—and stared at her in a way that made her near to blushing. "What?"

"Oh, I'm sorry." Tobimar looked embarrassed. "I didn't mean to stare, but... your eyes. They're just about exactly like Xavier's. I've never seen that precise shade of gray, and it's also their size, the intensity... Really, if I didn't know better, I'd swear you had to be related."

Suddenly she remembered that day, as they were approaching Zarathanton. "By the... I think I actually *saw* those five! A tall blond boy, two dark-haired boys, and two girls, all strikingly beautiful, and... yes, it *was* you, Xavier! I remember, because you looked so much like my sister Urelle."

"I look like your *sister*?" Xavier echoed. "Well... I hope that's good. I admit... we do look kinda alike. But given that we're from different *planets* I doubt we're actually related."

"Urelle?" Poplock's voice came from another room, over the sound of clinking—something small sorting through heavy silverware, she suspected. "Isn't your middle name—?"

"Uriel," Xavier said slowly. "That's... pretty weird." He suddenly glanced up. "Hey, I remember now! I saw *you* and... what, your mom, maybe? Leaving the Castle, right before we went in!"

Kyri felt a pang from Xavier's innocent mistake, but smiled. "That was my aunt, but yes, I was there."

Tobimar looked at the two of them again, obviously still struck by the similarities, then shrugged. "Another piece of a puzzle that we can't quite fit into the picture... yet. Anyway, let me go on..."

They had finished their meal by the time Tobimar was done; Poplock then came in to give his summary, and rest after what was obviously strenuous work. Kyri didn't feel entirely comfortable with the looting, so she didn't watch or inquire much. She knew the discomfort was silly; anything valuable Thornfalcon should be used against the false Justiciars, or destroyed so *they* couldn't use it. Still, the sound of someone cheerfully breaking open cabinets to root around inside and find whatever caught their fancy...

In some ways, Poplock's story was even more startling than Tobimar's. The idea of that minuscule Toad somehow disrupting the plans of a great demonlord, of destroying an entire hidden enclave of *mazakh* and worse, and rescuing Tobimar from certain death some years later, was both comical and sobering. But she'd seen all too clearly just how dangerous Poplock could be.

"And so we came in and found out Thorny wasn't nearly as nice a guy as he should have been, and kept him busy long enough for you to join us." Poplock finished. "So that's about it for me. Your turn, Xavier."

She realized quickly that his was the strangest tale of all, and one that she wasn't going to understand in full for a long time. But the important points of his venture—the pain of losing a beloved brother, grief and vengeance, a second chance granted, these she understood and empathized with so strongly it ached within her.

It also sent a chill down her spine. *There are far too many similarities here. Is that the doing of this Khoros? Or someone or something else? A force we haven't yet heard of?*

But Xavier continued his story—which of course dovetailed at times with Tobimar's, but then split off. "Then I got to the Broken Hills like you said"—he nodded to Tobimar—"and started looking. Of course, that little mountain range isn't so little up close, and I was afraid I wasn't going to find anything. I mean, at least this Idinus guy has a known address." He grinned, but his face was... tense, and the grin faded.

"What's wrong, Xavier?" Tobimar asked. "You didn't find him?"

"Oh, no, I found him all right. Well, I *think* it was him, even though it was a her when I met him. If that makes any sense?"

Tobimar nodded slowly, and so did Kyri. Kyri said, "In the legends, the Wanderer wears many faces. He's been old and young, man or woman, *Artan* and human and Child of Odin, wizard and warrior and sage. So yes, it makes sense. He's definitely a *man*, but he can assume many forms and will take those, and other names, when it suits his purpose."

"Okay. Well, she never *said* she was the Wanderer, but she kinda implied it." A shadow passed over his face again. "I can't... talk about everything she said. Some of it's personal to me, other parts are just for the others in my group. Anyway, after we were done talking, she told me that I needed to hurry, that you would need me soon. And she gestured and *poof!*, there I was at the near end of the Broken Hills.

"So I made my way towards Evanwyl, got into that town—Gharis?—yeah, Gharis, and you know the rest."

Kyri smiled, then became more solemn. "Mine's not quite as travelled a narration, I suppose, but there's a lot to tell you. For me... for me it started when my parents died..."

She was aware of Tobimar's eyes on her, and those of Xavier, and there was warmth and sympathy there that she knew was not feigned. After learning the Justiciars were corrupt, she'd wondered if she would ever truly be able to trust again, and known that just the thought was a dangerous one; someone who could have no trust would never know true justice. But she could sense that Tobimar was telling her the truth, that Xavier was as honest as she, and without them and their strange companion Poplock she would already be dead. And she remembered Aunt Victoria's words: "...*you will perhaps find the allies you need*..."

"...and I grabbed my Raiment and put it on, getting outside just in time to keep Thornfalcon from finishing you off," she concluded. "So Justice was balanced in the moment of our meeting; we saved each other from the same threat." She looked over at Xavier. "And then you saved us both, and together we finished the job. So once more, Justice was balanced in that moment."

Tobimar laughed and pushed away from the table. "Yes, I guess that's so!" He stood up, looking around.

"But these attacks you've described, and your quest...I agree with you. There must be some connection. Thornfalcon, these false Justiciars, Myrionar's silence, the assassination of the King," she stumbled over that, the idea that such a thing—which had not happened since perhaps the Fall itself—could have been accomplished, "...the attacks on the Great Forest and even Artania itself...and the five people from your world, Xavier, and this Khoros."

"I think he's trying to fight against whatever's in charge of these attacks," Xavier said. "I don't *like* him—even less, the more I've learned about him—but he's on the side of the angels, I think."

"Probably." Kyri thought for a moment. "The name is vaguely familiar. But why would Toron not *tell* you about me?"

"Yeah," Xavier said. "That's really bugging me, too. If he'd told us at the right time, heck, we might all have been going together."

"Except," Kyri said slowly, "you couldn't have caught up with me even if you'd known right away. Because Khoros himself made sure of that."

Tobimar frowned. "That's true. But let's think about it from Toron's point of view. He said that he was doing his best to also guess what Khoros wanted us to know and not know. If he was right, then there must be some advantage to us not knowing."

"Well, let's look at that," Poplock said. "If we'd known, we would've come up here knowing the Justiciars were bad. We'd have been weeks...no, still *months*, behind you, too. Knowing they were bad, we wouldn't have gone over to contract with them, so we wouldn't have gotten into the Temple and gotten their info." He looked over at Xavier. "You'd probably have stuck with us. Maybe wouldn't have met the Wanderer, or not until a lot later. Maybe we'd have gotten into a fight with one of these Justiciars by ourselves and gotten killed. Or we'd have been more careful sneaking around, and we wouldn't have been hot on Phoenix's trail, so we wouldn't have shown up in time to save her."

"And right now the Justiciars think you're on their side...or at least a dupe for them," Kyri said slowly. "We might be able to use that."

"*And*," Xavier said with a surprised grin, "none of them know *anything* about me. As far as your enemies are concerned, I don't exist. And while I'm going to have to get going *pretty* soon," he continued, "I'm not just bailing on you until I know this whole situation's under control."

Tobimar suddenly laughed. "And we're sitting here talking it all out without any reluctance. Don't you see how hard that would've been?"

Kyri blinked. *Of course.* "Even if I'd somehow beat Thornfalcon on my own, assuming I'd lived...I'm working alone. I have to be wisdom and caution as well as Justice and Mercy, and a battle with Thornfalcon would have made me terribly cautious. If you showed up claiming to be willing to help me, I'd have had to be even more careful. I'd have to spend days, maybe weeks, figuring out if I could trust you, or if you were part of the enemy's deeper game."

"Well, we *could* still be, I guess." Poplock said, voice echoing hollowly from upstairs.

"Anything's possible," Kyri admitted with a grin, "but Thornfalcon didn't expect an interruption, and certainly didn't expect to lose his head. And no one making up a story would *ever* have come up with *yours*, Xavier."

"Heh. No argument there. *I* don't believe this story sometimes, and I'm *it*."

Tobimar nodded, and seemed about to answer, then glanced out the window and started. "By the Seven...I think I'm starting to see some light out there. We need to go. There's still so much for us to talk about, and decisions to make...but not here, I think."

"No," Xavier said, "being caught in the mansion of a recently murdered guy doesn't sound like a good idea to *me*."

Kyri looked out, saw that the window did not reflect pure black, but had hints of shapes of the outdoors in it now. "You're right, Tobimar, Xavier. Poplock?"

The little Toad bounced down the stairs, stuffing some last little object into his neverfull pack. "I think I've got most of the stuff that's safe to take, valuable, and not traceable. I could set some of my flares—"

"No," Kyri said.

Tobimar nodded. "Of course, it's *your* right to—"

"I mean, no, we're not going to torch the mansion," she said slowly.

The other two goggled at her; a part of her almost laughed, because for a moment Tobimar looked nearly as pop-eyed as his Toad companion. "*What?*"

"I think we have a perfect opportunity here, but we have to leave the evidence for what Thornfalcon *was* in order for it to work."

Poplock frowned. "You mean I have to put everything *back*?" His distress was so comically exaggerated that Xavier failed to repress a snort of laughter.

She shook her head, and *did* smile. "No. We already argued that, and it's true that he had no heirs except the Justiciars. Since I'm the one true Justiciar, that makes it mine to give away... especially," and she was no longer smiling, "since he admitted to planning the deaths of my family, and *did* kill my brother... and with his monsters, a lot of other people in Evanwyl, too. Blood-debt, now paid. You didn't take anything of the evidence, and that's all that matters."

"Oh," said Xavier. "I get you. You're going to try the straight-ahead move."

Tobimar was looking at her speculatively, those brilliant blue eyes showing the beginnings of understanding. "You'll be taking a *drought-damned* risk, if you want to do what I think."

"Maybe... maybe not as much as you think," she answered, and felt hope rising. "Thornfalcon was bad through and through, and I suppose Bolthawk and Skyharrier might be too. But I *know* that wasn't true of Mist Owl and Shrike," *and I'm sure it's not true of Condor, please let it not be true,* "and even Thornfalcon was *shocked* to find out it was me. I can't keep that secret forever anyway; part of the reason it's worked at all is that they know where I went and why, and it would be almost impossible for me to *be* here again."

"Oh, oh, I think I see where you're hopping," Poplock said. "Might work. If we can do it right."

"It relies on what they already know—and what we know," Kyri said. "And on what I'm betting that innkeeper, Vlay, would have done after you left."

She could see Tobimar's brows lower, then raise in comprehension. "That *look*...he *knew* about Thornfalcon!"

"Makes sense," Xavier said.

"And if he knew *that*, he had to be one of their agents. Once he suspected what was going on, he'd have used one of the village messengers, sent someone straight to Evanwyl—the city—the man you saw, Xavier, and going probably to the Watchland, maybe to the Temple where the Justiciars would be sure to check in. He couldn't send anything to Justiciar's Retreat, that's not accessible if you aren't one of them, but the Watchland and the Temple would cover pretty much any chances."

Tobimar suddenly grinned. "And we can use that—and me— against them!" The grin grew sharper. "And with Xavier as a reserve."

"Something they'll *never* see coming," he said, with an answering grin.

The smiles, and the sudden certainty that they were *right*, wiped away the exhaustion. "Yes," she said, returning the smile, "I think we can. Because we have one other ally..."

52

Tobimar strode out of the forest, holding tightly to the ropes. A quick glance showed that Poplock was in place on his prisoner's shoulder, his slender but deadly blade resting against her neck. A glance ahead showed the main street. "You really *do* know your way around," he murmured. "We're practically *at* the Temple of the Balanced Sword." He had to trust Xavier was in his correct location, but that wasn't much of a worry; the native of Earth had proven his abilities to follow and stick with a plan—and improvise when the plan failed—enough in their journeys together. *I can trust him to do his part—or do nothing, if he's not needed, so he stays a secret.*

A shadow of a smile was just visible under the great beaked helm. Otherwise Kyri gave no sign of hearing, or of even being capable of much other than staggering along as she was pulled. Bindings tied her arms securely behind her back and wrapped around front; another line was connected to her legs in such a manner as to allow Tobimar to practically hobble her at need.

However, the blood streaking her armor, especially on the legs, showed that there probably *was* no need. She was limping and her shambling gait was that of a prisoner at the very edge of endurance and pain.

Tobimar knew he didn't look much better, with a cut on his cheek, blood on his clothes, dirt and sweat smeared across his face, in his hair, and other parts of clothing tattered and ripped. *We cleaned up, then we had to mess ourselves up again. And we* still *need to be ready to run as though the Hells themselves were on our trail, if this doesn't work.* Eating and the short rest they'd had during their talk had given him some reserves back, but they were all a long way from their best condition. But if this plan was going to work at all, they had to do it now.

Looking forward caused him to slow his pace for a moment. There was a *crowd* up ahead, dozens of people gathered in front of the Temple of the Balanced Sword. After a moment, though, he moved forward again. *I think this is just what we were looking for.*

In front of the crowd, seated on a beautiful gold and white feathered Sithigorn, was a silver and green armored figure with gold-blond hair. "*The Watchland,*" Kyri whispered.

The Watchland was addressing the crowd. "...will ride with as many of you are ready. Whatever we fear may have happened... will have happened, or not, long before we can arrive." As Tobimar got closer, he recognized two more elaborately armored figures: *Bolthawk and Skyharrier. No sign of Condor.*

Kyri was obviously puzzled...yet just as clearly relieved. "I did not want to fight Condor," she murmured. "I don't know why he isn't here now...but I am glad."

"So am I," Poplock said in Tobimar's ear. "One Justiciar just about whipped us all. Three would be entirely too much of a bad thing."

Tobimar made a gesture for them to both be quiet. Have to time this correctly...I think it's time to move.

"So," the Watchland continued, "we will move with haste and decision, but not rashly. We have..."

He trailed off, head raised to look down the road and staring in their direction.

The rest of the crowd turned to look, and a murmur began. Tobimar saw Skyharrier stiffen, then begin to move forward.

Tobimar ignored them, proceeded towards the steps of the Temple of the Balanced Sword. As he did so, the doors opened, Arbiter Kelsley emerging... and then stepping back in shock, nearly falling despite the cane on which he walked. "Adventurer Silverun...have you...is *this*...?"

"You asked that I find the one responsible for Mist Owl's death," Tobimar said, entering, hearing the rustle and murmur behind him as the crowd began to follow—and the sharper, ring-ing sound of two pairs of armored boots, not *quite* running but moving quickly indeed. *Another pair of heavier, armored steps right behind them—that must be the Watchland.*

About as good as we could hope... as long as Kyri's right about Kelsley. "You asked I do this, and so I have done. Before you is the slayer of Mist Owl and Shrike and—as of this past evening—Thornfalcon."

Kelsley was alternating his stare between Tobimar's prisoner, whose head was bowed, figure hunched, and Tobimar himself. "We had heard... a messenger had come from Gharis, with word that Thornfalcon might be in danger. I had hoped... But at least it is over now."

"Indeed it is over." Skyharrier's voice was grim and hard, and his face as stony as the pillars supporting the temple. Bolthawk nodded, brows dark over furious eyes, and the crowd murmured; it was an ugly sound. The Watchland, Tobimar noticed, said nothing, and his expression was analytical, not angry.

"And now, impostor, you will face us without a mask to shield you from the Justiciars and our certain vengeance!" Skyharrier's hand lashed out to rip the helm from the captive's head. "We shall see what manner of—*Great Balance!*"

Skyharrier fell back, shock replacing anger, the helm falling from nerveless fingers, as deep-sapphire hair cascaded down, hair crowned with pure silver-white, and beneath that the furious glare of Kyri Vantage, the Phoenix. *Oh, that was perfect*, Tobimar thought, and at the same moment felt a tiny weight scuttle up his back. *And now we're ready if it all goes bad.*

Kyri straightened, the bonds falling away, *burning* away in golden flame, and the crowd withdrew, the murmuring filled with disbelief and confusion now. "We shall indeed see," she said quietly.

For a long moment no one else moved; Skyharrier and Bolthawk's faces ran a gamut of emotions, and Tobimar realized Kyri had been right. *They may be very bad men, perhaps almost as bad as Thornfalcon, or they may not; but they never expected to have to face* her.

The Arbiter was the first to move. He stepped forward, eyes wide, and his voice shook. "Kyri? Kyri Vantage, child, is it truly you?"

She turned her head and looked down, and her expression softened; Tobimar could see a fond smile. "It is, Arbiter."

"But then..." He seemed at a complete loss for words, mouth opening, closing, and finally he found only one last word to speak: "... *why?*"

"That," the deep voice of the Watchland said, "is indeed the question, and a deadly one." The crowd murmured agreement.

Kyri turned fully to face the Watchland and then dropped to both knees. "Watchland, I am Kyri Victoria Vantage, inheritor of my house, Eye and Ward of Evanwyl. Will you hear me, Watchland? Will you truly hear me, in the name of the Balanced Sword, in the name of Myrionar, in the name of Justice with Wisdom, Vengeance with Truth, Mercy through Strength?"

He stared down, and Tobimar saw his eyes flick towards the two Justiciars, who were now recovering from shock and clearly trying to figure out the right response. Then he looked back to the girl kneeling before him.

Moments went by, and no one else dared move; even the crowd was silent, holding its collective breath, waiting to see what the Watchland would do.

Then his hand came down and touched her shoulder, lifted, brought Kyri to a stand to face him. "I am Jeridan Velion, the Watchland and Ward of Evanwyl. My Eyes are my strength and the Vantages are my heart. I will hear you truly, in the name of the Balanced Sword, in the name of Myrionar, in the name of Justice with Wisdom, Vengeance with Truth, Mercy through Strength."

Kyri bowed her thanks—and then whirled, finger jabbing like a spear. "Then I say to you that *these* are the true traitors, Jeridan! The Justiciars are corrupt and fallen. Thornfalcon *boasted* of it, for he *arranged* my parents' deaths, killed Rion with his own hands, and Shrike..." her voice caught for a moment, then went on, "Shrike was the one who cut down both my mother and father."

"*What?*" Skyharrier's face was a perfect picture of stunned disbelief, and the crowd echoed that shock. "How... how could you *say* such things, Kyri?" He looked to the Watchland. "Watchland, you *know* what she says is... insane. Impossible. You have *seen* our powers, you have fought beside us, you *know* us! I don't know what's *happened* to her, but..."

"... but she's completely off her head," Bolthawk finished, a look of tormented sympathy on his face. *By the Seven and the One, they're good. But I suppose being able to carry off such an act is something they've become very, very practiced in.*

The Watchland was now standing a short distance from them, the conflict before him mirrored on his face. The people in the crowd were murmuring, and Tobimar couldn't tell how the sentiment in that group might turn. He could see Kyri's gaze flicking from one group to another, studying them, judging.

"Sir," Tobimar said, "if I may?"

Watchland Velion raised an eyebrow. "If you can clarify this... horror for us, you may speak."

"I am Tobimar Silverun of Skysand," he said carefully; a nod from the Watchland showed that the older man understood what that name meant. "I am also an Adventurer—Zarathanton Guilded, sponsored by none other than T'Oroning'Oltharamnon ʰGHEK R'arshe Ness, Marshal of Hosts—and now, I should inform you, King of the Dragon Throne."

The Watchland stepped forward and tested the Guild Seal. "So you are—though your other words hint at news I would hear—later. Go on."

"Sir," Tobimar said, "I was hired by the Arbiter—for the Justiciars, ironically—to hunt down the killer of Mist Owl and, as it turned out, Shrike. I tracked the Phoenix and arrived, I thought, barely in time to rescue Thornfalcon.

"But it was entirely the other way around, and Thornfalcon very nearly killed me before Phoenix escaped from where Thornfalcon had imprisoned her." He looked into the blue gaze of the other man. "As he had imprisoned many others before. The evidence you truly seek is there, on his mansion grounds."

The Watchland nodded, then gestured for him to move. To Tobimar's surprise, he found himself stepping aside without even really thinking about it. *He's the ruler of a tiny country... yet he has that same...force...that my mother has, that Toron has. How strange.*

Kyri stood still as the Watchland strode to her and stopped no more than a pace away, gazing at her intensely.

Kyri met his gaze, then slowly turned her head. "Hello, Gallire, Lehi. It's a long time, isn't it, since that day in the Temple when we were doing the Balance?" She smiled fondly. "You've both grown so much."

Tobimar saw the two girls—twins, with dark hair twined with flowers—staring at Kyri in confusion. The second twin, Lehi, smiled slowly, and then her sister joined her.

Behind them, a man and a woman—obviously their parents—stirred, moved forward. "Yes, they have. And...we've watched them do that growing, thanks to you, Kyri."

"We do not," Skyharrier said, and his voice was gentle, not angry now, "argue against the courage, the valor, or the kindness of the Kyri Vantage we knew, or, in some ways, the one we see now. Tragedy can break any of us, and surely she and her family have seen tragedy beyond that which any should."

Subtle, and well thought out, Justiciar. Had he not known the truth, Tobimar was sure the words would have made him uncertain. The crowd was also torn, that much was clear, and that made things far worse. Kyri had made it clear she would tolerate *no* killing on their part of the citizens of Evanwyl, unless it was absolutely certain that they were knowing and willing accomplices to the false Justiciars. *If the crowd turns on us...*

"Tragedy can break us," Kyri agreed, pitching her own voice low, yet in a carrying tone that Tobimar knew would be heard far back in the mostly silent crowd, "but I was not *broken* by tragedy; I was only *driven* by it, and I did not make for myself this armor. I stand before you in armor of the Spiritsmith, new-forged for my name and station, the Raiment of the Phoenix."

"A bold and necessary claim," Bolthawk said, "for one who claims the station of Justiciar. But a claim hard indeed to prove, unless the Spiritsmith himself were present to support it."

A murmur was beginning in the crowd, and the words were not what Tobimar hoped. A consensus—either way—would be better than a division, a split, but that was what he was hearing. "...always helped us, never cruel, always *fair*..."; "...Justiciars *healed* me just last week, that's the power of the gods, you can't argue..."; "...daughter knew her all her life and she would *never*..."; "...if it's possible to fake being a Justiciar, how do we know which one..."

She swept the crowd with her gaze once more, then returned it to the Watchland. "Jeridan, you said once you knew us far better than I would have believed. You are the Watchland. You have watched us, and watched *over* us. Who am I, Jeridan Velion? You must judge me. Am I broken and mad...or am I the Phoenix?"

He said nothing, just looked at her for a long moment, as though by sight alone he could find the truth in the young Justiciar's eyes.

Without warning he whirled and pointed. "Lay down your weapons, both of you."

The false Justiciars stared in disbelief. "What? Are *you* gone *lackwit* now? How dare you—"

The Watchland's sword was in his hand, and the crowd was murmuring more loudly... and some of the eyes that now turned towards Skyharrier and Bolthawk were hardening. "I said *lay down your weapons*. Kyri Victoria Vantage, a Justiciar? That I can believe. A murderer, one who could kill three Justiciars, she *not* a Justiciar? That I do *not* believe."

Tobimar saw a conflicted mass of emotions crossing the faces of the two Justiciars... and Bolthawk glanced sharply off to one side.

Too late, Tobimar saw the figure at the rear of the crowd, a figure with a wand raising, pointing directly at Kyri, and there was no time, not even a fraction of a second to warn her, he saw the hand already steadying and light beginning as his eyes were widening, his mouth trying to open...

A thunderbolt split the air, singeing the heads of several in the crowd, screams rising, people dropping to the ground, with the lightning arrowing straight for the exposed back of Kyri Vantage, the Phoenix—

—And stopped dead in midair, caught on two leaf-green blades, cast aside like a parried sword-blow to spatter harmlessly against the thick, carved stone wall of the Temple. "Not a chance," said Xavier Uriel Ross, and the false Justiciars stared in shock at the impossible.

"And *now* the Balanced Sword speaks to me." The new voice cut through all others, louder than mere human speech, no longer shocked and uncertain tenor but as hard and cold as steel. Arbiter Kelsley stepped forward, and his face was like carven stone in his fury. "*Now* it speaks, and says but three words, and those words are your doom, Skyharrier, Bolthawk, for Myrionar says: 'She speaks truth.'"

Bolthawk was unmoving, perhaps unable to believe that the deception was coming apart in mere moments. Skyharrier, however, seemed to recognize a hopeless situation.

Great gold and white wings whipped out, wings edged with bladed metal, and the false Justiciar spun, forcing the entire crowd to duck backwards from the lethal span, making even the Watchland and Kyri leap back. At the same time he drew his bow forth, an arrow appearing from nowhere, already nocked, the golden bow being drawn—*he's aiming for* her! He couldn't get there in time, and Xavier was behind, protecting her from assassins in the crowd, not from the Justiciars in front, and it would be too late—

Blue-silver light *slammed* into Skyharrier, knocking the bow skittering away. "You shall harm *no one*," Kelsley said, and from his hands—and the great Balanced Sword behind him—another bludgeon of argent-sapphire power smashed Bolthawk backwards. "You have *betrayed* the Balanced Sword." Another bolt of power, even brighter, and Kelsley strode forward, cane discarded, his voice now thunder, his hands blue lightning. "You have *defiled* your names. You have spoken *lies* in the name of the Balance."

Even the Watchland was backing away, Kyri with him; no one dared stand between Arbiter Kelsley and the false Justiciars. Skyharrier's wings blocked the next blast—and the armor *shattered*. "You have tried to speak lies of this child, you have killed her family, performed only the gods know what unspeakable acts, and still you thought to trick the Watchland, trick us all?" Kelsley spread his arms wide, and Tobimar saw blood trickling from his nose, and remembered Kyri's story; the priest wobbled unsteadily, weakened or dizzy. "Never more. Never again." The false Justiciars saw him waver, took two steps forward, and Kelsley's head came up, proud and certain. "Not in *my* Temple!"

There was a blaze like burning diamonds in the sun and a concussion that staggered Tobimar, drove him to his knees. Screams and curses filled the air, and the Prince of Skysand blinked, desperately trying to clear his vision. Then he felt his jaw sag.

A *hole* had been blown clean through the Temple, in line with and above the great doorways, missing all the nearby crowd. Through the still-open doorway he could see Skyharrier and Bolthawk, nearly a hundred yards from those portals. Bolthawk was literally *smoking*, his armor almost completely gone. *He must have thrown himself between Kelsley and Skyharrier.* Skyharrier dragged himself to his feet, seeing the crowd turning towards them, and desperately grabbed up Bolthawk. He leapt skyward, great white-gold wings beating furiously. Arrows streaked in his wake, and from a crystal in the hand of a woman who had tears streaming down her face a flaming spirit was unleashed, burning its way through the air after him. *But even that's going to take a bit to catch him . . . and I don't think it can kill him.*

"Arbiter!" Kyri caught Kelsley as he slumped to the ground.

"Don't . . . worry," he said painfully. "It was . . . a dangerous strain . . . but Justice demanded it. I will live."

The Watchland sheathed his blade. "And *there* is the proof, even had Myrionar not spoken. A true Justiciar would have waited, for lies can be shattered by truth, and if the evidence you spoke of was not to be found, they would have been freed." He looked out to the crowd. "And the assassin?"

Xavier emerged from the crowd, with several of the citizens dragging a body that Tobimar recognized as the Gharis innkeeper, Vlay. "Dead. Sorry about that, but he was fighting to kill us."

"Do not concern yourself with it; death would have been his penalty in the end for such treason and dishonor." Velion turned and knelt. "My most abject apologies, Kyri Vantage. I had sworn to find your parents' killers ... and instead I have harbored them."

"Don't blame yourself," Kyri said, with a tired, relieved smile. "They fooled us all, and they must have had help." She wavered on her feet. Xavier didn't waver, but looked as though he probably couldn't move another step.

"By the Balance ... are you hurt?"

Tobimar had the distant, fogged feeling of utter exhaustion himself. "No," he managed to say, "we've just been going for more than a day and a half, maybe two days, with fights along the way..."

The Watchland caught Kyri's arm and helped support her; Tobimar found someone else—one of the Seekers of the temple—at his side; another was helping Xavier. "The Temple is closest," the Arbiter said, "and also most appropriate. You will rest." He smiled fondly at Kyri. "Time enough later for explanations.

"For you all have done the work of the Balanced Sword today."

53

"Boy, you look tired," Poplock said.

Tobimar also looked rather cross-eyed, but that, Poplock was willing to concede, probably had to do with the fact that the little Toad was sitting on top of Tobimar's head when he made the statement.

"Unlike you," Tobimar said with a tolerant grin, "*I* can't decide to take a nap when parts of the proceedings get boring. Parties crossed with debriefing the Watchland and other local lords, the Eyes, those are getting pretty tiring." He glanced askance to Xavier, who was leaning against the gate. "*And* I can't just go invisible and run off, either." Xavier grinned at him, showing no sympathy at all.

"*She* doesn't look tired," Poplock observed, seeing Kyri still talking to a small crowd that surrounded her at the entrance to the Watchland's castle. "Of course, this is her home country."

The Skysand Prince snorted. "*That* isn't it. And I think you know perfectly well how exhausted she is, even though they gave us a few days to recover before starting in. She knows that with the original Justiciars gone, she's *got* to show Myrionar's presence a *lot*. She has to be all the Justiciars in one." He gazed at the tall girl in the glittering armor, giving blessings of the Balance to each of the crowd, talking with them, nodding her understanding.

Poplock bounced his agreement, then slid down to Tobimar's shoulder. "I guess it wouldn't work at all if she wasn't someone they knew already."

"Not a sand-burned chance, in my opinion. The only way our confrontation at the Temple worked was that the Watchland and the Arbiter *knew* her family and couldn't believe Kyri could have gone entirely bad. Oh, I could see someone else finding a way to prove the *other* Justiciars had betrayed their faith, especially if they beat Thornfalcon and had the evidence—but they'd have a long, long time to prove themselves otherwise trustworthy, retain belief in the Justiciars as...hmm, as an *institution.*"

"Yeah," agreed Xavier. "And that seems pretty central to the way they work here, too. I mean, they've got a temple and that priest, but the Justiciars are the real symbol." He shook his head. "Still takes getting used to, that the gods really play a part in things..."

"...but," Poplock said, not without some "I told you so" in his tone, "you gotta admit Kelsley was pretty convincing."

Xavier nodded. "Your gods still aren't quite *my* idea of a 'god,' but I can't argue they've got some style, and boy, Kelsley's one *badass* bastard when he decides he's had enough and Myrionar's backing him."

Tobimar nodded. "I'm not sure I'd use your...particular language, but I certainly agree. About Evanwyl itself...I think you're right; if they lost the Justiciars, it might have finished breaking the faith entirely. So right now, that means Kyri's the only true symbol of Myrionar, so she's got to constantly keep herself looking confident, comfortable, wise, and just. I sure don't envy her *that.*"

Kyri had finally disengaged from the crowd and was striding at double-time to catch up with them. "Deserting your companion to save yourselves?" she inquired with a smile.

"On the contrary," Tobimar said lightly, "it was a force only a true Justiciar of Myrionar could face, and so we withdrew so as not to encumber you."

"Oh, indeed?" But she was still smiling.

"I was just waiting to say goodbye," Xavier said, and Poplock saw her smile dim.

"You have to go so soon?"

Xavier looked into the distance, squinting as though at something only he could see. "*Have* to?" he said slowly. "Maybe not. But...well, I've still got to get the answer to that question from Idinus himself, and that's one long, long hike across the continent. And I'll have to find my friends."

Poplock exchanged a knowing glance with Tobimar. Something the Wanderer had told Xavier still weighed on him, and it was something that the native of Earth wasn't going to share ... something that had to do with his companions, Khoros, and the deadly mission they were on. "But now, as night falls?"

Xavier nodded. "It seems ... right, somehow. Don't ask me why. You know, don't you?"

Poplock saw Tobimar nod slowly. "We share many things, Xavier Ross. Yes, I know. The course of the world is clear to you now, and it says you should be already on your way."

"Yeah." He turned to Kyri. "Kyri ... Phoenix ... you take care, okay? I'm not going to be around to watch your backs, and those two false Justiciars aren't giving up now, I'm sure of it."

Kyri gave him the full pirouette of the Armed Bow. "I shall be careful, Xavier. And you will always be welcome, in my home or at my side in peace or war." She smiled suddenly, and Poplock noticed an answering smile on Tobimar's face as well as Xavier's. "And perhaps you will come to know Myrionar one day, and we shall give you a new name as a Justiciar."

He laughed. "That'd be something, all right."

Turning back to Poplock and Tobimar, he slowly and with ceremony reached back to the two hilts with the seven towers and parallel blades graven upon them, grasped them, and drew forth his swords. The green blades came out and were brought before him, parallel as those on their hilts. "Tobimar."

Tobimar drew his own swords and held them in the mirror of Xavier's pose. "Xavier."

The two bowed slowly to each other, and then with a laugh sheathed their blades. Tobimar stepped forward and embraced Xavier; Poplock saw startlement in Xavier's eyes, a look of a young man rather taken aback, but a moment later he managed a faint grin and returned the hug. "Hey, don't get all sentimental on me," Xavier said.

"You are going to a place few return from," Tobimar said. "And you then seek to accomplish a quest that is almost unthinkable."

"I'm going to be one of those few," Xavier answered. "Believe it. And don't think you're never going to see me again. You will."

"I'll expect you, then."

"Only when you *least* expect me," he answered with a grin. "Okay, Poplock—keep an eye on *both* of these guys for me, all right?"

The little Toad bounced over and shook the extended hand between both of his. "As always."

"Well... then I guess this is goodbye." He gave one more reassuring grin. "For now."

They watched the slender, dark figure fade into the night; when none of them could see any more, they began walking again.

The three were silent for a few moments as they walked down the road towards Vantage Fortress, which Kyri was mistress of in the absence of her aunt. Poplock noticed, but did not comment on, the fact that the two humans were walking rather closely together. *They'll notice it themselves, when they're ready to think about it. That Watchland's already noticed, of course. I think he kinda wants to be doing the walking with her too.*

"I guess I'll—"

"When do we—"

The two had spoken at the same time and both broke off in the same instant, and both then tried to say "Go ahead" at the same time, and then, "No, you first," and at that point both of them broke into laughter. Poplock joined them.

Once the laughs had died down, Poplock said, "Since I'm the disinterested observer, I say *you* should start, Phoenix."

"Oh, *please* don't call me Phoenix, I get enough of that from everyone else."

"But it's so *funny* to see you twitch." The mock-glare she gave him was still surprisingly intimidating. "Okay, okay. Anyway, go ahead."

"You are a cruel little Toad," she said, still giggling. "Tobimar, I was *going* to ask when we had to leave."

Poplock had to hang on as Tobimar halted suddenly. "Leave? Um, I was about to say that I guessed I should find myself some more permanent rooms in town, since we were staying."

She shook her head. "No, no, Tobimar, you've got your own quest, and—"

"—and it's waited twelve thousand years, I think I can forgive a few more days, or weeks, or maybe even months, if the world will let us have them."

Kyri looked torn. "Well... I appreciate that, but there's so many terrible things going on..."

"And right now, we're not part of them," Poplock pointed out. "Not trying to sound like I don't care, but... I guess the real question is whether things are over *here*."

Kyri opened her mouth to answer, closed it, started to say something again, and then stopped, looking more thoughtful. The two humans started walking again.

"That's . . . not quite as easy to answer as I thought at first," Kyri said finally.

"What about the other false Justiciars?" Poplock asked.

"Our best guess is that they must have gone to Justiciar's Retreat; it's a place only the Justiciars can go to, hidden by all kinds of spells. I *might* be able to find it . . . but maybe not. *Something* was giving them the power to pretend to be Justiciars, and we know it wasn't Thornfalcon alone."

"No," Tobimar said slowly. "They were still using their powers after we know Thornfalcon was dead. And Thornfalcon also essentially *told* us that he used to be human and his 'patron' made him otherwise. Whatever was doing this not only isn't human, it's got to be immortal or close to it."

"That's the way I think it has to be," Kyri said after a moment. "Something that could slowly work its way in, corrupt the Justiciars, and then act as a . . . supporter, a patron, for the false Justiciars. This patron must have allowed them to take over the Retreat, and unless that patron *was* Thornfalcon, I'd have to guess the Retreat's secure from easy approach." She looked pensive. "On the other hand, the whole country now knows the truth. They can't set foot in the rest of Evanwyl without the alarm being sounded."

"What about that diary I heard about?" Poplock asked.

"Oh, *that.*" Kyri looked sour. "Well, it proves that we did the right thing in confronting everyone and pushing the issue, instead of waiting. Thornfalcon had kept a false diary somewhere that it was guaranteed to be found—and in a spelled safe, so it might have survived even if we *had* put his mansion to the torch. It was a perfect cover story—made it sound like he was simply weak and tempted into betraying the Justiciars as an individual. Even explains the Gateway in his house, in a way."

Poplock was, unwillingly, impressed. "*Drought*, he was a sneaky one. Brought those monsters in without anyone else knowing so he could get your brother killed while everyone was distracted, wrote a cover story to keep the Justiciars clean if he was caught— and if he was their boss, probably set up stories for them, too."

She nodded her head. "He must have assumed that if something *did* happen, he'd be cornered alone—in a group, almost nothing could beat them—and so if the others just kept their heads they'd be able to pass it off as a terrible, treacherous action by one weak member corrupted by the powers that lie beyond Rivendream Pass."

"That's where the Gateway went?"

"Sasha—our summoner and also a symbolist of some skill— confirmed it. She went over the remains and said the resonances show it goes to the north, straight through Rivendream and to... whatever lies on the other side."

She looked over to Tobimar. "We didn't really get a chance to talk before this night's party—how did both of you do?"

"It was *definitely* Condor who found Shrike's body before us," Tobimar said, and Poplock could see the girl wince in pained sympathy. "He ran off towards the west once he'd confirmed Shrike was dead. I'd guess he's at your Retreat too, since that was the same direction Skyharrier flew in. We did find a couple of witnesses who saw him moving straight as an arrow and, as one said, 'looking as though Death itself was on his back.'"

She looked torn. "I wish..."

"I know," Poplock said, at the same time that Tobimar did; the Toad continued, "but if he's got any chance for salvation, he's got to make the move. He's gotta know the truth by now; if he ever comes to meet with you, well, then you can decide to give him a chance."

"Is Evanwyl safe?" Tobimar asked. "Everyone else is at war, after all."

Kyri didn't answer immediately, as they walked up the broad steps to the entrance; the doors opened as the three reached them. "For now? I think so, actually," she said after a few moments. "If your guesses are right, these people were connected to the whole plan, and whatever their plan was obviously *didn't* involve immersing Evanwyl in the war, at least not right away. Now, we've disrupted their original plans, but right now they've *already* committed their forces to the largest countries on the continent—and off it, like Artania."

Tobimar laughed suddenly. "Of course. Since they never planned on it in the first place, they almost certainly haven't got anything to *spare* for Evanwyl."

"That's my take on it." They entered one of the downstairs sitting rooms and Kyri let the Phoenix Raiment flow off her and onto a rack nearby, then dropped into a large stuffed chair, now wearing the formal suit she had worn for the Watchland's dinner and dance. "*Finally* off my feet."

"Be fair," Poplock said, "you got to sit down during dinner. Of course that didn't mean you got to *rest*."

"You have *that* so very completely right, my amphibious friend." She leaned back and looked over at Tobimar, who had found his own chair—one that automatically shifted slightly to let him recline. Poplock bounced to a nearby end table.

"If you *are* staying, Tobimar," Kyri said, "there's no reason you can't stay here. There are plenty of—"

"Absolutely *not*," Tobimar said emphatically. "I've already been staying here with you long enough, given—"

"So I *was* right," Poplock said, very satisfied with himself; it wasn't often you got to win an argument weeks after you started it. "Your people really *are* silly on that subject."

As Tobimar went crimson, Kyri was obviously trying to control her laughter. She was not terribly successful. "Are you saying that in Skysand—"

"I . . . Toad, I swear I will . . ." Tobimar stuttered, then with an obvious effort shook himself and looked the tall girl in the eye. His face, however, remained the color of a sunset. "Yes in Skysand we have many traditions around men and women and how they interact, and it's . . . improper for me to stay in the house of a young woman such as yourself, unless we're, um, walking together."

"But—" Poplock could tell it was almost as hard for Kyri to avoid the obvious "but we *were* just walking together" as it was for him to point it out. "All right, I don't want to make it difficult for you."

"Thank you." Tobimar took a deep breath and visibly relaxed.

"Returning to the prior subject, let's take it as agreed that you both made commitments to support each other's missions," Poplock said after a moment. "Well, we've done a drought-damned good job of starting on your problem, Kyri, at least I think so. What I want to know is how close to *finished* are you?"

It was Tobimar who answered. "Not very," he said. "The real planners behind all this we don't even know."

"And Myrionar promised I would have my Justice and Vengeance in full measure," Kyri agreed. "The Balanced Sword has already delivered to me the slayer of my brother, and of my mother and father. But the being or beings who made it necessary and possible for that to *happen* are still out there."

"On your side," Poplock said, looking at Tobimar, "you're chasing legends, but you've actually got a better lead on it than any of your ancestors ever did, right?"

Tobimar looked surprised. "You know...you're absolutely right. I just didn't think of it that way. I'm now *certain* that our homeland was what you now call Moonshade Hollow. 'When justice and vengeance lay just beyond the mountains,' the fact that it seems to have gone bad in the last Chaoswar, the map showing it ringed by mountains, it all fits. More, the fact that old Khoros told me I would have to follow justice and vengeance—and I did, and it brought me here—tells me this *has* to be the right track."

"So," Poplock said, looking from one to the other, "you've *both* helped each other, and both your missions have moved forward, right? And for me," he added, "well, both of your quests and mine are connected." He bounced a nod at Tobimar. "We agreed what we *really* had to do—find out what was behind this, and get that word back to the people who could do something. We're closer now—and it's all connected."

"You're not saying we can stop now, though, are you?"

"Not by Blackwart's Chosen!" he answered, emphasizing that with a loud croak. "But these guys we're up against, they've spent...how long? Centuries? Maybe longer, maybe if they come from Moonshade Hollow they've been working on this for *thousands* of years.

"I think we don't need to rush, because that'll get us killed. We need to think out where to go next, and why, and what preparations we need to do before we go." Poplock bounced again and smiled. "And guess that means...it isn't over, no, but for *now*, it is."

Tobimar's smile lit up his face. "The *adventure* is over, you mean."

"Successful mission accomplished, Guild Brethren," Poplock agreed. "You completed the contract with the Temple, Kyri unmasked the false Justiciars and avenged her family, and me and Xavier got to save you both when the mud got *really* deep and sticky. Kyri's got to make sure her home's safe for a while, and we've got some research to do." He noticed a fly buzz by, snatched it out of the air with a quick tongue-lash, swallowed. "Sure, there's those renegade Justiciars hiding out, Thornfalcon's patron out there, whoever's behind these wars, and there's whatever scares the water out of you in that Moonshade Hollow... but those are all things for *later*. They're busy, and you've already smacked their strongest forces here down."

Kyri nodded, and Tobimar nodded with her. "You're right, Poplock," Kyri said. "Maybe there will *always* be another adventure waiting; that was something Aunt Victoria once warned me about, that once you became an Adventurer for real it was hard to know when you *could* stop.

"So we'll do what we have to do here together." She looked at the other two, and both Tobimar and Poplock nodded their assent. "And when the time comes, we'll go face the rest of *both* quests together."

Tobimar nodded emphatically and took Kyri's hand—and took one of Poplock's tiny paws in his other. "And until then," he said with a smile, "we won't let the adventures of tomorrow rob us of what we have today."

GAZETTEER FOR ZARATHAN

Overview

Zarathan (more properly Zahr-a-Thana, World of Magic) is a planet of generally Earth size and composition. It is presumed to be the source of all magic in all universes. The main continent (and the only continent commonly known) stretches approximately four thousand, eight hundred miles north to south and, at its widest, is about the same east to west (it averages between two and three thousand east-west over most of its extent, however). It can be generally divided into three regions: Southern Zarathan, which is most of the continent south of the Khalal mountain range; Northern Zarathan, which is everything north of the Khalals plus the very large island/miniature continent of Artania; and Elyvias, a subcontinent peninsula shaped something like a gigantic Cape Cod and separated from Southern Zarathan by the Barricade Mountains.

The history, geography, and peoples of Zarathan are all affected greatly by the apparently cyclical "Chaoswars," which bring periodic conflict to the world and are associated with massive mystical/deific disturbances which, among other effects, distort or erase memories and even records of prior events—up to and including those of the gods. Thus, while the generally known history of Zarathan stretches back over half a million years, clear records are rarely available for anything older than the most recent Chaoswar.

Countries

There are several countries on this continent, but it should be made clear that "country" on Zarathan is not quite the same as "country" in the modern civilized world of Earth. Most of the area claimed as a country's territory is actually relatively wild and untamed and dangerous; only cleared areas around cities and major roads tend to be safe for travel. The overall population of the countries is therefore much lower than might be expected, given that the average standard of living is closer to that of twentieth-century Earth in many ways than it is to the medieval era that one might first assume, seeing no factories and noticing that the sword is still a common weapon.

Following is a list of the important countries in *Phoenix Rising*:

STATE OF THE DRAGON GOD

Called variously the *State of the Dragon God, The Dragon-King's Domain, The State of Elbon Nomicon*, and other appellations, the actual name for this country is a very long string of Ancient Sauran words that, boiled down, means something like "The Country founded in the days of the Dragon-God's First Creation, That Endures Eternally." It is the largest country on the planet, stretching from the western edge of Southern Zarathan all the way to the Barricade Mountains in the east, and from the southern coast all the way to the Ice Peaks in the north. In a governmental sense, the State of the Dragon God might best be described as a theocratic libertarian state.

The capital of the State of the Dragon God is called in Ancient Sauran *Fanalam' T' ameris' a' u' Zahr-a-Thana T'ikon*, but commonly (and to the Saurans and Dragons, painfully) called simply "Zarathanton." It is the most ancient city, and the largest on the continent, with some buildings over five hundred thousand years old, and a population of roughly 200,000 inside and immediately outside its walls. Other important cities within its borders include T'Tera (also called the Dragon God's City); Artani (a city of trade with the *Artan* of the Forest Sea); Dragonkill; Bridgeway; Odinsforge (also the name of the mountain range in which it is set); Salandar; Thologondoreave (an independent city of the Children of Odin); Shipton (known to the Saurans as *Olthamian' a' ameris*); and Hell's Edge.

THE EMPIRE OF THE MOUNTAIN

Nearly as large as the Dragon God's country, the Empire of the Mountain actually straddles the Khalals, claiming much of the territory north of the Ice Peaks to the Khalals and some territory to the north and east above them. Ruled in unbroken power for hundreds of thousands of years by the God-Emperor Idinus, the most powerful wizard ever to live, the Empire has always had an uneasy relationship with its neighbors. While God-Emperor Idinus is not, strictly speaking, evil, he has motives and goals that are unclear to others, and this has led, on occasion, to war on a titanic scale. The capital of the Empire of the Mountain is Scimitar's Path, at the base of Mount Scimitar—tallest peak of the Khalal range at sixty thousand feet. There are several other cities, the most important of which are Kheldragaard to the west and Tor Port in the east. It is an ironclad theocracy, ruled directly by the Archmage himself from atop Mount Scimitar—where he remains virtually always.

DALTHUNIA

Dalthunia used to be an ally state to the Dragon God, a modest-sized country which broke away from the Empire due to a very bad set of missteps by some of the Empire's local rulers, eventually triggering a local revolution. For some reason the Archmage—after a short demonstration of his power that showed that if he wished, he could take Dalthunia back at any time—allowed Dalthunia to remain independent. At the time of the story, however, Dalthunia has been a conquered state—whether by internal revolution or some subtle external invasion is unclear—for a couple of centuries, and very little is known about it, other than that they do not welcome visitors. They clearly have powerful magic and probably deific patrons, because scrying and ordinary espionage have not been effective. The capital of Dalthunia is Kymael, named after the instigator of the revolution.

EVANWYL

A small country between the northeastern portion of Hell's Rim, the Khalals, and the Broken Hills, Evanwyl is an almost forgotten country at the time of *Phoenix Rising*; its great claim to fame used to be its connection to the civilization that lay on the other side of Heavenbridge Way, the winding but only useful pass through the Khalals. But that was before something happened during the last Chaoswar, something that turned the other side to the monstrous

Moonshade Hollow and turned Heavenbridge Way into Rivendream Pass. Now Evanwyl's only function is keeping the things that exit Rivendream Pass from entering the larger world. Governmentally, Evanwyl is a monarchy (ruled by the Watchland) with the monarch's power moderated by his subordinates and advisors the Eyes and Arms, and by the powerful influence of the faith of Myrionar, the Balanced Sword, especially as embodied in the Justiciars of Myrionar and the high priest called the Arbiter. The city of Evanwyl is the capital; its population is between four and five thousand people in total.

SKYSAND

Situated on the far northeast corner of the continent, Skysand is a country that is mostly desert with considerable volcanic features and with some interior and coastal oases (around which are built its few cities). A theocratic monarchy, Skysand is ruled by the Silverun family under a complex set of rules administered and watched over by the temples of Terian, the Mortal God. The capital is also named Skysand and is situated in a natural harbor with a periodically active but generally harmless volcano on the southern side. Cut off from the rest of the land by the high and volcanic Flamewall Mountains, Skysand trades by sea with other countries around the continent, its most prominent exports being magical gemstones, which are found in great quantity and diverse assortments in the desert and mountains.

ARTANIA

A huge island or small continent a thousand miles long and a few hundred miles wide, Artania is the claimed homeland of the youngest of the major species on Zarathan, the *Artan* (sometimes called Elves). Few other than the *Artan* are allowed beyond the capital city, Nya-Sharee-Hilya (which means "Surviving the Storm of Ages"); this city is run on rather militaristic lines but it is uncertain as to whether this reflects the overall government, or the fact that the city is often the focal point of invasion attempts.

WHITE BLADE STATE

Located in a circle of mountains in the far northwest of the main continent, the White Blade State is a rotating monarchy, with rulership cycling regularly between the ruling families of the five main cities. How the individual cities determine their ruling families varies, making governmental changeovers... interesting at times. Naturally, this also means the capital city changes with regularity. The "White Blade" is a symbolic, but extremely powerful, sword which is held by the current ruler; it is said to be the gift of the patron god of the White Blade, Chromaias, and each of the five cities are devoted to and named after one of the five gods of that faith: Chromaias, Stymira [Thanamion], Amanora, Taralandira [Mulios], and Kharianda.

AEGEIA

A small country walled off from the rest of the continent by the mountain range called Wisdom's Fortress, Aegeia is a theocratic state which is ruled much of the time by a council of twelve nobles, but at other times by the literal incarnate Goddess of Wisdom, Athena, in the capital city of Aegis.

ODINSFORGE RANGE/THOLOGONDOREAVE

The Children of Odin claim this as their homeland, and politically the entire mountain range is treated as neutral ground with the Children of Odin having priority in disputes. The area immediately surrounding the general location of Thologondoreave ("Cavern of a Thousand Hammers") is acknowledged to be sovereign territory of the Children of Odin; as the exact location of Thologondoreave is a well-kept secret from most people, complete with powerful enchantments and even deific protection, in practice this makes most of the Odinsforge Range their country, an island in the middle of the State of the Dragon King.

PONDSPARKLE

Possibly the smallest country in the world, Pondsparkle consists of one small city and the surrounding area near a small lake a few miles in extent. Pondsparkle is the permanent home for a large number (several thousand) of the Intelligent Toads and the site of the first and still primary temple to their god, Blackwart the Great.

Other Locations

ELYVIAS

Not, strictly speaking, a country, but a subcontinent, Elyvias used to be a larger portion of the continent, with additional area extending up nearly to Tor Port; according to legend, a battle between Elbon Nomicon and the Archmage Idinus caused a cataclysmic restructuring of the whole area, sinking a large chunk of the continent and creating the distorted conditions within. Elyvias has several countries and significant cities within its borders (Firestream Falls, Shuronogromal, Thunder Port, Thelhi-Man-Su, Zeikor, Artilus), but is severely cut off from the rest of the world both by the physical barriers of the Barricade Mountains, Blackdust Plateau, and Cataclysm Ridge, and by the mystical disruption called the Maelwyrd which surrounds the entire peninsula to a range of up to forty miles, with only a mile or two of clear-sailing space inside the Maelwyrd, near land. Magic also tends to work differently in Elyvias, and the civilizations there have developed differently in the last several thousand years.

THE FOREST SEA

Stretching from the Great Road and the Odinsforge Range in the east to the Barricade Range in the east, the Forest Sea presses against the Ice Peaks and surges around them in the east, up into the Empire of the Mountain. Stretching for three thousand miles, the Forest Sea is broken only by tiny enclaves within it and by the narrow clear-cuts around the cities and Great Roads. Somewhere within is hidden the Suntree, which the *Artan* on the main continent use as temple and center, but most of it is utterly unexplored, filled with danger and possibility.

"HELL" AND HELL'S RIM

Created, it is said, from a cataclysmic mystical confrontation between the powerful Demons and the Great Dragons in the days before human beings walked the planet, the region called "Hell" is a place of twisted, distorted magics, impossible conflicting terrain, and monsters found nowhere else. No coherent picture has emerged of the place within, and few even attempt to go there; passing Hell's Rim, a steep barrier of high peaks, would be too much effort for most anyway. The only pass through those peaks is sealed off by the fortress city of Hell's Edge.

ICE PEAKS

Like "Hell" and Elyvias, the Ice Peaks are a reminder of one of the conflicts of history, though long enough ago that the precise nature of the event isn't known. The Peaks are magical, solidified ice for the most part, meaning that they are beautiful, transparent or translucent, and very, very hard to pass, given they have nothing growing on them. They form one of the natural borders between the State of the Dragon God and the Empire of the Mountain.

People of Zarathan

Many different species share this continent—many relatively peacefully, others...somewhat less so. Following is a summary of the most significant peoples of this world.

HUMANS

Human beings on Zarathan are basically the same as they are on Earth. Generalists, humans are something of the chameleons of the civilizations, showing up in any profession, any part of the world, in large numbers. They are probably the most common of the intelligent species.

INTELLIGENT TOADS

Called the *Sylanningathalinde*, or "Golden-eyed," by the Saurans, the Toads claim to be the oldest of the intelligent species, even pre-dating the Dragons and Demons. They are in general a fun-loving but insular people, and mostly stay near to the pond they are born and raised in. Toads are given one name in their larval (tadpole) stage and, when adults, choose a significant second name. They vary tremendously in size, from dwarfed individuals a few inches long up to some four feet from nose to rump and weighing two hundred pounds.

SAURANS

Averaging eight feet in height with massive bodies, armored tails, heavy, clawed feet and arms, and a head sporting a very large fanged mouth, Saurans resemble nothing so much as a miniature Godzilla. They claim to be direct descendants of the Great Dragons, and the Ancient Saurans—somewhat larger and clearly superior in many ways—are supposedly ranked as equals with the Dragons. There are very few Ancient Saurans left. They are generally even-tempered, and a good thing, since when angered, they are terribly dangerous.

ARTAN

Very humanlike, *Artan* tend to be delicate in appearance, with hair and eyes of exotic colors; they are extremely controlled in emotional displays as a rule. They often live in wilder areas—forests and mountains—but not, despite some assumptions, because they like to live "close to nature"; they prefer to be hard to find, and have a sort of racial paranoia that they are still being hunted by some nameless adversaries who supposedly chased them from beyond the stars to Zarathan. The Rohila are technically the same species, but are otherwise separated from them in culture, behavior, and associations, aside from being also isolationist.

CHILDREN OF ODIN/ODINSYRNEN

Short, broad, tough as stone, these appear to be—and in many ways are—the classic dwarves. However, they are not a species of hard-drinking and fighting warriors, despite appearances and the fact that their patron pantheon includes Odin and Thor. According to their legends, they were literally created by Odin, who forged them in Asgard from the heart of a world, using Thor's hammer to do the striking. While their greatest city is indeed underground, the Children of Odin are equally at home above ground and are nearly as flexible in choice of profession and environments as human beings.

WINGED FOLK/SAELAR

Generally human in appearance but with a set of huge, compactable wings, the Saelar are almost certainly the result of some mage's experimentation a few Chaoswars ago. The records are, however, lost, and they breed as true as any, so they are now an uncommon but widely spread species, most heavily concentrated in the region of the Broken Hills.

MAZAKH

Often called "snake-demons," "snake-men," and other more derogatory terms, the *mazakh* were originally the creation of the demons they worship (the *Mazolishta*), who literally constructed them from a number of other species. In appearance, they are actually somewhat less snakelike and more like small raptorian dinosaurs. Generally raised in a hostile culture that trains them for warfare and lack of empathy, the *mazakh* are not inherently evil, and some leave the service of the *Mazolishta* and join the greater societies above; these are called *khallit*.

Gods of Zarathan

The gods and their choices affect nearly everything on the planet. There are, literally, hundreds if not thousands of deities worshipped on the planet; for purposes of *Phoenix Rising*, only a few are of great significance, however.

MYRIONAR

God of Justice and Vengeance, Myrionar is at the heart of the action. In the grander scheme of things, Myrionar is a fading god whose influence is vastly reduced from what it was, but that may be changing. Represented as a set of scales balanced on the point of a sword.

TERIAN

The Nemesis of Evil, the Light in the Darkness, Terian is also called Infinity as he is referred to in prophecy as "The Length of Space." A deity of unswerving good, Terian is also ranked as one of the most powerful of deities on anyone's scale. Represented by a human figure mostly in black with a cape or cloak clasped with a golden sidewise-eight figure, and head blurred/concealed by a blaze of light.

CHROMAIAS AND THE FOUR

Generally portrayed as good, the Chromaian faith is extremely flexible, especially as it manifests all aspects of magic and power. Symbolized by a four-pointed jack-like object with crystals of four different colors at the points and a clear diamond at the center.

EÖNAE

Goddess of the world(s), Eönae's focus is on nature, with control over the natural elements (earth, air, fire, water, and spirit) the most common manifestation of her power. She is frequently allied with **Shargamor**, a demon of water turned to the light, who is mostly focused on storms, streams, rain, and so on. Symbolized either by a woman (young, medium, old) with green and brown hair, or by her signature creatures, the **Eönwyl**.

ELBON NOMICON AND THE SIXTEEN

One of the most ancient pantheons, the head of this group of gods is Elbon Nomicon, Teranahm a u Gilnas (Great Dragon of the Diamond), supposedly father to all Dragons and a being of almost incalculable power. The Dragons tend to slow, long duty-cycles on Zarathan, either sleeping for ages or travelling to other planes of existence, with only a few physically present on Zarathan at any given time; it is, however, rumored that Elbon Nomicon's own home is at the center of the Krellin mountains at the extreme southwest tip of the continent. The symbol of each dragon is its chosen gemstone; Elbon's personal symbol is a stylized lighting bolt with rays extending out from it.

KERLAMION

The Black Star, King of All Hells, Kerlamion is one of the most powerful of the gods as well as one of the original Demons. He symbolizes destruction and conquest, and attracts only the worst sort of worshippers; he is, however, often quite active and those who please him may often get material aid. His symbol is, predictably, either a black starburst or a humanoid outline of pure black.

THE MAZOLISHTA

Great Demons who are the patron gods of the *mazakh* and other creatures of darker natures, there are several Mazolishta whose names are rarely spoken; the only one appearing directly in *Phoenix Rising* is **Voorith**, whose focus is life, forests, and such—in a corruptive and destructive sense.

BLACKWART THE GREAT

God of Toads (and anything else he happens to like), Blackwart manifests as a gigantic black toad, hence the name. While not powerful on the scale of many of the gods, he is much more savvy than many give him credit for (just like his people). He is symbolized by a stylized set of pop-eyes and a smile, or by a black toad figurine.

AFTERWORD

In many ways, the publication of *Phoenix Rising* is the most personally important and thrilling part of my writing career so far. Oh, the publication of my first book, *Digital Knight*, has a certain special something about it that nothing else will ever match, but the *roots* of *Phoenix Rising* are much deeper—even though the two books take place in the same overall universe.

The world that Kyri, Poplock, and Tobimar live in, Zarathan, was first created in 1977–1978, about 35 years ago. It's changed a lot, of course, but there are elements that have remained the same for decades. Most readers will notice—will have a hard time *not* noticing—that there are a lot of things going on in the book which aren't, precisely, covered, just touched on. That's because Zarathan is, to me, a living, breathing, complex world, and the world-shaking events that Kyri and her friends encounter require more than one team of heroes to deal with. There's room on Zarathan for many heroes—and many villains. There is the story of Kyri, Tobimar, and Poplock, which I call "The Balanced Sword"; there is the story of Xavier and his friends, which I call "Spirit Warriors"; and a third set of heroes includes none other than Kyri's little sister Urelle and young Ingram Camp-Bel in "Godswar." I know all their stories; with luck, I will get to tell them all as well.

I have always dreamed of having Zarathan presented to the world. It almost scares me, in a way; the only other people who've entered the world of Zarathan have done so in a very personal fashion, as people playing in the campaign for which Zarathan is the setting, where I can convey the world in the spoken word, with gesture and voice and hours upon hours of time; I can't be sure how well I succeed in mere writing. But if I've done it well enough, some readers—maybe only a few, maybe many—will see the Towers of the Six and One glowing with the colors of a thousand jewels in the setting sun, momentarily come face-to-face with a mighty child of dragons, hear the thunder of the voices of the gods, or just perhaps, smile at the wit of a tiny golden-eyed toad, and feel some of the joy and wonder that I do as I survey a world that exists only in my imagination...and the imaginations of those who have visited the World of Magic.

Ryk E. Spoor
January 30, 2012
Troy, NY
www.grandcentralarena.com